Figures it would be today...

Kalei glanced at the body of the dead Estranged woman, dark memories crowding in with her darkening mood. The woman's face was turned toward Kalei, her mouth half submerged in the pool of her own blood. She stared at Kalei with wide, unseeing eyes, her hand stretched out on the floor with obsidian nails. Those nails... they were all the proof Kalei needed to know that the woman was guilty. Those black nails proved that the woman was no longer a person; she was a mindless killer, bereft of any humanity. She was Estranged.

Estranged
Alex Fedyr

Estranged
By Alex Fedyr

Copyright © 2015 Alex Fedyr

Estranged is a work of fiction. All characters, events, and locales are figments of the author's imagination. Any resemblance to actual events or locales or persons, living or dead, is entirely coincidental.

To report any errors, please email alex@alexfedyr.com

Cover by Paula Thomas

Independently Published by Alex Fedyr

ISBN: 978-0-692-50960-9

To all of my teachers,
both in the classroom and out.
To my parents, my friends,
and the people I've met along the way...
This book would not exist without you.

CHAPTER ONE

Sacrifices

Kalei tried to ignore the shouts that echoed in the back of her mind. *Estranged...* She could still see those black-nailed fingers closing around her father's arm...

"Excuse me, ma'am. If you aren't doing anything tonight, we are holding a memorial to remember those lost on E-day. There will be a live performance from—"

Kalei pulled out of her reverie and realized that a young man in a nice pair of jeans and a button-up shirt was trying to push a pamphlet into her hand. She barked, "I'm on duty. Bug off."

His eyebrows jumped slightly, but he quickly moved off to find another victim.

"Lost on E-day..." The kid's word choice was spot on. They couldn't exactly say, "Died on E-day," when half the victims still lived Downtown. They might as well be dead, though. Better to just finish them all off and be done with it.

A car horn blared, and once again, Kalei's attention was dragged to the present. From where she stood, leaning against the bank on Fifth and State, she couldn't identify the source in the mid-day traffic jam. The tendency of the encroaching skyscrapers to amplify and distort sounds annoyed her. Then again, everything annoyed her today.

Marley laughed and smacked her on the shoulder. "Sleeping on the job, Officer Distrad?"

Kalei ignored him for a moment, pushing off from the building and scanning the crowd clogging the sidewalk. Professionals in suits, tourists with cameras, fanatics handing out pamphlets, fashionistas prancing along in their stilettos... for all appearances, it looked like just another day on Fifth. But she could easily spot the locals in the crowd, the anniversary weighing heavily on every one of them. Whether it showed in the slump of their shoulders, or the grim cast to their eyes, the screams of the past rang in everyone's ears today.

Kalei replied, "Sleeping on the job? Eh, no more than usual."

She finally looked at Marley, a fairly short figure, rounded at the edges, but not fat. Marley harbored an impressive collection of muscle beneath that soft exterior. Once, she had seen him throw down a man twice his size, just to make a point to the rest of the bar as he arrested the brawler for assault on a police officer.

Marley let the smile that always lurked behind his eyes break out, making his round face light up. "It's no wonder SWORDE doesn't want to hire a slacker like you."

"Is that so? Well, I'm not too worried. A numbskull

like you isn't going to be promoted anytime soon. At least I'll have good company."

Marley laughed again. Kalei wondered if he was trying to be extra cheerful to make up for her sour mood. "C'mon, Slacker. We're supposed to be on patrol."

The pair made their way down the sidewalk, cutting through the indifferent crowd. The day was unusually warm and sunny. Between the shimmering skyscrapers, Kalei spotted a narrow strip of bright, clear blue sky. The weather was much too nice for E-day. For once, Kalei was grateful for the perpetual gloom down on the streets. Even so, her hands sweltered in their black polyester gloves. Regulations stated she had to wear them at all times, but she didn't see what good it did to wear gloves when her short sleeves left the rest of her arm exposed. She was about to say as much when her radio went off next to her ear. "Estranged event reported at Sixth and Elm. Local units, please respond."

Kalei grabbed her radio and replied, "Officers Distrad and Douglas on our way, current location Fifth and State."

Kalei got the rest of the details over the radio as they ran: suspected Estranged, a young white female, small grocery store, shots had been fired.

The once-indifferent crowd of commuters and tourists stopped to watch Kalei and Marley run past. Kalei ignored them, focusing on the path ahead, dodging those pedestrians who didn't hear her shouts to get out of the way.

As they neared the last turn, cries rang through the air. A woman screamed, "Help! Please, my son is hurt!"

Kalei and Marley came around the corner, drawing their guns, alert for any sign of the attacker. They found a woman clutching a man by the front of his suit, shaking him, her eyes filled with tears, her voice filled with desperation. A white and blue sundress clung to her body, stained with streaks of blood. Sunglasses, forgotten, slid off the back of her head, hanging on as one arm caught in a tangle of her curly brown hair.

Kalei kept her gun pointed to the ground, unsure if the woman was the victim or the attacker. The sidewalk was empty, save for the struggling pair in front of the store. A few pedestrians lingered at the end of the block, watching; one young woman had a cell phone in hand, but the rest of the foot traffic moved to the opposite side of the street, studiously pretending they didn't hear the commotion.

Still held by the woman, the older man leaned back, a stethoscope around his neck, his hands poised to push her off, although hesitant to touch her exposed skin. He stammered, "Lady, please! I'm just an actor. I'm not a real doctor. I can't help ya."

The woman's hands were covered in blood past her wrists, dying the man's suit red where she held him. She said, "He's only five years old. Please, he needs help. If you can just—" She spotted the officers and released him, turning to Kalei instead. "Please."

She clasped her hands together and walked toward the officers.

There was too much blood; Kalei couldn't see if her nails were black or not. For all she knew, this could be the suspected Estranged.

"You need to help him. There is so much blood, he—"

Kalei held up her left hand. She said, "Whoa, whoa. Calm down. Tell us what happened, ma'am."

"There's no time! My son is bleeding!"

The shop door opened and a man poked his head out. He said in a thick accent, "You the police? Come. The boy is hurt. Come!"

As the man beckoned, gesturing urgently to Kalei, she could see that his nails were clear. She holstered her gun and stepped forward, but Marley stopped her with a hand on her shoulder. "Hey! You know protocol. We aren't authorized to go in there. We have to—"

"Let a kid die? Ease off—"

"I'm serious! They'll have your badge if you screw up again. Just— have some sense. It could be a trap."

"Estranged don't have the brains to set traps." She pushed past him, but he grabbed her again.

"How many times do I have to tell you, we're not Wardens, Kalei! We don't have the equipment–! You go in there and you're dead or unemployed. Just do your job. We need to set up a perimeter until SWORDE gets here."

Kalei pushed his hands off of her. "Last I checked,

Marley, I am still human. Fuck my job and fuck the Wardens. I swore to protect these people and that's what I'm going to do." This time, he didn't stop her.

Inside the store, two adults – one male and one female – lay dead on the ground. The female had her brains shot out. A shelf had been knocked over, spilling crackers and candy bars all over the floor; the shiny wrappers mingled with the pool of blood from the dead woman. The blood didn't bother Kalei. Fenn used to say that with a stomach of steel like hers, Kalei should have become a paramedic. Kalei always scoffed at that. She was better at causing messes than fixing them.

A second, smaller pool of blood flowed from a young boy who was crying on the floor where he leaned against a stack of soda boxes. His upper thigh was bleeding profusely through his tiny jeans. There were smudges of blood across his blue jersey, and as he pushed his red fists to his watery eyes, he smeared more blood across his cheeks.

Kalei knelt down, calling the information into her radio before grabbing a first aid kit from the shop owner. His hands shook as he babbled, "I didn't know the lady was Estranged, but when the gentleman went down, I had no time to think— it was self-defense, I promise!"

Kalei ignored the man and offered a few words of comfort to the child. With his mother's help, she pulled the boy away from the soda boxes, then laid him down on the tile floor. She might not be a paramedic, but she had enough first aid training to help this kid stay alive until they got here. Pulling a pair of scissors from the first aid kit, she cut the boy's pants back from the wound and pulled out a thick pack of gauze. While she worked, she asked the storekeeper, "How did this happen to the kid?"

"The woman, when she was shot, she knocked the shelf over. The boy was caught underneath."

Kalei nodded absently, assessing a four-inch slice on the boy's quad. He had already lost a lot of blood. A few more minutes and—

A siren wailed in the distance. Only SWORDE's vans made that particularly high, undulating sound.

They must have been in the area to get here this soon, Kalei thought.

Kalei clenched her jaw and applied the gauze to the boy's wound. The boy screamed in pain and punched at her arm. His mother sat beside him, soothing him and assuring him that everything would be all right.

Meanwhile, the sirens stopped. Kalei knew it was just a matter of seconds now before they kicked her out and took her badge.

Fucking E-day. Figures it would be today...

Kalei glanced at the body of the dead Estranged woman, dark memories crowding in with her darkening mood. The woman's face was turned toward Kalei, her mouth half submerged in the pool of her own blood. She stared at Kalei with wide, unseeing eyes, her hand stretched out on the floor with obsidian nails.

Those nails... they were all the proof Kalei needed to know that the woman was guilty. Those black nails proved that the woman was no longer a person; she was a mindless killer, bereft of any humanity. She was Estranged.

Kalei felt her fury rise as those dead eyes continued to stare at her, almost pleading as the black-nailed hand reached for her. The Estranged blinked.

Kalei jumped back and released the gauze.

The shop door burst open and two figures in full SWORDE uniform stepped in. They wore black from head to toe: helmets with blacked-out visors, polyester jackets, polyester pants tucked smartly into a pair of sturdy boots, complete with gloves covering each hand. They were both armed with assault rifles as they yelled for everyone to get back and put their hands up.

Kalei looked back at the Estranged body on the floor. The eyes were now closed.

One of the Wardens, female, judging by her voice, pulled Kalei aside. "Ma'am, I understand you are a police officer, but I need you to stay here until another Warden comes by to administer a test—"

Kalei wasn't listening to the Warden. Her eyes were still locked on the Estranged. She thought she saw one of the fingers twitch. If it got up, it could kill the shopkeeper standing next to it before anyone knew what was happening. "That body— I think the Estranged is still alive. You need to get—"

"Ma'am, this is now a SWORDE crime scene. You

need not concern yourself with—"

"I'm telling you, she's alive!" The mother and the shopkeeper jumped and stared at Kalei with wide eyes. The shopkeeper looked down at the Estranged body, slowly stepping away from it.

"Ma'am, if you could please step out to the van with me."

Kalei was furious. "That Estranged is alive! You're putting everyone in danger—" The Warden grabbed Kalei's arm above the elbow and pulled her toward the door. Kalei relented as she heard the insanity of what she was saying. There was no way the Estranged was alive; it was missing half its brain. But the eyes... Kalei shook her head. It must have been one of those weird post-mortem twitches, like rigor mortis or something. Kalei sighed. All this stress was making her loopy.

Outside, the police had already erected barricades to shut down the sidewalk and half the street. Within the circle of police stood the SWORDE van with the back doors flung open. The interior was pretty bare, just a pair of benches with lockers underneath.

The Warden sat Kalei down on the back bumper and pulled a kit from one of the lockers. The kit was red, with a wire sticking out on one side, ending in a clamp. The Warden said, "Sit still. This will just take a moment." Kalei tried not to flinch as the warden clamped the device onto the top of her ear. After a couple seconds, the device gave a quiet beep. "You're all clear. Please submit a report to your sergeant by the end of the day." With that, the Warden picked up the kit and returned to the store.

Kalei sighed and leaned forward, propping her elbows on her knees and placing her head in her hands. Today was such a shitty day. E-day was already shitty every year it came, but this year, it was particularly shitty. She sighed again, sat up, and hopped off the bumper. She spotted Marley along the barricade and walked over to him.

She was about two feet away when he turned around and said, "Why can't you just do your job like you're supposed to?"

"And why can't you mind your own business?"

"Dammit, Kalei, I'm serious. Ever since we were kids, you—"

"Give it a rest, Marley."

Kalei's cell phone went off, saving her the trouble of arguing with him further. She didn't even look to see who it was before she answered, "Distrad here."

"Kalei, once you are cleared by SWORDE, I want you to come straight to my office." The caller hung up. She had been expecting the call, but her stomach still turned to ice.

Marley noticed the change in her expression. "Was it the sergeant?"

"No, the captain."

Marley sighed. "Well, I'll put in a good word for ya in my report. Maybe he'll let you off again?"

Kalei grumbled, "Not likely. This is the captain,

Marley, not Sergeant Barslow."

"Well, good luck."

"Thanks." Kalei stepped past him and made her way through the barricade. The crowd on the sidewalk was tightly pressed together, and a couple of reporters tried to heckle her for information as she passed, but Kalei pushed sullenly by, ignoring them all. Most jumped out of her way freely, not wanting to be touched by the drying blood on her hands.

The full implications of what she had done were finally crashing in. Kalei's entire future was crumbling down around her because she wouldn't let a little boy bleed to death. The captain himself had called her cell phone, and Kalei couldn't think of anything more indicative of the trouble to come. What had this police force come to, that they would fire someone for saving a life?

Her phone went off again, and she automatically answered, "Yes, Captain?"

"Nope, not the captain. Just me." Kalei was relieved to hear Fenn's voice. But then the relief turned to dread as she realized... she would have to tell her husband that she was losing her job. "Why were you expecting a call from the captain? Are you in trouble again, Kalei?"

Kalei rubbed her hand lightly across her forehead. She wasn't officially fired yet; no need to tell him anything. "Don't worry about it. I'll tell you when I get home. So what's up?"

Fenn hesitated, clearly deciding whether or not he

wanted to press the issue. Apparently he decided not to. "Uh, yeah, I was just calling to let you know that we're going to have the girls again tonight. Qain is dropping them off at two."

Kalei wasn't sure if she had the energy to keep up with her nieces tonight. At two and four years old, they were anything but quiet, and tonight was the last night she would want kids around. But, she resolved that she could probably use the distraction after a day like today. Reading the girls bedtime stories and pretending everything was all right would probably be better than knocking down scotch and trying to sort out what career options remained to her. Not many, she was sure. Fenn was still making money with his graphics job, and they had a decent-sized savings, but she would need to find new employment soon...

"Kalei?"

"Yeah. Sorry, honey. That sounds great. I'll see you tonight."

"Are you sure everything is all right?"

"Yeah, fine. Look, I can't talk about it now. I've got to go. I'll be home for dinner, alright? Love you."

"Love you too."

Kalei hung up the phone, staring at the cement tile beneath her feet. She hated the twelfth of May. She hated E-day so much... First, it took her parents, now it was taking her job.... Kalei forced herself to take a deep breath. She closed her eyes, squared her shoulders, then resumed her walk to the station.

Kalei saw the captain the moment she stepped out of the elevator. He was sitting behind the desk in his glass-walled office. He spotted her as she approached, setting down a stack of papers and standing up to lean against the front edge of his desk, crossing his arms in front of him. His hair was grey, buzzed short along the sides with an inch more allowed at the top. His large frame loomed over the desk even as he sat, his lean-muscled torso perfectly erect as Kalei walked in. He said, "Close the door behind you, Kalei."

She obliged, the door latching to the frame with a resounding click, feeding her anxiety.

The captain looked angry enough to blow, but his voice remained quiet and even. "This is the third time you have been reported for breaking protocol and entering an Estranged crime scene. The first time, you tried to apprehend the criminal yourself. The second time, you gave some excuse about the suspect trying to escape. Each time, Sergeant Barslow has come to your rescue. Each time, he convinced me that you would not do it again. And now, you have made a third breach. You've used up all your get-out-of-jail-free cards, Kalei. If I had my way, I would sack you right here on the spot. But this is beyond you and me now. The people won't appreciate punishing an officer for saving a life, but neither will they appreciate rewarding an officer for consistently breaking the rules. This is an impossible situation you've put me in." He pushed off his desk and stood up, a full foot and a half taller than she was. Kalei felt her heart race frantically in her chest. She clenched her jaw tightly. "So, until I find a solution to this mess, you are suspended indefinitely. Hand me your badge and your gun."

The shock unlocked her jaw. "Indefinitely, sir?" She pulled her gun out of her belt and handed it to him. "As in, forever?"

The captain barked, "No, not forever, Kalei. As in, 'not defined.' As in, 'I have no fucking clue, so give me your badge until I make up my mind one way or another.'" Kalei obliged, and as he took the item, he said, "Now get out of my office. I expect you to fill out a report and have it on my desk before you leave."

Kalei stood there, stunned, her thoughts tangled in a dizzying whirlwind of emotions. She heard herself ask, "So, I'm not fired?" She slammed her mouth shut, silently reprimanding her mouth for asking such a stupid question.

The captain was already behind his chair, dropping her gun on the wooden surface of his desk, gesturing toward the door with his free hand. "Will you just get out of here?"

She jumped and hurried to escape, shutting the door carefully behind her.

Talwart stood just outside, hands in his pockets. He was a skinny man with a narrow face and fully dressed in his police uniform, although he usually never left the station. He typically spent his days managing paperwork and collecting gossip. He casually asked, "So, how did it go?"

Kalei thought about it for a moment, trying to make sense of what had just transpired. She gave up with a shrug. "I have no idea."

Even agonizing over every word she put in her report, Kalei still made it home well before two o'clock. She was grateful because it gave her a chance to talk to Fenn before the girls arrived. She still didn't know how she was going to tell him... but she knew there was no way out of it. She *had* to tell him.

She pulled her car into the garage and pulled the keys out of the ignition. She stared at the dashboard, still trying to find the words to explain what had happened. Would he be mad? *I mean, I know this is Fenn we are talking about, but how could he not be mad?* Her screw-up had just dropped all financial responsibility on him, and there was no way they could pay for their house on just one income... But that was just it. She wasn't even sure that she was out of a job. "Indefinite" was very... undefined... Would her sergeant find some loophole and convince the captain to let her stay on? Would he want to? Kalei had to admit, she had been nothing but trouble for the department since she started... Then she remembered, the captain had said that the people were involved now... did that mean that the press caught wind of the incident? What if the commissioner became involved? What if the mayor stepped in? The thought made Kalei sick...

Kalei stared at the white numbers of her speedometer, the pale simplicity of the font a sharp contrast to the grim possibilities swarming her mind. But the worst thought of all was the realization that she had probably blown any chance she had at becoming a Warden. Even with her high academy scores and her zealous determination, all of her applications to SWORDE had been rejected. And now... there was no point in trying anymore. There was no way they were going to admit her now... She would have to find a way that didn't involve SWORDE. There had to be a way for her to—

The door from the garage to the house opened. She looked up to see Fenn in the doorway, his soft brown eyes shining with concern as they found her. He was absolutely perfect in her eyes, a lean, not-too-muscled figure, with a strong, straight nose that didn't quite fit his soft mouth. He opened that mouth to say, "Kalei?"

Kalei clenched her jaw and forced herself to open the door. She wasn't ready to leave the shelter of the car just yet, but she had to face the music. She climbed out just as Fenn came around, and, without thinking, she wrapped her arms around his body, her head burrowing into his shoulder. She didn't realize she was crying until she heard him whispering in her ear, "There, there. It's all right... it's all right..."

When her tears slowed, he pulled back and looked her up and down. "Are you okay? Are you hurt at all?

What happened, honey?"

Kalei said, "Let's go to the kitchen. I need some water."

When they were settled at the dining room table, Kalei told Fenn about the event at the store, and what had happened with the captain. At the end, she said, "And the worst part is, the boy would have been fine if I hadn't gone in. SWORDE arrived right after we did. Sure, the kid would have been a bit worse for wear, losing a couple more ounces of blood, but he still would have been fine. I've screwed everything up for nothing."

Fenn held her hands and looked into her eyes. "It wasn't for nothing, Kalei. You had no way of knowing that SWORDE was going to get there so fast. You did the right thing. Don't doubt that."

Kalei looked at the tiles on the floor and said, "Yeah, but..."

"No buts about it, Kalei. Stop beating yourself up over this. So what if you lose your job? We'll be fine. I've picked up some new clients, we still have the savings account if it comes to it, but I don't think it will. I was watching the news after I called you. The mom has already showed up on every station, going on about a heroic police officer who came in and saved her son. The stations are eating it up, using it to prime their audiences for the E-day specials. There's no way the mayor could fire you after that. It would be bad for his election."

Kalei sighed. "Maybe you're right."

Fenn said firmly, "I am right. Now change out of those work clothes and help me child-proof this house before the little terrors get here, eh?"

Kalei laughed quietly. "Okay." She obligingly changed into a pair of shorts and a blue tank top, the lighter clothes a nice relief from the heat after running around the city in her uniform. But as she went around the house cleaning up and moving candles to the top shelves, she couldn't keep her thoughts from the Estranged in the store, of the way those eyes reminded her of her mother's wide eyes... except her mother's eyes never closed that night... it was hard to believe it had been seventeen years...

They say time heals all wounds, but Kalei knew better. Her wounds only festered with age. She could still remember the very first E-day, the day when the Estranged first showed up in the city. One had shown up on their doorstep in the form of a young man, and that man had taken her life away from her with a hug.

He was tall, with lean muscles and a smooth, strong chin, and brown hair just long enough to fall into his eyes. Even as her parents' faces faded from her adult memory, the young man's face was burned into her mind's eye forever. His strong, angular face with his wide, naïve eyes... He had walked through the door and hugged Kalei's mom, then reached out to touch her dad. It was a simply, almost friendly act. But he was Estranged, and that touch— the skin of his arms wrapped around the skin of her mother's neck, the skin of his hand closed around the arm of her father... That was all it took to shatter Kalei's world.

The young man had fallen to his knees, his hair falling forward to veil his eyes as he doubled over and sobbed over the fresh corpses. Not his friend, though. The killer had a companion, an even taller, bleach-blond man who walked into the room with a fresh energy in his step, and a wide grin on his face. And as he walked through the room, the blond man kept laughing and laughing in a high-pitched shriek that made Kalei want to scream...

The doorbell rang, and Kalei jumped, nearly dropping the glass dolphin she held in her hand. She quickly placed the decoration on the mantel and walked over to the door.

"Auntie!" As Kalei opened the door, Kas immediately ran in and hugged Kalei at the hip.

Kalei smiled and rubbed the small girl's head as she greeted her brother-in-law. "Hey, Qain, how's it going? I hear you are taking another trip?"

Qain was half a foot taller than his younger brother, with an identical nose. But where his brother had soft brown eyes, Qain had steely grey eyes, which always narrowed slightly, as though he was repressing a great deal of stress. He sighed. "Yeah, they've got me going to Takaio this time. It could be a while. Sorry for dumping the girls on you like this..."

"No, not at all. It's always a pleasure to have them."

Qain smiled politely and handed a sleeping Teia over to Kalei.

Fenn came up to the door, greeted a bouncing and babbling Kas, then looked up and said, "Hey, brother. How's it going?"

"You know, the same old. Well, I'd better get going. I'm sure you four have an exciting night ahead of you. Bye, girls. Thanks again, Fenn."

"No problem. Have a safe flight."

Kalei shut the door as Qain made his way back to the driveway. She looked at Fenn and said, "That's odd. He wasn't even surprised that I'm home early."

Fenn shrugged. "Last-minute trip. He's probably got a lot on his mind."

Kalei nodded. "True."

Teia stirred and rubbed her eyes. "Auntie?"

"Yes, sweetie?"

Teia's eyes flew open. "Auntie!" She flung her arms around Kalei's neck, and it was all downhill from there. The girls were absolutely radiating energy, and they didn't give Fenn or Kalei a moment's rest as they tracked down all of their toys and demanded that their hosts play with them. Kalei and Fenn happily obliged, with Fenn slipping away a few hours in to start making dinner.

The girls were already beginning to crash by the time dinner was served, and Kalei was feeling pretty worn as well. Teia was practically falling asleep on her plate, and Kalei began fighting off the ghosts and anxieties that began to creep back in at the edges of her mind. She could even hear the blond man laughing as the memory of that night began to replay in her mind, unwilling to give her a moment's piece on this anniversary. The laughter went on and on and Kalei was starting to wonder if she was losing her mind when Kas said, "Auntie, who's laughing?"

Kalei's head shot up and she looked at Fenn, who shrugged. Realizing the laughter was real, she ran to the living room and pulled back the curtains. The blond-haired man was standing on their lawn, laughing. He stopped when he saw Kalei, his face growing with a wide grin.

Terror robbed Kalei of her limbs, her lungs, even her voice. It crushed in across her chest, pouring down through her veins. She couldn't move. She couldn't breathe. She couldn't think.

Fenn stirred at the table behind her. "Honey, what is it?"

Power rushed back along with a fresh wave of horror. "Fenn! Grab the girls! NOW!"

Kalei didn't have time to explain. Luckily, a loud BANG at the front door did it for her. *Shit! He's not alone.* She pulled the curtains shut and ran to the office to retrieve her silver 9mm pistol from the safe. When she returned to the living room, Fenn had Teia sitting on the couch as he wrestled with her shoe, trying to get it onto her fidgeting foot.

Kas was sitting on the floor beside Fenn, crying as

the Estranged continued to bang on the door. Keeping one eye on the source of the banging, Kalei walked over to her niece and gently rubbed her back. Kalei's determination threatened to melt away as she saw the tears in Kas's small brown eyes. Kalei took a deep breath. "Kas, remember what Auntie told you about the Estranged?"

Kas sniffed. "They're bad people who want to hurt us."

"Yes, and right now, they're the ones knocking at the door, so we've got to be really quiet so they don't get us, okay? Quiet as a mouse."

After another sniff, Kas seemed to be holding her breath as she whispered, "Okay."

Kalei placed her hand on the child's shoulder and gave it a soft squeeze. Kalei looked Kas in the eyes and said, "Now I need you to take care of your sister and follow Uncle down to the car. Can you do that for me?"

"Yes, Auntie."

Kalei smiled in spite of herself and turned around to tell Fenn, "Don't worry about the shoe. Just get the girls to the car and—"

The window shattered as two Estranged burst into the living room. Without hesitating, Kalei gave them each a bullet to the brain and told Fenn, "Get the girls to the car. NOW!"

Fenn scooped up Kas and Teia and ran for the garage door, the girls screaming in his arms.

A dozen more Estranged were climbing through the

window, surprisingly agile and quick as they jumped through it. Kalei could feel the adrenaline rushing through her veins as the Estranged closed the distance between them. She shot the first four down, then ran after Fenn as the rest stumbled over their comrades' bodies. She ran into the garage, slammed the door shut behind her, then grabbed a nearby stepladder and wedged it under the handle.

She leaned her forehead against the white door for a moment, catching her breath and willing her heartbeat to slow down. Behind her, a small voice asked, "Auntie, are we going to die?"

Kalei instinctually slid her thumb along the gun and put the safety on before she turned around to see Kas staring at her with wide, terrified eyes. Kalei closed her own eyes against the surge of tears the little girl's question had created. Kalei opened her eyes again, kneeled down to Kas's level, and said, "Everything is going to be okay, sweetie. Don't you worry." She just wished she could believe what she said.

Kalei looked past Kas to see Fenn still struggling to get a screaming Teia into her car seat. "Fenn, do you need help?"

"Nope, I got it," he called back— *BANG!* The garage door shuddered against its rails as something crashed into it. Kalei wasn't surprised they would try getting in that way; she just wished they would have taken longer to think of it. Fenn pulled himself away from the back seat, shutting the door as he pulled out the keys and said, "Hurry up and get in. I'm driving."

Kalei was loath to give up control of her car, especially in a dire situation such as this, but she had to admit it was necessary. "Alright, I need my hands free to shoot anyway." She scooped up Kas and rushed her over to the other side.

"Auntie, I can walk on my own—" Kas screamed and Kalei's gut jumped as the garage door crashed against the rails again. Kalei glanced at the door and saw a massive influx of metal where it had been hit. She doubted it could withstand another strike like that. The thought wasn't comforting.

She turned her attention back to Kas as she opened the car door and set the girl down. "I know, sweetie. I'm sorry. Climb in and get your seatbelt on. I need you to be a big girl and keep your sister quiet, okay?"

A third hit slammed into the garage door, punctuating the end of Kalei's sentence. The door buckled and sagged, but, against Kalei's earlier assessment, the rails continued to hold. Kas scrambled into her seat, and once her legs were clear, Kalei shut the door and hurriedly climbed into the car herself.

Teia was not in agreement with the situation. As Kalei sat herself in the front seat, all she could hear was Teia in the back, screaming for her daddy. Kas tried to get her little sister to calm down, but screaming "Be quiet!" at Teia just added to the chaos. Another crash coupled with a metal ripping sound blasted through the garage and the door finally crashed to the floor. Both girls fell silent.

Kalei looked over her shoulder and saw the silhouettes of six Estranged pouring through the breach against a backdrop of the setting sun peeking above the house across the street. It was almost beautiful, but the circumstances cast the scene in a menacing light. Fenn put the gearshift in reverse and hit the gas.

The car bumped as it ran into their assailants and slowed as the tires tried to find traction on the remains of the garage door. In any other car, Kalei would have been nervous, but she had faith in her four-wheel drive. Fenn gave it some more gas and the vehicle found its way over the obstacles. Kalei flicked the safety off and turned to watch for the next wave of attackers. When the tires cleared the bodies of the first few, another dozen Estranged ran at them from the yard. They charged the car, punching and pounding and climbing onto the moving vehicle.

Kalei reflexively checked on the girls and found them staring at the windows like little statues, wide-eyed with fear. The Estranged shot into the living room, the Estranged under the tires, the Estranged pounding at their windows... Kalei knew this night would haunt these girls for the rest of their lives. Kalei felt her jaw clench as her hands tightened into fists. She cocked her gun and opened the sunroof.

Kalei was already climbing onto her seat, sticking her torso through the sunroof as they reached the end of the driveway. As she pulled the gun free of the car, she saw a middle-aged man push a young girl aside and jump onto the hood. His hair was long and thick, falling down his back in a thick, greasy lump. The remnants of a checkered tie hung from his neck, and his slacks were ripped and shredded to the point that they could no longer reach his knees. Despite all that, he was the picture of health: plenty of flesh on his arms and gut, plenty of strength in his legs, and a desperate hunger in his eyes. On his chest, he had a few small tattoos hiding behind the erratic swinging of his tie, but Kalei didn't have time to figure out what they were. This man's bare hands were more dangerous than the weapon she held, and she wasn't about to let him near those girls. She lifted her gun as the man scrambled across the hood, reaching for Kalei. His black-nailed fingers twitched with anticipation as they closed in on their target, the deep black of the nails gleaming from beneath the grime like obsidian.

Seeing those nails brought Kalei's own childhood trauma to the forefront and sent a renewed wave of rage coursing through her body. She squeezed the trigger with a satisfied smirk.

His head snapped back and his body tumbled off the moving car, into the clawing arms of the dirt-smeared men and women who climbed up after him. Kalei took them out one by one until the slide on her gun slid back and stayed there. *Out of ammo.* But it didn't matter; only one Estranged remained. The teenage girl with her heavy, smeared makeup and her bedraggled brown ponytail didn't stand a chance as Fenn switched into first gear and charged down the road. She lost her grip on the spoiler and fell away, hitting the pavement and rolling in a swirl of torn sweatshirt and jeans.

Kalei looked up as the girl's body slipped into the distance and spotted three more figures pulling into the road on street-class motorcycles. *Seriously?* She returned to her seat and continued to watch the bikers in the side mirror. She knew they were Estranged because all three bikers were helmetless, shirtless (even the one woman), and they were coming straight at the car with the kind of hell-bent determination that could only be from an Estranged after a high. It didn't make any sense. Why were there so many? She pushed the questions from her mind and focused on what mattered. Opening the glove box, she stuck her hand inside where she found napkins and registry paperwork and tire gauges, but— "Honey, where's my revolver?"

"I didn't want Teia to find it, so I put it back in the gun safe."

Kalei took a deep breath and pushed her palm into her forehead. Now was not the time to argue. This wasn't the end of the world. Instead, she stuck her hand back into the glove box and started rummaging through the papers. Once more, she came up empty handed. "Where are my spare magazines?"

"In the house with the rest of the ammo. I cleaned the car last week, remember?"

Kalei threw her empty gun at the dashboard and

yelled, "Well, it's a damn good thing I don't have any
bullets, because I could shoot you!" Kalei regretted
those words the instant she heard them come out of her
mouth. The whimpering in the back seat grew a little
louder as Fenn grew silent. "I'm so sorry. I shouldn't
have said that..." But it was no use. The damage was
done.

She turned around and checked on the bikes. The
Estranged were right on top of them now, just a couple
feet behind the spoiler. No ammo, no weapons; just a
car holding what little family she had left. She looked
back at the girls and her heart broke as she watched
the tears slide down their small faces. Kas protectively
clutched her little sister as Teia quivered.

Then heartbreak turned to determination as Kalei
steeled herself for the plan forming in her mind. Fenn
wouldn't like it, but it was the only way she could keep
these girls safe. She said, "Kas, Teia, Uncle Fenn and I
love you very, very much. You'll get to see your daddy
soon; Uncle will take care of you." Kalei's emotions
threatened to overwhelm her, but she clenched her jaw
and stuffed them back. "Everything is going to be okay,
alright?"

Kas nodded, grimacing as she squeezed a couple
more tears out of her watery eyes.

Kalei turned to Fenn. "Whatever happens, I need
you to get them out of here."

"What are you talking abou—"

"I need you to keep the girls safe— that's all that

matters right now. Take them to the police station, call your brother, tell him what's happened. I'll meet you there."

"Kalei, I—"

"…I love you." She gave him a kiss on the cheek and saw his anger soften as his confusion deepened.

Balancing his attention between Kalei and the road, Fenn said, "I love you too. But, honey, I don't understand what you are talking about. You and I are in this car together. You don't have to tell me all this. *We're* going to the police station, *we're* going to call Qain—"

By this time, one of the motorcycles had pulled even with the car. It pained Kalei to hear Fenn say *we* when she knew she would be abandoning him. She mouthed one more "I love you" before opening the door and slamming it into the nearest bike. The motorcyclist wobbled and quickly lost control, his machine crashing into the blur of pavement. Without looking back, she jumped out after it.

CHAPTER TWO

Darkness

A practiced tuck-and-roll protected Kalei from the worst of the fall. That, and the very healthy bush she crashed into. For once, Kalei appreciated her neighborhood's obsessive attention to gardening. The Estranged, on the other hand, was worse off. His neck and head lay at an awkward angle to the rest of his body, and the front of his skull had caved in. *The government has helmet laws for a reason*, Kalei mused grimly.

She looked back over her shoulder to see the blue car disappear as it took a right at the end of the street. She was relieved. Her biggest concern was that Fenn would try to come back and talk her out of it while the remaining Estranged closed in on them, but he had listened to her. Only for the girls' sake, she was sure.

The next part was a gamble. The two bikes; would they turn back or would they continue their pursuit? Kalei wasn't sure she could catch up to them if they continued after Fenn, but she told herself that her familiarity with the neighborhood would allow her to cut them off at another intersection. Fortunately, she didn't have to test that theory because the Estranged dropped their speed for a moment and doubled back for her. *Typical predators.* She was hoping they would go after the easier target. Now it was just a matter of eluding them.

Kalei sprinted over to the downed bike and extracted it from the dead man's grasp, carefully avoiding his exposed skin. He might be dead, but she was still wary of him. Once the bike was erect, Kalei threw her leg over it, kicked it into life, and took off just as the others started to catch speed again. The thrill of speeding across the pavement on two wheels poured a new surge of adrenaline into her veins along with a vibrant sense of optimism. Not only were Fenn and the girls going to be all right, but this was going to be *fun.*

Blondie was still MIA, though. He wasn't standing in any yards, he wasn't riding either of the bikes, he wasn't following in any car. His absence didn't sit well with Kalei, but she pushed it out of her mind as she tried to put more distance between herself and the last two Estranged.

She twisted the throttle, but instead of gaining power, she started losing it. The bike began to slowly die beneath her. Her optimism quickly faded to dread as she looked down and saw that the entire left side was demolished. The plastic and metal framework was so twisted and torn that she was surprised the bike was still functional. In fact, she was surprised the thing hadn't exploded beneath her the second she fired it up. When she had made her plan, she didn't count on the bike taking so much damage in the crash.

Fuck! She looked back at the other bikers and assessed the situation. They were gaining on her. Not surprising. Side by side, elbow to elbow, they rode at her. Kalei looked forward, formulated a new plan, and prepared to act.

Without warning, she dropped one foot to the ground, whipped the motorcycle around, and released it. The momentum pushed Kalei off balance, causing her to fall backwards onto her butt, yet the new plan had worked. The bike crashed into the ground and skidded across the pavement, straight for the Estranged. With no time to react, the bikers slammed into it and were thrown violently into the air. Kalei first watched with triumph, then alarm, then horror as one of the bodies flew right at her. She scrambled backwards as fast as she could, then dropped onto her back as she realized the Estranged woman's momentum was going to carry her over Kalei, not into her. But it wasn't enough. The woman's bare, flailing arm brushed against Kalei's exposed knee as she sailed over her.

Pain ripped through every cell in Kalei's body.

***

The light at the corner of the television blinked one, two... five times, then the black screen came to life with light and sound.

A fair-haired woman sat before a fake cityscape backdrop as she continued in mid-sentence, "...news coverage on this seventeenth anniversary of E-day. We just spoke with news correspondent Jim Neilly from the scene of the attack, and now we have Professor Laney Daskalov of the Alundai University joining us to help answer the question: what exactly does this all mean to the people of Celan? Professor Daskalov, thank you for joining us."

The screen split so the newscaster's face could share the screen with another, dark-haired woman. This newcomer occupied some sort of office, with shelves full of books and unidentifiable knick-knacks filling the wall behind her. The Professor smiled and replied, "Thank you for having me."

"So, Professor, let me ask you: now that we have witnessed what seems to be the first organized attack from the Estranged since E-day, what kind of implications does this have for further attacks, and how can those at home protect themselves?"

"These are questions I have been asked many times, even before this latest attack. As far as implications, I expect we will see a lot more activity from the Estranged. We now know they have the capacity to be organized, and this makes them even more dangerous than before. So in light of this, my advice to your viewers is this: Lock your doors. Don't let anyone in without checking their nails first. This includes your friends, your cousins, even your own children, because to be perfectly honest, anyone can become an Estranged. I cannot emphasize this enough: *You cannot know who to trust until you have seen their nails.*"

Joanne-the-Newscaster replied in a light, incredulous tone, "You're saying we can't even trust our own children?"

Professor Daskalov answered, "That's right, not even our children. Because, you see, the second someone is touched by an Estranged, they are gone. Whether they die or not, they are gone. The few people who survive to become Estranged are no longer the same innocent friends we once knew. Sweet little Suzy down the road will no longer be smiles and sunshine once her nails are black. If the Estranged-Suzy sees you, she will do everything in her power to kill you."

Joanne leaned forward and clasped her hands together. "What causes that?"

The Professor hesitated briefly. "What? The change, or the need to kill?"

Joanne paused, then shrugged. "Both, I suppose."

"Unfortunately, what little we know about Estranged is very complicated. We do not know whether it is a disease, a parasite, or something else entirely, but we do know for certain that it targets the limbic system in the brain. In layman's terms, the presiding theory is that every Estranged is occupied by something we call the darkness. Now, we don't know why, but we believe that the darkness, in a sense, embodies and enhances the negative emotion that resides within us: sadness, anger, destructive cravings... So when an Estranged touches another person, their darkness seeks out these emotional centers within the other body and immediately floods these areas of the brain. If the victim cannot withstand that initial rush, they die. But if they survive, they begin generating darkness on their own and become Estranged themselves. For the survivors, all thoughts of family, food— everything falls away in the face of a single-minded drive to obtain that limbic excitation they received when they were converted. In other words, a high."

"A high?"

"Yes. It was discovered in a recent test that when an Estranged touches another person— Estranged or Untouched; doesn't matter— they receive a high that we have found to be well beyond anything modern drugs have achieved. This is what the Estranged are after when they attack the community. To put it in perspective, several years ago, a pair of scientists named Olds and Milner performed an experiment in which rats received a controlled electrical impulse to excite the limbic system in the brain. If you recall, this is the same system that is targeted by the darkness in Estranged. Every time the rats pressed a lever, they received this limbic excitation, and it was found that the rats began ignoring food and sleep in preference to pressing this lever until, eventually, they died of exhaustion. However, the dose these rats received is minimal compared to the excitation Estranged are receiving from the darkness."

Joanne's hand was over her heart as fear and concern lightly played across her face. "It's a good thing we have SWORDE. Actually— does SWORDE really quarantine Estranged? Or do they—" Joanne stopped herself and looked at somebody behind the camera.

Daskalov finished the sentence for her. "Do they kill them? Honestly, I can't say what SWORDE does with the Estranged. As far as I know, nobody has definitively seen an Estranged leave Downtown, for good reason, of course. Perhaps that should be your next *FactLine* story? 'The Mystery behind the Fence.'" Daskalov laughed at her own cleverness.

Joanne responded with a laugh of her own and replied, "Perhaps you're right, but we'll leave it to our editors to decide. Well, thank you for joining us, Professor. Coming up..."

A hand closed around the remote and picked it up from the worn, wooden desk. An old fountain pen rolled to the side as it was knocked away by the rising controller. The thumb— with a black flower swaying gently within its nail— pressed the power button and the television went silent.

***

Kalei woke up facing an abandoned city street. She

only glimpsed the cracked grey pavement and heard the eerie silence before a deep, piercing dagger drove into her heart, forcing her to close her eyes against the pain. The sting was so acutely emotional that it felt alarmingly physical, catching her unaware and making it painful to breathe, making it impossible to even think. She bent forward and clutched at her chest, clenching her jaw as she tried to shut it out.

Gritting her teeth, Kalei forced herself to take a few deep breaths. One, two, three breaths and she started to regain her senses. Then it all came back. The attack, the car, Fenn, the girls— Her eyes flew open and she heard herself call out, "Fenn!"

Her voice echoed off the pavement and bounced off the abandoned structures around her, but she heard no response. It didn't make any sense. She didn't recognize any of these buildings. The cracked pavement, the abandoned, trashed cars on the sidewalk...

She looked up, and up, and up as her eyes followed the lines of the towering, crumbling skyscrapers. A soft breeze brought her the scent of salt and dead fish. Between the buildings, she could see part of the Alundai mountain range watching from the west. *Downtown. I must be Downtown.* The end of Celan's peninsula used to be the center of it all. Now it was cordoned off and— like the frostbitten tip of a toe— left to die. This was Estranged territory.

Kalei's head began to spin, and a growing headache threatened to rip her skull apart. None of this was right.

How did she get here? What had happened to Fenn
and the girls? What was she doing Downtown? Kalei
pressed the heel of her left palm into her forehead,
and then placed her right hand on the pavement as
she prepared to push herself off the ground. Through
the crack in her half-opened eyes, she saw black
fingernails. Her own fingernails were all black. Kalei's
mind locked. Everything within her froze as a fresh
wave of daggers ripped through her lungs and down
through her gut. Again, she doubled over, unable to
breathe. Her thoughts slowly began to turn as she
hunched there, choking for air. *I'm... I can't be...*

Kalei's vision blurred. She fell forward and caught
herself with both hands. Both black-nailed hands.
The coughs became more violent as her lungs began
to function again. She didn't know how long she sat
like that, her entire body shaking as cough after cough
ripped through her throat, but eventually, the coughs
subsided and she began to breathe normally again. She
listened, suddenly exhausted, to the sound of her own
breathing. Everything seemed so surreal. It felt like
there was some... thing inside of her, moving through
her body like a watery serpent bent on destruction. And
even as it moved, she felt more of its body pouring out
of a chasm in her chest, spreading and expanded as it
lay claim on her body. *Perhaps this is just a* really *vivid
nightmare,* she assured herself. Then, in the renewed
silence, she heard the sound of a shoe scuffing against
pavement.

Kalei sat up abruptly and pulled away from the source, pressing her back into the brick wall of the nearby building. A few feet away from her stood a young man with dark hair. Her eyes didn't linger on the figure for too long; she looked past him to see if there was anyone else. She suddenly felt very exposed; she felt that any minute, a group of Estranged could attack her, and here she was on the sidewalk, totally unaware and unprepared. She checked the street, she checked the sidewalk on her right, she peered warily into the shadows of the abandoned cars, but she didn't see anyone else. Kalei heard a shout in the distance, but it was too far away to be related to her and the new visitor. They were alone. She wasn't sure if the revelation made her relieved or more anxious.

A renewed wave of pain brought Kalei's attention back to her condition. It rolled through her like a flood of angry lava, pouring through her veins and melting through every inch of her body. Her head bowed and her eyes locked on the pavement as she tried to regain control. The stranger was still there, probably some curious bystander who had found something new to look at. She managed to rasp, "Get the hell away from me."

She heard the young man take another step forward. His voice carried a certain authority when he said, "Tell me what happened."

The odd question sent another wave of dizziness through her skull, and she almost lost hold on what little control she had regained. Kalei clenched her jaw for a brief moment as she waited for the world to stop spinning, then opened her mouth to spit a wad of phlegm onto the ground. She said, "What the hell do you know? Why should I tell you anything?"

"I need to know," he simply stated.

This new guy was grating on Kalei's already raw nerves. "You don't need to know anything. Just get the hell out of here!"

"I need to know about the attack on your household. You and I both know that attack wasn't random."

Kalei went rigid. Her pain coalesced into rage, and she used the fresh wave of energy to push herself off the ground and look him in the eyes. "What do you know about it?" For the first time, she got a good look at his face. His features seemed familiar. She recognized— Kalei froze. *His face...* Standing before her was an exact picture of the boy Kalei remembered from seventeen years ago. The boy who killed her parents.

She saw the arms of this man wrapping around her mom. She saw her dad falling... "You murdering son of a—" Without bothering to finish her sentence, she swung her fist at his exposed face.

The young man didn't react to her retort, and as her fist neared his cheek, he continued to hold her eyes with his own. The pure sorrow within those steel grey eyes almost stayed Kalei's hand. Although his eyes were dry, she felt as though she were looking into the heart of a soul that never stopped weeping. Her fist finished its arch.

Her knuckles slammed into the flesh and bone of his cheek. His whole body rocked to one side and he spit out a tooth. The sudden, physical contact brought Kalei back to her senses. She remembered who she was facing, and she recalled her hatred. Whatever she thought she saw, it wasn't there. This young man was an Estranged and a murderer.

As he recovered from her first blow, Kalei went in for another, but this time, he caught her wrist. She hadn't even seen him move. Then she realized she couldn't move herself. The entity within her, the thing that had been ripping her apart... it locked. Every inch of her body was soundly frozen. Not even her eyes could move away from the hand that held her tight.

She wanted to scream, she wanted to run, but she couldn't even widen her eyes at the terror of being imprisoned within her own body. She stood at the verge of a complete mental breakdown, but the young man interrupted her thoughts. "Shhh... Calm down."

His attempt to calm her only enraged Kalei. She hated the fact that he had caught her this way, she hated the fact that the murderer was trying to calm her, but mostly, she hated the fact that the monster was touching her, and there was nothing she could do about it.

Unable to perform any of the physical actions she wanted to – and unwilling to think about what would happen next – Kalei focused her attention on the hand that held her, the one piece of the world left to her.

The young man's nails weren't anything she expected. They weren't the flood-black nails she had remembered from the hand that killed her parents. They had... flowers. A single, intricate black flower painted onto each and every fingernail. Six delicate petals atop tall, slender stems, all writhing in a tortured dance. They literally moved upon his fingers, doing the one thing she *couldn't* do. She found herself lost in their motion, wishing she could be free with them... Eventually, the flowers slowed and paused.

The young man broke the silence. "Do you remember the other man from E-day? Was he there tonight?"

Abruptly, Kalei felt her mouth loosen as she regained control of her lips and voice. She moved her jaw experimentally, then let her anger poison her voice as she said, "Yeah. That murdering, no-name bastard. He was there. Are you sorry you missed out on the party? Or were you hiding in the bushes?"

"Xamic Kahli."

Kalei would have blinked if she could. "What?"

The young man's voice was toneless as he answered. "That's his name."

"I don't give a fuck what his name is! I don't know what you and your friend have going on, but I will put an end to each of you before you can lay a finger on the girls, Fenn, or anyone else in this damned city."

Out of the corner of her vision, she saw him look away. The flowers began to writhe again. He said, "You will never see them again."

For a moment, everything went quiet. "What?" He couldn't mean— he couldn't be talking about Fenn. He couldn't be talking about Kas and Teia. "What the fuck are you saying?"

"Make peace with that." He released her arm and turned away.

The moment his skin left hers, she felt full control over her body return. Her arms dropped to her sides. She should have gone after him, she should have demanded answers, exacted revenge –but all the anger was gone now. Instead, she felt the power go out of her legs. She slumped to the ground, free, but still utterly powerless. She knew what he was trying to say. They were dead. All three of them. It was over.

Nothing mattered. Nothing made any sense. From that moment on, everything passed in a blur. Words were spoken. Words were shouted, but none of it mattered. Nothing mattered. Hours? Days? Not even time meant anything anymore.

Numb. She wished she was numb. Instead, intense pain accompanied her every movement, her every moment. It started in her chest. A sharp knife that pierced her heart and spread throughout her body. What felt like dozens of dull, tearing razors bore down relentlessly on her body, piercing her through, ripping her to shreds until Kalei wanted to reach in and pull her heart out to be rid of it all.

But the pain propelled her. It wasn't something she

had ever encountered, and yet, it wasn't entirely alien either. It was familiar, as though all those nights she had cried alone had suddenly jumped forth and set up shop in her veins. And with the desolation of losing Fenn, with the anguish of failing to save the children, it had coalesced into a raging demon that tormented her incessantly. It consumed her.

Then it all went away. A hand, just one hand with those black-tipped fingernails reached out and touched her. The pain was gone. From the place on her shoulder where skin had met skin, a sudden... relaxation spread throughout her body, like a soothing wind sweeping through and dousing the fire. Then it went further. It picked up her heart and carried it high into the air, sending it singing through the sky. The rest of Kalei followed with sheer, unimaginable elation. She moved even further away from the world. She moved into the clouds and kept on rising higher and higher. Anything outside that sensation ceased to exist. It became the center of her world, it became her new life, away from all the loss and sorrow.

But when the trip to the clouds began to wear off, when reality began to creep back in, only those black-tipped fingers could bring back the clouds. She needed their touch. She needed to wash away the pain, to wash away this decrepit world. Black-tipped fingers; that was all that mattered.

Hand after hand slipped through her palms. An arm, a shoulder, anywhere that skin could contact skin was

enough to bring the high rushing back. Kalei didn't
know up from down. She didn't know who she was, or
what was happening to her life. She didn't care. All she
knew was that touch that lifted her to where the pain
couldn't reach.

Another hand, another high. Kalei reached for it,
but an alarm tried to sound in the back of her deafened
mind. Kalei reached anyway, desperate to claim the
promised ecstasy. She heard a scream, but she was
almost there. The hand tried to pull away, but Kalei
wouldn't let it; she needed it. Her hand closed in on
the other. Then, somehow, it registered. The fingernails
weren't black. A gunshot went off.

Kalei awoke to the sensation of a pounding
headache. A woman's voice kept asking, "Are you
okay? Hello? Kalei? Are you okay?"

The voice sounded oddly familiar, yet different.
Kalei tried to place it, but the relentless hammering in
her skull only increased with the effort. She wanted to
just roll away and block it all out, but the voice kept
pestering and pestering; it wouldn't let her rest. So,
Kalei opened her eyes. Leaning over her, silhouetted
against the blue sky, Kalei saw a face that finally placed
the name.

"Lecia?" Kalei hadn't seen her since elementary
school, but here she sat, grown up Lecia Ma'Lory,
complete with soft blonde hair, a cheeky smile, and
enough layers of clothing to hide her lean curves and

make her look like someone's grandmother. Beneath the woman's brown cardigan, Kalei saw a thick red shirt and another yellow turtleneck peeking out above the collar. Add some brown slacks and a pair of mittens, and here sat a young woman wearing a blind old lady's wardrobe. Kalei couldn't believe how ridiculous the girl looked.

The last time Kalei saw Lecia, they were in the fifth grade, arguing over whether or not Estranged had souls. The argument hadn't been particularly philosophical. In the end, Kalei punched the girl in the face for disagreeing with her. As a result, Kalei was transferred to another school – this was her fifth such offense – and Kalei hadn't seen Lecia since. She didn't regret it either. Lecia had always been ridiculously stubborn in her opinion that Estranged weren't all bad. Kalei couldn't stand it.

Then Kalei remembered something more immediate: the hand with the clear fingernails. A wave of panic hit her, but before Kalei could say anything, a sudden wave of nausea made her roll over and heave. It was a painful, wrenching process, especially as there was nothing in her stomach to expel. As the spasms slowly subsided, Kalei let out an exasperated curse, and then asked, "What happened? Did I kill—" Kalei almost heaved again. "My hand, I think I touched..."

Lecia's smile widened. "No worries." Her voice was cheerful as she held up a handgun, shaking it in midair like she was showing off a new toy. "I stopped you before you could do any damage."

"What? Wait—" Kalei shook her head as she tried to clear it. The nausea gave way to the more familiar stabbing in her heart. Kalei wished she could go back to the nausea. "What are you saying? Did you shoot me?" She glanced down at her body in search of some sign of blood or damage. Despite the internal agony that ripped through her, outwardly, she was fine.

Lecia's tone was so sweet it was starting to piss Kalei off. She said, "Yup, I shot you right between the eyes." She smiled again and pointed the gun at Kalei's forehead, innocently closing one eye as she looked down the sights at Kalei. She whispered a soft *"Bang"* before pulling the gun back and setting it down beside her.

Kalei flinched at the blatant disregard for gun safety. This woman had clearly lost her mind. Nonetheless, she could feel something warm on her face where Lecia had pointed. She reached up above the bridge of her nose and her fingers found something wet and sticky. She pulled her hand away and saw blood. Her hand quickly shot back to her face, where it searched for the source— the injury— but there was none. The skin beneath the blood was completely smooth.

Lecia watched the process with gentle concern. "If you don't believe me, you can check the back of your head. You were a cop. You know what firearms do to a person's skull at close range."

Kalei's hand moved to the back of her scalp and she

felt... skin. Her hair was gone. This time, there was no blood, just smooth, fresh skin.

Was Lecia implying – it wasn't possible. If it was – the thought was absolutely horrifying. Although as much as Kalei didn't want to believe, it made sense. She recalled the woman she saw in the store, the Estranged that had closed her eyes, even though she should be dead...

Could Estranged really – could they regenerate themselves?

Kalei tried to wrap her head around the idea, but before she could make another mental step, the pounding in her head turned to a screaming siren and it was all she could do to squeeze her eyes shut in an attempt to block it out. She couldn't think, but her emotions still ripped and roiled through her. Kalei's sense of helplessness, confusion, and frustration grew, but the heightened emotions only fed the— whatever it was that was consuming her from the inside out. She hunched over and grabbed at her skull as she tried to find a way out of this madness. Her breathing became ragged; a harsh whisper slipped through her lips. "What is happening to me?"

She hadn't expected an answer, she hadn't even meant to say anything, but she heard Lecia's voice answer, calm and reassuring. "It's the darkness."

Kalei squeezed her eyes tighter; every muscle along her body was beginning to seize and contract. She forced herself to respond past the internal hell that was trying to bury her. Maybe if she could just keep her attention on the conversation, she could climb her way out. She demanded, "The what?"

"The darkness." Lecia was kind and eager in her response. "When the Estranged touched you—"

"He turned me into an Estranged. Fuck! I know!" Kalei clenched her teeth as the daggers sharpened at her rage.

Lecia replied, "I'm sorry. I understand you know a lot about Estranged. You used to be a police officer, but—"

"Used to?" *Fuck!* Kalei bowed even deeper into her crouch. "I *am* a police officer! I am Kalei Distrad, member of the 39th Distri— Gah!— CPD!"

Lecia paused for a moment. Kalei couldn't see past the dirt-smeared skin of her knees on the pavement, but she knew Lecia was watching her. Kalei tried to fight down the pain inside, she tried to make it go away— anything— *black-nailed hands – No!* There were no Estranged around, and Kalei was not about to kill Lecia. The thought made her nauseous, and she felt the pain grow with her desperation. She heard Lecia quietly reply, "No, Kalei. You are Estranged now. I'm sorry, but whatever you were before... you have to let it go."

"Shut up!" Kalei screamed. But even as she said it, she knew Lecia was right. Kalei placed both hands flat on the pavement and watched as they slowly clenched into fists. Her partner Marley, her coworkers, her neighbors, even the young lady at the coffee shop she frequented; that entire world was lost to her now. Just like Fenn, Kas, and Teia... Flower-Boy was right. She would never see them again. Any of them, dead or alive. Kalei always knew the name *Estranged* was a fitting term for those cast out from society by those black-nailed hands, but now she *knew.* She could feel the accuracy of that name down to her core. She was Estranged now. Her whole life, although it lay just on the other side of the fence, was gone.

She felt a soft pressure on her shoulder. "Don't!" Kalei quickly pulled away and turned on the woman. "Stay away from me! Do you have a death wish?"

Lecia held up a gloved hand. "It's okay. I—"

"No!" Kalei glared, holding firm until the woman let her hand fall into her lap. But Lecia wasn't entirely resigned. She fixed Kalei with a stubborn stare, and they remained like that for several moments, each silently willing the other to back down and face the truth. Of course, Kalei knew their versions of the truth differed tremendously. In Kalei's mind, she was already as good as dead from the moment her nails went black, and she knew Lecia needed to get out of Downtown while she was still alive. But Kalei suspected that Lecia was probably here because she thought she could save everyone. That was Lecia, off to save the misunderstood with her cheery smiles. But the woman's efforts were pointless. Nothing could make Kalei's black nails go away. Not even a happy little chat polished off with a nice pat on the shoulder.

Lecia relaxed and broke the silence. "We never could get along, could we?"

Kalei leaned back and rubbed an aching muscle in her hand, the newest addition to her collection of negative sensations. "Of course not. You always wanted to save all the Estranged."

"And you wanted to kill them."

Kalei turned away and studied the morning fog, which still clung to some of the distant buildings. Of course she wanted to kill Estranged. Who would want to let them live? They took Downtown away from the city of Celan, they took away daughters and brothers and mothers...They stole everything that was good in this world, leaving behind the darkened corpses to remind everyone of just how dark their world had become. "They don't deserve to live."

Out of the corner of her eye, Kalei saw Lecia raise an eyebrow. "So you don't deserve to live?"

Kalei clenched her teeth. "No. I don't."

Kalei turned back and saw Lecia drop her gaze to her hands as she said, "I'm sorry..." After a moment, Lecia looked up at Kalei, but this time, there was hope in her eyes. "But you don't have to feel that way— I can help!"

"And what the hell makes you think you can help me?" Kalei growled.

Lecia sat up a bit straighter, a goofy grin growing on her face. "I'm an unofficial Estranged counselor."

Kalei scoffed. Why did this not surprise her?

"Unofficial? That means no one's stupid enough to pay you, right?"

Lecia lost her smile and picked up a note of defiance as she said, "Well, there isn't any institutional recognition yet, but that's going to change when I publish my book."

Kalei couldn't take this naïve little woman seriously. "Ha! A book?" The words came out easily, but Kalei quickly shut down as a fresh wave of pain rushed back into her skull.

Lecia drove on. "Yes, a book. Is that so hard to believe? I want people like you to understand that there are more to Estranged than just highs and death."

Kalei didn't hear her. Her own breath became labored again. She could feel the sharp bite of a craving creeping in. It started in her heart and seemed to work its way into her arms, causing her muscles to twitch and clench at the impulse to just grab one hand... *Gah!* Kalei fought it. She reminded herself that Lecia had almost died by her. Of course, the girl had it coming, considering she was wandering Downtown alone, but nonetheless, Kalei refused to let herself be the one responsible for the inevitable. As much as she couldn't stand Lecia, she had to admit that nobody deserved what she was going through, not even this stupid little woman. So Kalei fought the aching need, and the need retaliated by sending sharp muscle spasms through her body. Kalei tried to pull herself back to the conversation, hoping to distract herself again. "I don't care what you're spouting; you need to get out of here. You need to leave Downtown before you get yourself killed. Do you really think all your counseling and your books are really going to help anything? Because they aren't." Kalei let out a groan and pulled her arms close as she fought off another spasm.

Lecia looked to be conflicted between concern and frustration. "Look— will you just listen to me! I can help you, I promise."

Kalei raised her eyes to meet Lecia's and growled, "The only thing I need from you is another bullet to my head."

Lecia quietly asked, "You want to die?"

Kalei didn't even have to think about it. "Yes."

Lecia scooted another inch closer, but Kalei pulled away. She said, "You already know that can't happen. "

Kalei let out another groan. "Since when are Estranged immortal?"

"They always have been." Lecia shrugged as she continued, "People just don't want to believe it. They see an Estranged die on the street and they don't want to see him or her get back up. So they let themselves believe that they won't. Of course, SWORDE does a good job of —"

"I don't care!"

Lecia paused. She looked into Kalei's eyes this time. "I think you do."

Kalei buried her head in her arms. "I don't. I don't care, I just need you to go away."

Silence fell. The spasms had subsided, but now the muscles along Kalei's arms slowly began to clench harder and harder until she felt like the flesh would burst from her skin. And still it continued. No matter what she did, she couldn't fight it. The sharp pains, the spasms, the aches; it all kept coming back at her in one form or another. "What's doing this to me?" she asked weakly.

"The darkness."

"The darkness? You're saying that bullshit they spout on the news is—" Kalei paused to curse as a particularly vicious stab of pain wrenched at her hip. "You're saying sad emotions are ripping me to shreds right now?"

"Well, they aren't really emotions anymore. I mean— yes, you still have emotions, and yes, the darkness is driven by sadder ones, but the darkness is... kind of a living thing now."

"What? You mean I have something living inside me?"

"Well— it's not really a *thing*. It's still you, it's—" Lecia let out an exasperated sigh. "This is so hard to explain."

Kalei pushed her fist into the knot in her hip. "With you telling it, it's hard to understand."

Lecia paused for a moment to collect her thoughts, and then said, "The exact 'what' doesn't really matter. All you really need to know is that the darkness is inside you now, and that is what's causing the pain. It is also the thing that causes the highs and all of that."

This was all too much. Lecia, the darkness, the pain... With labored breath, Kalei asked, "Why?"

Lecia leaned forward and rested her head on her hands. "We don't know."

Kalei clenched her teeth. She felt hot tears building in the sides of her eyes. She thought to herself, *So it was the darkness, huh?* Some negative emotion-feeding *thing* that wasn't a thing had taken away the three remaining people she loved in this stupid world... "This is all so friggin' pointless." She angrily brushed the tears out of her eyes with the heel of her palm. "They didn't deserve to die by this bullshit."

"Oh yeah. I'm so sorry about your parents— and your sister. You know—"

Kalei was pissed at Lecia's thick head. "Not them!" She paused as she was reminded of the loss of her first family. "Not just them... but my nieces." She sniffed defiantly. "And my husband."

"Your husband?" Lecia's voice was painted with confusion as her eyebrows met. "I heard about the attack on your house, but all the reports said there were no casualties. Well— that is— except for you. Fenn and the girls were taken into SWORDE custody."

CHAPTER THREE

Introductions

The revolving door had deteriorated to nothing more than a twisted frame and a pile of glass. Kalei stormed past, heedless of the shards that tore at her bare feet. The only thing she could feel right now was rage.

The foyer was large— more like immense. The ceiling rose at least forty feet above Kalei's head, inlaid with delicate artisanal moldings and bearing a ragged, gaping hole where a chandelier once hung. The marble floor was cracked directly below the cavity, and all around the walls were dirty and missing chunks of plaster with a few scattered paintings hanging at odd angles. On the back wall, four elevator doors stood in silence with so many dents and scratches in their tarnished metal that Kalei doubted they still functioned.

After casting a glance over all this rotted grandeur, Kalei spotted someone sitting at the desk off to her left. Whoever it was either was very short or was sitting in a very low chair because all she could see was the top of their head.

She crossed the room and discovered he was short.

Or rather, he was a kid. A kid who looked to be no more than ten years old, lounging with his feet up on the counter. She couldn't believe it. Lecia had told her this place was SWORDE headquarters, but instead, she found an abandoned hotel with a lazy brat. She wanted to kill Lecia for this sick prank, but the girl was already long gone on some deranged mission. Kalei approached the worn marble counter, her anger growing like a ball over fire, expanding with the heat until it threatened to explode.

"Where the fuck is SWORDE?" she demanded.

The boy calmly took his feet off the counter and set down the book he had been reading. Despite his short stature, he looked somewhat stately in his tailored suit. A brown and black silk tie tucked neatly into a well-fitted, chocolate-colored vest, and a white dress shirt sat beneath it all and covered his arms down to his wrists. A matching brown jacket hung on the back of the chair, and the entire ensemble stood at odds with the boy's black, springy hair.

As his hand released the book, Kalei's attention was drawn to his exposed fingers. A surge of energy spiked up her neck, and Kalei's head involuntarily jerked to one side to release it. As soon as the rush was gone, more bursts began to arise in her arms, in her legs, in her fingers... Kalei clenched her fists and tensed her muscles, doing her best to suppress the energy that accompanied a fierce urge to grab that small boy's hand. Seeing the dark rectangles in his nails didn't help her battle. Knowing that he was Estranged, her mind worked to justify the innocence of grabbing that hand for just one, small high... But Kalei needed her mind clear. She needed to make sure her family was okay.

Kalei pulled her attention away from the hand and looked at the boy's face instead.

The boy met her eyes with a calm, scholarly gaze and answered, "This is SWORDE. May I help you?" His voice was composed and quiet, despite the slightly higher notes his youth added to his formal accent.

Kalei found the child-playing-grownup to be insulting. "Yeah, fucking right. A brat sitting in a hotel? Do you think I'm an idiot? We both know this isn't SWORDE, so tell me where SWORDE headquarters is!"

The boy studied her for a moment, then his chin inclined slightly as recognition lit in his eyes. He said, "Ah, I know who you are." He leaned back in his chair and interlocked his fingers across his small abdomen as though he were a professor examining a new student. Kalei's attention was once again drawn to those hands, both sets of digits fitting together like pieces of a puzzle. The aching desire in her heart strained to be fed by just *one* touch... Kalei clenched her fists harder and felt all the muscles in her arms ache as she fought against the impulse. Her head jerked again to release a fresh influx of energy.

The boy continued, "If I have judged correctly, you think you know all about SWORDE. When you were an officer of the law, you saw us quite nearly every day, calling upon the Wardens to deal with the Estranged incidents as they popped up throughout the city. It must have been quite difficult for you to let someone else protect the citizens of Celan while you stood by, tasked with keeping the curious onlookers out of harm's way. As I recall, you have submitted an application to SWORDE every quarter since you joined the force, am I correct?"

The surging energy and Kalei's anger coalesced into one massive rush, and her ears became overwhelmed by a drawn-out shriek, like metal dragging against metal. She slammed her fist into the marble counter, pouring all of her pain and emotion into the blow as she yelled, "How the fuck do you know!"

"Didn't he tell you?" said a voice from the other side of the foyer. "You're in SWORDE Headquarters."

She turned around and saw a man in full SWORDE uniform step out from one of the elevators. Despite being covered from neck to toe in black, his helmet was off so she could see his sturdy, masculine face topped with light, short cut hair. Next to him stood—

"*YOU!*" Kalei's lips twisted into a snarl.

The teenager with the flowered nails stood beside the uniformed man. She was furious to find the young man here, to find him fraternizing so calmly with a Warden. To have him address her in such a condescending manner. Kalei started forward but then stopped herself. She was still wary of him after their last encounter on the street. Her parents' murderer and his companion casually stopped where they stood just outside the closing elevator doors. The door screeched and rattled as it slid along a broken rail until finally it came to a stop with a resounding bang.

Kalei was the one who broke the silence. "What the fuck are you doing here?"

"I'm the Director of SWORDE."

"Like fuck!" Her head twitched violently. "Where is Fenn?"

"He isn't any of your concern anymore."

"You let me think he was dead!"

His reply was a flat, emotionless statement. "It's better that way."

A harsh, heavy sort of pain grabbed and dragged at Kalei's chest. "Is it? Is that really what you think! What about the girls? What about their dad? Does he even know what happened?" The darkness pulled even harder. She bent over and clutched at her screaming heart. "The fuck ..." she finished weakly.

Kalei heard hushed whispers echoing off the cold walls. She looked up and saw two women and a man at the edge of the foyer, just inside the hallway. One of the women, a tall, black-haired lady in a SWORDE uniform, was whispering to her shorter, casually dressed companion. All three of them watched Kalei closely, as though she were a new act in a show. More people began to press in behind the first three, but Kalei didn't pay attention. She was more interested in the hands of the second woman. Her small, exposed hands. They had what looked like a black raindrop on each nail. Another set of hands behind her had zigzags; yet another had what looked like eyes.

Unable to control the impulse, Kalei lunged at the small woman. Yet she hadn't made it more than a foot before she relentlessly tore her eyes away from the woman's hand and planted her feet on the cold marble to halt her momentum. The sudden reversal threw Kalei onto her backside.

Denying herself the hand and the high released a massive backlash from the darkness. It ripped through Kalei's body like so many razorblades pushing though her veins. She screamed out as she tried to contain the furious slicing that ripped at every muscle, every bone, every— curling up in a ball, she resisted a growing urge to reach for the hand again, just to be rid of the battle.

She heard the murderer's footsteps as he approached. She saw his feet stop at the edge of her vision. "You're an Estranged now. If you see Fenn, he will die."

Kalei lunged at the teenager, this time not holding back. "I'll fucking kill you!" But before she could make contact, his companion grabbed her wrist and redirected her momentum, using it to spin her around and pin her fist to her back. Then, with a tremendous amount of force, he cut her feet out from under her and slammed her into the ground. Kalei thought she heard her jaw crack as she hit the unforgiving surface.

The teenager hadn't moved a step. He said stoically, "You're welcome to kill me. But you can't."

"What? You don't think I can find a bullet big enough?" Kalei struggled and twitched beneath her captor's grasp. "Don't worry. I'll find it, and when I do, I'll slaughter you all!"

Unfazed by Kalei's screaming, the young man stated, "It's not a bullet."

Kalei grew still for a moment. She retorted, "What?"

"There is a way to kill Estranged, but it's not a bullet."

Kalei snarled, "Too scared to tell me what it is? Tell me and I'll kill you right now!"

"I already told you, you can't." Kalei's head twitched violently and smacked into the ground. A sensation like an icepick tearing through bone shot through Kalei's jaw, confirming it was cracked. Dazed, she heard Flower-boy continue, "Get yourself in check."

The teenager was already retreating from the room when Kalei called after him as best she could through her swelling jaw, "Where tha fugh is Fenn!"

Without turning or changing his stride, he casually replied, "You'll know when I'm dead."

The teenager left the foyer.

Kalei's captor and the boy from the desk escorted her to one of the rooms on the second floor. The boy explained that she was not a prisoner; she was free to come and go as she pleased.

The boy told her, "When you feel you are ready, we can teach you how to control the darkness. Or, you can go live in the district as you were, pursuing highs and living out your days as you please. In either case, the choice is yours."

Kalei stopped glaring at the uniformed man to turn her attention to the kid. At this point, her jaw was fully swollen, and it felt as though half her face was being pounded over and over again with a giant hammer. The growing migraine didn't help anything either. Kalei kept her mouth shut and snarled at the boy.

He replied, "Terin didn't lie to you. There is a way to kill Estranged, and we can teach you that as well. But that knowledge is restricted to those who become Wardens of SWORDE, for your own safety. If you accept our offer, you are welcome to become a Recruit in our program."

Kalei opened her jaw just wide enough to mumble, "Go to Hell."

They shut the door behind her.

The room was large. Where she stood could have been considered a living room, and a door off to her left suggested a bedroom. Kalei's eyes swept over a stately, wooden coffee table snapped in two and leaning at an odd angle against the near wall. A sofa was buried in a small mountain of its own guts; foam, springs, and feathers strewn about like a day-old pile of snow after

Christmas. All around the room were smaller piles of glass and ceramic shrapnel where the mirrors and artisanal pieces of the room had met abruptly with the floor and other hard surfaces. On a table against the right wall, a single crystal glass stood among the ruins of the other whiskey glasses and decanters, which had once made up an elegant set. In its day, this room had been grand. Now, it was a cage for animals.

Kalei didn't know why they put her in this room. She didn't care. She just needed –*a hand*– No. She just needed time and quiet to sort out the chaos that raged through her.

Kalei charged through the room, heedless of the various kinds of shrapnel that dug into her bare feet. Then Kalei dropped down into the far right corner, where she put her back against the two walls where they met. For a moment, she watched the pair of doors opposite her, the front door and the bedroom door, wary of the possibility that someone might come out to... *I don't know, but I'm sure I wouldn't like it.* Then her head twitched violently, and in a burst of energy and emotion, her fist reached out and slammed into the wall. Infuriated, frustrated by these impulses, Kalei clenched her unruly fists and watched the knuckles strain against her skin. She waited for a count to three. Then, she counted to ten. After that, she pulled her knees to her chest, clasped her hands together in front of them, and bent her head forward to rest in the quiet space she had created. Once there, she bid her body to be still.

The moment Kalei closed her eyes, her mind was thrust into a battleground. The war ripped and rang through every nerve, every muscle in her body. It sent impulses to her limbs and drove energy vibrating through every cell. Kalei struggled to contain it, but behind her efforts, she felt a deep and biting despair. She felt a fierce conviction that there was nothing left. No power to her name, and no reason to reclaim it. She had lost everything. Fenn. Family. Everything. She was Estranged now. Her world was dead.

Then she remembered how she had almost killed Lecia. It all happened so fast, there wasn't time to pull back her hand. If Lecia hadn't... it could've been so easy. Taking a life was so easy, so effortless now. Kalei was appalled by the thought. Her stomach heaved at the thought. But it was true. That could have been Kas or Fenn's hand. Now that she knew Fenn and the girls were alive, she knew it was possible. She remembered Teia holding out her hand to Kalei with a small ladybug cupped in it... Kalei would not allow herself to lose control again.

So instead, Kalei immersed herself in the pain. After a while, the addiction lost its hold amidst the quiet, endless violence. It faded, and it became no more than a distant echo to Kalei's dark thoughts.

She opened her eyes then, and she found herself lying on the floor. As she moved to sit up, she felt a series of stabbing sensations— *in* her feet? She looked down and saw shards of glass and splinters of wood lodged into the soles of each foot, wedged beneath layers of dirt and dried blood. She reached down to scrape the blood away and found that the skin and muscle had healed around the objects. No swelling, no redness, no sign of any injury aside from the random items protruding here and there. It was unsettling to look at.

Kalei braced herself for what came next. She gripped the first piece of splintered wood firmly between her thumb and forefinger. It appeared to be a piece off the coffee table, a solid chip of pine with slivers sticking out at odd angles where the wood had broken off from the polished body of the table. Only an inch of the wood could be seen before it disappeared into the soft flesh of her instep. With a deep breath, she ripped it out. Blood and pain blossomed from the new hole, and Kalei cried out and nearly bit her tongue off as her teeth clamped together. Yet strangely, this new pain was welcoming. It was almost... good. She grabbed the next piece and continued with her grim task, and all the while, the enraged flesh distracted Kalei's senses from her inner torment. It was a relief to be away from those darker battles, if only for a moment. But as soon as the fragments were free, the wounds quickly recovered and the external pain subsided, allowing the darkness from her heart to flow back in. For every sharpened fragment she pulled out, she resisted the urge to reapply it elsewhere.

When at last her feet were free of their contaminants

and the final wounds had healed— unnaturally fast—
Kalei wanted nothing more than to curl up in her
corner and die. Instead, she pushed herself off the floor,
carefully made her way across the room, and grabbed
the door handle.

Kalei didn't know how many times the sun and the
moon had passed by her window, nor could she say how
many meals she had skipped. Neither hunger nor sleep
plagued her anymore. She looked back at the cracked
window at the far side of the room and saw only a
warped reflection from the single fluorescent light that
shone from the ceiling. It was too dark outside to see
the world without, but somewhere in the distance, she
could hear the screeching of a hungry bat. She didn't
care. She opened the door.

In the hallway, a figure in full SWORDE uniform
spotted her. As the uniform stepped forward, a stern
woman's voice came through the visor. "This way."
Without waiting to see if Kalei would follow, she turned
and walked down the hall.

Kalei followed, for lack of anything better to do.
The woman led her through the battered hallway and
down a grand set of carpeted, rotting stairs— which
smelled terrible, like someone had poured milk down
the walls and left cabbage out to spoil. The mold and
spores that squished beneath her feet only served to add
to the cacophony of smells. It made the musty, dried
blood smell of her room seem like a basket of roses.

All the while, Kalei's escort didn't say a word. Kalei

was grateful for the silence. She had enough going on within her own skull without having to worry about anyone else's bullshit. They walked along another hallway, passing a series of heavy wooden doors with small windows, and each with a small placard beside the door that read, "Conference Room." Most of the rooms appeared to be empty, but occasionally, Kalei would spot a person or two lurking in the corners or sitting at a table.

The room Kalei was shown into was as simple as all the others: four walls with peeling wallpaper leaning over an old, abused table like aged corporate directors looking down upon some old plan or proposal. At the head of the table sat the little boy from the foyer wearing a blue suit similar to his brown one. To his right sat an old woman with frayed white hair standing at all angles on her head, and a heavy brown coat that looked to be a size too large sat on her shoulders. She seemed to be shaking from head to toe. *It's not that cold in here*, Kalei thought passively.

The boy looked up. "Ah! There you are. Mar here is a bit ahead of you, but I don't think she will mind slowing her lessons while you catch up."

Kalei's escort was already retreating down the hall. Kalei watched her go and then looked at the little boy. "Where is Fenn?"

"He is safe. That is all you need to know." The boy stood up and flashed Kalei a smile. "Won't you join us?"

Kalei clenched her jaw. She had expected as much. SWORDE wasn't going to give her a straight answer. She nodded to the old woman. "What is this?"

"Training," he responded cheerfully.

Kalei didn't return his enthusiasm. "Why?"

"It is requisite; all Recruits must go through it. You should join us. I assure you, it will not be a waste of your time."

"I think it would be," Kalei replied apathetically. "I have no intention of joining the organization that killed my parents and kidnapped my husband."

The old woman looked up and brusquely shouted, "Shut up! Your stupid whining is breaking my concentration, you little bitch!"

The boy calmly reassured the old woman and set her back to her task with a few small words. Then he turned back to Kalei and said, "Come now. SWORDE had nothing to do with your parents' deaths. The organization wasn't even founded until the following year."

Kalei was disconcerted by the fact that he knew exactly when her parents were murdered. "Perhaps, but the man who founded SWORDE had everything to do with it, and there is no way in hell I am working for him." Kalei was fed up with their games. She turned and left the odd pair to their lessons.

Nobody stopped Kalei as she found her way to the main exit, not the boy or anyone else. This time, the front desk was empty as she carefully stepped through the shattered doors and into the night.

The cool breeze was nice, like a distant whisper carrying the scents of the sea to Kalei's nose to calm her despite her battle with the darkness. Kalei could feel it now that the addiction had faded. The darkness beat against her: a steady, consuming drum that made her body its home and brought her nothing but misery. She could see no point to it. There was no point to any of it.

Kalei wandered the cold streets, the rough bite of the pavement on her bare feet an echoing reminder of the shards that had been ripped out just minutes before. Kalei watched the cracked asphalt pass beneath her and tried to make sense of it all. Everything was a mess. It was as though she finally fell asleep that late night and now she couldn't wake up.

She thought about the trip to the park with her two nieces. Kalei felt as though it had happened only a couple days ago. But something told her it had been much, much longer since she had seen them.

And only SWORDE knew where they were now. The story might be that they were in Victim Protection, but what did that mean? The truth was, it could mean anything. Once people went into Victim Protection, they were never heard from again. For all Kalei knew, Fenn could be dead. The girls could be slaves. Or worse. They could be Estranged like Kalei. She didn't want to think about it.

And then there was the attack that brought her here. Kalei had been on the scene of many attacks, if only to keep the peace, and she had never heard of more than two or three Estranged being involved in one attack. A couple dozen indicated something more, something organized. Estranged didn't just get together and buy a couple motorcycles before attacking a random house. No. And it couldn't be a coincidence that Xamic was there either, on the anniversary of her parents' death.

But why? And why was it that when she woke up, the other guy was there, the teenager with the flowered nails? None of it made any sense.

The only thing she did know for sure was that SWORDE was a sham. The people in Celan thought they were being protected by SWORDE. Heck, Kalei had even idolized them growing up; they were the only ones who could do anything against the Estranged. And now she knew they were Estranged themselves. The thought made Kalei want to vomit. She felt betrayed. She felt infuriated.

The list of people Kalei needed to kill had just gotten longer.

After her parents died, Kalei had decided that she would exterminate every Estranged in existence. Not just for revenge, but to protect everyone in the city. When she was ten, she used to sneak out at night with her foster mom's old revolver, searching for the black-nailed monsters so that she could exterminate them all.

But Kalei never found an Estranged on those excursions. Most nights, she never met anyone on the streets. Some nights, a stranger would find her and bring her back home. Kalei always resented that. At school, she heard about Estranged attacks all the time, but somehow, she was incapable of being at the right place at the right time. More than anything, she wanted to stop those attacks from happening. Even as young as she was, she didn't want any more people to suffer the way she did. Of course, there was always the possibility she would fail and fall victim to an Estranged. If that happened, she'd always hoped she would be dead instead of turned. The gaping hole that was created when her parents died left her okay with leaving this world behind.

Then one day, she was climbing out the bathroom window when she met a boy her age. He was lost, crying, and utterly shocked when he saw her sneaking out of the house. "What are you doing! It's night time— get inside!" His arms were clenched close to his chest. His head quickly checked left to right and then returned to Kalei. "You're going to get killed! I'm going to get killed! Big brother said Estranged come out at night and go after— Oh man, I don't want them to eat me!" And with that, the boy burst into tears.

Kalei dropped down to the grass with a soft thud and retorted with all her nine-year-old confidence, "You idiot, Estranged don't eat people! Besides, they come out in the daytime too. It's not like they're nocturnal."

The boy looked up at her and snuffled. "Nocturnal?"

"It means they only wake up at night, stupid, which they don't. So stop whining." She pulled out her foster mother's gun and stormed off into the street.

The young boy panicked. "What are you doing!"

"I'm going to shoot an Estranged," Kalei yelled back.

"What!" The boy was totally bewildered. He ran after her. "You can't do that! They're bigger than you! You'll die!"

"Yeah, right. I'll shoot 'em before they can even get close!" she retorted arrogantly.

The boy started crying, louder and harder than before. He caught up to her and clung to her arm as he blubbered, "Please don't go after the Estranged, please!"

That night had changed things for Kalei. The boy refused to move until Kalei went back into her house, but when Kalei tried to ditch him, he followed her doggedly, too terrified to be left alone. He followed her for an hour before Kalei realized he truly didn't know his way home. She might have been willing to sacrifice herself in the pursuit of Estranged, but she didn't want this sniffling little boy to get hurt. She asked the boy for his address, but he wouldn't tell her. He wasn't just scared for himself. The tight grip on her forearm, determination in his eyes despite the trembling of his jaw; it occurred to Kalei that he was scared for her too. Until she promised to stop hunting Estranged, he wouldn't allow her take him home. But she refused.

And thus, a long and loud debate between nine year olds ensued. It was a sign of the times that no one dared step outside to scold the two kids.

"Why do you have to kill Estranged?" the boy insisted.

Kalei's hands clenched into fists, the gun tucked safely into her belt. "Because they killed my parents!"

"So! That doesn't mean you have to kill them. That's what SWORDE is for. Didn't you hear? They built a big huge fence in the city and they've been throwing Estranged in there and keeping them locked up!"

"They shouldn't be locking them up; they should be shooting 'em," Kalei replied sullenly, crossing her arms.

The boy became animated, eager to share his knowledge. "They do that too!"

Kalei's arms unfolded and a smile slipped onto her face. "Really?"

"Yeah! I saw it in the newspaper! They do it all the time. Not even the police can fight Estranged anymore. Only SWORDE can take 'em on!"

The boy's enthusiasm became infectious. Kalei's grin widened. "Really!"

The boy nodded, all knowing. "Yeah, because the police aren't strong enough to stop the Estranged. They keep dying. That's why my mom says no one wants to be police officers anymore."

"So. The police are just wimps! Anyone can kill an Estranged. It's easy!" Kalei held up her borrowed gun proudly.

"Have you killed an Estranged?" the boy asked in wonder.

"Maybe yes, maybe no," she replied.

The boy caught on. "You have not!"

Kalei's lip pouted out defiantly and her eyebrows came together. "So! I will!"

The boy's eyes widened. "But— but what if they kill you?"

"They won't," Kalei replied, her eyebrows returning to normal and her chest sticking out boldly.

The boy started to cry again. "But if the police keep dying, then that means you'll die too! I don't want you to die! Don't go after them, please! I don't want anyone else to die. Not you too!"

Kalei relaxed, concern growing in her eyes for the first time that night. "Who else died?"

"My— my best friend Freddy," the boy sniffed.

"Oh," Kalei said.

The boy cried for a while longer, and then suddenly he became enthusiastic. "Oh! I know! You can join SWORDE! Then you won't die and you can kill all the Estranged you want!" He grinned at Kalei, eager for her approval.

"Why can't I just kill them now?" she asked sullenly.

"Because you'll die," he pointed out sternly, glaring at her through puffy eyes.

Kalei considered him for a moment, then decided she wasn't going to win against this whiny boy. "Fine, I won't kill any Estranged until I join SWORDE."

That was the night she met Fenn. That was the promise she made to him. Now what was she supposed to do? SWORDE was run by the very people she had been determined to kill.

CHAPTER FOUR

The Other Side

Kalei passed beneath streetlight after streetlight, watching the night close around her when she passed under a burnt-out lamp, and then letting it retreat again as she stepped into the light of the next one. She felt anger, frustration, and pure hatred. She hated the bastard who killed her parents, she hated SWORDE, she hated the world, she hated herself. She wished she could take a knife, stab it through her heart, and then tear the blade down across her abdomen so she could reach in and rip out all the stupidity, futility, and stabbing pain that resided within her.

Kalei passed by the hollow husks of restaurants, shopping centers, and a decimated children's museum. Sitting on top of these corpses stood the ever-present skyscrapers, penning Kalei in and blocking out the sky, making the night feel all the darker. Kalei's eyes skipped from one building to the next, taking in what little she could see of their crumbling stone and rusting metal. She wished every one of these structures were on fire, burned to the ground so the people of Celan didn't have to be haunted by these dark memorials anymore. She hated it; she hated it all. Still, she walked on in the cold, dark night.

"Oh hey! Kalei!"

Kalei saw Lecia approach from an intersection up ahead, but she didn't respond. Lecia dodged a dormant delivery truck that sat deserted in the road, and gave a small Smart car a wide berth as she made her way over to Kalei.

Kalei watched as Lecia navigated the car-littered street, surprised an Estranged hadn't jumped out of one of the vehicles to attack the woman, and alarmed at the possibility. Lecia came up to a solid walk of four sedans and a sports car, all smashed bumper to bumper. Apparently, the woman decided the best way around the pile was through it, because she opened the door to the nearest car and climbed into it.

Kalei stopped watching and marched over to the heap of metal. "Are you some kind of stupid!"

The car door nearest Kalei shuddered and then popped open. Lecia climbed out, head first. "What?"

"How did you know there wasn't an Estranged sleeping in there, huh? And what the hell are you doing down here in the middle of the night?"

Lecia smiled as she brushed off the dust she had picked up from her excursion. "Research never sleeps. So, how are things going with SWORDE?" She looked up at Kalei and grimaced, "Sheesh, you'd think they'd at least give you some decent clothes. Why are you still wearing those grubby PJs?"

Kalei looked down at herself and saw she was still wearing the same shorts and tank top she had worn on the night she was turned. Only now, they were brown, frayed, and half the shirt over the left side of her stomach was missing. Kalei was appalled. But not nearly as appalled as she was at Lecia's implication that she was involved with SWORDE now. She clarified, "I'm not with SWORDE."

"Really?" Lecia seemed confused, her eyebrows came together. "You've been gone for two weeks. I just assumed—"

"Two weeks?" Kalei repeated. That didn't seem right. And yet— "How long has it been since the attack?"

"I'm guessing you mean the one that turned you Estranged? Let me think..." Lecia paused and muttered the names of months while absent-mindedly counting them out on her fingers. "Almost a year and a half now."

A year and a half? Had it really been that long?

Lecia continued, "So, why aren't you going to work for SWORDE?"

Kalei felt the muscles in her neck tense. "I'm not going to answer that. Wait, you know SWORDE is Estranged?"

"Yeah, of course. I can't get anyone outside the fence to believe me, though. Everyone seems to think I'm a coot."

"Well, you are."

Lecia huffed up. "Am not!"

Kalei laughed, and Lecia folded her arms stubbornly. Then Lecia said, "How am I supposed to get people to listen to me if none of you will take me seriously?"

Kalei shrugged. "Stop being a coot."

Lecia scowled at Kalei. "Oh, now that's real helpful. Anyway, what are you up to now? The last time I saw you, you were all gung-ho about finding your family. Did SWORDE tell you anything?"

"No." Kalei was done talking to Lecia. The woman seemed to have a talent for getting on her nerves. Kalei turned and started to walk back to the sidewalk.

Lecia didn't get the message. She followed Kalei, keeping pace at Kalei's shoulder as she went on. "Well y'know, Tusic might have some information. I hear they've been investigating SWORDE, super-secret though, off the books—"

Kalei looked at Lecia. "Tusic? You mean the GPS company?"

"Yeah, Landen Franklin has his own organization of Estranged, kind of like SWORDE. Except they operate outside the fence and they don't get along with SWORDE very well. This one time—"

"Why would Landen Franklin have an Estranged organization?"

"Didn't you know? He's Estranged too. I guess he doesn't agree with the way SWORDE does things, so he formed his own group, but he can't get the government to hand Estranged policing authority over to him, so he's been keeping the whole thing hush-hush for PR reasons. But they still have people all over the city, he even—"

"You can't be serious."

Lecia blinked. "I am."

Kalei stopped walking and looked Lecia in the eyes. There was no way Landen Franklin was Estranged. The story went that after E-day, when the Estranged appeared in Celan and the ships stopped coming to port, the city's economy nearly collapsed. Then Landen Franklin showed up, bought up some dirt-cheap property, and manufactured some of the first GPSs in the world. He made a fortune. And then he poured that money back into the city. He dredged up the East Lake, which had formerly been unusable as a harbor, and built a brand new port away from Downtown. Then he beefed up the existing railway system, he funded a dozen non-profits, he paid for a new town hall – after he was done, the new port was full of ships again and the city's tech industry was booming. He saved Celan. And everyone in town considered him to be a hero for it.

And now Lecia was trying to tell her he was Estranged?

Lecia returned Kalei's stare with a stubborn glare and said, "Don't give me that look. Think about it: Landen Franklin has not been seen in public in fifteen years. Why?" She paused and gave Kalei a chance to respond. Kalei wasn't biting. "Because he's Estranged! He would look exactly the same as he did fifteen years ago!"

"Have you seen him in person?"

"Well, no."

"Then how can you say for certain he's Estranged?"

"Well— because—" Lecia sighed. "Look, why don't you come with me and meet one of the Tusic guys? Ask them yourself."

Kalei crossed her arms. "Why would I want to do that?"

Lecia shrugged. "What else are you going to do?"

Kalei considered her question for a moment, then unfolded her arms and said, "Fine. Lead the way."

Lecia gave a small jump and shouted, "Yes!"

As Kalei followed, she said, "Don't you ever get tired? It must be four o'clock in the morning."

"Of course I do. I'm still an Untouched, silly. I've just switched my sleeping habits around is all."

"An 'Untouched'?"

"Yeah." Lecia turned around and started walking backwards as she addressed Kalei. "Yeah, it's what people on this side of the fence call non-Estranged. Wow, you really don't know anything, do you?"

"And you really should watch where you're going."

Lecia continued to walk backwards, "Nah, I'm fine. I know this city like the back of my—" Sure enough, she tripped. Unable to offer any assistance, on account of Lecia being Untouched, Kalei sat back and watched as Lecia untangled herself from a fallen telephone pole. Kalei covered her grin with a hand placed casually across her mouth. The grin was quickly wiped away, though, as sudden burning sensation blossomed in her left lung, as though someone was pouring hot coffee into it. Kalei dropped her hand and remembered what she was.

Having finally found her feet again, Lecia stood up and resumed their journey. As Kalei stepped over the telephone pole, she asked, "If Tusic operates in the city, how does Landen keep his people from attacking Untouched?"

"Uh, well, from what I understand, Landen keeps them on a pretty tight leash. Rumor has it he's brutal to anyone who break the rules."

"How brutal?"

"I don't know. The guys were too scared to tell me."

Kalei scoffed. "They probably just fed you that bullshit to get rid of you."

Lecia's eyes widened and she looked at Kalei. "You really think so?"

"I don't know. I've never met the guys. But I know you, and that's what I would do."

Lecia huffed, "You're so mean!" and picked up her pace, leaving Kalei to catch up.

As they walked, Kalei was... well, miserable would be an understatement. Her anger had subsided for the most part, but one other thing remained: the conviction that existence was futile. By allowing herself to live,

Kalei could only bring death and despair to this world. But dying wasn't an option because she still didn't know how to kill her Estranged body. For the time being, Kalei was forced to accept that her existence was unavoidable. And if it meant bringing death and destruction to the world, then she knew where she would deliver it. But SWORDE would have to wait; she still had to find out what they had done with her family. If Fenn and the girls were alive, Kalei didn't want SWORDE hurting them to get back at her. She had to make sure they were safe first.

Lecia and Kalei reached the edge of the city, where a ten-foot-tall chain-link fence overlooked the ocean and sealed off the old docks.

"Why did they bother to build a fence around the water?" Kalei asked.

"Well, the local fisherman kept finding people drowning in the ocean, and when they went to rescue the person, well, they died. Nine times out of ten, the drownee was an Estranged. There's even one story that a couple Estranged were carried away during a storm and showed up months later on Dostralean Coast. SWORDE decided it was safer to extend the fence and keep the Estranged out of the water."

"Ah."

Kalei looked up at the fence. The metal seemed brand new, and a curling line of razorwire gleamed as it caught the light of a nearby streetlamp. A slight hum suggested it was electric as well.

Lecia noticed Kalei's inspection of the fence and said, "They pump electricity through it around the clock to keep Estranged from trying to climb over. The razor wire is just for show. It wouldn't really slow down an Estranged."

Kalei looked at Lecia. "I already know that."

Lecia smiled. "But what you don't know is that *I* have a solution for electricity." She pulled her book bag forward and started rummaging through it until she produced what looked like the clamps from an old jumper cable. Except, instead of a cable connecting the two, each of the clamps had their own homemade device jerry-rigged onto them. It looked like someone had taken the battery pack out of a half dozen cellphones and applied a lot of duct tape. "A friend of mine made 'em for me," she said proudly.

Kalei jibed, "What? Couldn't convince the Wardens to let you in the front gate?"

Lecia giggled. "SWORDE frowns upon Untouched visitors." She chuckled some more at her own joke and then walked over to the fence. A narrow hole had been cut through the chain-link, although both sides of the hole still came together and prevented anyone from passing through without touching the fence. Lecia reached out her hands, held the clamps to either side of the gap, and, turning her head away, she quickly clamped the devices onto the metal. As she did so, she hastily jumped back, shaking her hands as though trying to get something off. Lecia took a look at the hole, and then at Kalei. A broad grin spread across Lecia's face. "There." She proudly placed her hands on her hips. "The clamps have negated the electricity around the hole. After you!"

Kalei wasn't exactly comfortable with going first, but if anyone was going to be a guinea pig against an electric fence, why not the undying? She got down on her knees and tentatively touched the metal. It felt warm to the touch, but it didn't bite.

"Well, go on," Lecia urged. Kalei shot her a glare before pushing back the chain-link and crawling through.

On the other side, the vast stone walkways spread out for about a quarter mile to Kalei's left and right. Jutting out from the walkway every few hundred feet were massive concrete docks reaching out into the water until the dark night consumed them. The water seemed dark and menacing as it swirled and crashed against the man-made structures, slowly ripping them apart piece by piece. On the nearest dock, Kalei could see that the sea had already claimed several feet of the pier where the cement had cracked and fallen away. The pieces that remained jutting above the water's surface watched her with gleaming barnacle eyes. Kalei turned away and watched Lecia crawl through the fence. She had no clue where the small woman planned to take it from here.

Having safely cleared the fence, Lecia brushed herself off and led Kalei to the next dock over. Taking a flashlight out of her bag, Lecia turned it on and took a small set of service stairs down to the water's surface. There, sheltered in the shadow of a massive, rusting cargo ship was a small dingy, bouncing and bobbing on the waves, a bright counterpart to its companion.

"Ta-dah! My ticket in and out of Downtown! Isn't she a beauty?"

The dingy was built entirely out of wood, and from what Kalei could tell in the light of the flashlight, someone had tried to paint it blue. But the paint had been applied haphazardly, missing wide sections here and there, and whatever paint had managed to make it onto the boat was already peeling away, exposing the dark, rotting wood underneath.

Kalei replied, "Yup, a real beauty."

Lecia pulled the boat closer and climbed in easily. Kalei took a long, wary look at the craft before climbing in after her, struggling not to let the boat tip under her added weight.

Once they were out on the water, Kalei started to realize what a bad idea this was. Not the fact that they were a couple girls taking a small wooden boat out onto the deepest lake-harbor in the entire continent, although that was plenty stupid in and of itself. But she was more worried about what would happen when they landed in the city. There were real people out here, and if Kalei was among them... then they could die.

Lecia had only just pushed the boat off the rocks when Kalei started to climb out. "I'm going back."

"What?" Lecia struggled to keep her balance as Kalei moved across the dingy. "No! Sit down. You're going to tip us over." But the boat was moving fast, and already they were a few feet from the rocks and drifting. With the cargo ship blocking out most of the light from downtown, the water looked cold and sinister as the tips of the waves caught the stray orange light from Lecia's flashlight and reflected it back at them. Sitting back down, Kalei resigned herself to the journey.

"How far away is this meeting spot?"

"Not far. After we land, it's just a couple blocks that way," Lecia said, pointing into the night.

As Lecia rowed away, Kalei warily watched the hulking, groaning hulls that made up the Ship's Graveyard of Westlake.

Eighteen years ago on E-day, the docks were one of the first places to be attacked. Caught unaware, and unable to pull out on the low tide, many of the ships lost half their crew to the Estranged before an alarm was raised. According to the stories Kalei had heard, most of the survivors had made it out by sheer luck.

Moments before the first attack, one man had jumped off the bow of a cruise liner, showing off at a party. When he came to the surface and heard shouts up above, he had assumed it was in reaction to his spontaneous leap. But when the shouts turned to screams, he quickly realized something was wrong and managed swim to shore before any of the Estranged spotted him.

Others were less lucky, sealing themselves into watertight holds to wait for help, only to suffocate before anyone arrived.

Kalei's eyes skipped from one hull to the next, dozens upon dozens of boats and ships, and she was reminded of just how many people had lost their lives in this place. A cold shiver ran down her spine. Even Lecia had the sense to keep the silence as she quietly rowed the dingy past the floating graves.

Eventually, they broke free of the docks and ventured out onto the open water of the harbor. The boat rocked and swayed, often tipping to alarming degrees as it was caught by the larger waves, but overall the trip was uneventful. About twenty minutes later, the floor of the dingy gave a muffled protest as it hit rock and sand.

"Here we are!" Lecia announced brightly.

While Lecia camouflaged the boat, Kalei waited and watched the bright skyline of the new city, clenching and unclenching her fists as she eyed the gleaming lights of the new skyscrapers.

When Lecia was ready, they climbed up the rocky shore and entered the part of the city known as "The Grey Zone" because of its proximity to Downtown. The most notable aspect of the district was its dirt-cheap property prices because the area was known to get occasional Estranged attacks from Downtown escapees. Only the truly desperate dared to live here.

The shops and office buildings were only marginally better maintained than the buildings that populated Downtown. In this late hour of the night, the streets were empty.

Until, true to Lecia's word, they saw a man just a couple blocks in from the water.

The guy wasn't much to look at. He leaned with his back against one of the brick buildings and one leg up against the wall. He was skinny and wore only jeans – no shirt. With no muscles to display either. Along his right arm, a tattoo of a Chinese dragon wound its way up to rest its oversized head on his shoulder; on the left side of his exposed chest, a cluster of three small black stars had been inked in. His head was bald, aside from a short Mohawk down the middle.

With black-nailed fingers, he pulled an unlit cigarette from his mouth and threw it on the ground as he demanded, "What the fuck is this about, Lecia?" He stomped on the roll of tobacco and rubbed it into the pavement with his shoe, making eye contact with Kalei. She met his glare with her own.

With a hesitant glance over her shoulder, Lecia pointed at Kalei and said, "I, uh, have a friend here who's interested in the Tusic Organization."

The man broke eye contact and looked Kalei up and down. "What the fuck do you want with Tusic, bitch?"

Kalei stood her ground. "I was thinking about joining up. But after seeing your sorry ass, I know I have the wrong place."

That didn't go over well. Pissed, he started to cross the distance between them, spitting and cursing until his phone rang. She never knew a gangster to stop in mid-rage to answer his cellphone, but this one did. He glanced at the caller ID and blanched. Suddenly shaking, he tapped the screen and answered the phone. In a tone far more polite than the one he had used with Kalei, he said, "Hey, um, ahem, hello, Boss. What? Oh. Uh huh." He grew a few shades paler. "Right." He turned to Kalei, and with an apologetic, "He, uh, wants to talk to you," he offered her the device.

"Who is it?" Kalei asked, not even reaching for it.

His lips curled back for a moment, but then he quickly stuffed the snarl away and said in a controlled voice, "You want to join up with Franklin so bad? Here he is."

Confused, Kalei took the phone. "Hello?"

"Hi, Kalei. Landen Franklin here. Sorry about my associate. Recruits are in short supply these days. So what can I do for you?"

Landen Franklin had a distinctive voice that could make anyone optimistic just by hearing it, and this was definitely it, but there was no way the man himself would be calling her up in the dead of night on some punk's phone. Voice changers were easy to acquire these days, and it wouldn't be hard to get a voice sample for a famous person like Franklin.

"What kind of game is this?"

"Excuse me?" The voice was genuinely confused.

"Why the hell would Landen Franklin be calling me up? You'd better drop the act, asshole. I'm not gonna play."

She heard a laugh on the other end as the gangster frantically mouthed, *What the fuck are you doing!*

The voice said, "Sorry, there seems to be a misunderstanding. What can I do to convince you that I'm Landen Franklin?"

"You could start by getting your ass down here."

He laughed again. "Sorry, I can't do that. How about this? Just a second." There was a pause as she heard his phone hit a hard surface, and then a beep went off in her ear. His voice was more distant when he said, "Okay, Kalei. Look at your phone."

Confused, she did as he asked. Somehow, he was able to remotely activate the video chat on her phone. And there he sat, Landen Franklin, the spitting image of his portraits from over fifteen years ago. Only, instead of shaking hands with someone important, or signing a big check for the needy, now he was lounged back in an office chair with a shuttered window behind him. A lamp on the desk lit his face in a soft orange light. "Okay, so now you know that I am who I am, and obviously you are still you. So, how is Estranged life treating you?"

Kalei was a bit bewildered to be talking to Landen Franklin, but that didn't change anything. "Cut the crap. How do you know me?"

"Your grandfather and I go way back. And right

now, I need your help."

"Which grandfather? My mom's side or my dad's?"

"Last name Demir, your mom's side. I'm guessing you never got a chance to meet him?"

"Of course not. He took off when my mom was a baby. Not exactly a great guy."

"Well, you didn't know him like I did. Before I started Tusic, your grandpa taught me everything I needed to know. In fact, if it wasn't for him and his partner, I would never be where I am today."

Kalei eyed him warily. His body language told her he was telling the truth, but... "There's no way you and my grandfather were buddies."

Franklin shrugged. "Sorry, Kalei, I don't have the time to dig into the past and explain to you what did and didn't happen, so let's move on to something I think you will understand. SWORDE is too powerful. They have too many secrets, and for the sake of this city, we need to take them down."

Kalei wholeheartedly agreed with him, but she needed to see where he was coming from first. "What makes you say that?"

Franklin leaned forward onto his desk and said, "You ever hear of SWORDE's Victim Protection Program, Kalei?"

"Of course."

"Do you know what happens to people who are entered into this program?"

Kalei swallowed a batch of saliva that had become

uncomfortably wedged in the back of her throat. "No."

He studied her closely for a moment, both hands interlocked in front of him as he watched her through the phone. It was true, his nails were black. Then he unlocked his hands, leaned back, and said, "Neither do I. Of course, I've heard some rumors, I have some ideas, but the truth is, *no one knows*. And that's how SWORDE operates. With secrets. When they confiscate the body of a victim, it is never seen again. When they arrive on the scene of a crime, nobody is allowed beyond the tape. Even the Wardens themselves all wear masks. That is not how a branch of the government should operate. This city deserves to know who is entering that burning building to save their child. When a family member dies, they should be allowed to bury the body and properly grieve their lost loved one. Or if the person has turned, they should know that too so they can protect themselves from a possible attack. SWORDE is protecting nobody with these secrets, least of all the people in the Victim Protection Program. For all we know, those people could be dying at the hands of the very same Estranged who are supposed to be protecting our city. But I want to put an end to all of that."

Kalei clenched her jaw, and she felt her jaw muscle flex and strain beneath her cheek. When he paused, she asked, "How?"

"I need someone to get into SWORDE and start uncovering those secrets. I'm working on a device right now that, once plugged into SWORDE's main computer, will upload all of SWORDE's files directly to the 39th district police station. It's going to take some time to get the device ready, but it will also take time for this person to get close enough to SWORDE that they can gain access to those computers. Will you be that person for me, Kalei?"

"What makes you think I'm the one to do it?"

"There are people within SWORDE who want to see you become a Warden. You won't have any problem getting in."

"Who?"

"The less you know, the easier it will be for you to avoid suspicion."

Kalei's jaw flexed and relaxed. Flexed and relaxed. Here was an opportunity to get everything she wanted. As a spy, she could find the whereabouts of Fenn and the girls. By exposing SWORDE, she could take them down. But it seemed too good to be true. "What's in it for you?"

"A safer city," he replied.

"One where you're in charge of the policing with your Tusic group, right?"

Franklin sighed. "I'm not going to lie to you, Kalei. Right now, that is the plan. The truth is, I just don't trust anyone else to do it."

"And why should I trust you?"

"Why not? You've seen what I've done for this city. I've been in every magazine, every newspaper, I've been on every channel. Out of all the things you've read or heard about me, do you have any reason to think that I'm not fit for the job?"

Kalei recalled the stories. In them, she had heard inspiring tales about Landen Franklin, of course, but there were also character flaws she tended to disagree with, such as his lack of funding for SWORDE and other anti-Estranged groups. Although now, she could see why. If she had to choose between the two Estranged, between him and Flower-boy, the answer became clear. "No. You seem to be the better candidate."

"So, will you do it?"

"Sure."

CHAPTER FIVE

Recruited

Kalei returned to SWORDE. Stepping over the threshold again, the knot in her gut pleaded with her to turn and run the other way. This was a bad idea, and she knew it. She was never a good liar, she was never particularly good at being stealthy, and now she was going to be a spy in the home of a murderer? She could feel her hands shaking. Kalei clenched them into fists. She had to do this. It was a necessary evil if she wanted to take down SWORDE.

A new person was at the front desk, a young woman with storm clouds on her fingernails. She was happy to escort Kalei to Erit, stepping out from behind the desk and leading the way with a warm smile. She didn't even ask Kalei for her name.

The warm welcome set Kalei further on edge. She expected she was being led to an ambush. Down one of these halls, a door would open and she would find herself overwhelmed by hungry Estranged, and they would drag her away to— Kalei stopped her imagination from carrying the nightmare further.

They wouldn't ambush her. Surely, they wouldn't? She remembered what Franklin had said; someone in SWORDE wanted her to become a Warden. It must be someone with some pull in the organization. She remembered how sincere Erit had been when he had offered her a chance to become a recruit. Could he be that person? Or was he a puppet for someone else's agenda?

They arrived at the conference room. Kalei recognized it as the same room from her last visit. The woman smiled and left Kalei with a warm "Best of luck." Kalei wondered why the woman thought she needed luck. What did this training involve?

Kalei swallowed back her concerns and opened the door. She was surprised to find Erit and the old woman exactly as she had left them, sitting at the end of the table, working away at their lessons. Did they ever sleep? Then it occurred to Kalei, she couldn't remember the last time she had slept since becoming Estranged...

The boy looked up from his work and said, "Ah, you're back. Always a pleasure to see you. Have you changed your mind about becoming a Recruit?"

Kalei paused. This was it. Time for the lies to start. Time to become a SWORDE Recruit. She swallowed hard, trying to mask her nerves with a more cheerful tone as she answered, "Yeah, I did."

"Excellent! Come. Have a seat." He indicated the seat to his right with a smile and a light pat of his hand on the wood of the table.

As Kalei moved to take her seat, someone came to the door. It was the man from the foyer— the one who'd pinned her when she attacked the murderer. "Hey! What do you think you're doing?" he demanded, walking up to Kalei, still fully uniformed and holding a helmet in one hand.

Kalei remembered her first week at the police academy. Lesson one: don't show weakness. She plopped down into her chair and looked up into his face as she crossed her arms. "I'm a Recruit," she replied stiffly. "I hear you people are in short supply of 'em."

The boy said, "Walker, this has been approved. Now would you kindly leave us to our lessons?"

Walker replied, "*Was* approved, and then the girl refused and took off. I don't think that—"

"Walker," the boy interrupted again, retaining his mild-mannered tone. "If you have a problem with this, I suggest you take it up with Terin. You have no business here."

"Erit, you know better than I do that—"

"Walker." A slight edge crept into Erit's voice. "Go."

Walker shut his mouth and scowled at Erit, then turned and left.

When he was gone, Kalei asked, "Who's Terin?" *Let the spy work begin*, she thought to herself.

The boy replied, "The Director. You may recognize him by the flowers in his nails."

"Ah." Kalei regretted becoming a mole already. She

preferred to keep her demons anonymous.

And thus, Erit, the little boy with the arrogance of a teacher, took up his role. As Erit and Kalei worked, Mar, the old woman on the opposite side of the table, sat by and worked on some "exercises" Erit had assigned to her. From what Kalei could tell, all she did was stare at the wall. Kalei quickly dismissed the old woman as she tried to feign interest in her own lessons.

"SWORDE," Erit intoned. "This, as you may know, is an acronym, standing for the organization's full and official title: The Special Wardens of Retrieving and Detaining Estranged. Now, SWORDE has a long and tragic history, going back some eighteen years to when the Estranged first appeared in the heart of the city..."

Kalei lost track of his words. She was lost in her own mind as the calmness of sitting made it more difficult to block the darkness out. It drained her. She felt as though the darkness had grabbed hold of her existence and had begun dragging her down into the void...

Bang! Kalei's reflexes kicked in and she jumped to her feet, knocking the chair aside. In front of her stood the old woman, with both palms flat against the surface of the table. A small crack in the worn wood spoke of the force the woman had brought to it when her hands crashed down. Mar lifted a veined, accusing finger to Kalei's face. Kalei resisted the urge to knock it away. "You need to take this seriously, young lady." The old woman's hand shook, and her face flushed red as a snarl grew at her mouth.

Kalei looked straight into the woman's craggy old eyes, "I am." She turned away from the lady, retrieved her chair, and forced herself to sit back down. She looked to the little boy. "You were saying?"

Mar didn't take kindly to being ignored. She lunged across the table at Kalei, but before her bony hands wrapped around Kalei's neck, Erit stopped her forward momentum with a single hand on her shoulder. Then, using that same small hand, he pushed the enraged lady back into her seat as though *she* were the child. Kalei couldn't be sure if this was a testament to Erit's strength, or to the old woman's weakness.

Through it all, Erit remained calm and amiable, a bemused tutor through and through. He patted Mar kindly on the shoulder, set her back to her assignment with a few kind words, and then moved to stand behind his own chair. "So, Kalei, what can you tell me about the work SWORDE is tasked with?"

Kalei pulled away from her thoughts and begrudgingly took on the role of obedient student. "Basically anything the police are tasked with, except their jurisdiction, is Estranged. Any Estranged found outside of Downtown are to be collected by SWORDE. Any incidents caused by Estranged are handled by SWORDE. And once SWORDE has the Estranged in custody, they are tasked with keeping them Downtown and maintaining the peace within the fence."

"*We* are tasked with keeping the peace," Erit

corrected as he stepped around the chair and sat down again. He leaned back and brought his hands up to his face, forming a teepee in front of his nose. He peered out at Kalei, studying her, deep in thought.

Kalei tried to ignore his scrutiny and found herself staring at the wall much like Mar was. Her heartbeat raced. She wondered if he suspected. Did he know about her meeting with Landen? What if...

He said, "You know, you handle the darkness remarkably well for someone who has just arrived."

Kalei released the breath she was holding. "From what I heard, it's been over a year."

"Ah, hardly." He leaned forward and waved his hand. "You were high for most of it—that does not count." Kalei gave up trying to find out where he got his information. "Look at Mar here," he continued. "She has been on this side of the fence for a couple years now. She has been working and learning with us for almost a month. Around the effort it takes to maintain control, she can hardly spare enough of her concentration to form a full sentence." Mar glared at him out of the corner of her eye. "My apologies, Mar, I did not mean any offense. Would you care to join our discussion?"

She growled, "No. I'm not going to join your fucking discussion." She seemed to be making a point of articulating a whole sentence. She returned to staring at her wall.

"It's not that becoming Estranged makes us stupid.

It is because the darkness is so vastly overwhelming. Not only do we have the addiction to contend with, but there is also the severe physical and emotional pain that comes when we don't feed that addiction. The pain alone drives most people to exist in a constant state of high as a form of evasion, or coping. That aside, those who have the will and the genetic predisposition to resist the addiction have to fight with the darkness for control of one's body and even of one's own emotions. The expression of this conflict is different for everyone. For some, it manifests in violent outbursts." He nodded to Mar. "In others, it becomes a debilitating depression."

Kalei glanced up from her limbo. She knew which category she fell into.

"It takes a great deal of focus to function around such obstacles." Erit paused and shook his head. "Alas, here I am rattling on while I can see you are slipping away from me. It is time to start with the more practical aspect of our lesson. May I?" He pointed to Kalei's right hand and waited for her answer. Instinctively, she started to pull it away. He smiled genially. "I am not going to hurt you. And do not fear; I am not seeking a high. This is merely for demonstrative purposes."

Kalei reluctantly held her hand out between them. He easily picked it up in his own and ... nothing happened. Kalei was amazed. For the first time since she had become an Estranged, she was touching the skin of another person without... anything. No surging high erupted at the touch, no overwhelming sensations, just... a touch. Kalei was relieved, even a little excited. Erit gave a small laugh. "That wasn't the lesson. I was just taking a moment as I remembered something I had forgotten to— oh, never mind, I will tell you after."

And then it happened. Something entered her body. It started where their hands touched and moved up her arm. It was like the darkness, but... different. Her own darkness grabbed and pulled at this new entity, trying to rip a piece free. But this thing resisted the attacks and instead pushed her darkness back. It felt... great. As Kalei's darkness retreated from her arm, she began to feel relief. Her arm felt normal again. She'd forgotten what it was like to be without that deep, aching throb. Then, quite abruptly, the other force pulled out and Kalei's darkness slammed back down her arm. A small cry escaped her lips as the pain came with it.

When she looked up, Erit was standing on the table, holding someone's wrist. She didn't think he was capable of being angry, but there it was, etched fiercely on his young face. She turned around to see whose wrist he held. A young woman — Kalei guessed she was in her late teens by the soft curve of her cheeks and tightness of the skin under her eyes – stood behind Kalei. She wore a red blouse that was a size too small and buttoned up more to support her breasts than to contain them. Her short brown hair sported streaks of black and fell into her eyes. She laughed at Erit. "Wha'? I just wanted ta say hi."

Erit threw her hand away from him and stepped forward. "No. I believe we both know that was not your intention. Get out of here, Shenaia."

Shenaia slowly moved backwards toward the far corner, hands up, a slight sway in her step. Half seductive, half seemingly intoxicated. "Is this far enough?" she asked silkily. Then she waved at Kalei and raised her voice in a mocking, "Hiii, Kalei! How's it crackin', sista!"

Kalei could have smacked her forehead into the table. Another person knew her name. "Does everyone in this fucking place know who I am?"

Mar shot a glare across the table. "I don't know who the fuck you are, and I don't give a fuck neither."

Kalei saw Shenaia open her mouth to speak, but Erit interrupted, "Mar has it; not everyone knows your name. Although your show in the foyer a couple weeks back did nothing to improve your anonymity." He had regained his composure for the most part, but he continued to glare at Shenaia.

Oh yeah. That. Kalei remembered screaming beneath Walker's grip in front of a crowd of people.

Shenaia seemed perturbed by some silent exchange with Erit, but then she laughed and yelled, "Haha, dat was great! You were kickin' and punchin'... an' man, did you make Walker jump when you took a swing at Terin! Ha! Beautiful!"

"Shenaia was there," Erit clarified.

"I gathered as much," Kalei replied dryly.

Erit walked to the edge of the table and stood between Kalei and Shenaia. The fresh crack squeaked under his weight as he passed. "Okay, Shenaia, you've had your fun. Now be on your way."

Shenaia pulled away from her corner. "I don' think so." She crossed over to the seat directly in front of him and sat down. "I wanna be a Recruit."

Erit's composed mask threatened to slip again. "Come, Shenaia. You are not interested in becoming a recruit. Recruits and Wardens alike are required to be sober around the clock. We both know you hold your precious highs too dear to give them up for a life of work, be it for the common good or not."

Shenaia leaned back and crossed her arms. "Who says I need ta be sober ta be a Warden?" Erit didn't give. Shenaia sighed and rolled her eyes. "You know what? It don' matta." She uncrossed her arms and held them up in surrender. "I can be sober."

Erit jumped off the table and turned away from the young woman. "Hardly." He began to walk back to his seat at the head of the table. "SWORDE doesn't have any need for the likes of you."

"Oh, but I think you do." Shenaia leaned forward, her cleavage all too apparent through her red blouse. "I have knowledge and skills dat I know you would *love* ta use and abuse." The little boy didn't seem the least bit interested. "Besides," she leaned back again and threw her arms behind her head. "Terin won' say no."

Lovely, Kalei thought to herself, disgusted. *She must*

be sleeping with the bastard.

Erit conceded. "Fine." He sat down, leaned forward. "Let me put this in terms you can understand." Erit pointed his index finger at Shenaia's face, pronouncing every word clearly. "You are to stay the *fuck* away from the other Recruits. Can you manage that?"

A cocky smirk crept onto Shenaia's face. "Sure thang."

CHAPTER SIX

Water on the Floor

Shenaia's promise lasted all of five minutes.

"Sorry for the delay—" Erit began.

"Hey there, school boy, don't forget to teach me too," Shenaia called from the far end of the table.

"You are not forgotten, Shenaia. As of this moment, you are to wait until you come down from your high. Can you do that for me?"

"Roger that, Teach." She rested her head on her hands and watched Erit and Kalei intently. Kalei turned away to face Erit, but she could still feel Shenaia's eyes on the back of her neck.

Erit squared his shoulders as he continued to watch Shenaia, and then he broke his gaze and turned back to Kalei and said in a quiet voice, "Rule number one in SWORDE, Kalei. *Never* trust an Estranged." Erit returned to his seat, casting another glance at Shenaia.

Kalei raised an eyebrow. "But—"

"You'll recall earlier when I asked for your hand? Your hesitance was the correct response. Of course, given as I am instructing you, it is asked that you lend at least some level of trust to the validity of what I am saying. Then, one day when you are finished with your training, you will be assigned to a team, and that team will ask for some amount of trust as well. Nonetheless, to work and live among Estranged you must learn to *never* give your full trust to any one Estranged. When you work with an Estranged, you are not only dealing with the individual, a trustworthy soul perhaps, but you are also dealing with their darkness. The darkness is not an idle entity, Kalei. It works for its own ends. Much like any parasite, it wishes to thrive."

Kalei stared at him. "You've lost me."

Erit sighed. "I suppose I have not yet explained the mechanics of the darkness. When our hands touched, what did you feel?"

"Nothing."

"And then?"

Kalei hesitated, trying to find the words to describe it. At the time, she had felt excitement and relief as the darkness was pushed away from her arm. Now that it was over, she felt as though this whole exercise was stupid. She didn't see the point. She didn't see any reason to go along with some ten-year-old's games. She didn't even know why she agreed to join SWORDE anymore. Franklin, SWORDE, all these people; it was all stupid. She just wanted to go find a place to sleep. She wasn't tired, but she couldn't think of anything else worth doing in this damn world.

Erit leaned forward, "Kalei—"

"Can't you see you're boring her?" Shenaia's voice interrupted.

Erit stood up abruptly as Kalei heard Shenaia's footsteps approach.

The footsteps stopped behind her chair, and Shenaia called out, "Come on, girl. Let's go raid the closet!"

Erit stood up. "And what makes you think I'm going to let you take her?"

"Because I want to," Shenaia replied. Kalei saw a cell phone fly over her head toward Erit. He caught it. "Take it up with Terin if you've got a problem."

Kalei heard the slides from a pair of guns clicking into place. She turned around to see Shenaia aiming two pistols at Erit.

"I'll take her by force if I have to."

Erit glared at her for a moment. "If you lay a single hand on her—"

"She'll be fine!" Shenaia replied, holding the guns out for a moment longer. She looked at Kalei and nodded her head toward the door. Kalei took the cue and obligingly stood and started moving toward the exit. As Kalei walked past her, Shenaia holstered the weapons in their concealed places behind her back and said, "I'll bring her back safe and sound, little boy."

"You know what I mean, Shenaia."

She raised both arms as she shrugged. "What? I can't control what she does. If she jumps me to get a high—"

"Shenaia!" Erit's voice was strict.

Shenaia dropped her arms. "Fine." She turned toward the door and casually raised one hand into the air to wave goodbye. "But only 'cuz Terin told me to play nice."

Shenaia took Kalei down the hall and up a different set of stairs than the ones Kalei had come down originally. Kalei went willingly; she didn't have the energy to object.

Along the way, the walls they passed sported chipped and flaking paint, but were otherwise bare. Occasionally, they passed a spot where the paint was lighter, usually in the shape of a perfect square. Presumably, these lighter patches marked the places where paintings had once hung, and in some cases, it seemed that their removal had been violent as the squares sometimes sported massive holes in the plaster.

Then Shenaia stopped at one of the many doors that lined the hallway. She flashed a grin at Kalei and opened it.

Kalei was met with a massive room that had been cleared of all furniture and debris. The room wasn't pristine, but relative to the rest of the hotel, it was sparkling. The walls and floors were bare, but for the most part, clean and undamaged. The ceiling was entirely intact, and the windows along the far wall didn't have so much as a scratch. In the center of the floor stood more than a dozen racks of clothes and accessories. Tall racks, short racks, bright colors, subdued shades; rack after rack labeled by size and type.

"What's all this for?" Kalei asked apathetically.

"According to them that writes the checks, this is all for undercover missions. Wardens can blend in, go anywhere, be anyone. Sounds hella fun, right?" Shenaia leaned in closer and lowered her voice. "But you want the real answer?" She paused as her smile widened. "This is my fucking closet! Haha!" Shenaia left Kalei and fervently descended upon the racks.

Kalei wasn't comfortable with the thought of Estranged going undercover in the city. She filed the subject away as something to share with Landen Franklin, but otherwise, she let the subject drop.

"OO! How are we going to dress you up, Sister? Celebrity appeal or backstreet whore? Oh! You would look so damn good in a cocktail dress!" Shenaia flitted from one rack to the next, pulling out and replacing one garment after another.

Kalei found a chair in the corner and sat down. She didn't want to raise suspicion by asking about the undercover operations, not that Shenaia would know anything anyway, so she brought up another subject instead. "Why do you want to be a Recruit?"

Shenaia squealed, "Because it sounds like fun!"

"You think it's fun being an Estranged?" Kalei asked.

Shenaia held out an orange shirt and looked it over. "Hell, yeah!"

A flash of rage overwhelmed Kalei. "How the fuck

can you say that? People die because of us!"

Shenaia swiftly turned her back to Kalei and put the orange shirt back. She stood there for a moment, not speaking, not moving. Then she said, "Hey, we've got it good, sis." She turned around, and the smile was back on her face. "We've got bodies that never die! Looks that never age! And we can get a high that takes us higher than any drug on the planet! How can you argue with that?"

"Try endless pain! You think death is something to laugh at? What about the people who are left behind! What about the families ruined? You think that's something to laugh at?"

The smile slid from Shenaia's face. "... no." A couple of hangers clicked together as she resumed sifting through the clothes. She shrugged. "Maybe that's why I want to join." Another pause. She turned and started on another rack. "Hell, that's why I quit Tusic."

Kalei was surprised. "You used to be with Tusic?"

A couple more hangers clicked. "Yeah." Shenaia took up a deep breath and her upbeat energy returned as she resumed her search. "Man, they knew how to party! None of this sober crap. Them boys knew how to keep a good high on the down-low." She turned and faced Kalei. One hand danced to the tune of her story. "They could walk around high as a kite and you wouldn't even know it by lookin' at 'em. Landen tells 'em to go out and get shit done, and boy, they got their shit *done*. Don't need to be sober for dat. And

SWORDE wants everyone to stay clean? Ha! They can't touch Tusic, even with all this high and mighty goody-two-shoes shit."

Kalei had imagined Tusic to be straight-laced, but now this girl was telling her that they ran around high as a bird? She couldn't believe it. Kalei wasn't sure she believed anything that came out of Shenaia's mouth. But that being said ... Kalei found that she had about as much information on Tusic as she did on SWORDE: not much. Perhaps even less.

Kalei asked, "If it was so great, then why'd you leave?"

Shenaia shrugged. "Eh, it's over. Oh! I've got it!" Shenaia emerged with a flowing summer dress. "Put this on!"

"It's almost winter, you idiot."

"So. We're Estranged, sis! The cold can't hurt us!"

Shenaia had a point. While Kalei still felt hot and cold, it didn't really bug her anymore. The steady throb of the darkness made it simple to block out a trifling discomfort such as the weather. Still. A summer dress? Kalei stood and walked over to another rack where the labels indicated her size. She grabbed jeans, a black tank top, and a jacket. Then she went to the bathroom to change.

"Spoil sport!" Shenaia called after her. "Hey! Take a shower before you put those on!"

Kalei obliged. She didn't want to, but she knew it was necessary. She stepped in under the faucet and the hot water slid down her shoulders and turned black before it slipped into the drain. A year's worth of dirt and grime would do that.

As she worked, Kalei's heart was weighed with stone. Not only that, but her arms and legs felt like they were twenty pounds heavier, and every movement felt like a chore. Nonetheless, she raised her weary arms to wash the shampoo into her hair, and she slid them to her face to scrub the grime off of her skin.

Where Lecia had blown her brains out, Kalei's hair was growing back as a short accumulation of fur hidden beneath what remained of Kalei's longer hair. Kalei pulled at the longer strands, but the dense mass of knots wouldn't yield. Kalei wrenched and yanked, and as the tangles held firm, her frustration grew.

Finally, she gave up. She sank down to the shower floor and began to cry beneath the water. Her sobs were covered by the sound of the water, and her tears were washed away even as they appeared on her cheeks. The shower allowed her to be utterly alone with her misery.

At the heart of it all, she missed Fenn. There were other people she had cared about. Her nieces, her old coworkers, her partner... But not like Fenn. Nothing could make her life whole the way Fenn did.

Kalei laughed to herself. Yeah, there had been days when she wanted to strangle him for spilling water all over the bathroom floor. But now... Kalei watched as the water from the shower splashed against the side of the tub and turned back to travel toward the drain...

Now she would give anything to see his puddles.

A harsh knocking came at the door. "Kalei! Stop taking your sweet time and get your ass out here! I wanna see you in your new clothes, girl!"

Kalei shut off the water and walked over to the sink. She grabbed the porcelain with both hands and looked at herself in the mirror. Her eyes were red and swollen but fierce as they glared back at her. Her skin was pink and raw where she had scrubbed it, and her brown hair sat piled atop her head in a massive lump. As she looked at herself, the grief in her eyes slowly turned to rage, and from rage into pure hatred. She reached past those hateful eyes as she opened the cupboard. It held an array of toiletries, tweezers and such, and on the top shelf sitting next to a couple bottles of baby powder, she spotted a cardboard box with the picture of an electric razor. Kalei decided the knots in her hair weren't worth dealing with.

CHAPTER SEVEN

Trust

Shenaia was thrilled with Kalei's new haircut. "I knew I liked you! Man, you should've let me do it, though. I could've made it look so good!"

"It's shaved. How could you have possibly shaved it any better?"

"There are lots a' ways to shave a head. You make some parts shorter, longer – it coulda looked good! You shoulda told me!"

Kalei shrugged. "There was nothing to tell. I did it, it's over."

Shenaia pouted. "Fine." She started walking toward the door and waved for Kalei to follow. "C'mon. Let's go play hooky before teacher comes snoopin' for us."

Kalei followed. "Hey, you've been here a while, right?"

Shenaia stepped out into the hallway and checked both directions as she said, "Yeah."

Kalei casually asked, "Do you know if there are any computers around here?"

Shenaia's eyes brightened. "Just one. But, girl, you

wouldn't believe how big this thing is!" She slapped her hands together. "Yeah, dat's a good idea. Erit will never find us there. Follow me. I'll show you where they hide the brains 'round here."

Shenaia took Kalei further down the hall and stopped in front of a set of elevators. After seeing the elevators in the foyer, Kalei didn't see any reason to trust these deathtraps. Quite frankly, she didn't think Shenaia was going to prove her otherwise. "Why don't we take the stairs?"

"The stairs won't take you there. Trust me." Shenaia hit the call button and the doors to their left slid open.

What was Erit's first rule again? Kalei climbed into the elevator.

Once the doors shut behind them, Shenaia pulled out a small service key. "Hehe, took this off Walker the other day. Dumb bastard, probably doesn't even know it's missing!" She put it into the hole beneath the buttons, turned it, and hit "12" and "13" at the same time.

"Two floors?" Kalei asked.

"Nope, just one. Ever heard of nine-and-three-quarters?"

Kalei was baffled. "You read?"

"Of course I read! I may be street, but I ain't stupid. I call dis floor twelve-and-a-half."

"Twelve-and-a-half?"

"What? You got a problem with that?"

Kalei shrugged. "Nope, no problem."

"You judging?"

"I'm not judging."

With a light *ding!* the elevator doors opened. As the doors receded, Kalei found herself looking at a vast library of computer servers. She only knew what they were from the documentaries she had watched with Fenn. Otherwise, they just looked like tall metal cages with shelves of black boxes inside. The boxes themselves weren't featureless; they had ports and buttons and small lights ranging from a dull yellow to bright green, and several menacing red ones. Server after server lined the walls like ominous sentinels, blinking and whirring at them from the chilly room. A narrow aisle stretched between them and Kalei and Shenaia followed it to an opening in the collection. Beyond the aisle was a small space about ten feet wide and twenty feet across where all the servers had been moved aside to form a small room. In the far corner stood an office chair and a plain oak desk, just four legs with a flat surface to hold a black keyboard and mouse. Behind the peripherals sat six thin monitors, stacked above one another in rows of three and angled toward the chair. From behind the screens, dozens of wires cascaded to the floor and slithered off into the forest of hardware.

"What do they do with all this?" Kalei asked as she peered into the shadows between the towers.

"This is how they control Downtown. Keep da fence juiced, spy through ev'ryone's fancy jewelry..."

Kalei stopped investigating and looked at Shenaia. "Fancy jewelry?"

"Yeah, didn't you notice?" Shenaia tisked and rolled her eyes. "Sis, since when do you wear studded earrings?"

"Those are the only kinds I wear."

"What?" For some reason, Shenaia seemed to find this offensive. "Fine, but since when do you wear them one at a time? Didn' you notice the stud in your left ear when you were shaving your pretty little head?"

Kalei had noticed. At the time, she had written it off; there was no telling what had happened during the year and a half she was high.

Kalei put her hands into her jacket pockets. "What are you getting at?"

"That, girlie, is how they watch you."

"What?"

"Yeah, they watch all the Estranged that way. That ain't no earring. That's a camera."

That was it. Kalei was sunk. If the thing in her ear really was a camera, then that meant they knew about Lecia, they knew about Tusic, they knew about her plan...

"But those things are useless as shit!" Shenaia said as she plopped down into the chair. The joints creaked beneath her weight, the wheels protesting as she dragged herself closer to the desk. "Them cameras are never pointin' in the right direction, they's always buried beneath piles of hair, they's fuckin' useless as—"

"How do you know?"

Shenaia looked over her shoulder at Kalei. "I've played around with the system a bit." She turned back to the computer and pulled the keyboard closer. "The thing ain' exactly password protected. Guess they figured the fancy elevator was enough."

If they were as useless as Shenaia said, then perhaps... Kalei asked, "Do they save the video? I mean, for multiple days?"

"Damn right they do. What, you think these big-ass computers are just for looks? Here, lemme show you." Shenaia started clicking and typed a command or two.

The five outer monitors continued to show various feeds from the city: a burnt-out storefront bobbing up and down as the camera moved, a motionless pile of bodies in a dim hallway, and a few more that were too dark to distinguish. In all cases, the feeds were black and white, but the definition was crystal clear. In the top left monitor, a small blue window displayed a series of numbers and codes in green, all of which meant nothing to Kalei, but it was the lower middle monitor where windows began closing and opening. The first few windows closed before Kalei could see what they were, and then another opened with a blue background and grey square that prompted "Identification Tag Number" with a blinking cursor in a white box waiting for the response immediately below.

Shenaia spun the chair around and said, "Turn around. Lemme see the back-uh yo earring."

Kalei didn't like the idea of turning her back to Shenaia. "Why?"

"So I can see yo tag number." Shenaia turned away and "tched" again. "Fine, I'll use mine."

"No, wait." Kalei turned until Shenaia could see the back of her left ear. If she wanted to find out how much SWORDE knew, then this might be the only chance she would get.

"Yeah, now we talking!"

Kalei turned back around when she heard typing at the keyboard.

"A'ight, when do you want? Any day, any time. We got a whole year to play with!"

Kalei feigned contemplation. "Let's start out with... yesterday at about—" she thought back to the display on the phone during her conversation with Landen. "Four a.m.?"

Shenaia looked at Kalei. "Really? No 'what happened the day I got tagged?' Not even curious about dat huge ice storm when ev'ryone was all snugglin' up to one 'nother?"

Ice storm?

Kalei shook her head. "Just do it."

Shenaia "tched" again. "Fine, is yo cam."

Shenaia entered in a few commands and then the video in the top screen flickered and switched to a new image. In this new shot, all they could see was black with occasional patches of lighter grey.

"Dammit! See what I mean? Yo hair was in the

way." Shenaia fast-forwarded and rewound, but it was all the same. "This is bullshit. Give me another day!"

Instead, Kalei asked, "Does it have audio too?"

"Nope. Shit, I'm glad they don'." She gave an exaggerated shudder. "That video woulda been hella worse with audio."

"What video?"

Shenaia glanced back at Kalei and, for the first time since Kalei had met her, she seemed uncomfortable. Her mouth curled like she had just eaten something bitter and her eyes looked over Kalei's face and then quickly darted away as she turned to face the desk again. She drummed her fingers nervously against the wood a couple times before saying, "Look, Terin didn' want me to tell, but—" She spun back around and paused when she saw Kalei again. She chewed on her lip for a moment, then sighed and said, "Shit, you're goin' to find out anyway. You and Mar are probably the only ones in the whole damn town who didn' see it."

"Shenaia, what are you talking about?"

"Uh—" Shenaia spun the chair again and made two revolutions before she stopped and said, "Look, you know when them Estranged attacked yo place? Some son a' bitch broke into the CNB news station, used their system to hack the ear cams, and then streamed the attack onto ev'ry screen in Celan."

The darkness within Kalei stirred and swelled as it fed on the sudden influx of rage that poured through her veins "Who the fuck—!"

Shenaia grimaced. "I don' know. The guy—"

"Terin!" Kalei looked away from Shenaia and her eyes scoured the monitors with their haphazard shots of Downtown. "He owns this fucking place! It's his cameras; he—"

"It wasn't me."

Kalei spun around and looked down the aisle. The elevator door was beginning to shut as Terin walked past the towers.

Kalei took three steps toward him, then stopped. Terin continued to walk until he reached the edge of the small room, then he stopped too.

Kalei didn't dare cross the four feet between them, but that didn't stop her from lashing out. "You're a fucking liar! If it wasn't you, then who the fuck could've done it?"

"The cameras' inventor."

"Oh, so you're going to throw the blame to someone else, huh? And who the fuck is that? Sorry little boy, but 'Great Estranged Inventors' wasn't a topic in my history class. "

Terin put his hands behind his back and straightened his shoulders. "You know who it is because you told me he was there."

"Who? Blondie?"

"Yes, Xamic."

"So what're you saying? One day he just gets up and decides it's a good idea to swarm a house with Estranged?" Kalei raised her arms and mocked a male voice. "'Hell, while I'm at it, might as well jack a news station and transmit the whole thing so everyone can have a good laugh.' Is that it?"

Terin casually looked away and studied one of the towers. "Something like that."

"What the fuck aren't you telling me? Why'd Xamic pick my house?"

Terin looked her in the eyes. Kalei saw nothing in the steady gaze of his stone grey irises. They were as stoic and unyielding as the Alundai Mountains.

He answered, "To send me a message."

Kalei didn't break eye contact. "What message?"

"Six feet of dirt isn't enough to bury history."

Kalei blinked. "What the hell is that supposed to mean?"

Quietly, he asked, "Why do you want to join SWORDE?"

Kalei glared at him. "Don't redirect me with a question."

"I answered your questions. Now answer mine."

"No you didn't!"

As though nothing had transpired, he repeated the question in the same even tone as before. "Why do you want to join SWORDE?"

Kalei clenched her fists. "Because I'm just waiting for the day when I get to watch your carcass bleed."

"You can do that any time. Here's a knife. Go right ahead." From his back pocket, he produced a pocketknife, which he flicked open with a jerk of his wrist and offered to her.

Kalei looked away from the knife and snarled, "You know what I mean. Ripping you open is only satisfying if it ends with you dead."

Terin didn't reply. He simply folded the knife shut and returned it to his pocket.

Kalei said, "The first day I came here, Erit said you guys would teach me how to kill Estranged if I become a Warden. Is that true?"

"It is."

"So even though you know I will kill you, you'll still teach me?"

"You won't kill me."

"How the hell do you know?"

Terin replied, "You aren't strong enough. You never will be."

"Like shit! You have no fucking clue what you're dealing with! Once I know how, I am going to come after—"

"Kalei, don't—" Shenaia started, but Kalei turned on her.

"Shut up, you fucking Estranged!"

Shenaia stood up and took a step toward Kalei. "You're calling *me* the 'fucking Estranged'? Last I checked, you were Estranged too, bitch. You'd better get that through your pretty little head before you get yourself hurt."

"Where'd the mask go, Shenaia? I thought you were trying to be my friend? Yeah, fucking right, you were just waiting to catch a sweet high from a newbie. Am I right?"

"Fuck you! I'm trying to help you! You don't know jack shit about who—"

Terin appeared between them, but before Kalei could react, she felt his hand on the back of her neck and her entire body went rigid. Shenaia froze too.

Terin said, "Shenaia, give me Walker's key and get out of here." He released his grip on her neck and Shenaia's body relaxed again. She continued to glare at Kalei as she dug a hand into her pocket, produced the key, and dropped it on the floor. She broke eye contact and walked past Kalei to the elevator.

Once the elevator door shut, Terin removed his hand from her neck. Control returned to her limbs as he walked over to the computer, sat down in the creaking chair, and began to click through the blue program.

Kalei asked, "Why was my family used to send you a message?"

Terin didn't turn around or pause in his work as he said, "What are you going to do when we're all dead, Kalei?"

"Answer my question."

"Erit will still teach you to kill Estranged once you are qualified."

"Not that question!"

He continued to type. "What would you do if you knew where to find Fenn?"

Kalei could feel her rage escalating again. "Answer

my fucking question."

Terin spun around and yelled, "YOU ANSWER MINE!"

Kalei froze. She had never heard Terin raise his voice before. His words seemed to hang in the air. She wanted to answer, she tried to think of something to say, but his steely glare terrified her.

He closed his eyes, and when he opened them, the glare was gone, replaced with his usual stoic composure. He calmly repeated the question, "What would you do if you knew where to find Fenn?"

Kalei said, "I'd make sure he's safe."

"And then what?"

"I would leave."

"Why?"

"Because I don't want him to die."

Terin turned back to the computer and put his right hand on the mouse, but he didn't move it. He said, "It doesn't work like that. If you attempt to find Fenn, I will kill you myself."

He dismissed her.

CHAPTER EIGHT

Dancing with the Past

Kalei didn't remember what happened after that. A week later, she woke up in what Erit called a "Recovery Room." This, of course, was just a fancy name for the demolished rooms of the hotel, like the first one she had visited with the broken glass. This room was a sibling to the first Recovery Room she'd stayed in. The metal nightstand was dented and had two legs missing, a pile of grey plastic, frayed wires, and chunks of sanded pinewood sat where a TV should have been. Kalei sat in the bloodstained remains of a shredded feather bed. The smell wasn't great. Her first instinct was to check her feet for glass. She was both relieved and disappointed when she found none.

What do I do now? Cold, late fall air poured in through the shattered window, drawing Kalei's attention to the overcast sky. She watched the swollen, low-hanging clouds roll silently past the enormous Terondac Mountain, its slate peak reaching for the grey clouds without quite touching them. But the clouds and the mountain only reminded her of how bleak and desolate the world had become.

Kalei took a deep breath and remembered something her mother had taught her before she died. Whenever Kalei had a problem, her mother had insisted, "Start by listing what you know." It was a silly exercise, but doing it always made Kalei feel closer to those days at the kitchen table, talking to her mom about everything from life to homework.

So Kalei leaned back against the wooden headboard of the bed and started gathering facts. It was hard to do with the darkness pounding at the back of her skull, but she tried anyway.

I know the names of five people within SWORDE now, and I know the name of my parents' killers. And I know that one of them is the Director of SWORDE. Kalei took another deep breath. *I know that SWORDE will train me to be a Warden, and I know where they keep their central computer. Good. Now when Tusic is ready with the device, I can take it straight there, after I get my hands on a key. But how am I going to manage that?* Kalei's eyes scoured the cracked plaster on the ceiling. One piece looked dangerously close to falling on her foot. She closed her eyes and focused her thoughts. *Walker and Terin are the only ones with keys, and getting close enough to either of them to steal a key without notice doesn't seem likely. When the time comes, I'll just have to take it by force... I hope Terin wasn't lying about them teaching me to kill. I don't care what he says, he's going to be the first person I execute.*

*In the meantime... looks like the only thing for me to do
is join this damn recruit program.*

Kalei pulled herself out of the bed, went downstairs,
and returned to training. The whole gang was there:
Erit at the head of the table, Shenaia at the opposite
end, and Mar still sitting to Erit's left. Shenaia tried to
say something when Kalei stepped in, but whatever it
was, Kalei ignored her as she walked past Shenaia and
sat down in her seat across from Mar. Shenaia got the
message and didn't say anything further.

While Shenaia sat in what was essentially time out,
Mar grunted at her blank wall, and Erit taught Kalei
how to pull back her darkness. In their earlier lesson,
when he had pushed Kalei's darkness back, it turned
out he had done it using his own darkness. Now Kalei
had to learn how to pull back it back on her own. It was
tricky at first. Grabbing the darkness was like trying to
grip the smooth exterior of a skyscraper as she plunged
to her death. There were no handholds, only the havoc-
inducing darkness spinning through her mind the whole
way down. This made it impossible to concentrate. But
eventually, she got it. Break one of the windows and
you'll find a bloody handhold. And once she did, she
yanked hard and shoved all of the darkness into a small
knot within her chest.

The pressure immediately built within the mass
of darkness, and before she could push the last shred
into the knot, her entire body screamed as a sensation
like a thousand suns exploding ripped through her. The

next thing she remembered, Erit was standing over her, explaining how the darkness was like an agitated, carbonated beverage: it should never be bottled.

He helped her up.

So instead of bottling the darkness, Kalei had to learn how to vent the steam. First, she would pull back the darkness. As she did so, the black would retreat from her fingernails and she could feel some small amount of relief in her arms. That was the most rewarding part of the process. Then she would have to reintroduce a small amount of darkness into her nails, or even redirect it elsewhere if she could, but that took more concentration. So she watched as a controlled dose of darkness crept back into her fingers.

Erit explained that eventually she would have to come up with some sort of shape or design through which she could channel her emotions. This would serve as an outlet for the darkness and would help focus her control of it. For example, one member of SWORDE had a sun on each of her nails and the weather could become cloudy, rainy, or even windy, depending on her mood. Erit himself had the spines of books on each finger, the titles of which would change to whatever he felt appropriate. When he told her this, Kalei took a glance and saw the title *Robinson Crusoe* delicately etched in italics on each book. She couldn't imagine the amount of control that would take.

For herself, Kalei started with a single line that stretched from the base of her nail and reached out into

open space. It took a week for Kalei to make that line
stable. It would blur, it would bleed off into the rest
of the nail, and at the slightest noise in the room, her
concentration would break and her nails would flood
black again.

But after about a week of working at it around the
clock, she mastered the technique. One of the perks
of being an Estranged was that she never got tired or
hungry, which left her with far more time to work. Of
course, Erit still forced her to take a break every now
and again, during which she would usually wander the
hotel or shut her eyes and force her body into a light
sleep. Kalei wasn't sure how it was possible that she
could sleep when she wasn't tired, but she was grateful
for the opportunity to take a break from the world, if
only for a little while.

On her excursions through the hotel, Kalei explored
the various rooms, saw a few scuffles between Wardens
and new arrivals, and learned where the key points of
interest were. The building had a rec room, an indoor
shooting range, an armory, and – rumor had it – they
even had a prison in the basement. Kalei didn't try
looking for it just yet; she mostly preferred to explore
the empty upper floors where she didn't have to deal
with the screams of unruly newcomers, or the watchful
eyes of the Wardens.

She knew she should be mingling with the other
recruits, gleaning what information she could from
casual conversations and so forth. That was what spies

were supposed to do. But it was more peaceful upstairs.
And some of the rooms, although incredibly dusty and
rotted, were still intact. Kalei enjoyed the opportunity
to peer into the untouched world of almost twenty years
ago. The faded grandeur spoke so much to what was
lost on E-day.

In one room, on a brown metal desk, sat a crumbling
notepad in which few words were still legible: *million-,
aeroscience stock se-, Friday afternoon, 3:30 pm.*
In another room, spoiled cosmetics on the bathroom
counter sat beside a short stack of black and white
photos that held a beautiful, smiling woman showing
off a flowing ball gown. Several of the pictures had
already been signed with the fat black marker that sat
beside it.

On her fourth excursion into the hotel, Shenaia had
jumped up and asked to go with her. Kalei had allowed
it, and as they walked, Shenaia apologized about
the fight. The girl sounded sincere, but Kalei wasn't
sure what to think of the apology. She saw the way
Erit watched Shenaia warily. Whether it was because
Shenaia was a former member of Tusic or because he
simply didn't trust Shenaia not to jump after one of
the recruits for a high, Kalei couldn't tell. Common
sense told her this girl was trouble, but Kalei's gut said
Shenaia was someone she wanted to be close to. Kalei
wasn't sure which to trust.

So Kalei didn't say anything in response to
Shenaia's apology, and the girl seemed to take the

silence as "Apology accepted." Shenaia then went on
at length to tell Kalei all about a new gun she recently
bought off a Warden, and how it would go nicely with
the rest of her collection of vintage revolvers, but how
she really wanted to start getting more guns for her rifle
collection because she only had six of those... Kalei
quickly tuned her out.

When Kalei went back to her lessons, she started
to focus on bending the tip of the line in her nails,
twisting it in on itself until it ended with a simple whirl.
Satisfied with the design, Kalei stopped tinkering and
left it at that. At first, she focused simply on holding
that shape. Then she began to let it tighten and flex with
the pulse of her darker emotions. Slowly, it began to
take a mind of its own, thrashing and undulating when
she became frustrated, or calmly tightening when she
regained her composure.

Erit moved Kalei on to multitasking while she tried
to hold the pattern. At first, he would try to carry a
conversation with her. Then he made her solve simple
math problems.

Once everyone had progressed to Kalei's level – for
somehow, she had passed both Mar and Shenaia just a
couple days in – they moved on to physical activities.
A walk around the room turned into a routine of
jumping jacks. Then, finally, a game of dodgeball. Mar
had a wicked arm. She had floored Erit with the ball
more than once. Kalei was quick enough to dodge the
worst of them. Shenaia, on the other hand, kept taking

hits from Mar as she struggled to explain to the old woman that the game was not free for all. When that didn't work, she left the old woman's team and started throwing balls back at her attacker.

Going shooting for the first time was Kalei's favorite part of training, although she didn't enjoy it nearly as much as Shenaia did. The girl not only brought her own gun to the indoor range, but she brought her collection. A dozen suitcases and briefcases held at least two dozen weapons from every manufacturer Kalei had ever seen, and then some. And according to the grinning teen, this wasn't even a tenth of what she owned.

"Aren't they the *shit*!" Shenaia squealed as she opened up the eighth gun case.

"Yup, shit pretty well sums it up," Mar mumbled as she looked over a double-barreled shotgun from case number three.

Shenaia reached into case six and pulled out a long-barreled revolver, swinging it around to point at Mar. "Hey! Don't patronize my babies!"

"Ho there!" Kalei tried to smooth things over. "No need to point that at anyone."

"What?" Shenaia's wrist flopped to the side, the barrel casually aimed in Erit's direction. "It's not like I'm going to shoot her."

"Rule number one about gun safety, Shenaia," Erit said as he eyed the revolver. "Never point a gun at anything, or anyone, you do not intend to shoot."

Thankfully, Shenaia's arm and the gun dropped to her side. "Who needs gun safety? It's not like a bullet is going to kill any of us anyway." In one swift motion, she raised the gun back up, swung around, and without even taking a moment to aim, she let off six bullets at the nearest target. From what Kalei could tell, Shenaia had given the paper man two eyes, something of a mouth, and a small hole where any manly parts would be.

Over the severe ringing in her ears, Kalei heard Erit say, "As a Warden, you will be working among Untouched as well as Estranged, and they will not recover from an accidental bullet wound as well as you or I. In order to become a Warden, you must learn to respect gun safety, Shenaia."

Shenaia tossed the revolver onto the table. "Yeah, yeah..."

This time, Kalei got her earplugs in before Shenaia could reach for the shotgun.

Sitting at a poker table in the hotel lounge – aka: the rec room – Kalei and Erit faced off. The table sat in the back corner of the room, and Kalei could see the whole lounge spread out behind Erit. Two more poker tables lined the hall to the right, a couple pool tables sat in the middle of the room, and at the far end sat two couches back to back, each facing a TV. The room was full, and the sound of movies, pool cues, and general conversation filled the lounge, but Kalei ignored it all as she studied her opponent over her small mountain of poker chips.

Erit had a fair-sized pile himself. The two players each had split the chips nearly in half over the course of the game. Mar, who had been knocked out early, dealt the cards. The game was Texas Hold 'Em. House rules stated you had to play with at least one hand exposed on the table. That was what killed Mar. She might have had a poker face, but her nails sure didn't. Mar had chosen a smiley for her emblem. As they played, she had tried her best to maintain a neutral line for the mouth, but the occasional twitch at the edges gave her away every time.

Shenaia had chosen a steering wheel for her nails. It was supposed to turn different directions, but for most of the night, it had taken her entire focus to maintain the outline. Her poker chips hadn't kept her company for very long either.

Kalei still had her simple swirl with its long stem anchoring it to the base of her nail. She had developed a subtle pattern throughout the night: a slight squeeze of the swirl for bad hands, a slight loosening for good ones. Erit had picked up on the pattern, but now was time for the end game. She planned to use the pattern to her advantage.

Mar dealt the cards. As Kalei reached out to look at her own, she mentally prepared to give her swirls a slight squeeze when she lifted the cards. As she lifted the edges, she saw a pair of aces. *Sweet!* Belatedly,

she remembered to look at her nails. Not only had she
remembered to squeeze the swirls, but she had squeezed
them so tight that they were now black circles on her
fingers. Casually, she flexed the lines back open again
and looked up to see Erit's reaction. He watched her,
one eyebrow raised.

She didn't even bother to look at his nails. The
damn books were useless.

Kalei tried to downplay her excitement at seeing
a pair of aces in the pocket. When Mar prompted her,
she casually checked. Erit, testing the waters, raised her
with a couple red chips. Kalei moved quickly to give
off the appearance of being anxious, and called. Mar
drew the next set of cards.

A Queen of Spades, a six of Hearts, and a Jack of
Spades.

Hoo, that's dangerous. A queen and a jack of the
same suit meant it was possible for Erit to get a straight
flush. If he had the King and Ace of Spades, he could
get a royal flush, the best hand in the game. But that
wasn't likely. Her partner Marley had once told her the
odds of getting a straight flush were one in 650,000.
Kalei only remembered because they had argued about
it at length on one of their patrols.

Kalei checked. When Erit raised again, she feigned
a slight squeeze before calling.

Then came the flop: the King of Spades.

Three cards of the same suit, all in a row. Even if
Erit just got a flush or a straight, he would beat her

pair of aces. Unless... was one of her aces a spade? She didn't dare look. Instead, she looked at Erit. He looked at her. Kalei checked. Erit raised again; this time, he doubled his last two bets. Kalei called.

The turn came and both players watched Mar as she reached for the next card. The old woman lifted it from the deck, took a peek for herself, showed it to Shenaia, who was now watching over Mar's shoulder, and then grinned as she set it on the table.

A ten of spades. Without even checking her cards, Kalei went all in. She'd done it. Somehow, she had hit those one in 650,000 odds and landed a royal flush. All spades! She was grinning so wide her cheeks hurt.

Erit smiled too, although his grin was more composed. "Nice try. But I shall call your bluff and take the pot." He flipped over his cards. A pair of nines, one of which was a spade. That gave him a straight flush, king high.

"Nope." Kalei smiled triumphantly and turned over her own pair. "Royal Flush!"

She began to reach for the chips when Erit said, "You may want to check again." Kalei looked down at the red and black inked aces. Hearts and clubs. She had two aces, but neither was the right one.

"I'll take these off your hands," Erit said as he cleaned her out. Luckily, they hadn't been playing for anything more than pride.

After neatly stacking his prize on the table before him, Erit addressed his defeated students. "Now, it seems that you have all come a long way in these last few weeks, and Terin has noted your progress. While I feel that *some* still need work," he glanced at Shenaia, "Terin feels that you are all ready for the more practical levels of training, such as fighting, combat tactics, etcetera, etcetera." Mar grunted her approval. Shenaia returned to her seat on Kalei's right and glowered openly at Erit. Kalei, formerly slouched and recovering from her defeat, now leaned forward with renewed interest.

"Does 'etcetera' mean killing Estranged?" she asked.

"That will come *after* you become a Warden." Kalei sat back in her seat again, dejected. Erit continued, "Now, before you can fight an Estranged, you must first understand the mechanics of what happens the moment one Estranged touches another. In that instant, the darkness from each Estranged reaches forth and rips a piece from the other individual's darkness. Then, it returns to its original body where it devours the new piece. In Estranged, this results in a high. In Untouched, this foreign entity ripping at their dormant darkness is the trigger that releases their darkness and begins the process that can either kill them or turn them into Estranged."

Erit paused to evaluate the effect of his explanation on his students. After a moment's silence, Mar's jaw flopped open to spout, "What?"

Shenaia took it upon herself to explain, holding out

her hands as she said, "I have a chocolate cookie, and you have a chocolate cookie. We hold out our hands and I take yours while you take mine. Then we eat them."

"Oh, I get it," Mar rumbled.

Shenaia turned to Kalei and said, "Y'know, cookies sound really good right now."

Kalei agreed, then asked Erit, "Can we even eat cookies?" She couldn't recall eating anything since becoming an Estranged.

Erit sighed. "Yes, you can eat. But you don't need to. And if you do, your body will process the food as normal and you will have to use the facilities. Which I strongly advise against."

"Why is that?"

Shenaia answered, "Because they don't have any fucking toilet paper in this entire Goddamn district!" She turned an accusing eye to Erit. "How could you let me eat an entire fucking plate of burritos and not tell me that we don't have any Goddamn toilet paper?"

"I told you not to eat it."

"That doesn't mean jack! Out-of-toilet-paper is need-to-know! Dammit!"

Erit turned away from Shenaia's ranting. "It seems we have drifted off topic. Let us proceed to the fitness room to commence our combat training, shall we?"

On their way up to the third floor, Erit explained how several rooms had been converted into fitness rooms. Walls had been knocked out, wrestling mats added to the floors, padding installed along the walls, but no weights or treadmills. Estranged were pretty much frozen in the bodies they were converted in, so no amount of exercise would make them stronger. Instead, the fitness rooms were primarily intended for training reflexes and combat skills.

When they finished climbing the final set of stairs, Kalei followed Erit out of the stairwell and into the hallway. The flat, green floor was ripped and torn at regular intervals in front of the open doorways along the hall, the cuts and tears reminding Kalei of a remodeling project she had seen at a friend's house, leading her to suppose that construction work was probably the cause of this damage too. As they passed the open rooms, Kalei saw that they were indeed padded with light blue mats across the entire length of the floor and halfway up the walls. The padding on the floors appeared to be made of a sturdier material than that on the walls, but both seemed newer than the rest of the hotel, albeit worn with years of use.

Erit took them to one of the smaller rooms and handed out long-sleeved workout shirts, pants, gloves, and even cloth ski masks that reached all the way down their necks. He insisted that they tuck in the garments wherever the seams met so that not an inch of skin was showing when they were done, apart from around their mouths and eye sockets.

Shenaia made a comment about being dressed for

robbing a bank, then the students waited for Erit's instructions, sweating before they even threw a punch.

"I understand that the level of combat experience among you three varies considerably. Kalei was trained traditionally by the local force, Shenaia has what she would call 'street' training, and Mar has almost no combat experience at all."

Mar scoffed. "Yeah, right. You don't get to be my age without learning how to knock a few heads around."

Erit ignored the comment. "To rectify this, we will go through the basic hand-to-hand fighting styles that are accepted and used by SWORDE."

For Kalei, this meant the rest of the afternoon was a test of patience. She went through the motions as Erit instructed, she listened to Shenaia argue with everything the instructor said, and she tried to help Mar wrap her head around the importance of fighting stances.

"Why don't I just stand here and punch you in the face?" Mar asked. "Why do I have to do all this weird shit with my feet?"

"Because when you stand like that, your abdomen is an open target. If you turn to the side, then there will be less for your opponent to hit."

"They won't be hittin' nothing after I knock 'em on their ass!"

Kalei sighed. It was a very long afternoon.

Once the physical training started, the recruits got

their own rooms and started to receive weekends off. That first Saturday, they all went their separate ways: Shenaia disappeared into the city, Mar would go do whatever it was Mar did, and Kalei would head down to the shooting range to blow off some steam. By the time Sunday came around, Mar joined Kalei at the range, muttering about having nothing to do.

The next weekend, Shenaia joined them with a dozen pistols, and after they blew through a small mountain of ammo, the range officer cut them off and kicked them out, so they went up to Shenaia's hotel room where the two younger women taught Mar how to disassemble and clean a gun. It was an important thing for Mar to know, although Kalei suspected that Shenaia just wanted an excuse to put the work on someone else.

After they cleaned the first pistol together, Shenaia went to the closet and came back with three more pistols, one for each of them.

"Where the hell do you get all of these?" Kalei asked incredulously.

"Don't worry about it," Shenaia replied with a grin.

Kalei took one look at the .50 caliber handgun Shenaia plopped onto the bed and decided not to ask again.

Kalei took the pistol Shenaia had assigned to her and went to work. She got as far as pulling off the slide when she heard Shenaia ask, "So, Mar, why do you wanna join SWORDE?"

"I don't wanna talk about it," the old woman

grumbled as she pushed a wire brush down the barrel of the revolver.

Kalei noticed that Mar had forgotten to take off the cylinder. She reached over to take the gun. "Here, let me help you—"

Mar pulled it out of her reach. "No, I've got it." She noticed what Kalei was getting at and started to pull the cylinder off.

Shenaia started up again, "If you don't tell me, I'll pull out my hollow points and see how many it takes before you talk." Again, she smiled.

Mar stared at her blankly. "What are hollow points?"

Kalei replied, "Not something you want to learn about first hand. It's probably better if you just answer the question."

Mar grunted and went back to work on the revolver. The smiley on her nails took on a deep frown, and its new eyebrows alternated between sharp downward angles and a level plane. Shenaia started to get up from the bed when Mar finally answered with a barely audible rasp, "The past doesn't matter. What matters is, I'm gonna set it right." She picked up an oiled rag and made a couple of swipes down the barrel of the gun. Her smiley's mouth flashed into a full frown, then an angry grimace, then struggled to maintain a flat line. Kalei glanced at Shenaia, and Shenaia met her eyes. They would let it lie at that.

After a moment, Mar looked up and asked, "So

what about you girls? Why do you want to join SWORDE?"

Franklin's plan flashed through Kalei's mind, she thought about her desire to wipe Estranged off the planet, and she thought about her hatred for Xamic and Terin... but instead, she answered, "I've spent the last six years of my life protecting the people in this city. I'm not going to stop now just because the darkness shows up in my nails." Kalei hadn't forgotten about all of the trouble-makers and screw-ups, all of the victims and civilians she met in her former line of work... some hated her, some loved her, but in the end, she was able to make a difference in their lives... what she did meant something to the world. Kalei had never realized that before. Joining the police force had just been a means to make her way into SWORDE. The people she worked with were just coworkers. But the thing was, they weren't just co-workers.

Every Thursday, Debbie would visit Kalei in the locker room to talk about the latest episode of *Professor Where*, and Talwart was always shining his flashlight in her eyes, or pretending to check if she was intoxicated. Even their chief would sometimes come out and joke with them for a few minutes before brusquely sending them on their way. And then, of course, there were all those hours she had spent on patrol with her partner Marley... After being with these people five days a week for the last six years, they had become her family. And she missed them all. But thanks to the darkness, she could never get that life back.

Mar asked Shenaia, "What about you?"

Shenaia shrugged and looked at Kalei. "I became a Recruit because I care about my family."

Mar and Kalei glanced at each other and started laughing.

"Hey, I'm being serious, guys!"

Kalei wiped a tear from under her eyes. "Sorry, but the thought of you, being all lovey dovey—" She started to laugh again.

When Shenaia started to load the .50 caliber, Mar and Kalei ran for the door.

After two weeks of patiently walking through the basics, Kalei was beyond ready to start throwing some real punches. In fact, she was tempted to pick a fight with Mar just to speed things up. But, luckily, Erit gave them the go-ahead to spar before Kalei had to resort to such tactics.

Kalei and Shenaia were paired off first.

As the two walked out into the center of the mats, Erit preceded the match with a few words. "No need to worry about hurting one another. We are all Estranged here, so I can assure you that any injuries, mortal or otherwise, will meet with a swift recovery. Now fight!"

They didn't circle or dance. For a moment, they simply stood there. Shenaia playfully stretched her neck from side to side while Kalei shifted her weight to the balls of her feet. When Shenaia smirked, Kalei raised an eyebrow.

Shenaia feigned a lunge to Kalei's left, and then swung at her right. Kalei dodged easily. It was a tactic Kalei had seen many times. Somehow, it reminded her of her childhood, when she would— Shenaia ran at Kalei and cocked her right arm back for another punch.

With all the confidence that came from years as a cop, Kalei blocked Shenaia's first punch, grabbed the second one, and then twisted Shenaia's arm behind her back while kicking in the back of her knees. The counter-attack would have been successful, except that in mid-kick, Kalei lost her grip on the darkness. It went punching through her limbs, slammed into her head, and left her dazed and doubled over. Shenaia readily escaped, but she must have lost control as well because she ripped off her gloves and charged after Kalei with the ferocity of an animal ready to feed, the whites showing in her eyes, her lips bared in a ferocious snarl. Erit intervened, small as he was, and with an arm around the woman's abdomen and a small leg behind her calf, he easily threw her to the mat.

Both Recruits were sent to opposite sides of the room to recover while Erit worked with Mar on her stances.

As she sat in her corner, Kalei was forced to face the fact that the darkness would not be so easily tucked away and forgotten. Some battles never ended, no matter how much training you put into them. Even now as she tried to regain control, she could feel it pulling, digging, and consuming her soul from the inside out. The all-too-familiar sensations burned at her heart and spread once more. She struggled to pull herself away, but she only felt it sinking deeper into her bones.

Slowly, she put the darkness back under her control, but the leash was tenuous. She stood up to fight another round.

Over the next few weeks, Kalei eventually learned to maintain control while sparring with Mar. Yet always beneath the skin, she could feel the pressure of the darkness and the slight tang of its presence in her heart. She resented its presence even as she knew she would never be without it.

Shenaia was having trouble too. She would disappear for hours, days at time. When she returned, she was usually disheveled, disoriented, and a bit too quick in her movements. Kalei recognized the symptoms of an addict, but she didn't say anything. Erit would have to be the one to kick Shenaia out; Kalei had no authority. And she knew Erit wasn't an idiot; she knew he saw what was going on. But still, much to Kalei's aggravation, the boy kept his silence.

Combat practice moved slowly. Even working day and night with their tireless bodies, it took nearly a month before Mar and Kalei could spar without losing control. For Shenaia, it took another four weeks.

Fighting Shenaia was the hardest challenge for Kalei. She had scuffled with gangsters before; it was part of her job description as a cop. They were scrappy fighters, with no regard for the rules or etiquettes of more civilized combat. Shenaia was much the same, except that she took it to a whole new level. Not only did she have no regard for the conventions of fighting, but there was cunning and experience there too. Add a bit of unnatural ferocity to her style, and Shenaia was a beast. In an even fight, she would have won every time. But with the darkness in the mix, Shenaia always lost control first.

During the fifth month since Kalei had entered the recruit program, Kalei and Shenaia were able to extend the length of their matches while maintaining the darkness. As they fought round after round, neither woman would submit to the other, leading to long, drawn-out battles of will. Shenaia even broke her own arm once to get out of Kalei's hold. But the intense level of fighting that passed between them consistently brought the two women to their limits, and Shenaia would consistently cave first. Sometimes, she would simply collapse. Other times, the darkness would turn her into a monster, ripping at mask and glove to reach Kalei's skin. Erit, somehow, was able to tame the beast every time.

Then, one Tuesday between bouts, Shenaia began to pace fervently, muttering to herself as she went. Kalei picked up on a few words, "–need it, just one more..."

There it was. Confirmation for what Kalei had been suspecting for weeks. She walked over to Shenaia and stood just inches in front of the young woman, interrupting her pacing. "You need what? What was that you just said?"

Shenaia glanced at Kalei, then furtively dodged to the right as she responded, "Ai-air, that's what I said, I need air..." She stepped out of the room.

Kalei made to follow, but Erit stopped her with an outstretched arm. She turned her fury on him. "What the hell are you doing? Why are you letting her get away with this! This isn't some game, Erit."

"Kalei, you have to understand. Not everyone can handle the darkness as well as you. Wait– Listen to me. Shenaia has been an Estranged for far longer, and under much different circumstances. She has spent the last decade in an environment where highs are accepted, encouraged, even. Rewriting those old habits will take time. I hate it as much as you do, but it is necessary."

Kalei pushed past him and walked through the door. She decided she needed some air. Real air.

She made her way through the broken foyer doors and sat on the curb, looking out over the desolate, cracked street. The pavement had split and crumbled so much over the years that it looked more like a dried-out riverbed than an actual road. Holes had appeared and swallowed the tires of abandoned vehicles. Patches of dirt attempted to nourish scraggly dandelions. Large slabs that refused to break jutted out at odd angles where the soil beneath had sunk and shifted. Overall, the elements had done their fair share of work over the last twenty years to render the street back to nature.

A moment passed as Kalei took it all in, and she was relieved to be alone. Then she heard something. A slight shuffle of cloth as someone moved behind her. Then,

"I'm sorry."

Kalei turned around to see Shenaia leaning against the building. Kalei asked, "What?"

"I'm sorry– I..." Whatever she had meant to say faded into silence.

Kalei let it. She turned away from Shenaia and resumed studying the bleak scenery.

After a few moments, Shenaia spoke again. "Who were those girls?"

Kalei didn't even turn around this time. "Excuse me?"

Shenaia's voice was quiet. "The girls in that video – in the car when you were attacked. Who were they?"

Kalei spared a glance toward Shenaia. "They're my nieces."

"Wait – nieces?"

Kalei was surprised by the shock in Shenaia's voice.

She turned to look at the young woman. "Yeah, my husband's brother's kids."

Shenaia let out her breath. "Oh, right. I thought—" She laughed. "Never mind." She looked up at the sky for a moment and Kalei returned her thoughts. Then Shenaia asked, "What are their names?"

"Kas and Teia."

"Beautiful names."

"Yeah, I thought so."

Another pause fell between them. Shenaia said, "Why were they at your house that night?"

A bitter knot clenched at Kalei's stomach. *If Qain didn't have that damn meeting in Takaio...* Kalei explained to Shenaia how Fenn's brother worked a lot, so they would watch the girls quite frequently. Of course, Qain earned enough money that he could have afforded a nanny, but he preferred to leave the girls with family when he went out of town.

Before she knew it, Kalei was rambling about the girls' bedtime routine with its shadow puppet stories and their "My Little Dreams" night light. She recalled the time that Kas had helped Fenn build her new big-girl's bed. She talked about the hundreds of ways Teia had annoyed her bigger sister, and how it had reminded her of her own childhood with her big sister Jenna.

And then she was talking about Jenna. About the big sister who was always there for her, who was always screaming at Kalei to get out of her room. Jenna used to pretend to take the bigger slice of pie just to see Kalei get angry, and then when Kalei was worn out from trying – and failing – to beat up her bigger sister, Jenna would switch the plates around and give Kalei a fork. Kalei loved that. She hadn't really cared about the bigger piece to begin with, but when she finally got it, when her sister gave it to her, the piece somehow became... special.

So many stories over so many years, and they all just came spilling out as Kalei sat on that curb, talking to the pavement as though it were listening. She forgot Shenaia was even there. After a while, the stories fell silent and Kalei watched the present creep back in where the past had filled the air.

Shenaia said, "It sounds like you had a beautiful life."

Kalei didn't look at her. "I did."

CHAPTER NINE

Promotion

Two months later, Kalei walked along the perimeter fence, and Mar quietly matched pace at her shoulder. It was a fresh day. The rain had just cleared and spring was making itself known. Birds flitted back and forth over the chain-link fence, heedless of the border they traversed. Past the razor wire, Kalei could see the open ocean, brilliant blue with huge cargo ships and a few scattered fishing vessels sailing into East Lake Bay on their way to and from New Port. The ships gleamed as the light glinted off various metal instruments and objects. The bright sunlight reflected off a rolling ocean wave, blinding Kalei. She looked away.

Mar rasped, "Ya think that one will be a problem?" Kalei looked at where the old woman was pointing and saw a lone figure standing on the street corner, anxiously shifting her weight. The person was wearing far too many layers than was appropriate on this warm day. Even from this distance, Kalei could see the winter coat bulging as it tried to contain the bulk of several shirts, causing the figure's torso to look oddly disproportionate to its legs.

Kalei almost laughed. "Of course she will. That's Lecia."

Lecia glanced over her left shoulder and saw the two Wardens. She jumped slightly, as though the sight of the pair had surprised her, then she immediately turned away and started speed walking toward the nearest alley.

Before the woman took more than two steps, Kalei called out, "Hey!" She pulled off her Warden's helmet.

Lecia glanced back at the Wardens again, this time tensing up as though she was preparing to run, but then she noticed– "Kalei? Is that you?" Lecia called back.

"Yup," Kalei replied as they approached.

Lecia looked her up and down. Kalei stood still for the scrutiny, fully covered with the standard black polyester from head to toe. Minus the helmet, of course. Lecia's eyes lit up. "You're a Warden now!"

Kalei shrugged. "Apparently."

"So? Does that mean they taught you how to kill Estranged?"

Kalei's grip on her helmet tightened. "No. Supposedly, I need to be an experienced Warden for that." She consciously loosened her grip and felt the swirls in her nails relax as well. "If you ask me, they're just stringing me along. But, it doesn't matter. That's not why I'm here anyway." Kalei knew Lecia understood what she meant, but neither of them said it out loud.

Mar pointed at Lecia. "You. Come on." Mar turned and led the way.

"What she means," Kalei interpreted, "is that we have orders to escort you out of the district on sight." She made a sweeping motion with her arm, as if to say, "After you." Then she said, "It doesn't mean we can't talk on the way."

Lecia pulled her attention away from Mar and seemed to remember Kalei. "Of course! You know—"

"Hold on." They made a few slow steps as Mar trudged on ahead of them. Once the old woman was out of earshot, Kalei picked up the pace again and said, "You know, you really shouldn't hang out Downtown. I can come to you."

"It's not like I come Downtown just to find you. Besides, most Estranged are too zoned out to really come after me. The typical pattern I've observed is that they find a few other Estranged and settle in for a long series of highs. I could jump up and down in front of them and scream my name, but if I'm more than ten feet off, they won't even bother."

"Fascinating. Well, anyway, does Landen have the device ready? Have they learned where my family is?"

"Not that I know. My contact with Tusic changed his number right after your meeting, and I haven't been able to get in touch with any of them since."

"Then how the hell am I supposed to communicate with Landen?"

"I don't know. Maybe this is his way of making sure

you don't blow your cover." Kalei started to make a retort, but Lecia continued, "Anyway, I've been trying to dig up information about your family on my own, but all I could find out is what the news reports already say: that your family is safe and in Victim Protection. All the reporters I talked to have their sources locked down tight."

Kalei paused and chewed absentmindedly on the inside of her cheek for a moment, then said, "Have you tried the police?"

"No, I didn't think about that." Lecia grinned and eagerly asked Kalei, "Do you think I should?"

"Yeah, ask for Marley. Tell him—" Tell him what? By now, everyone at the police station would know Kalei was Estranged. It wasn't hard to piece together when they didn't have a body. Even Marley wouldn't listen to anything she had to say now... "Just, ask him for the police report regarding the attack. You might find what you need in there. If he tries to say no, just tell him it's for your book. He's a sucker for authors and journalists. He thinks they're his type." She laughed.

"Thanks, I will!" There was a moment's pause. Lecia's cheeks began to turn red. She looked down at her shoes and then back at Kalei. "So, who is Marley?"

Kalei glanced over at Lecia. "He used to be my partner when I was on the force." She held up her hand before Lecia could say anything. "And before you get any stupid ideas, I'll let you know he was my foster mom's grand-nephew. We're practically siblings."

"I wasn't thinking anything stupid!" Lecia retorted a bit too indignantly.

"Yeah, right. Everyone does. It doesn't take a career in law enforcement to learn that one."

Lecia pouted. "You're always so negative."

Kalei shrugged and watched Mar's back as it swayed with the steady motion of her march to the front gate.

Lecia said, "Whatever. It's my turn now. You promised you would let me interview you for my book."

"Yeah," Kalei sighed. "I did." Normally, Kalei would have done anything she could to avoid the woman, but when Lecia had offered to look for Kalei's family in exchange for interviews, Kalei could hardly refuse.

Lecia's head bounced in a quick nod. "Yes, you did. So what did it take to become a Warden?"

Kalei explained the process of bringing the darkness under control, shaping the nail designs, moving on to physical training, and so forth. All the while, Lecia badgered her with more questions.

"But you knew how to fight already, didn't you?"

Kalei reached back and ran a hand through her two-inch-long hair. Kalei had noticed the other day that it was growing back with black highlights, although, much to her relief, it was still predominantly brown. Kalei said, "Well, fighting is different as an Estranged. It's like a balancing act... and once you start fighting *with* the darkness, that's a whole 'nother story."

Lecia's eyebrows scrunched together. "*With* the darkness?"

"Yeah. You know how the darkness works, right? When two Estranged touch hands, their darkness reaches out and grabs a piece of the other's." Kalei decided to use Shenaia's example, "Kind of like if you and I each had a cookie in one hand, and I grabbed your cookie while you grabbed mine. Then, when I eat the cookie, A.K.A, when my darkness absorbs your piece of darkness, it releases the high. But there are ways to defend against that. I can solidify my darkness — or close my hand around the cookie – so that you can't get it. But if I don't strengthen my grip enough when we come into contact, your darkness can mix in with mine and start trying to pull out a high. But that's still no big deal, because so long as I am still touching you, I can cut off that contaminated piece of my darkness and push it into you. Kind of like cutting off a hand and throwing it to the wolves."

"From cookies to amputated hands." Lecia grimaced.

"Eh, that was the first example that came to mind."

Lecia shivered and said, "Well, it made your point. Since when did you get so smart?"

It was Kalei's turn to grimace. "Guess I've been spending too much time with Books."

"Books?"

"Yeah, sorry. I mean Erit. When we became

Wardens, we were told to stop using our real names over the comms and start using nicknames based on the patterns we chose for our nails. Erit is Books, I'm Swirls, and Mar over there is Smiles."

Lecia laughed, despite the fact that Kalei was being serious.

"So what's your plan now?" Lecia asked.

Kalei checked to see that Mar was still out of earshot. "Well, I guess I'll just keep on gathering information for Tusic until they contact me. And so long as you keep looking for my family, I'll share that information with you too." The gate was only a hundred feet away now. "But this stays between us. Don't go publishing anything until this is all over."

"Of course!"

Being a Warden was hardly interesting so far. Most days were spent patrolling along the fence or sparring with Mar and Shenaia to keep sharp.

It was just another Tuesday. Lecia was already well on her way, and Kalei walked along the humming fence, watching chain link after chain link pass to the sound of Mar's grumbling. Her mind wandered from topic to topic until it flitted through Lecia's interview questions and settled on the memory of her final test to become a Warden.

It was... different.

Terin had stepped into the room and walked over to the center of the training mats, not quite sucking the air from the room with his stoic nature. He stopped when he reached a seam in the mats that divided the room perfectly in half. With his hands in his pockets, he looked each of them in the eye, then said, "You're done with basic training. But we can't promote you to Wardens until you pass a test, so here it is: go into the district and shake hands with an Estranged. We will be watching through your ear cameras." He walked back to the door.

Erit stepped forward from where he stood by the wall and added, "Of course, the Estranged you shake hands with cannot be affiliated with SWORDE." Before the recruits could grasp what either of them had said, Erit waved his hand with a "Best of luck!" and followed Terin out of the room.

Several moments passed in silence, until Shenaia said, "What the hell kind of test is that?"

Kalei raised an eyebrow as she continued to stare at the door. "Who knows?"

Mar added, "Who cares? I'm just gonna do it and get this damn training over with." The old woman tore off her ski mask, flung it in a corner, and marched out the door.

Shenaia looked at Kalei, a grin on her face as she said, "He didn't say nothin' about doin' this thing solo. Let's go, little sis! Although I wanna stop by tha closet first. There's no way in hell I'm passin' no test in these damn sweats!"

Kalei followed as Shenaia pranced out the door.

"What makes you think I'm the little sister? I'm at least a decade older."

Shenaia looked over her shoulder and smirked. "Trust me, you ain't no big sister ta me."

"Do I need to set you straight, little one?"

Shenaia scoffed. "Go ahead and try!"

Out in the street, Kalei glanced left and right as she tried to make sense of where they were. It occurred to her that she had never spent much time outside of SWORDE HQ, except that time when Lecia had taken her to Tusic. Kalei's sense of direction in the Downtown district was a bit lacking.

She asked, "Where do we find other Estranged?"

"The theatre. They always at tha theatre." There was no hesitation in Shenaia's stride; she was already halfway down the block before Kalei caught up to her.

Kalei replied, "I'm not going to ask."

They had been walking for about half a mile when Kalei told Shenaia, "You know, I'm guessing the entire point of this exercise is that we *don't* get high from touching them."

"Don't you worry 'bout that." Shenaia pulled a pair of Warden's gloves out of her back pocket. "If you're nice, I'll let you borrow 'em when I'm done."

Kalei raised an eyebrow. "Isn't that cheating?"

"Well, ain't you a goody two-shoes? Did Terin hand you a freakin' rulebook before he left? No." She pulled the left glove down firmly over her wrist. "No rules, no cheatin'."

They took a left down an alleyway, and as they emerged into a parking lot on the other side, Shenaia pointed out, "There." On the far side of the parking lot stood a flat, square building with burnt-out lettering above the entrance which read: *C-n-ma*. And sure enough, huddled against the outer wall like smokers out for a puff, sat three Estranged.

One man wore nothing but a pair of grimy briefs, and he sat with his legs sprawled out while the sun gleamed off his balding head. The second man was only marginally better dressed, sitting cross-legged and wearing a pair of basketball shorts, but he had enough hair on his chest and limbs to make him look like he was fully clothed. And both men possessed an ample supply of belly fat, which sprawled over their waistlines like some ill-conceived clay creations.

Then there was a little girl, probably no more than six years old, wearing a faded yellow sundress. A ponytail hung limply from the back of her head as she looked to the sky with closed eyes and hummed a cheery song to herself. She was small and flexible enough that her hands held on to her bare feet as they moved back and forth to the rhythm of her humming.

Shenaia laughed. "I think we found Erit's girlfriend."

Kalei rolled her eyes. "Stop being stupid. Let's just shake their hands and get out of here."

Holding up a gloved hand and wriggling her fingers, the teenaged girl said, "Watch how it's done."

"No thanks."

The two women crossed the parking lot and made their way over to where the Estranged sat. Shenaia headed for little girl, while Kalei picked the hairy man as her target. She didn't want anything to do with Mr. Boxers.

When they came within a few feet of the Estranged, the three opened their eyes and looked for the source of the scuffing noise Shenaia made as she walked. Their eyes lit up when they saw who it was, and they reached out eagerly to the newcomers.

Kalei stepped up to the hairy man, pulled the darkness back from her arm, and offered him her hand.

His two hands latched onto her one. As his fingers closed around hers, a grin spread across his face, revealing black, rotting teeth. His excitement was palpable, but nothing happened. Kalei sealed the handshake with a quick up-down, then tried to withdraw from his hold. The man's smile slid from his face, and creases began to appear on his forehead as his eyebrows came together in anger. Before Kalei could break free, his grip tightened and he started to yank on her arm with impossible force, like a small child trying to yank their favorite toy out of the bushes. Kalei almost lost her balance, but she caught herself on the brick wall with her other hand. Off to her right, she heard the shrill notes of a temper tantrum starting up.

Kalei delivered a solid kick to the man's ribs, yet he didn't seem to notice. He just kept yanking and yanking, his lip curling as he redoubled his effort. Kalei thought her arm would pop out of its socket any moment. Then the bald man decided to take an interest and began crawling toward the party. *Dammit!*

Kalei looked back at Yanker and tried to concentrate despite the constant jolt-jolt of the man's persistence. She reached in, ripped off a piece of darkness, and shoved it down her arm. She pushed it out her hand, into the man's palms, and kicked him in the chest as it hit. She pulled her arm free just in time to catch a tackle from Mr. Curious.

Kalei hit the ground hard, forcing the air out of her lungs. The little girl's screams became frenzied, like a wild chimp, furious that her meal was trapped inside a glass box.

The bald man had her arm. *Shit!* Kalei's control of the darkness had slipped in the attack, and now she could feel a high racing up her arm from where he made contact. Kalei severed the connection with all the darkness below her shoulder, and, just like with the first man, she shoved it into her attacker's hands. As his head rolled back and a grin blossomed on his face, Kalei pulled her arm away and struggled out from under his weight.

A gunshot ripped through the alley. Kalei looked up in time to see the little girl fall to the ground, her brains splattered across the bricks of the cinema.

Kalei regained her feet and shouted at Shenaia, "What the hell did you do!"

"Wha'? She didn' feel a thing. She'll be fine," Shenaia said as she calmly holstered her weapon.

Kalei closed the last few steps between them and grabbed Shenaia by her shirt. "That wasn't necessary."

The teenager grabbed Kalei's hand and shoved it off. "What're you so worked up about? She was Estranged! No harm done."

Over Shenaia's shoulder, Kalei could see the little girl's body crumpled against the wall, like a doll propped up for teatime. The child's delicate jaw hung open. A bead of blood escaped from the red hole in her forehead and traced a jagged path through the light layer of dirt on her ivory skin.

Kalei said, "That doesn't make it right."

Shenaia gave a harsh laugh. "What the hell do you care? I thought you wanted all Estranged dead, Little Miss High-and-Mighty." Shenaia grabbed her left glove by the wrist and peeled it off, then did the same for the right. "And what about all 'highs are bad' shit? Look at your guys!" She finished removing her glove and pointed at the two men lying against the theatre with wide grins on their faces. "They're high as the fucking moon! Don't go preaching to me about what's right, you fucking hypocrite."

Shenaia smacked the gloves against her open palm and walked back across the parking lot.

CHAPTER TEN

Freedom

Kalei, Shenaia, Mar, and Erit sat in the back of a windowless van, rocking back and forth with the motion of the moving vehicle. The bleak interior with its two benches reminded Kalei of the first time she had sat on the back bumper of one of these vans, getting tested while she wondered how much longer she would be keeping her job. So much time had gone by since then, so much had happened... the incident felt more like a dream than a memory.

They were on their way to their first Call. Kalei sat next to Shenaia, and as she watched Mar grunt at the straps of her helmet, nearly elbowing Erit when one of the straps came loose, Kalei couldn't help but wonder if this was a good idea. They were still Estranged, all of them. Could a little bit of training really change anything? Who knew what Mar had done in her past? It wouldn't surprise Kalei to learn that the old woman had killed someone, Estranged or not. It made sense, back at the hotel when Mar had said she was going to make things right. Maybe she was trying to redeem herself for past crimes? Why else would the old woman be so set on learning to suppress the darkness?

But suppression was not erasure. Once they were out in the city, it would be too easy for Mar to hurt innocent people. Take away her weapon, tie one hand behind her back; it wouldn't matter. Mar was Estranged. Let her have her pinky and she could wipe out an entire city block in the span of ten minutes.

Kalei wasn't sure she was ready for a Call. There was too much at stake.

"What the hell is a 'Call' anyway?" Shenaia blurted, breaking the silence.

Erit hadn't explained much when they left headquarters. He showed up at the Lounge and told them to suit up, Terin had orders for the team to take their first Call. So they did.

Irritated, Kalei saved Erit the bother of explaining. "It's when the police call SWORDE to alert them—" Kalei glanced at Erit. "—to alert *us* to an incident involving Estranged. The police will secure the area and wait for Wardens to arrive."

"Precisely," added Erit. He leaned forward to address his students. "We will go in as a four-man team, with me as the leader, of course—"

"Shouldn't you be teaching?" Mar butted in.

Erit closed his eyes and took in a deep breath, then he opened them and propped his right hand on his knee as he told Mar, "There are plenty of people who can teach as well as I. Terin has assigned me to lead your team, and so I shall. Now, from what I understand, an Estranged has attacked the West Hill apartment complex on Lake Street. The building has been evacuated, although the occupants are in quarantine until we can confirm that they are not Estranged."

"Is that really an issue?" Kalei asked. "Some of them are victims, for Pete's sake. Why make the police coral them into pens like cattle if—"

"Not every Estranged is a blubbering zombie, as you well know. It is possible that the attacker may be hiding among our victims, posing as an Untouched."

Kalei leaned back and diverted her gaze to the rear doors. "Makes sense."

Erit continued, "Our task today is to locate the Estranged who attacked the complex, disable him or her, and relocate them back to the Downtown District along with any corpses. We must submit what bodies we find to the Containment and Observatory Department to ensure that they do not decide to wake up in the near future and become Estranged themselves. Now, any further questions?"

Leader perhaps, but always the teacher, Kalei thought to herself.

Kalei returned her attention to Erit and asked, "Do we know for certain that just one Estranged is in the complex?"

"We do not."

Shenaia scooted forward on her seat, a big grin on her face as she said, "What if the guy is hot? Damn, I love bad boys." The van grew silent as the three other occupants openly glared at her. Shenaia's grin fell from her face as she rolled her eyes. "Okay, alright, go back to your little policy-chat or whatever you're doing. Forget I said anything."

Erit shook his head, then replied to Kalei, "Reports are vague at best. You will find that with most any Call. Once the word 'Estranged' gets out, panic tends to run rampant among the witnesses, and the local police can offer very little assistance from the sidelines."

"Sidelines?" Kalei couldn't keep the edge out of her voice. "Yeah, they're on the sidelines because Terin got cozy with the mayor and forced all the officers out of—"

"My apologies, Kalei," Erit quietly interrupted, holding up one hand to stop her. "I did not mean to offend. I understand the difficult position the police are in, I do. If anything, I commend them for respecting the laws in place, even as it bars them from helping those to whom they are sworn to protect. But you and I both know that it is for the best." He held Kalei's eyes with his own and waited for her response.

She looked away again. "Yeah, of course."

The sound of screeching brakes filled the compartment as the van slowed to a halt. Shenaia used the momentum of the stop to fall dramatically into Kalei. Kalei pushed the girl off and gave her a glare, then picked up her own helmet from the bench and pushed it down over her head.

"Helmets on," Erit reminded the other two as he put on his and waited to see that they were all similarly suited. Kalei felt the magnet in the back of her collar *snitch* into place as it connected to her helmet. She ignored the other three Wardens and watched the edges of her visor as the WARCOM system came online. When it flickered to life, she could see four small icons in the left corner of her visor and a slight crackle told her the audio was now live.

The four icons displayed a black smiley face, the spine of a book, a steering wheel, and a swirl: a live feed of the team's nails. Shenaia's steering wheel flicked happily back and forth on some cheery drive, Erit's book read *The Puppet Masters*, and Mar's smiley face kept its mouth flat-lined, but its eyebrows arched in a deep scowl.

Erit opened the doors and they stepped outside.

It was Kalei's first time outside the fence since she had officially become a Recruit with SWORDE. She stepped out into the grey day and listened to the light rainfall against her helmet. Looking past the raindrops multiplying on her visor, she could see the apartment complex ahead. She was standing at the edge of a cluster of tall, repetitive brick buildings reaching for the sky with about as much character as the grey clouds that hung over them. Less, actually.

Meanwhile, the second building on her left was cordoned off with caution tape, and a handful of locals crowded the yellow ribbon to get front row seats to the show. There, a man with a thick brown jacket and a baseball cap, both hands in his pockets, stood on his toes to see the entrance of the apartment building. A middle-aged woman in her sweats asked a police officer for information, holding an umbrella as she hugged her heavy sports jacket closed with her free hand. It was the typical crowd Kalei was used to from her policing days.

Within the caution tape, stretching out across the open area between the police cars and the apartments, stood an expanse of dirt that could hardly be called a lawn. The squat tufts of grass were clearly the minority. Across the yard, cement paths wandered this way and that, not lending much to the greenery despite the hardy clumps of weeds that made their stand in the many cracks and crevices.

Standing huddled at the intersection of these paths stood a dozen scared people surrounded by a half dozen police officers. The officers questioned the civilians with soft voices and notebooks in hand, while the civilians alternately nodded nervously and demanded answers. Nothing had changed since she left. The same scene, the same people, the same helplessness pervaded. Except now, she wasn't helpless.

She spotted Dwaro among the officers and walked over to him.

"What's the situation?"

He spun around so fast Kalei almost pulled her gun. He gaped at her for a moment, his eyes dancing across her visor as they tried to work out some burning question. "Uh, a woman heard screams. She, uh—Kalei, is that you?"

Shit. Kalei tried to think of something, anything she could say that would change his mind. But she couldn't open her mouth. Even if she tried to change her voice, she had worked with this man for years. He would know her voice anywhere. *Obviously.*

They stood there for what felt like a year, Dwaro watching her incredulously as he waited for her response, and Kalei with her mouth working frantically, trying to answer his question without speaking. Kalei was on the verge of creating some absurd bastardization of sign language when Erit finally showed up.

"What the hell are you doing? Get over there with Wheels." Kalei nodded, relieved, and walked over to Shenaia, who was laughing, of course.

"Haha! You made Books say 'hell'! Haha! That was great!" Kalei rolled her eyes and accepted one of the assault rifles from Mar. Estranged might not be killed by guns, but it stopped them all the same. No one likes to get shot.

Erit joined them and gave the signal. "Let's go."

As the Wardens walked into the building, it didn't take Kalei's eyes long to adjust to the dim light. In front of her, on the opposite wall, stood two elevators, and to her left and right, hallways led down to the first-floor apartments. Mar and Erit went to the end of these halls and secured the fire exits while Shenaia and Kalei began to clear apartment after apartment after apartment.

For most people, additional closet space is a perk; for Kalei, it was just one more nook to check. And these apartments could boast a *lot* of closet space.

The first floor showed nothing. So, they took the stairs up to the next floor.

Kalei saw Shenaia's wheel take an erratic 180-degree turn. Shenaia said, "We have to do this for ten freaking floors! Why the hell don't we have more people for this shit?"

"Budget cuts," Erit replied sarcastically. Wardens didn't get paid a dime for what they did.

"Fuck you and your budget cuts. I'd rather be sitting in the van than marchin' up and down these damn hallways," Shenaia retorted. That being said, Shenaia continued to march up and down the hallways with Kalei, clearing each of the apartments.

On the third floor, they stepped into a room that was completely dark. Not unusual, but when they tried to flip the switch, nothing came on. Per protocol, they pulled out their flashlights, attached them to the top of the rifles, and proceeded with caution.

The beam of Kalei's light slid over a large couch, a wooden end table, and cast a huge shadow on the wall as it caught the lamp. She worked her way around the living room while Shenaia checked the closets, but both came up empty, so they continued down the hall.

Before they reached the first door, Kalei heard something: a muffled, choking sound. Kalei signaled for

Shenaia to stop. The sound was hard to pinpoint with her helmet on, but she didn't dare remove it. Instead, she moved slowly to the first door on the left and gently pushed it open. The sound grew louder. She raised her rifle, and the beam of light from the flashlight revealed a bed covered in a thick blue comforter and, on the other side, tucked between the bed and the wall, the top of someone's head.

Kalei moved toward the far wall, her flashlight trained on the person as she yelled, "Put your hands up! Make any sudden movements, and I *will* shoot."

Instead, the head ducked down and the choking noise grew louder. Kalei tucked her rifle tighter into her shoulder and placed her finger on the trigger, but as her line of sight broke clear of the bed and she could see the full body of the person, she saw a crying young boy. His hair covered his face as he hugged his knees tightly to his chest, his shoulders bouncing to the rhythm of his sobs. Kalei lowered her weapon.

"Is he Estranged?" Erit asked over the radio when Kalei reported the discovery.

Kalei crouched down next to the boy and put one hand on his back. Shenaia moved in behind her and pointed the flashlight at the boy so they could see.

Kalei said, "Hey, it's okay. I'm not going to hurt you." She continued to talk to him as she gently pulled his hands away from his legs.

Shenaia reported, "No, he's not Estranged."

"Okay, you and Swirls escort him back to the van

and check him out. Smiles and I will continue the sweep."

"Roger that."

Rubbing the boy's back, Kalei asked, "Hey, where are your parents?"

The boy hesitantly looked at Kalei through a break in his dark hair, his eyes still puffy, his lower lip quivering. Kalei estimated he was no more than eight years old. He didn't say anything, he just stared at her dark visor with wide eyes.

Kalei reached back and removed her helmet, smiling at the boy as she said, "It's okay. You can tell me."

The boy continued to stare at her.

Shenaia propped her gun against the wall so the light still shone on them and removed her helmet as well, kneeling down next to Kalei. She said, "Hey, come here, kid."

The kid glanced at Shenaia briefly, but then returned to staring at Kalei. Shenaia whispered, "Hey, put on your helmet and get out of here. I think he recognizes you from the TV."

Kalei tossed Shenaia a wary glance, put her helmet back on, and then retreated to the far wall. Far enough that the boy couldn't see her, but close enough for Kalei to keep an eye on Shenaia.

"Kid, time to go. Get up."

"No."

"No?"

"The cop girl said she was going to shoot me."

"Kid, we Wardens. We the good guys. Now c'mon."

"No."

Shenaia put her helmet on, reached back for her rifle, and tossed it to Kalei, saying, "Hold this."

Kalei caught the rifle, but with the flashlight now pointing at the ceiling, she didn't see what happened next. She heard the boy cry out, and then Shenaia stepped into the light with the kid slung over one shoulder, kicking and screaming and punching her back with both fists.

Shenaia didn't seem to notice as she took her rifle back from Kalei with her free hand and led the way out of the apartment.

Once outside, they took the boy straight to the van. His shouts and screams garnered a lot of attention from the crowd, but luckily, the open back doors shielded them from unwanted attention as Shenaia put the boy down onto the back bumper. Kalei pulled a blanket out of one of the lockers and draped it around the boy's shoulders. He immediately pulled it tightly around himself, pulled his legs inside, and glared at them from his shelter, only his neck and head visible above the brown wool.

Kalei touched Shenaia on the shoulder and spoke softly into the radio so the boy couldn't hear. "You go ahead and give him the test. He could still be an Estranged. I'm going to grab the other kit from up front and start testing the other victims."

"Gotchya."

Kalei walked over to the passenger door of the van and gave a nod to the driver as she opened it. Beneath the seat sat the green testing kit she was looking for. She reached down and started to pull the kit out, but it caught on something.

Kalei bent over to take a look, but as she did so, her helmet bumped into the floor mat and wouldn't allow her to see anything below the edge of the seat cushion.

This motherfucking piece of—

Kalei glanced over her shoulder to make sure no one was around to see her, then she ducked back into the shelter of the van and removed her helmet.

They really need to consider switching to masks, Kalei thought to herself as she took a moment to pull an earbud from the collar of her suit and tuck it into her ear. If Erit tried to radio her and found out her helmet was off, that was one lecture she would never hear the end of.

Kalei looked under the seat. The small red box, molded from plastic with a handle at the top, was wedged behind some sort of lever that jutted out from the chair's frame. Kalei reached in, grabbed the handle, and attempted to move the box around the bar, but the kit was too big. It was at least an inch wider than the gap between the bar and the seat. *How the hell did they get this thing in here?*

She slid the kit as far to the right as she could, then she placed her left hand on the seat cushion to give herself more leverage, and she gave the kit a hard yank. With a loud *snap!* it came free.

That didn't sound good.

"What's going on?" The urgency in Erit's voice made her jump.

"Nothing! I, uh--" She looked over her shoulder and realized Erit wasn't there. It was her radio. "Uh, I was just getting the second kit, and—"

"What is Wheels doing? Why did her nails just go full black?"

"What!" Kalei dropped the kit and ran toward the back of the van just as a scream pierced the air. She reached Shenaia and saw the boy slumped over in her arms. Kalei was furious. "What the hell did you do!"

Shenaia was rocking back and forth, stroking the boy's hair, muttering, "I'm sorry. I'm so sorry." The young woman's eyes were stretched wide open and her pupils were fully dilated.

Kalei opened her mouth, but she heard a shout behind her. "Kalei!" She looked back to see Dwaro running towards her. *Shit!* Her helmet was still in the front of the van. "Kalei, what happened?"

The yard fell silent as everyone looked at the van. Time seemed to slow down. Kalei saw Dwaro closing the distance between him and Kalei, one long stride after the next, she felt her heart pounding against the inside of her chest, and for two more heartbeats, she did nothing as Shenaia continued to mutter behind her.

Then the silence was broken by a deep, throaty

laugh that carried across the yard and echoed off the cold brick walls of the complex.

Time kicked back into motion. Kalei turned away from Dwaro and looked past the open door of the van. In the heart of the crowd of onlookers stood the hooded man she had spotted before, now shoulder to shoulder with a half dozen new spectators. His hood was pushed back, and he held his stomach as the laughter sailed out of his grinning mouth. His bleach-blond hair caught the light and stood out bright against the gloomy scene around him.

"Get away from him! NOW!" Recognizing Xamic and the danger he posed, Kalei sprinted toward the crowd. The people around him were confused, bumping into each other and pushing away from Kalei, clearly unsure which "him" she was referring to. Then they started to run in terror when Xamic reached up and stroked a hand across the cheeks of a middle-aged woman and a young man. The pair fell like rocks.

Then Xamic bolted, the laughter shifting into a higher pitch.

Kalei didn't slow her stride, pushing through the crowd and charging after Xamic. He ducked down a narrow alley between the apartment buildings, and disappeared for a moment in the shadows. Kalei followed, catching sight of him exiting the other end. She covered the twenty-foot stretch and followed him into the open.

About thirty feet of flattened dirt stretched out

before her and ended at an aged chain-link fence that leaned away from its posts, sporting several holes where it had been cut or pulled up for someone to crawl through. Xamic slipped through one of those holes and ran toward a toppled boxcar. Track after rusted railway track covered the ground for as far as Kalei could see. The track nearest to her bore a mile-long cargo train, the majority of the cars still standing despite the proliferation of rust covering nearly every inch of the yard. But the section of five cars directly in front of her, the section Xamic was running toward, was toppled as though some giant had taken his massive hand and pushed them over. Beyond that, Kalei could see the remnants of a train wreck, with boxcars crushed and twisted, and piled at odd angles from a high-speed collision. Kalei couldn't decide if it looked more like a pile of discarded toys, or a misguided piece of modern art.

This had once been the busiest railway juncture in Celan. E-day had put an end to that. A hijacked train crashed into the yard, traffic to West Lake came to a complete stop, and later, when Franklin built a new train yard on the East Side, the West Side railway became obsolete. Home only to runaways and rogue Estranged. A place for society to bury its dead.

Xamic reached the toppled boxcar, ten feet tall even on its side, and vaulted it easily, as though it were a small turnstile in a subway. Kalei's pace slowed momentarily, then picked back up as she spotted a gap between the cars on her right. She lost sight of Xamic, but he was still easy to follow. He kept *Whoop!*-ing like a frat boy on his way to a tailgate party. The sound carried easily across the abandoned yard.

Kalei skirted the massive pile of train cars, and on the other side lay several more tracks with trains still standing. Kalei slipped between the cars, and as she ran, she occasionally saw Xamic jump up onto the trains, shouting and skipping from boxcar to boxcar. Even with his antics, he was still faster than her, and the gap between them grew wider. Kalei ducked her head and pushed her legs to run faster. Her breath was labored, her legs were beginning to ache, but despite all that, she didn't feel tired. If anything, she felt determined.

The rail yard was coming to an end. Xamic and Kalei had cleared the trains and were now sprinting across the open ground toward a twenty-foot cement wall marking the border to the freeway.

Xamic didn't slow. Kalei didn't either.

When Xamic arrived, he used his momentum to sprint up the side and easily launch over the barrier. Kalei tried to follow, but made it only halfway up the wall before she fell away. She looked around, spotting a maple tree growing beside the barrier about ten feet to her right. Its leafy green canopy reached about forty feet into the air, and its middle branches reached over the fence to watch the traffic on the other side. Kalei ran over and began climbing.

She was about halfway up when she heard glass

shattering, tires screaming, and horns blaring as metal slammed into metal. Kalei scrambled to climb the last few branches, then shimmied over to the top of the wall.

Looking down, she saw about twenty cars – ten on each side of the freeway – slammed together in two mangled piles. At the heart of the collisions, the metal was so twisted and mangled, it was hard to tell where one car ended and the next car began.

Xamic stood on the cement median, watching her. He held out his hands and smiled, as if to show off his masterpiece. Then he hopped off the median and ran into the mess.

Kalei swung off the branch and dropped into a ten-foot pile of freshly dug dirt that sat to one side of a construction site. Her feet sank straight into the pile like it wasn't there, and the dirt came almost to her neck before she stopped, pinning her arms to her body. Cursing, Kalei fought and kicked her way out until she broke free and ran out onto the freeway after Xamic.

Kalei jumped, dodged, and climbed over the wreckage as she ran. An SUV lay on its side, windshield shattered, the driver hanging limp, suspended by the seatbelt. Whether the woman was alive or dead, Kalei couldn't tell.

She kept running, trying not to look too closely at the carnage she climbed over. She sidestepped the remains of a hot rod, catching a glimpse of white-walled tires before looking away, and as she passed, she felt a sharp bite as something caught on her arm, sinking into her flesh. Without looking or slowing, she ripped her arm free and charged forward.

Once she was clear of the first crash site, she spotted Xamic on the other side of the highway, leaning against the hood of a yet-untouched Smart car. The owner stared at the pile-up before him with wide eyes, seemingly unaware of Xamic's presence. Xamic waited for Kalei to hurdle the median, then galloped off into the traffic jam he had created.

As he went, Xamic shattered windows and windshields left and right using a metal tire iron he had picked up. Screams rang out in time with every crash of shattered glass; some people climbed out of their cars and ran in the opposite direction.

Xamic continued to shout and carry on, occasionally stopping to take out a tail light or bash in a hood. The activity slowed him down, allowing Kalei to catch up.

As the distance between them closed, Kalei put on more speed. The sound of his destruction became louder, and she could see the families and commuters cowering in their cars as she ran past. Kalei clenched her jaw and closed the last few feet between her and Xamic.

Xamic spun around and took a deadly swing at her skull, but he missed her head as she dropped her torso and tackled him low in the abdomen. They both went crashing to the ground.

Xamic didn't struggle as Kalei climbed on top of

him, pinning his arms to the cement with her knees. Nor did he protest when she grabbed him by the throat. He didn't seem to mind when the blood seeped out of her flayed right bicep, down her arm, and colored his neck red. Instead, he smiled.

"Y'know, the black in your hair really brings out your eyes. You have your grandfather's eyes."

She punched him in the face.

"You want to get physical, huh?" The ease and strength with which he moved made Kalei feel like a child as he tossed her off and reversed positions. Now he sat on top of her stomach with his hand on her neck.

Kalei snarled "You fucking—!"

"Shhh." Kalei's jaw locked. She could feel his darkness inside her, slowly creeping through her body and taking control. Her own darkness tried to bite and attack the invading mass, but his simply brushed the pestering blows aside as it continued to pour into her. He laughed. "The darkness is mine, sweetheart. You can't use it against me."

The sheer amount he sent into her was overwhelming. Yet even as the flow of darkness stilled, Kalei could feel that the opaque well within him was still full.

He smiled again. Kalei glared at him, then tensed as she felt his darkness tear a piece from hers. He leaned his head back and sighed deeply, as though enjoying a deeply refreshing beverage.

A brief moment later, he rocked his head forward

and said, "You can tell Terin that I will be taking the dessert for myself. Once it has finished baking, of course." Xamic grinned at her again.

Kalei tried to move her arms, she tried to use her darkness to push him back, but she couldn't. She was trapped within her own body. It was a similar experience to the day Terin first found her downtown, when Terin had immobilized her by freezing something – presumably the darkness — within her.

But Xamic was different. Xamic was invading her. Kalei could feel his darkness within every inch of her body, holding her tightly beneath his control.

He leaned his head in close to hers. She couldn't even wrinkle her nose against the smell of stale earth and fresh death. "You know, Fenn is a nice guy. He won't stop talking about you, even after I told him what you are." Xamic slid his left hand up to her chin as he slipped his right hand behind her skull. Then he snapped her neck.

CHAPTER ELEVEN

Trapped

Kalei woke up screaming. She kicked off a blanket and sat up. The room was entirely bare, aside from the cracks in the walls and the light streaming in through the window. Kalei found herself in the middle of the carpeted floor, a red comforter askew beside her. She recognized the Recovery Room; she had been here several times, dropping off out-of-control visitors. It was weird to realize she was one of them. Again.

She held up her hand and flexed her fingers as she watched the black swirls assume their places on her nails. She felt as though Xamic was still inside her. She felt tainted.

At the thought of Xamic, her stomach seized, and she rolled over to dry-heave as her gut tried to expel its nonexistent contents.

When she was done, she sat back down beside the blanket and wiped off a glob of spit from her lips. Still a bit dazed, she tried putting the pieces together ...

Fenn is a good guy... even after I told him what you are.

The memory hit Kalei like a fist to the stomach. She doubled over for a second time, only this time, she kept her jaw clenched shut. When she recovered, she headed straight for the door.

Kalei tore through the halls, yelling for Terin all the way. He didn't respond, but that didn't matter; she knew where his office was.

When she reached his office, she had enough presence of mind to use the door handle, but the door still slammed into the wall with enough violence that the doorknob left a hole.

Somewhere along the way, Kalei had picked up a vase. She couldn't remember grabbing it, the trip down the hall was one angry blur, but the vase was there in her hands. So when she saw Terin lounging behind his desk, playing with a fountain pen, she didn't hesitate to chuck the piece of pottery at him. He easily dodged it, which infuriated Kalei further, but she remained rooted in her place by the door as she demanded, "Where is my family!"

Terin leaned forward and set the pen delicately upon his worn, wooden desk. His face darkened as he propped his elbows on the table and interlocked his hands in front of his face, but he didn't answer. He didn't even look at her.

Kalei took another step into the office and continued, "Xamic knows where Fenn is. If he hasn't already, he's going to—"

"Xamic does not know where Fenn is." Terin's

tone was flat. "I reviewed the recording from your ear cam. I can tell you for a fact that he is not going to kill your family. Xamic is messing with your emotions. You should forget about what he said."

"You weren't there! You didn't have him—" Kalei cringed and faltered at the memory of Xamic's hand around her neck. She clenched her fists. "He knows. And I need to stop him before he can lay a hand on those girls. Are you going to tell me where they are or not?"

He didn't answer as he continued to maintain his thousand-yard stare.

Kalei muffled a frustrated scream. "Fine! I don't need you. I'll find Fenn myself." She spun around and started toward the door.

Terin called after her, "I warned you before." Kalei stopped. She heard his chair drag against the short carpet as he stood up. "If you try to find Fenn, I'll have to kill you."

Kalei turned back with a snarl. "Go ahead and try."

Before Kalei could react, Terin had her by the neck, lifted her off the ground, and slammed her against the wall. Her elbow struck the side of his TV and it crashed into the floor with a dull *crack*.

"You want to know how to kill Estranged?" Kalei was surprised by his sudden attack, but she was even more surprised when she saw the tears in the corner of his eyes. The tears contrasted sharply against his rage. Terin's grip tightened around her throat. "I'll show you how to kill an Estranged."

His teeth clenched, the muscles in his jaw flexing, and he glared into her eyes. Kalei felt her heart race, her breaths came rapidly as she strained against the pressure on her windpipe. She could feel his nails sinking into her flesh as the weight of her body pressed against his hand. But Terin didn't move, and his darkness didn't advance.

After several more erratic heartbeats, Terin looked away. He loosened his hold and let her slide to the floor, keeping his fingers wrapped around her neck. Kalei heard him mutter, "I never wanted this for you."

Then he looked back at Kalei, steel in his eyes. He drew his arm back and slammed her skull into the wall, sending the room spinning into darkness.

Kalei could feel her face pressed against something cold and smooth. The pressure of the object against her cheek and shoulder seemed to be holding her erect.

The joints in her legs complained as they sat tucked beneath her at awkward and painful angles. She couldn't fully stretch them out because her feet were already pushed up against something solid behind her. Confused, Kalei opened her eyes and pulled her legs forward into a more comfortable position.

She found herself sitting in a glass tube. It had a cement floor with a perfect circle of glass sealing her in on all sides. She had barely enough room to move her elbows, no more.

Looking past the glass, Kalei realized she wasn't alone. Another dozen tubes lined either side of the long hallway, each with another person – another Estranged – within. They were like so many test subjects, lined up for study. Some of them slept, some of them cried, some of them shouted intermittently or banged on the glass with bloody knuckles. Kalei might have done the same, if she didn't already know it was pointless.

She knew where she was. This was solitary confinement. Built several levels below the basement of headquarters, this was where SWORDE put Estranged who were too dangerous to wander the district on their own. She had been given a tour during training. At the time, she had wanted to kill every one of them for being murdering bastards. Now she wondered how many of them were like her: people who had simply pissed off Terin.

But was she really in here because she had pissed him off? It was more likely he had discovered her connection to Tusic. *Dammit!* She had grown pretty lax about where and when she met Lecia. It didn't surprise her that they had found out. Kalei had never exactly been trained for espionage.

She reached her hand out and traced the curving line where the cement and glass came together to form her cell. She knew the cement wasn't holding the tube up. Apparently, the ground beneath was hollow, allowing the glass to slide up and down using some mechanism below. But all Kalei could see was a small black gap between the two surfaces, no larger than the width of a wedding ring. She pulled her hand back.

Kalei knew she couldn't break out. Erit had offered her the chance to execute these dangerous inmates if only she could crack the glass. Even with a pistol at close range, she couldn't make a scratch. In fact, she nearly killed herself when she tried.

She leaned her head back against the tube and looked up at the featureless, cement ceiling. The only things to interrupt its monotonous grey expanse were the bright lights recessed into the cement at regular intervals, drawing a straight path along the center of the hall. Kalei's eyes traced the path of the lights to their beginning, and then her eyes slid down to settle on the heavy steel door that marked the entrance to the prison.

What is happening out there? Is Fenn really all right as Terin said, or is Xamic on his way to kill him now? Perhaps he was already dead.

Kalei punched the glass. *No!* She refused to believe that. She refused to accept that he was. Even if—No. Fenn and the girls were alive. She remembered Xamic's darkness within her, the way it resonated with his innermost thoughts while he held her hostage. When he spoke, she could sense the emotions – the truth behind his words. Xamic knew Fenn was alive, and he knew where to find her husband. But his intentions didn't feel like death. They felt like... excitement? Elation? That couldn't be right. Perhaps she had just imagined it.

But where is Fenn? And the girls? Kalei furrowed

her brows. *What about their father?* Kalei shifted
her weight in an attempt to find a more comfortable
position. *Come to think of it, what did they tell Qain
when he came back from his trip to Takaio? Had they
kept him from seeing his daughters, or did they take
him into protective custody as well?* Kalei couldn't see
that going well. Qain was a high-profile employee for
a high-profile company. There was no way he would
allow them to take him off the map.

But then again, being a high-profile employee for a
high-profile – international – company meant it would
be easy for Qain to pick up and move. Were they even
in Celan anymore?

Kalei tried to imagine Fenn lying on some beach
somewhere without her. It was hard, not only to
imagine him alone, but to imagine him leaving without
her. She knew Fenn; he wouldn't have left without a
fight. They must have told him that she was dead, *or
what if Xamic really had told him that I'm...*

But what did she know? She wasn't there when they
enrolled him into Victim's Protection. What if he just
skipped into the office, happy to be free of his nagging
wife?

Kalei shook her head. *Stop it. You know that wasn't
the case. He loves me, and I love him. He wouldn't do
that.*

*But that was then. What about now? It has been two
years since the attack...*

Kalei remembered the night before her first day at

the police station. A hundred thoughts had run through her mind, each more bizarre and paranoid than the last. What if she spilled coffee on the police chief? What if her partner was a smelly old man? But there was one thought that was more plausible and scary than the rest. What if she died on the job?

It didn't happen all the time, but it happened. Kalei started to think about what the world would be like if one day she just... wasn't here.

A sudden fear had grown inside her and she woke up Fenn. She told him that if she ever passed away, be it that day or a hundred years off, she wanted him to remarry. She didn't want him to spend the rest of his life miserable over the woman he had lost. She wanted him to find love again, to be happy, to live his life. She wouldn't let him rest until he promised.

Fenn had run his hand through her hair, looked her in the eyes, and told her he would never love another woman the way he loved her. She was the only one in the world for him. But if this was what she wanted, then he promised he would find love again, even if it could never touch what they had, and he wanted her to do the same.

When they made those promises, Kalei had never imagined she would become... this. Estranged. She was dead to Fenn, but at the same time, she was still very much alive.

She knew he should forget about her; it was better for him that way. But what if he had listened to her?

What if he had found some woman to comfort him through his grief, to hold his hand, to keep his bed warm at night...?

Kalei's hands began to tremble. She began to fidget with the diamond ring on her left hand, its largest diamond sitting on the white gold band like a queen announcing her shining presence to the world, while a trio of smaller gems framed it on either side. Its beautiful design brought back memories of a candlelit dinner and a question she had been breathless to answer...

Kalei gritted her teeth against the tears streaming from her eyes and the painful tightening of her throat. The swirls on her nails began to bleed and blur. The biting pain in her heart turned into a cruel stabbing and twisting that made her stomach clench. When the sobs came, she couldn't stop them.

She sat like that for ages. It could have been a week or a year; she had no way of knowing. Time didn't make itself known in this damned dungeon.

Then she heard a few shouts and calls from her fellow inmates at the far end of the hall, followed by the steady rhythm of two boots thumping against cement. She lifted her chin off her chest and saw a Warden approaching. She watched the dark figure's advance with dead eyes.

The Warden stopped at Kalei's tube. Kalei raised an eyebrow at him as she heard a grunt, and then the

Warden pulled off his helmet. It was Wexley, the old weapon master. Well, Shenaia called him old – the man was in his late fifties, his hair not entirely turned to grey yet. Not that it ever would, considering the man was Estranged. Kalei knew him well from all the time she had spent at the range. She only belatedly remembered that he was in charge of solitary too.

As Wexley tucked his helmet under his arm, he grumbled, "Fuck protocol. This ain't exactly by the book to begin with."

Kalei smiled in spite of herself. She hadn't realized how desperate she was for information until she saw the man. "Hey, Wexley. How's it going? What's going on out there?"

Wexley studiously ignored her, walking over to the wall behind her tube where steps had been carved out of the cement. The steps created a slight, curving path that hugged the back side of her tube and climbed all the way to the open top about twenty feet above.

Kalei persisted, "Hey, Wexley. C'mon. At least tell me what you're doing. Shenaia and I took good care of your guns. Yeah, we might have burned through a lot of ammo, but we always cleaned up, helped you out around the range. C'mon, Wexley. Don't give me the silent treatment."

When he reached the top of the staircase, Wexley pulled something out of his pocket and dropped it into the tube. Kalei watched the small white package grow larger as it dropped. She held out her hands to catch it, but the object moved so fast it shot between her outstretched fingers and hit Kalei's knee with a soft thud. The package split open, splattering brown refried beans across the glass and hitting Kalei in the face. Kalei wiped the mess from her cheek and opened her eyes in time to see a burrito slide out of the white wrapping and fall limply to the ground.

Wexley returned to ground level and told Kalei, "Shenaia thought you'd want some food. Hell if I know why, but she wouldn't leave me alone 'til I gave it to you. Don't recommend eating it, though. There's no way in hell I'm cleaning out that cage when it comes back 'round." He winked at her. "Unless, of course, you got a little sugar to spare."

Kalei snatched up the remains of the burrito. "You can tell Shenaia I don't want her fucking burrito!" She attempted to throw it out of the tube, but within the confines of the glass, she couldn't pull her arm back far enough to make a decent throw. The burrito weakly flew several feet up the tube and then came falling back down, nearly hitting her again. Kalei managed to dodge this time, and it hit the floor with an unpleasant squelch.

Wexley laughed and said, "Well, have fun with that. And you're right, you girls were pretty kind to my guns. And pretty kind on the eyes too. Thank you for that." He winked again and turned to leave.

"Hey!" Kalei screamed. "What's going on out there? Is Fenn still alive? Wexley! Wait!"

Without stopping or slowing, Wexley yelled back,

"Just be glad you got that much. I'm not allowed to talk to inmates, y'know." He reached the door at the far end of the hall and disappeared through its frame.

Kalei's world shrank once more to the size of her small glass circle. Except now she had company. She would have kicked the burrito, except she didn't want the damn beans all over her shoe. Not that they didn't already cover half her pants and most of the cell. Kalei sighed and smacked her forehead against the glass. After a moment, she reached up her hands and held its surface beneath her open palms. Then she slowly pulled her fingers closed, wishing she could pull the barrier away like a curtain. But it stood, impervious to her desires.

She looked down at the lump of tortilla-wrapped beans. *This is what I have become: the butt of some slut's pranks.* This time, Kalei really did kick the burrito.

She regretted it immediately. The lump became a brown smear across the bottom of her cage. It looked like shit. Kalei tried to wipe it off her boot, fighting the urge to gag as she did so. Then she noticed something.

Within the mess of beans sat a square chunk of hardened plastic, small enough to fit comfortably in the palm of her hand. When she wiped off the beans, she found it was white underneath, with smooth, rounded buttons bubbling up on one side. It looked like some kind of remote.

What the hell is this, Shenaia? A remote to nothing?

This is sick. I'm not anybody's monkey in a cage to be laughed at! Kalei flung the device into the wall. It ricocheted off the glass, hit her leg, and then landed in the pile of beans. Kalei turned her back on it and looked out at the hall.

Her cell felt smaller now, as though the burrito mess was crowding her. She wanted to get out – she had to get out – but she couldn't. She knew that.

Across from her, a bearded man sat cross-legged in his cell with one leg pulled up at an odd angle so he could chew on his toenails. Disgusted, Kalei turned away.

She stared at the ceiling for a while, played thumb wars with herself, even attempted to clean up the burrito mess with her jacket. Once everything was scooped off to one side, more or less, she sat down again. Only now, she had to sit at odd angles since her burrito-filled jacket was claiming a fair portion of what little space was left to her.

Left with nothing better to do, she picked up the remote again. She cleaned off the worst of the beans and read the buttons: "OPEN ALL," "CLOSE ALL," "LOCK DOWN.".... As her eyes scanned down the list, it dawned on her. This wasn't a remote to nothing — this was the remote for the cages.

Kalei felt something sharp pull at her finger, so she turned it over. A long crack ran down the back, presumably from when she threw it at the glass. *That can't be good.*

She turned it back to the front. She ran her thumb along the cool, smooth buttons, glanced around the hallway, took a deep breath, and looked back at the controller.

She took a final breath to steady her resolve, moved her thumb to the "OPEN SINGLE CELL" button, and pressed it.

The glass fell away into the floor, sending a soft breeze up into Kalei's face as it descended. When the tube was low enough, Kalei jumped out of the circle and stretched her arms as far as they could go. It felt great.

As she lowered her arms, Kalei noticed her bearded neighbor stretching as well.

That's not right.

His glass tube had disappeared. She glanced down the hall and saw they weren't the only ones. Along the entire expanse of the prison, inmates were jumping, shouting, or dazed as they discovered their freedom. She immediately grabbed the remote from where she had dropped it on the ground and started mashing the "CLOSE ALL" button. The tubes didn't return. It seemed the remote had sustained more damage than just a crack.

Kalei dropped the remote in favor of punching the closest inmate. She started cracking skulls left and right in an attempt to contain the building riot.

Then the door at the far end of the hall opened up. A dozen Wardens charged in, the front row pushing back the growing mass of bodies with their riot shields as the Wardens in the back row tossed canisters of tear gas into the fray. Kalei dropped her latest victim and ran in the other direction.

After shoving and kicking her way through the swarm, Kalei arrived at a narrow door just as it opened. Two Wardens stepped out, no riot gear, just pistols at the ready. Kalei stepped wide of the first Warden's gun and slammed him hard under the ribs. Then she shoved the Warden into his companion and bolted past the both of them to run down the stairwell.

From the moment Kalei became a Recruit, she had studied the building's escape routes in preparation for the day she would betray SWORDE. If Landen Franklin hadn't taken so long to contact her with the device, she might have had her chance. But it was too late now; she wouldn't be getting a second shot at those computers.

Kalei's research told her the nearest exit was down: through the sewers if she could get to them.

She grabbed the railings and used them to catapult herself from landing to landing, skipping stairs entirely, a trick she had learned from chasing down criminals in the city.

Several flights later, the stairs ended at a service tunnel. There were no more lights ahead, only an exposed live wire dangling from a power box at the end of the hall. The wire's sporadic sparks lit the floor in fits, as random and bright as lightning. By these spurts of light, Kalei could see that the walls and ceiling were covered in pipes stacked side by side like so many logs building a cabin. Many of the pipes appeared severely rusted, and some jutted out or hung from the ceiling at odd angles.

Kalei glanced over her shoulder, listening to the clatter of the two Wardens above, then she charged into the tunnel, heedless of the danger as she ran through the dark. Unable to predict the next burst of light from the wire or the location of any obstacles in her path, Kalei was lucky she didn't snap her neck.

At the end of the hall, Kalei stepped wide of the arching wire and entered a large storage room. The brief flashes of electricity from the hallway showed her a space crowded with rusty utility shelves, each spewing its own array of tools and rotted cleaning supplies. Kalei made her way to the back corner as fast as she could, tripping and cursing the whole way in the unreliable light. Behind a collapsed desk, she found what she was looking for: an access ladder to the sewers. It looked like a short, cement mound with a manhole cover on the top.

While the sound of running boots started to echo down the hall, Kalei pulled the manhole cover off the opening, climbed onto the ladder inside, and replaced the cover above her.

The lighting was even worse inside the manhole. Suspended on the ladder in complete darkness, the brief flares from the wire were too faint to give any meaningful illumination. Instead, they only impeded

Kalei's eyes as they tried to adjust to the darkness.

Kalei paused on the ladder for a moment to catch her breath. She tried not to think about what the slimy substance beneath her hands could be. She tried not to imagine what was producing the smell of chemicals and rot. Instead, she covered her nose with her shirt, took a couple more deep breaths, and focused on finding her next handhold as she made her way down.

She was two steps down when her foot slipped. Kalei fell. She frantically attempted to grab the ladder again with her left hand, but the slick metal slid from her grip, sending her down a few more feet until she shoved her right hand between the rungs and hooked her arm around one of the bars. Kalei cried out in pain as the rung pulled sharply against the inside of her elbow, nearly pulling her arm out of its socket, but she finally stopped falling.

Kalei leaned her forehead against her arm, adrenaline pumping through her body and her darkness whirring through her head like a crazed monkey. During the descent, her shirt had slipped off her face and now she was breathing the putrid air of the sewers again. Her stomach threatened to hurl.

Before Kalei could collect her senses, a light came on. The sudden illumination blinded her and nearly caused her to lose her grip again. She blinked and cursed, and when her eyes finally adjusted to the light, she looked over her shoulder to find Shenaia standing at the bottom of the manhole with a flashlight.

Above, the sound of shouts and crashing utility shelves marked the arrival of the Wardens.

Kalei hissed, "Shut that off! They'll see it."

Instead, Shenaia shielded it with her hand, reducing the light to a dim glow. Kalei accepted the compromise and silently focused on finishing her descent.

When she reached the bottom, Kalei spun around and shoved Shenaia. "What the hell is this? What do you think you're doing here?" Kalei struggled to keep her voice at a whisper.

Shenaia replied in an equally strained whisper, "Hey! I'm tryin' ta help you, sis. Didn' Mama eva teach you, you shouldn' bite the hand dat feeds you?"

"I don't want any help from a murdering addict. You could've left me in there for all I cared, but now that I'm out, I need to find my husband, and there's no way in hell I'm letting you anywhere near him." Kalei walked past Shenaia and into the tunnel.

The tunnel itself was seemingly endless in the dim light of the flashlight. To her right, the tunnel stretched on for a few hundred feet before disappearing into the black, and to her left, it was much the same. Lining the tunnel were two narrow cement walkways on either side, and connecting the two was a long, rusting metal catwalk. Kalei crossed the bridge without heed, intent on the service door on the other side. She made it about three steps across when her foot fell through the floor, sending a chunk of rusted metal into the wash below. She heard a faint splash and the smells rising from the putrid water wafted up, stronger than ever. Kalei coughed and paused to pull her shirt tighter over her face.

Behind her, she heard Shenaia stepping onto the walkway.

"What the—? Get off!" Kalei turned and waved at Shenaia to go back, but the young woman continued to walk onto the bridge. Kalei whispered, "This thing can't hold both of us, you idiot."

Shenaia was close enough to whisper back, "Yes it can, dumbass. Just gotta watch where you walkin'." Shenaia shone the flashlight upon the catwalk, illuminating patches where the rust was lest prolific, and the metal seemingly more sound. Shenaia started to walk past Kalei, but Kalei grabbed her by the shoulder and spun the young woman around to face her.

Kalei said, "Get the fuck out of here."

Shenaia knocked Kalei's hand off her shoulder as she replied, "Dat's what I plan ta do, sis." She reached into her pocket and pulled out a set of silver, jangling keys. "See dat door over there? It's locked, and you ain't goin' through it without me."

"Really? You think I'm going to take you with me just because you managed to pick a pocket?" Kalei grabbed for the keys, but Shenaia pulled her arm back and closed her hand around them.

"Did that cell make you stupid?" There was a shout followed by the loud screech of the desk being moved up above. Kalei knew what that sound meant: the

Wardens had found the manhole. Shenaia said, "You can try ta take this from me, but you don' have time. You can try to find Fenn on your own, but you don' have time. Tusic are the only other people in dis city who might know where Fenn is, and I can take you straight to 'em."

"I can find Tusic on my own, thanks."

"You don't have time!" The words came out as a yell. Both women fell silent and looked back at the ladder. For a moment, the only sound was the sluggish flow of the putrid water below. Then they heard the harsh dragging sound of the manhole cover being pulled back. Shenaia stepped forward and grabbed Kalei by the shirt. "Listen, little sister; we can get out of here, find Tusic, and get ta Fenn within the hour. Are you gonna take my help or not?"

Kalei knocked Shenaia's hand free and glared at the young woman's heavily shadowed face. "Open the damn door."

CHAPTER TWELVE

E-Night

Out in the city, Shenaia worked her "persuasion" on a few of the Tusic grunts. Some methods violent, others not-so-violent, but in every case, she found an excuse to pull out one of her guns. The teenager was seemingly in love with her pair of silver etched pistols, and she didn't seem capable of resisting the opportunity to show them off. It had started when Shenaia put her gun to the head of a gangster, demanding information on the section manager's hideout. Then they moved on to the section manager's office where Shenaia switched tactics, leaning over his desk to show him the new modifications she had added to the slide.

Kalei was revolted by the whole show. The section manager was a stout pile of rolls sitting behind a cluttered desk, with probably no recollection of what it felt like to have a chin, and here Shenaia was, leering over the man as if she wanted to have his babies. Kalei told herself that it was all just an act on Shenaia's part, and hoped it was true.

But Kalei's mood grew darker as the section

manager told them he had no information on Xamic or Fenn. Kalei was about to step forward and throttle the man, assuming she could find his neck among all the lard, but then he smiled and told Shenaia something useful: Landen Franklin would be at his mansion hosting "E-night" tonight.

"'E-night?" Kalei asked.

The manager looked at her incredulously. "Yeah, you ain't never heard of 'E-night'? Shit, how long you been keepin' this one under a rock, Shenaia?" He wiped the sweat off his brow with a damp kerchief and explained, "Landen opens up his mansion every year on the E-day anniversary for this massive party. Invitation only. A lot of high-class Untouched come by to get turned into Estranged."

Kalei was stunned as several thoughts went racing through her mind. *Today is E-Day? Already? Shit, it figures the day I break out had to be E-day... Wait– What was that other thing he said? There's no fucking way.* "You seriously want me to believe that Landen Franklin, savior of Celan, throws parties to turn people into Estranged? That doesn't sound like him."

"Sure it does. You just don' know 'im."

Kalei scoffed and resumed her silence while Shenaia and the manager finished up. Once they were back on the street, Kalei asked, "He's joking about the E-night thing, right?"

"Nah, Landen does it every year. He acts like the damn thing is better than Christmas too."

"You're shitting me."

"Nope."

Kalei stopped and looked into Shenaia's eyes, searching for some hint of the punchline she wasn't getting. Shenaia gazed back, her eyes dead serious.

Kalei threw her arms up in resignation. "Okay, so why the hell would a bunch of rich Untouched show up to be turned into Estranged? Don't they realize there's a good chance they could die?"

Shenaia shrugged and gave a noncommittal "eh." She answered, "Rich people like risks. I dunno, I've seen just as many of 'em fall as walk, but for some reason, the dumbasses keep climbin' up to the stage thinkin' they're the exception to the rule."

"You mean you've been to these parties?"

"Of course, I—" Shenaia gave Kalei a sideways glance. "It's complicated." She started to walk down the street again.

Kalei scoffed and followed Shenaia. "Right. Whatever."

Shenaia slowed a bit, looking at the street sign, and then checking over her shoulder. "Y'know, we should probably wait 'til tomorrow."

Kalei matched her pace and tried to spot what the young woman was looking for. "Like hell. You're the one who said we don't have time."

"Yeah, that was before I knew it was E-night. Landen ain't the most... *rational* guy on E-night."

"I don't care what kind of guy he is. I just need him

to tell me where to find Fenn. Now would you stop checking street signs and take me to the damn place already?"

Shenaia stopped at the corner and hesitated.

"You said you wanted to help me. Then do it."

Glancing at Kalei, Shenaia stepped out into the street. "I ain't sure you'll call this help."

Kalei followed, aggravated by Shenaia's resistance. "Just take me to the damn mansion!"

"That's what I'm doin'!"

The sky was turning a deep shade of blue, and a couple satellites were already glowing on the horizon when they arrived at the base of Chodai Mountain, where the wealthy built their estates. The night was warm, but a cool breeze made the temperature just perfect. Shenaia and Kalei began their ascent to where Landen had built his abode.

On either side of the road, wide-open fields butted against thick stands of pine as the terrain sloped upward toward the imminent peak. Only one mansion was visible about a quarter mile back, its sprawling, four-storied expanse tucked within a lavish green garden and lit by strategically placed floodlights.

The mansion's property was circumvented by a seven-foot-tall, wrought-iron fence, which yielded to stone where it met with the boundaries of its neighboring properties. These other properties were similarly fenced, and although Kalei could not see the homes, presumably because they were tucked within the trees or behind hills, Kalei could count at least six other unique properties as they ascended.

Kalei looked from one imposing fence to the next, some ornately built with rocks from the mountain, others built as solid walls of granite, and she remembered what the manager had said about the rich wanting to turn Estranged. With that in mind, she couldn't help but wonder how many of these estates were miniature versions of Downtown: places where Estranged happily enjoyed their highs behind a secure boundary.

Kalei furrowed her brow and looked at Shenaia. "Wait, the manager said this party was invitation only. How will we get in?"

Shenaia kept her eyes straight ahead as she walked up the winding road. "Don' worry. They'll let us in."

"What's that supposed to mean?"

Shenaia looked over her shoulder at Kalei, anger driving the words from her lungs. "Jus' what I said: don' worry." She turned her attention back to their path.

Kalei let it go. She was too tired to keep bickering.

The night was quiet. Their footsteps echoed across the pavement as an airplane hummed through the darkening sky above. Crickets were beginning to sing their song, and off to the west, a couple frogs added their voices to the melody. It wasn't until about fifteen minutes later that Kalei could pick out the sound of a muffled beat up ahead. As they drew closer, she could pick out more of the notes in what seemed to be a very upbeat, cutting edge song. Whatever they were doing up there, they definitely weren't sleeping.

They crested a hill and the gate to Landen's estate came into view: wrought iron like most of the rest they passed, but twice the size at nearly twenty feet, and elaborately wrought to draw out the three-star emblem of the Tusic Company.

As Kalei and Shenaia walked up to the grand barricade, two women stepped out through a smaller side gate to greet them. The women wore tactical combat suits, black from neck to toe, complete with black polyester gloves. Despite the seemingly practical nature of the outfits, the clothes were fit to each woman's body in a way that accentuated every curve. Kalei didn't doubt that these women could fight off intruders, but she suspected their function was more heavily weighted toward impressing guests. One woman was a brunette and the other a blonde. Although their hair was tied back into ponytails, the tails were long enough to fall around their shoulders in a soft cascade of curls.

The blonde bouncer called out to Kalei and Shenaia as they approached, "Good evening, ladies."

In an equally elegant tone, Shenaia replied, "Good evening."

Kalei caught her jaw as it dropped.

The brunette woman asked, "Shenaia? Is that you?"

"One in the same."

Kalei was silent, her eyes bulging as she watched the exchange.

The brunette playfully demanded, "Where have you been? Last I heard, you had joined SWORDE."

Shenaia smiled sweetly. "You heard right."

"So it's true!" the blonde chimed.

"Yes." Shenaia stopped in front of the women and said, "Melody, Samantha, I would like you to meet Kalei."

The blonde – Samantha – her eyes lit up as she looked at Kalei. "You mean your sister? Oh! It is such a pleasure to finally meet you, Kalei! Shenaia has told us so much about you!"

Kalei managed a smile as the woman came up and shook her hand.

They started to ask questions, but Shenaia politely cut them off. "Excuse me, ladies, but we really do need to get going. It sounds like the party has already started without us."

"Of course!" Melody opened the side gate for them. "Go right ahead. Make sure to come back and see us again, Shenaia. We missed you."

Shenaia smiled again. "I missed you too. G'night!"

Melody smiled back. "Goodnight."

Kalei followed Shenaia into the yard, trying to regain her bearings. Her head felt like it was spinning on a carousel after watching that bizarre exchange, but what she found on the other side of the fence made the carousel spin even faster. They weren't standing in a yard. They were standing on a bridge, and for as far as she could see, there was not an ounce of dirt, just a seemingly endless crystal blue pool that was beautifully illuminated by the lights built under the bridges.

The bridges themselves were not arched or sloping; if anything, they were more like docks: white, pristine docks that wound through the yard like paths in a garden. Parallel to Kalei's path, the road continued from the gate to the house, heedless of the change in terrain. The paths and the pool weren't the most striking thing either. In the center of it all stood a three-storied mansion, one central square with the facing wall constructed entirely of glass, and two slightly smaller squares to the left and right, built of the same white stone as the walkways. And from the roof, along the entire length of the building, water fell in a single, shimmering sheet, turning the entire structure into a beautiful waterfall.

And through that sheet, and through the glass of the central building, Kalei could see that all three floors were packed with guests, and even the roof had another hundred or so guests dancing upon it, along with a live DJ, suggesting that more paths and patios spanned a pool up there.

Shenaia broke Kalei's reverie as she said, "Ugh, gag me."

Kalei blinked at the woman, unable to articulate an answer. She must have been staring, because Shenaia asked, "What?"

Kalei pointed at the pool, at the waterfall, at Shenaia, then finally managed to say "They-you- where the hell did you learn to talk like that?"

Shenaia reached back and absentmindedly scratched her head. It was comforting to see Shenaia return to her usual street-punk persona. She sighed. "That's how normal people talk, right?" She shrugged. "I can be normal."

Shenaia stepped onto the nearest bridge, but Kalei didn't budge.

Shenaia looked over at her. "Okay, the Shenaia you're used to is something I picked up from my friends in high school. I wasn't raised to talk like a G-zone kid any more than you were."

"G-? But they called me your—"

Shenaia cut her off. A group of guests from another path had spotted Shenaia and were making their way over, shouting greetings and pleasantries while they closed the distance.

Kalei didn't say a word as the three women and the two men, all dressed for a formal occasion despite the informal music, chatted and cooed over Shenaia and Kalei as they walked together to the mansion.

Kalei felt severely underdressed for the occasion. More than that, she felt like this was all a dream. She wanted to splash some of that pool water on her face to find out if this was really real, but they were already at the waterfall. A short overhang above the doors diverted the water to either side, creating a rift in the sheet for them to walk through. As they passed beneath the overhang, Kalei held her hand out to the waterfall and felt the cool, clear liquid run through her fingers.

Not a dream, then, but still no easier to believe.

A man in a black tuxedo met them at the door. "Kalei, Shenaia, it's good to see you. Landen Franklin will be with you ladies in just a moment. Here are your gloves." He handed them each a pair of black silk gloves. "We ask that you please wear them for the night, at least until after the main event." Kalei followed Shenaia's lead and put them on. "While you wait, you are welcome to a drink at the bar, hors d'oeuvres are being served by our lovely ladies, and if you have... other tastes, just say the word and I shall be happy escort you to another room where such is being offered."

Shenaia waved him off. "No thank you." The two excused themselves from the man and their new friends, then walked into the party.

This first floor had more than a dozen low, soft black couches – not that anyone was using them. Sure, there was a man in the company of four lovely ladies making use of the couch on the far wall, but, for the most part, the guests stood. The music was mildly more subdued than it was outside, although four large speakers scattered throughout the large room relayed the music from upstairs. Kalei couldn't tell if this room was supposed to be a living room or a foyer, but either way, it seemed to be made for partying. The front and back walls were made of glass, while the clean, white sidewalls were broken by a single door each. On the right, caterers came and went. To the left, guests slipped in and out, giggling and furtive. The rest of the guests gathered in a dozen tight clusters, chatting, laughing, and sipping their drinks of choice. Judging by the drinks Kalei could see, they seemed to have decadent tastes; three women in a cluster to her left held tall glasses filled with red wine, while their male companions drank from heavy whiskey glasses filled with an amber liquor.

This definitely isn't a beat-cop barbecue, Kalei thought to herself.

Kalei noticed that only about half the guests wore black gloves like her own, while other guests left their hands remarkably bare: no watches or rings, or even nail polish. The pattern was so absolute, with every guest falling into one category or another, that Kalei had to wonder at the significance of it.

Shenaia and Kalei stood at the edge of the crowd, looking for any sign of Franklin. That was when Kalei heard a voice she recognized amid the pounding notes of the music. Obeying her ears, she stepped around a flirting couple, and saw him standing with his back to her as he chatted with a couple of women. *No way, it can't be...*

Kalei walked up to the man and tapped him on the shoulder and he turned around, flashing a smile when he saw her face. Kalei almost didn't recognize him with the grin; she had never seen one on the man's face. But she recognized the strong jaw and the stern eyes.

"Qain, what are you doing here?" She glanced at his two companions, twin brunettes who eyed her suspiciously over their wine glasses. "Where are Kas and Teia?"

The woman on the left asked silkily, "Qain, who is your *Estranged* friend?"

She reached out a hand to Kalei as Qain replied, "Deviah, Denae, this is my sister-in-law, Kalei." Kalei was reluctant to shake hands, but she decided it would be harmless while she was wearing the gloves. Besides, these women looked like they would take any excuse to skin her alive, so she obliged to the courtesy. "Kalei, these two lovely ladies are the CEOs of Nexware."

Shenaia stepped up to stand at Kalei's shoulder as the women exchanged, "Nice to meet you."

Attempting to find the manners appropriate to the venue, Kalei said, "And this is Shenaia, my- associate."

The two women laughed, their voices high and airy. Deviah said, "Associate, that's a good one."

Denae asked Shenaia, "You're still using that name? I thought you would have outgrown it by now. Just because you cannot age doesn't mean you cannot mature." The woman laughed, playing off the insult as a joke.

Kalei whispered to Shenaia, "How do they know we're Estranged?"

Shenaia whispered back, "What do you think the

gloves are for?"

"Oh." Kalei looked at the twins with fresh eyes. No gloves. It seemed they were Untouched.

Shenaia replied to Denae, "It's boring to stick with the things we're born with. I see you agree with me. You picked up a new pair of breasts since the last time I saw you."

While the women bantered maliciously, Kalei glanced at Qain's hands, expecting to find them as bare as the ladies'. But they weren't.

"Qain, what the hell!" Everyone stopped to stare at her, but Kalei didn't notice. She only saw the black gloves on his hands. "When did you turn Estranged?"

Qain raised his eyebrows in surprise, then brought them together again as he mused, "Uh, I would say... sheesh, I can't remember exactly. It's been years..."

"Years? It can't be years. Just last year you were bringing Kas and Teia over for us to babysit—"

Qain laughed out loud. "I knew it was a mistake when Landen sent you into SWORDE as his..." Qain glanced at the two women, and then smiled at Kalei, "...close friend. You still don't know about the girls? Those aren't my kids. Landen had me put up the ruse so I could keep an eye on you."

Kalei grabbed him by his shirt. "What the hell are you talking about?"

Qain took off his black glove, reached his hand up, and grabbed her arm. His fingernails held no patterns or smileys. They were full black. She shoved him off before his darkness could find her. "So Teia and Kas aren't your kids? Then whose are they!"

The crowd shifted and Kalei heard Landen's voice behind her. "That's a good question. The truth is, we don't know who their parents are. They're simply a pair of orphans we rescued from the orphanage."

Kalei spun around and to look at him. Landen Franklin was a bit shorter than he looked in his pictures, but he was still a couple inches taller than she was. And he hadn't aged a day since she last chatted with him a few months ago. Although today, he wore a trim black suit – not quite black-tie, but very sharp. He continued, "It was very difficult keeping my men away from those two. But you know how that goes, don't you, Shenaia?" He grinned at her, but Shenaia met his attention with a level stare.

Kalei interrupted the exchange. "So what? It was all a joke? Some kind of sick game?"

Landen set his glass down on a nearby waitress's platter. "I wouldn't call it a game. It was more of a means to keep in contact. Family visits are much more personal than a security camera on the wall, not to say that we didn't take advantage of both opportunities. Speaking of family, I'm betting you are here to find out where your husband is, right? Don't worry, he hasn't left the city. I made sure of that. I believe they kept the kids penned up with him too. As for their exact location, well, I'm afraid I can't share that information with you. But..." He waved the subject off with a sweep of his hand. "This isn't the place to be talking about family disputes. This is a party! I think it's time to kick things off. How 'bout you?" He smiled at her, his face radiating energy and excitement.

Kalei pressed her hand against her forehead in an attempt to drive back a growing headache. "No." Her head was spinning. Why the hell was he keeping tabs on her? And what did he mean when he said that he'd made sure Fenn hadn't left the city? But what pissed Kalei off the most... "Why the hell would you take two innocent girls and put them in harm's way! Raising them around a bunch of Estranged?" Kalei spun around and walked up to Qain, her face just inches from his. "And you. How could you lie to your brother! What happened to the venturing entrepreneur Fenn was always looking up to? The big brother who was always doing everything bigger and better because he was just so awesome like that. Where the hell is he? 'Cuz he sure as hell ain't you!"

Qain laughed and leaned back. "Oh, I'm still at the top of the food chain, sis. I'm on the Board of Directors for the number one tech company in the world. I've got ladies, I've got drinks, and – even better than all the rest – I've got top access to the best stuff in the whole damn city." He wiggled his black fingers in front of her nose as he grinned maliciously.

Kalei pulled her gun. Behind her, a couple of voices cried out and the crowd pulled back as sudden as a quickly drawn breath. Then everyone froze.

Kalei glanced over her shoulder. Shenaia had her gun drawn too, aimed straight at Landen Franklin's head. Franklin and a half dozen of his guards scattered throughout the crowd had their own guns and returned the favor. For the most part, everyone bore standard issue pistols, but Landen's revolver was twice the size, silver, and polished to a reflective sheen. There was no branding it, the gun was clearly custom made. The overall design was as sleek as any sports car's, with the cylinder shaved down until just enough metal remained to hold the bullets, and a deep red ink was painted into every streamlined etching along the barrel.

Kalei lifted one hand up in surrender and, with the other, she slowly placed her gun on the floor, turning to face Landen as she did so. She glanced at Shenaia, who still held her gun at the ready. Kalei forced a polite smile onto her face, stood up straight, and said, "Come on. I'm sure your guests don't want to start off the night with bloodshed."

Franklin looked off to the side, knitting his eyebrows together quizzically, then he looked back to Kalei and replied, "You know, I have to disagree. I think they do." He pulled the trigger.

Kalei heard the sound of a voice blaring over a speaker. The thick distortion the microphone added to his voice reminded her of the time she went to see a comedian with Fenn. The man had pranced back and forth across the stage, sending the entire audience into fits of laughter with his quips.

But this voice wasn't telling jokes. He sounded serious, impassioned, excited. She tried to focus her attention to hear what he was saying, "...proven ourselves to be the best this city has to offer. Every single person in this room has the power to make a difference in this city. And we already have. Take a look around, between the tech and port industries, Celan has the biggest economy of any other city in Dendara. Why? Because we made it that way."

Kalei's head was groggy. She couldn't fully wrap her thoughts around what he was saying. She couldn't even make sense of where she was. She felt like she was... floating. Her arms and legs hung limp before her, but they came in contact with nothing. Around her, she felt... nothing. The only thing she felt was a tight pressure across her chest and hips.

In the background, somewhere out in the nothingness, the voice continued. She recognized belatedly that it was Landen Franklin's voice. "... isn't the only valuable resource in this city. We are a valuable resource to this city. So why should we let our resources go to waste? Why should we lose our minds and our bodies to the ravages of old age? Why should we let everything we are, and everything we've built fade away just because time has decided we're done?"

Kalei forced her eyes open, tired of being left in the dark. She saw another pair of eyes about forty feet below, peering back at her. She blinked and realized she was looking at a lion. Abruptly, she yelled and tried to pull back, but there was nothing to grab, nothing to push off. Instead, her sudden movement sent her spinning as she realized she was dangling by a harness, with the cord attached firmly to the center of her back. And beneath the harness, she was appalled to find that someone had dressed her in tight blue, polyester shorts with a black halter bikini top. The harness fit awkwardly around and under her breasts, acting more as a push-up bra than an actual restraint. Around her, the world slowly slid by and she saw curtains, a dark recess with lights and scaffolding, and then – an audience. About fifty to a hundred people looking up at her. She glanced down again and realized she was dangling above a stage, with the lion penned in a small glass enclosure below her.

Kalei knew she had to find a way out. Her hands scrambled to find the clasps of the harness. She knew she could survive the fall, even if it was a forty-foot drop. *I mean, I'm Estranged. I survived a gunshot to the head. A little fall should be nothing.* Her racing heart didn't seem to agree.

But as her hands closed on a clasp, she noticed the lion shift with anticipation below, and she realized that it wasn't the fall she would have to worry about.

At the head of the stage, Landen Franklin turned around, a small microphone pinned to his shirt. He saw her and smiled as he said, "Ah, our first guest is awake. See? This is what I'm talking about. Not even a bullet could quench the fire in this young woman." The crowd roared and cheered in response.

Kalei tried in vain to stop herself from spinning, but the world continued to turn, and as the clapping died, Kalei found herself facing the left half of the stage. Lying on the floor, dressed in halter-top and shorts to match Kalei's, complete with a harness strapped around her chest and a cable stretched out slack behind her, was Shenaia.

"Shenaia!" Kalei didn't know why she called out. Perhaps it was just to make sure the young woman was alive. Seeing her lying limp like that awoke fierce emotions of fear and concern in Kalei that she didn't know she could feel toward the teen. "Hey! Shenaia!" Kalei couldn't see if her efforts were working. She was already spinning away.

But she heard Landen say, "Ah, I see your sister is stirring as well."

Kalei yelled at the curtains, "Why the hell are you guys always calling her my sister!"

Landen and a few members of the audience laughed. "Kalei, you can't be serious." As Kalei turned again to face the crowd, Landen walked over to the front of the lion's cage to look up at her. The lion stood up, eying the man hungrily. Landen looked into her face, and Kalei glared back at him, hungrier than the lion. After a brief pause, Landen laughed again. "You really don't know. Kalei, that's your sister Jenna over there."

Kalei didn't have a response. Even as he finished

saying it, her spinning harness turned her to look at Shenaia. She was starting to sit up now. Her short hair was mussed, the heavy makeup was smeared... at this distance, it was hard to see much more detail than that. But now that he said it... it had been almost twenty years since Kalei had seen her sister, even if she was alive... but now that he mentioned it, there was no mistaking the way she held herself, the set of her jaw as she clenched her teeth, and if there was still any doubt—

Shenaia abruptly leaped after Landen. "Franklin, you son of a bitch!" The harness stopped her attack, but the way she fought and pulled against it brought a memory to the forefront of Kalei's mind. A bully had pulled Jenna by her backpack, and she had fought against the restraining straps with the exact same stance, the exact same swipes of her hand as Shenaia did now. The bully had gone to the hospital and Jenna was suspended for a week. This really was the nineteen-year-old version of her sister Jenna. How could she not see it...? Then again, she had never expected to find that her older sister was younger than her. Yet before Kalei could fully grasp the idea, the harness spun Kalei away from her sister, and she found herself facing the curtain again. Kalei wasn't sure if it was the spinning or the roiling emotions that made her nauseous.

Landen addressed the audience. "Ladies and gentlemen, I give you our honored co-hosts for this evening: Kalei Distrad and Jenna Kendrick." The

crowd cheered and clapped amiably. Landen walked
back across the stage and presented the lion with
an outstretched arm. "And let us not forget our dear
friend, the honorable and ferocious Max!" Again, the
crowd cheered and clapped. The renewed energy in the
audience had sparked Max's interest, and he began to
pace the front of his cage, licking his jowls as he beheld
the noisy morsels.

"And now, let's get on with the main event. Jared,
will you come up here, please?" Kalei's spin was
already turning her away from the theatre, but out of the
corner of her eye, she saw a man in the third row stand
up.

Kalei was facing Jenna now, and the young woman
was quickly working at the straps on her harness while
everyone's attention was on Jared. She managed to get
one leg loose when Landen Franklin said, "Jenna, don't
be a spoilsport. Here, before you take that off, let me
show you what it's for. Ted, can you take off the safety
for me?"

Kalei turned her head to try to see what Ted was
doing in the shadows behind Jenna, but her endless
rotation carried her too far around to see. She was
getting tired of this game. She tried to reach up and
grab the cable that held her, which was fairly more
difficult than she had imagined, but right as her hand
closed around it, she heard a click and dropped. She
had probably fallen no more than a few inches when
the harness pulled her to a stop again, but those three

inches were enough to scare her shitless. She didn't want to mess with the cable anymore. She felt the full terror of every foot of empty space between her and the stage. Adrenaline pounded in her veins and she closed her eyes to try to block out the height, but the darkness only added to the sensation of spinning and made her stomach heave. She opened her eyes again and saw that she was now turning back to the center of the stage where Landen stood facing the audience with Jared on his right and Jenna on his left.

Franklin said, "Okay, so we've got the safety off. Now, Jenna, you see your sister up there? Wave hi for me." Jenna didn't wave. Neither did Kalei. He continued, "Ah, a couple of spoilsports. Anyway, keep an eye on your sister and take a step forward." Kalei couldn't see them anymore, but the cable hoisted her a foot higher. "Now take a step back." The cable lowered Kalei back to where she started. Landen said, "You see how this works? Every time you take a step back, your sister drops closer to Max. He's a bit desperate for company, so I don't recommend letting her get too close to him. You're still welcome to take off that harness if you want, but I'm not sure Kalei will appreciate you for it." He laughed, and the crowd laughed with him.

Kalei heard Jenna mutter, "I'll keep it on, thanks."

Landen said, "Sorry, we didn't hear you." Kalei spun back around in time to see him walk to the front of the stage and accept a microphone from a stagehand. He walked back to his place and held the microphone out to Jenna. "Can you repeat that?"

Jenna squared her shoulders, pulled a smirk onto her face, and joked amiably, "You talked me into it. I hadn't realized how sexy this harness is. Maybe if you're lucky, I'll let you try it on sometime." The audience laughed, but Landen just smiled stiffly.

"Anyway, none of you came to see two sisters play with a lion, although we could call that icing on the cake. Tonight is E-night!" The audience approved enthusiastically. Landen continued, "So, on my right, we have our dear friend Jared. This man is terminally ill. His body has already begun to decay, his strength is fleeing him, and every day from here on out, he is doomed to watch as he wastes away into nothing. Unless Jenna here can cure our man."

The audience cheered again as Landen offered Jenna the microphone. *Jenna...* Kalei thought. *This is so weird, Shenaia is so... but Shenaia is Jenna, and Jenna is Shenaia.* Kalei's head was spinning faster than the harness. She turned her attention back to the issue at hand: escape. She searched for something, anything she might be able to grab on to, but the curtains that sailed by were more than ten feet out of her reach, and she doubted she had enough cord to inconspicuously swing over there.

She heard Jenna ask, "What kind of disease do you have, Jared?"

Jared responded confidently, "I'm Untouched."

Jenna laughed. "You have issues if you think being

Untouched is a disease."

Landen saved Jared the trouble of responding, "Of course it is. Name one Untouched man who doesn't have to fear dying in a car crash, or can withstand the ravages of cancer, or can say with confidence that thirty years from now, he will be every bit the man he is today?" Kalei came back around in time to see Landen step up and address the audience. "You know that saying, 'If it's not broken, don't fix it'?" He paused while several people in the audience nodded. "You know what I say? We are broken, but we can fix it!"

The audience roared in approval.

Landen walked back to his guest and co-host. "Jared, step up and shake Jenna's hand to find out what it means to be immortal."

Jared stepped forward, his eyes locked with Jenna's. She hesitated and started to step back. Kalei dropped an inch.

Landen said, "And don't forget, if you deny Jared, then you'll reward Max."

Kalei cursed as she lost sight of Jenna and Jared, then yelled, "Shut the fuck up, Landen!" The audience laughed. Kalei continued, "Drop me in the cage, Jenna." The name felt odd on her tongue. "We both know it doesn't have as much bite as you." The audience laughed again.

But as the laughter died, one voice continued to ring out in a deep, undulating laugh that steadily rose in pitch until its owner seemed to be crying. The theatre went quiet and as Kalei came back around, she saw Xamic sitting in the center aisle, wiping tears from his eyes.

Landen said, "It wasn't that funny, Xamic." The people laughed quietly.

Xamic pulled himself back to his feet and said, loud enough for everyone to hear, "What? The thing Kalei said about the lion?" He gave a short snicker. "That's not what I was laughing at."

Landen watched Xamic warily but maintained his composure. He smiled amiably and said, "What's so funny?"

"What's so funny?" Xamic replied. Kalei couldn't see them anymore, but she heard Xamic jump onto the stage. "What's funny is that you can dangle a girl above a lion, make some comments about the glory of being Estranged, and still call this entertainment. This entire setup is a joke! There's no edge, no excitement. Little Maxxie over there is a poor substitute for real suspense."

Kalei glanced down at Max and found him lying in one corner of his enclosure, closest to the crowd. It seemed he had lost interest in her. She watched him for a moment longer before a sudden wave of vertigo forced her to look away.

Landen asked, "Okay, then what would you do?"

Out of the corner of her eye, Kalei saw Xamic wander over to Max as he said, "First," he pulled several pins out of the joints holding the lion's cage together, "I would unlock Max's door and see how long it takes him to figure out he's free."

A security guard ran up to tackle Xamic, but the blonde man stopped him with a hand to the guard's throat. Kalei couldn't see Xamic's eyes, but the guard's eyes were suddenly bulging. Somewhere in the theatre, someone screamed. More guards appeared, guns drawn.

Kalei wondered if the distraction would buy Jenna enough time to get them out of this mess. Kalei hated to admit it, but Jenna was her only ticket out now. There was nothing she could do from her dangling perch. She tried to grab Jenna's attention, but the young woman's eyes were still locked on Xamic.

Xamic tsked at the guards and dropped the first guard's body. Landen signaled his people to lower their weapons.

Landen said, "Xamic, what are you—"

"Then!" Xamic shouted the word to be heard over Landen's microphone-aided voice. "I would place explosives beneath five of the seats and set them to detonate at random times between, oh, 12:30, 12:45, somewhere thereabouts. But— well, I've already done that."

A hush fell over the theater. No one, except Kalei on her spinning wire, moved. Someone screamed as a small bomb went off in the balcony. The explosion was just large enough to destroy three seats and mangle the people sitting in them.

Xamic shouted, "Here we go!" While panic broke

out in the theatre, he jumped over to Landen and snatched the microphone away. "And then, just when I have you all at the edge of your seats, I would remind you not to leave them just yet. Because, ladies and gentlemen—STOP!"

The theatre went silent again. "People, please, need I remind you, there is a lion in our midst? And look, you've disturbed his nap." Indeed, the lion was up and pacing again, unaware as of yet that he could be free with just a bump against the transparent wall. Everyone watched the lion warily, scared to move a muscle lest they draw his attention.

To a subdued audience, Xamic said, "Just a moment." They waited. One heartbeat. Two. Then several red lights revealed themselves in the ceiling and started flashing, adding a red, pulsing light to the room. A resounding *thunk* echoed from all the entrances. Xamic smiled and said, "Then I would activate the security lock-down protocol so that none of you can escape while I chase you down and rip the delicious darkness from your corrupted hearts." The audience had been still before, but now it was as though everyone had been turned to stone, with eyes that contorted with rage and terror. Xamic threw his arms up and yelled, "Welcome to E-night, bitches!"

Kalei couldn't see the stage anymore, but she heard a gunshot, immediately followed by something that sounded like a piece of wood snapping. She heard Xamic laugh while members of the audience gasped or cried out.

She came back around in time to see a guard in the third row shoot again, three times. Head-heart-groin. Xamic's body shook with the impacts, pieces of his flesh bursting out behind him, but he didn't fall. When the guard was done, Xamic shook his head, splattering blood and gore onto the stage, the hosts behind him, and the side of the lion's enclosure. He said, "God, that itches," unzipped his jacket, and reached up under his red shirt to scratch beneath the hole in his clothes.

Another bomb went off in the front row, scattering debris and catching the curtains of fire. The lion threw himself after the fresh blood on his cage and won himself free of his captivity. Landen tackled Xamic, and people screamed and ran for entrances.

Kalei didn't see what happened next because her attention was focused on the ground that was now rapidly approaching. The cord at her back still held her securely, but she was dropping at a pace far faster than she was comfortable with. All the while, her harness kept spinning, and when her spin brought her back around, she looked up to see Jenna running towards the stage entrance where her wire came from.

Kalei wanted to be excited, she wanted to believe that Jenna had found their ticket out and was working on a plan. But as she watched her sister run into the shadows backstage, Kalei could only see Shenaia running away to save her own hide. It didn't matter that everyone called them sisters, she couldn't deny that the young woman over there was her sibling, but she still couldn't see the Shenaia she knew stepping up to be the Jenna she remembered.

About ten feet above the stage, Kalei's descent stopped.

The Jenna from her childhood wouldn't leave her there; she would come back and make sure Kalei got out of the harness. Kalei waited for her spin to bring her back around. Shenaia, on the other hand, would give no fucks. Kalei looked for the backstage entrance where her sibling had disappeared, but the smoke from the curtain was already filling the theatre. The heavy haze caught and amplified the strobes of light from the security beacons, nearly blinding her in the process.

She shielded her eyes, but she couldn't make out any sign of Shenaia or anyone. And she felt not so much as a twitch from the wire. The entire world around her melted away as the flashing red cloud consumed it all, leaving her abandoned, spinning aimlessly in her own personal corner of hell. Within the smoke, she heard the lion snarl and several choked screams as people died. She wasn't sure if the victims belonged to Max or Xamic.

Taking matters into her own hands, Kalei reached down and started undoing the harness around her legs. When her legs came free, her weight shifted painfully to her chest, and she quickly moved her hands to the straps across her upper body. Her fingers had just found the first metal clasp when the wire above her went slack and Kalei dropped to the ground.

Hitting the stage felt like taking a hammer to every inch of her body at once. The hammer hit her knee and both elbows with particular violence as she threw her arms out before her, then it took a lighter, albeit no less solid smack to her temple.

She lost all sense of focus. Everything grew darker, and as she lay there fighting to remain conscience, like a drowning victim trying to stay afloat, she noticed a bit of black tape stuck to the floor in front of her. It seemed to dance and flash as it reflected the red waves of light, pulsing urgently again and again as though it were trying to remind her of something very important.

Sounds came to her ears quietly, as though they had to pass through a wall of cotton to reach her. Somewhere in the distance, she heard someone shouting her name. Then someone roughly lifted her from the ground into a fireman's carry. Distantly, as though it were happening to another person, she felt the exposed skin on her stomach press into the skin of her rescuer's shoulders, and the darkness leapt forward to pull and tease at the darkness of the other person. She thought she could feel a high coming on, but she couldn't be sure. She felt like the world around her was just a dream, and the only shred of reality that remained to her was that scrap of tape. Except her piece of tape had been replaced with tightly stretched blue polyester. It took her a moment to wrap her head around the change in scenery...

Jenna.

CHAPTER THIRTEEN

Memory Lane

Kalei began to slip in and out of consciousness. She remembered the smoke receding, but the flashing red lights persisted. She remembered awakening to the sounds of screaming and crashes, but her grip on the world slipped again before she could make sense of it.

She floated through a dark, murky haze, somewhere in her mind. There was no up, no down. Eventually, she heard a metallic screeching in the distance. It seemed to be coming closer. It became louder and louder until it seemed to fill her skull with noise, and even then, the sound continued to grow. Kalei launched herself upright, frantically searching for the source of the sound. But before her eyes could focus, she was overwhelmed with a wave of dizziness and nausea. It was all she could do to put her head between her knees.

"Whoa, easy girl." Jenna's voice sounded close, and Kalei felt her weight pushed forward, as though they were on a vehicle that was stopping. Kalei took a deep breath and the dizziness abated, but the screaming headache and nausea remained. She opened her eyes.

She was sitting on a plush leather couch, and behind her, to her left, were two matching leather armchairs. Between them was a sleek, metal coffee table. But the walls behind the chairs didn't make any sense. They were a shining, silver color, a shade that matched the coffee table, but the windows were oblong, and beyond them, she could see the passing grey walls of a tunnel. The screeching brakes, the tunnel out the window; she could have sworn she was on a subway. But she was sitting on a leather couch. Kalei began to wonder if she had taken brain damage from the fall.

Jenna sat in one of the armchairs across from Kalei. She still wore the bikini and shorts, but somewhere along the way, she had picked up a pistol and a pair of black gloves. If anything, the new additions seemed to complete her outfit.

Jenna said, "We're on Landen's personal light-rail. He built it between his mansion and the Tusic office."

That made sense. But if this was Landen's light-rail... the details started to come back to her in a flash of images and sensations. Kalei jumped off the couch.

Jenna jumped up with her, arms out to catch Kalei if she fell over, and she said, "Ho, easy, sister. You feelin' a'ight?"

Kalei looked around. "If this is—Where's Landen? What happened?"

"Don' know, don' care. We got out of there, you're safe, tha's all tha' matters. I say fuck everyone else."

The train gave a final lurch as it stopped. Kalei

pitched forward, catching herself on the arm of the couch. Jenna stepped up to help her, but Kalei waved her off. Then, with a click, the power shut down, followed by shouts outside the door.

"Shit, the assholes caught on to us. Quick, out the window. Go. Go!" Kalei ran to the window and pulled the escape release. For a recovering head trauma victim, she felt surprisingly alert. The only pain that lingered was the bite of the darkness running rampant through her body. *Oh. Yeah.* The darkness had probably finished the recovery process for her.

The shouts had turned to grunts as the guards started to pry the door open behind them. Kalei shoved the windowpane out of the frame and scrambled through, falling haphazardly onto the cement and fresh glass below. Jenna followed; a wave of bullets ripped and exploded through the air above her as she stuck the landing with a perfect tuck and roll. She was already on her feet and running as Kalei finished pulling herself upright.

Jenna fired a couple shots back at the train as she ran, shouting, "Come on! Let's go!"

Kalei ran after her sister, the guards behind them returning shouts and bullets of their own. The tunnel was completely dark ahead, and soon it was all Kalei could do to make out Jenna's outline in the fading light. Luckily, the ground was flat and even beneath her feet, or else she was sure she would have tripped.

She caught up to Jenna, and the young woman

greeted her with an increase in pace. "I can get us to the surface, but I dunno where we gonna go after that. No way in hell we can use a Tusic safe house now."

Kalei panted, "You said we're by the Tusic building, right?"

"Yeah."

"I know a place." Kalei suggested an abandoned office that wasn't more than a mile from the Tusic building. Kalei knew it because when she was a cop, she had visited the building several times to bust kids who were breaking in to vandalize the place.

Jenna led Kalei into a narrow service tunnel as she asked, "Untouched kids? What if they show up?"

The shouts of the guards were far behind them now, but the sounds of their boots echoing down the tunnel still put Kalei on edge. "They won't. They haven't gone back since one of them was turned Estranged there."

Jenna nodded and stopped to climb a ladder. Unlike the ladder in the sewers, this one was clean and dry. Kalei appreciated the minor luxury.

They emerged in an empty alley, the sky above them still dark and shining with the few stars they could see from the city. Kalei suddenly realized how conspicuous they looked in their halter-tops and short-shorts, but decided that no one would look twice at a couple of prostitutes slinking around the city at night. She helped Jenna replace the manhole cover, and the two women disappeared into the streets.

A chain-link fence surrounded the building, sagging and peeling away from its posts as though it was losing the energy and the desire to hold on to its life. Kalei and Jenna stepped over a section that had already met the ground and crossed the dirt-packed, weed-strewn yard. Off to their left sprawled an old parking lot, faded and cracked with a pile of garbage collecting at one corner where the wind had blown it. Ahead of them rose the office building, roughly ten stories of bricks, elaborate stonework, and broken glass. Although neglected, it still didn't look as desolate as the towers in Downtown. The stone moldings on each level of the high-rise sported only a few cracks, and more than half the windows were still intact. From what Kalei remembered, this building hadn't been abandoned for more than ten years.

Inside, fallen ceiling panels and chunks of plaster were strewn across the floor between scattered walls of misty construction tarp. Kalei and Jenna found a staircase and made their way up to the seventh floor before calling it quits. Kalei sagged into a wadded pile of the plastic sheeting, shaking from head to toe.

After looking out the window to make sure they weren't followed, Jenna noticed Kalei's condition and walked over to her. She knelt down and gently took one of Kalei's hands into her own gloved one. On some fingers, Kalei's swirls were twisted and contorted, and on others, they were completely gone in a wash of black. "Shit, Kalei," Jenna said softly. With an effort, she let go and sat back. "Man, I jus' wanna hug my little sis, but we is showin' so much skin I'm surprised I ain't gettin' a high just by lookin' at you. You and I are every schoolboy's wet dream right here."

Kalei gave a small laugh. "It's still hard to believe my big sister Jenna is so vulgar. And so little."

"Little, my ass! I'm still five years older than you!"

"Maybe, but you've still got the body of a puny teenage girl. I could break you like a twig."

"I'll believe that when I see it!" Jenna laughed.

Kalei gave a weak smile. Then she sighed, leaning her head back against the wall and closing her eyes. It was too much to take in. Shenaia, her sister, Landen, a maniac... the only part she found believable about the last twenty-four hours was the way Xamic had swooped in and started killing people like it was some sort of sick sport. If that was believable, then she really needed to get her head checked.

After a long pause, she heard Jenna's voice crack as she asked, "What happened?"

Kalei opened her eyes and looked at Jenna. One glove was now off, both hands sitting in her lap as she studied them. The wheels on her hand spun and veered just as haphazardly as Kalei's own thoughts. "What do you mean?"

"The night Mom and Dad died. How'd it happen?"

Kalei sighed and rubbed her forehead. She didn't want to go there, not now, not ever again. But if anyone had a right to know, it was Jenna.

"Mom was getting ready to cook dinner. It was Asian night. You were at a friend's house and I knew rice was your favorite, but I hated the stuff, so I decided that we shouldn't have Asian night. So I took Mom's rice cooker and hid with it in the closet." Kalei smiled. "I hid the rice cooker in a box, I piled shoes on top of my lap, I even put a coat over my head so no one could find me. Mom found out I was missing and it turned into a game of hide and seek. She was laughing and making a big deal about checking behind the couch, threatening to unleash the tickle monster if I didn't come out." Kalei laughed. But then, the smile faded.

"There was a knock at the door. I took the coat off my head peeked through the slats in the closet door to see Mom walk over to the front window. When she saw who was at the door, her smile disappeared and she called Dad over. Dad heard the sharp edge in her voice the same as I did and he came running into the living room saying, 'What? What is it?' Mom seemed upset, confused. She lowered her voice and said something to him. They talked quietly for a minute, but I couldn't hear what they were saying. Dad started smiling and he started to rub her arm. I think he was trying to tell her that it was okay. But then he went to look out the window, and his smile disappeared as well. Mom and Dad looked at each other, confusion and concern mirrored on both their faces. I almost came out of the closet to ask what was going on, but then the doorbell rang. I hunkered down in the shoes and watched as Dad took a deep breath and opened the door.

"And there he was, Terin, exactly as he looks today, with Xamic standing behind him. He took one look at Mom and his eyes widened. They stared at each other for a moment, Mom and Terin. Xamic was smiling like an idiot in the background, and Dad stood behind Mom protectively. Then Terin stepped forward, and before Dad could stop him, he hugged Mom. She went limp. Dad put a hand on Terin's arm to pull her away, but then he screamed. I had never heard a man scream before, and Dad's scream was terrifying. And that was it. Terin stepped back and they both fell to the floor like dolls. But Terin... something crazy, something totally happy washed across his face." Kalei's eyes fixed on the memory in the distance. She sat like that for a moment, staring into the past with her mind's eye. She could still see that ridiculous smile on Terin's face. She could still hear Dad's scream ringing in her ears... She closed her eyes and continued, "When Xamic stepped into the room, Terin seemed to wake up. He froze when he saw them lying there. Xamic said something like, 'How does it feel to be free?' I don't know if that's right, that's just how I remember it. Anyway, Terin began sobbing and pulling at Mom's body. He pulled her into his lap and started rocking back and forth, holding her head close and talking to her like she was going to wake up... I didn't know what to do. I was so scared...

"I think I started crying, because Xamic heard

something and came over to the closet. I didn't think I could get any more scared, but I became so terrified that I started to claw at the back wall of the closet, as though I could make a door appear and escape. I heard Terin scream, there was a lot of crashing, and then it went quiet. After a few minutes, I gathered enough courage to look through the slats again. Xamic and Terin were gone. All that remained were Mom and Dad's bodies on the floor in front of the open door. It felt like an eternity sitting in that closet, crying my eyes out, unable to take my eyes off their corpses. Sometimes, it feels like I never left. But I guess I did. The next thing I remember, I was in the police station and some detective was feeding me candy and fishing for answers. Not that I ate any candy, and I don't think he liked my answers." Kalei shrugged, staring at her nails, losing herself in the full wash of black that painted them. The pain from the night bled into the pain of the darkness and threatened to rip her in half. She muttered, "Now you know."

They were both silent. Jenna nodded her head quietly. After a while, Kalei started to re-draw the swirls on her nails as she asked, "What about you? They told me you were dead. We had your funeral and everything..."

Jenna pulled her glove back on, clenching her fists lightly as she said, "Nothin' so dramatic. I was at Brandy's place — you remember Brandy? Anyway, so Landen shows up in a cop uniform and says somethin' happened to you guys. He wasn' famous yet. Tusic didn' get big 'til after E-day. So Brandy's parents had no fucking clue he wasn't a cop. He showed the badge and everythin'. Anyway, so Brandy's parents let him take me to come see you. I mean, why not? They had no fucking way o' knowin'..." Jenna uncrossed her legs and pulled one knee up to her chin, resting her head on it for a minute before she went on, "But he didn' take me to you guys. He took me to his apartment in the city. He said you was all dead and he was gonna be my new dad from here on out. I believed him. Hell, I was twelve, I didn' know..." She paused again, watching the grey clouds gather outside the open window. "All those years..." She tucked her head behind her knee and started crying. "I'm so sorry, Kalei. It's my fault, it's all my fault...You should never... I'm so sorry, sis." Her crying turned to weeping.

Kalei's swirls were back in place now, but they began to flex and dance. "Whoa, whoa. What are you talking about?" Kalei slid down onto the floor in front of her sister.

Jenna sucked in a sob. "I didn' know you were alive... I hated Landen, I hated that he wouldn' let me leave the penthouse without a guard, I hated tha' he wouldn' let me be Estranged... He was fuckin' suffocatin' me. I told him, if he would jus' let me be Estranged, he wouldn' have ta worry about anyone hurtin' me. I would be immortal! Ev'ry year at E-night, he would go on about how great bein' an Estranged was. But he wouldn' let me be one. It was total bullshit! He was never a dad to me, more like a fuckin' Warden..."

Kalei kept her silence.

"So when I was nineteen, I snuck out and met with some o' his thugs. I'd been hangin' out with them for years at that point. Usually jus' at the house, but sometimes, I snuck out an' caught up with them. They were pretty cool bout helpin' me avoid Landen, but I found out later they were reportin' back to him on every fuckin' step I took... what good friends they were. When I found out, I was pissed. Even sneakin' out of tha house, I could never be free of that bastard. But if I could jus' be Estranged, if I could just get someone to give me a touch, I could leave and say a big 'fuck you' to 'em all! Of course, none of Landen's guys would do it. They was scared shitless of what Landen would do to 'em. But one guy, Garron, he wasn't scared o' nothin'. He was just loyal as fuck. And he would..." Jenna trailed off. The tears came back. She sat there, crying. Kalei clasped her hands together and held them in her lap. She stared at her black swirls and wished there was something she could do to comfort her sister.

Eventually, Jenna silenced her sobs and sat up straighter. She stared at an abandoned soda can for a moment and clenched her jaw. Finally, she said, "I touched Garron when he wasn' looking. Landen made sure I was there to watch when he killed him." Jenna looked down at her hands again and the muscles in her jaw twitched.

Kalei waited. She picked at the hem of her shorts. Then she asked, "What does this have to do with me?"

Jenna looked up at Kalei, her glare fierce as the corners of her eyes glistened. "You don' get it, do you?" She shook her head and looked up at the ceiling. "Landen was using me to keep Terin off his back. So long as I was Untouched, SWORDE wouldn' – it's my fault Landen dug up Xamic, it's my fault your family was attacked, it's my fault my little sister is a fucking Estranged!" She picked up the soda can and flung it behind Kalei.

Kalei heard it clang as it ricocheted off the beam. "Hey! Whoa, easy there." The voice was male.

CHAPTER FOURTEEN

Making Friends

A young boy, probably in his early teens, judging by his short, scrawny build and lack of facial hair, entered the doorway behind Kalei. His dark hair shot out at odd angles, as though he'd just rolled out of bed. He looked a bit like a scarecrow beneath his baggy jeans and T-shirt, but he had a square, somewhat handsome face. If Kalei looked at him from the neck up, she could believe he was an athlete. She looked down at his hands to check his nails: full black.

He said, "Sorry to interrupt. It's just—you threw the can and I—"

Jenna shouted, "How long have you been there? You been eavesdropping?"

"I've been here the whole time, but I wasn't listening, I promise I—"

Kalei ignored him and asked Jenna, "What did you mean, 'Landen dug up Xamic'?"

Jenna glanced over at her sister, but before she could say anything, the boy interrupted, "Uh, hey." He glanced over his shoulder at a pile of decimated electronics. Phones, computers, keyboards; all piled in one heap. Somewhere within the mound's depths, a red light was flashing. The boy looked back at the girls and said, "You might wanna know, there are some Wardens coming up the stairs."

Kalei asked, "You serious?" Before he could answer, Kalei turned back to Jenna. "SWORDE only uses the earring for tracking, right?" She and Jenna had torn out the ear cameras when they escaped Downtown.

"Yeah. I mean, as far as I know," Jenna replied. "But Landen—"

"Girls," the boy interrupted again. "Sorry, but I've really got to go. You can come if you want. I, uh... I'm assuming you don't want the SWORDE peeps to find you. But I know a back door we can use... uh, that is, if you want to come with me."

Kalei looked at Jenna and shrugged. She stood up and said, "Alright."

The boy fidgeted nervously, his eyes locked on Jenna's breasts as he said, "Well, it's not really a back door so much as a really good hiding place."

Jenna growled, "Jus' shuddup and lead."

The boy's eyes snapped up to her face and he said, "Right! Um, yeah, follow me." They walked a few steps past the tarp where Kalei had originally been sitting, then the boy turned around and offered Jenna his hand. "I'm Josh, by the way."

"What the hell? This ain't no time to get high, kid," Jenna spat.

Josh was abashed. "What? I mean, I know we can't touch normal people, but I thought touching other Estranged is—"

"Have you ever touched another Estranged?" Kalei asked.

"No, I..."

"Good. Keep it that way." She pointed forward and Josh obligingly turned and continued to lead.

On the other side of the desolate space, Josh entered the men's restroom. Jenna glanced at Kalei with an eyebrow reaching for the ceiling. The two women stopped outside the broken doorway.

Meanwhile, Josh headed to the second stall and yanked and pulled on the toilet until finally it moved free, revealing a hole in the floor. Josh straightened up and ran a hand through his hair. "Uhh..."

"What?" Jenna demanded.

He glanced at them and then quickly looked away. "I don't think we can fit more than one person in there."

"Are you serious? You didn' think of that before?" Jenna looked like she was about to strangle the kid.

"I—well, usually it's just me. I didn't plan on—"

"You didn' plan on havin' two girls walk in on your lovely little shithole of a home?" Jenna looked him up and down. "I can see why."

Kalei interjected, "Hey, cut it out."

Josh turned red and started studying the floor tiles. Jenna watched Kalei, crossing her arms and waiting for her to say something. Kalei glanced from Jenna to Josh.

The boy looked up at them briefly, then hastily turned away to study the stalls. Kalei turned away and said, "Come on, Jenna. We've gotta get out of here."

The girls took one step for the door before Josh blurted out, "There's another place we could hide."

Jenna turned back. "Is it another hidey-hole excuse to cuddle?"

"Jenna!"

"What?"

Josh responded, "No, there's plenty of space. I promise."

A few minutes later, standing on a six-inch ledge seventy feet above the ground, Kalei had to acknowledge that there was definitely plenty of space. Perhaps too much.

The sun was directly above them in a clear blue sky, creating a bright reflection off the apartment building across from them. Kalei couldn't decide which was more annoying, the blinding light or the steady wind. But then again, it was an improvement on listening to Jenna bitch at Josh. Kalei had positioned herself between the two for a reason.

Jenna yelled, "How the hell did he convince me to get out here?"

"Shut up! Do you want the Wardens to hear us?" Kalei called back.

"What? We're just a couple birds squawkin'! Ain't no one in there can hear us!"

Something below caught Kalei's eye. Against her

better judgment, she looked down. Far below, three
small ants in SWORDE uniform milled around the
entrance, standing close to their van in case they needed
to use it for cover. One of them looked up. "Shit! They
spotted us!"

Jenna rolled her eyes. "No they didn't! They can't
see shit from down there!"

The window to Jenna's left slid open. "Do you
believe me now?" Kalei asked.

"Shit!"

Josh was already moving. He turned around on
the ledge and reached both hands up to the next ledge
above, pulling himself up to the next floor. He called
back, "Come on!"

Jenna paled. "Aw, shit."

Kalei laughed. "Look at it this way: it's not like
you're going to fall to your death."

"I hate you both!" Jenna replied, latching onto the
building and turning herself around.

At the window, a Warden stuck his head out, saw
Jenna, and shouted, "Hey!"

Out of the corner of her eye, Kalei saw Jenna jump
and lose her grip. Kalei's immediate instinct was to
reach back and help her sister, but she had already
pulled her upper body clear of the next ledge and she
couldn't free up her arm in time to reach back for her
sister. She struggled to pull the rest of her body onto
the ledge, frantically pulling and kicking in an effort
to move faster. When she was finally clear, she looked

back and saw Jenna hugging a gargoyle and yelling at the Warden, "Fuck you!"

Kalei laughed.

Kalei shifted back from the ledge and grabbed the windowsill with her left hand, leaning forward to offer Jenna her right.

Jenna said, "I ain't no freaking pansy. Get the fuck out of here." She grabbed the ledge, stooped as low as she could without letting go, then launched herself so hard and so fast that she flew over the ledge, over Kalei, and in through the open window. She landed on her feet, much to Kalei's surprise, then turned around to smile at Kalei and Josh, casually flopping down on her back. Panting, she said, "I fucking hate heights."

Josh and Kalei climbed in after her. Kalei nudged her sister with her shoe. "Get up. We're not done yet. Josh, what's the quickest way out of here?"

"Out of here? Wait, we can't leave. All of my stuff is here. I—"

Kalei cut him off. "SWORDE knows we're in the building. They won't leave until they've turned over every toilet in this dump. We have to get out."

Josh stared at her for a moment, chewing on one corner of his lip as he puzzled something out. Finally, he said, "Fine, let's go." He turned and jogged across the open space of the barren eighth story. Jenna hopped up onto her feet and the two followed after him.

Josh found a flight of stairs, glanced down, and then headed up. Kalei raised an eyebrow, but followed without question, but Jenna was more vocal with her objections.

"No more heights."

Josh didn't look at them as he continued up the stairs. "No, I just have to grab something."

Kalei might have been okay with following Josh through an odd escape route or two, but she was not okay with running back into a burning building for the kid's blankie. "We don't have time for your keepsakes. We have to go."

He kept climbing. "It'll just take a minute."

"I don't care how long it will take. It's too long. If you're so set on rescuing whatever it is, then tell us the way and we'll let ourselves out."

Josh stopped and looked back. "You'd abandon me like that?"

Jenna replied, "Yup."

Josh's face grew serious. "You guys are cold."

Jenna laughed and retorted, "We're gals. Guys don't come as cold as us."

Kalei snorted.

Josh started going back up the stairs. "Alright, go ahead then, ditch me."

"Which way?" Jenna asked.

"Figure it out yourselves. Why should I help a pair of cold-hearted women?"

Kalei sighed and told Jenna, "Let's just follow him."

"No, let's find our own way."

Josh had reached the top of the stairs and was

walking through the door-less frame. Kalei glanced at him and then back at Jenna. Her sister was probably right for once, but that didn't mean Kalei was going to listen her. The thought of ditching the kid just felt wrong. "I don't want to leave him. The kid doesn't know what he's doing, he could get into some serious trouble."

"He's thirteen! He's Estranged! It's what they do!"

"He's thirteen about as much as you're eighteen. What if he wanders off and starts shaking hands with people? What if Landen picks him up? What if Terin throws him into a glass tube for helping us? We can't let that happen."

Jenna shifted her jaw back and forth as she considered Kalei. "Fine."

They started heading up the stairs.

When they cleared the stairwell, they found that the walls on this floor were still intact, creating a long white hallway in front of them. Even the carpet was still there, a very tight weave with geometric patterns of blue and green squares. At the far end of the hall, two pairs of boots stepped out onto the carpet, filled with a pair of Wardens. They were maybe fifty feet away when they spotted Kalei and Jenna on the stairwell, and without missing a beat, they raised their weapons, shouting, "Hold it!"

"Dammit!" Kalei and Jenna dodged back into the stairwell. Kalei hadn't spotted Josh in that brief moment, only the Wardens.

Jenna yelled out, "Josh! Where the fuck are you!"

They heard his voice call out from nearby, "Over here!" Kalei poked her head out and identified the source as the second door on the left. The Wardens were already on their way.

"Here." Jenna slapped a pistol into Kalei's hand.

Kalei looked back and saw that Jenna was still holding the original gun from the tunnels. Kalei had forgotten all about it. But if Jenna had that gun, then— "Where did you get a second gun from? And where the hell did you hide it? Last I checked, these short shorts don't have holsters."

Ignoring her, Jenna crawled up the stairs to stand behind the narrow strip of wall flanking the door. She said, "Shoot their kneecaps."

Kalei dropped the question and climbed to the opposite wall, readying her weapon.

Jenna nodded at Kalei and shouted, "Go!" Both girls leaned out and shot at the Wardens. Kalei's shot missed the kneecap, but caught the first Warden's shin as he ran, sending him face-first into the floor. Jenna hit both knees on his accomplice.

Before the echoes of the shots had cleared the air, Kalei and Jenna were sprinting down the hallway. Kalei's target picked up his gun, but Jenna sent a bullet through his wrist. His cry filled the air as the gunfire died out, and then that too faded away to the sound of ringing in Kalei's ears. The report of gunfire in a narrow hall had not been kind to her eardrums. She half

expected to find blood pouring out of her ears if she
was so inclined to check, but she wasn't worried about
it. Even as they ran, the ringing was dying down.

The sisters ducked into the room, gasping for breath
as Josh slung a black bag onto his back. Jenna wheezed,
"What the fuck is so important... that I just wasted...
four fucking bullets!" She took another, deeper breath
and continued, "You plan on buyin' me ammo when we
get out of this shithole?"

The room was cleaner than most of the others; the
walls were finished, the wiring for the lights and outlets
was complete, and a couple of old but undamaged desks
lined the far wall, with a single plastic chair sitting
before the one on the right.

Josh replied, "Uh...I don't know where to buy
ammo, but—"

New voices shouted in the hallway, accompanied by
the sound of thumping boots.

Kalei turned to check and saw two more Wardens
coming down the route their companions had taken.
They ducked into the first door on the right, using the
doorway as cover as they trained their guns on Kalei's
hideout. The helmeted figure on the left shouted, "Drop
your weapons and come out with your hands up!"

Kalei pulled her head back in and said, "Shit, they
got here fast."

CHAPTER FIFTEEN

On the Road Again

Kalei looked to Josh. "Which way?"

"We have to go through the hall and back down the stairs," he said, pointing.

"Dammit. Jenna, get over here." At Kalei's request, Jenna joined her sister, standing on the opposite side of the door from Kalei.

"How many?" Jenna asked.

"Just the two."

Jenna nodded. "Got it. I'll take left." They swung out into the open doorway and shot at the Wardens. Jenna caught hers cleanly in the shoulder, and as the force knocked him back, she sent her second bullet through his now-exposed heart.

Kalei's bullets mostly found the plaster wall her Warden was hiding behind, but that didn't seem to matter, since one of those bullets made her target cry out and fall to the floor.

Kalei turned back to Josh. "Come on!" She pushed him out in front of her and ran after him.

Jenna caught up and commented, "Your firs' guy is

gettin' up. That leg don' look like it's buggin' him no more."

Kalei replied, "Then take care of it."

As Kalei and Josh started to descend the stairs, Jenna spun around and took out the Warden's right knee, but not before a bullet grazed the side of her face. "Dammit!"

"You all right?"

"Yeah." Jenna wiped at the blood that began to spill above her right eye.

Josh's voice echoed in the stairwell as he called back, "Why didn't you just shoot them in the head?"

Jenna plodded down the stairs after them and said, "They're wearing bullet-resistant helmets, you dumbass!"

Josh nodded to himself. "Oh. Right."

They took an exit on the right, crossed another abandoned floor, down the stairs, to the left, another right...

Several flights later, they finally arrived at the first floor and ran for the exit. Kalei and Jenna kept low and headed for the walls at either side. Kalei thought Josh was following her. She had overtaken him in the sprint, but when she looked for him, she saw that he was standing in front of the open door, watching her with confusion as he said, "Why are you—?"

His head snapped forward and the blast of a gunshot ripped through the air. He crumpled to the floor.

"Fuck!" Jenna mopped her blood away from her eye

and leaned out to return fire. She pulled back just as a bullet whizzed through the doorway. "It's Terin."

"What?"

"It's fucking Terin!"

"Shit." Kalei reached out and snagged the edge of Josh's pants leg, using it to pull his limp body away from the gunfire.

Jenna frowned at Kalei, fresh blood pooling in the crease between her knitted brows. "What are you doing?"

Kalei finished dragging Josh and propped him against the wall. "We're not going to leave him here."

"Why the fuck not?" Gunshots continued to ricochet off the floor and walls. Jenna returned a few of her own.

Kalei ignored Jenna and checked her pistol. The magazine was still half full. She popped it back in and chambered a round.

Jenna said, "Fine, we're taking the kid, but I sure as hell ain't carrying him." She took another shot, then her gun made a sharp *click*. Jenna tossed the weapon away. "Hey, gimme your gun."

"What? Why?"

"Cuz I'm out. Now give it."

Kalei slid her gun over to Jenna. "It's just Terin, right?"

"That's what it looks like. Though fuck knows how he managed to land that shot on Josh." Jenna caught the gun and tucked it into the back of her shorts. When she pulled her hand away, the gun was replaced by a grenade. "This should keep him busy."

"Where the fuck did you—?"

"You ready?" Jenna looked at Kalei with an eager grin growing on her face. Kalei wasn't sure if she should be more concerned with where the grenade came from, or the fact that she was related to this madwoman.

"Hold on." Kalei stooped down and picked Josh up in a fireman's carry. "Okay, ready."

Jenna tossed the grenade, waited for the explosion, and then sprinted out into the dust and debris. Kalei was hot on her heels.

Running through the dirt cloud, Kalei's eyes burned and her shoulders ached as Josh's bony weight dug into her muscles. She soon lost sight of Jenna, but Kalei kept running, hoping she was running in the right direction.

She made it a few more steps, wondering if this could have an end, when the ground dropped out from under her. Her foot fell through open air, then abruptly found the pavement several inches lower than she was expecting it to be. Her knee buckled and she almost dropped Josh, but she caught herself with her right leg and kept on running.

The dust was finally beginning to fade on the wind. She looked around for Jenna and heard her sister curse loudly. Kalei found the young woman's silhouette several feet to the left, picking itself up off the ground next to what appeared to be a tire. Kalei slowed and called out, "You all right?"

"I'm fine. Just keep running." A bullet ricocheted off a patch of dirt beside Kalei. She picked up the pace, running straight for an old pickup truck parked on the other side of the road. Her breathing became labored, and Josh seemed to feel heavier with every step, but she pushed forward, diving behind the truck as another bullet pinged off the hood.

Jenna was already there, crouched beside the cabin with the gun in her hands. Kalei lowered Josh to the ground. "He had a clear shot. Why'd he miss?"

Jenna smiled at Kalei, blood running down one knee in addition to the gash that continued to weep above her eye. The red on her face was mixed with dirt, painting a grotesque mask streaked with handprints where Jenna had wiped the mess from her eyes. She said, "You've never seen Terin shoot, have you?" Kalei shook her head. "To say that he sucks ass would be an understatement." Jenna handed over her gun. "Keep him busy for a sec." She wiped at her eye again and opened the door to the truck.

"What're you—?" Kalei had to scoot back to avoid getting hit by the door.

"Don' worry 'bout it," Jenna said as she crawled into the cabin.

Kalei flicked the safety off and said, "Whatever." She popped out of cover and sent a couple shots at Terin and the van he hid behind. One-two, she ducked and waited for his return fire. She heard the bullets hit the cement and wood of the abandoned strip mall just behind them. Jenna wasn't lying; he really was a terrible shot. She stood up again, three shots this time, then the slide on the gun kicked back and stopped. She retreated to the shadow of the truck.

Meanwhile, violent ripping and crunching sounds were coming from the truck's cabin. As Terin's shots ricocheted off a nearby tree, Kalei moved over to the open door. Lying on the floor of the truck was Jenna, sprawled out on her back with a large piece of plastic from the steering column sitting to one side. Her arms worked methodically as she ripped out wires and used a knife to cut through choice colors. Kalei tapped on Jenna's boot and showed her the gun. Jenna nodded, a red wire held delicately in her mouth, then went back to work.

Kalei's old instincts told her to grab the handcuffs and march this bitch off to the station. Kalei had to remind herself that she wasn't a cop anymore, and seeing as she was already a fugitive, there was no harm in adding to the record. Kalei asked, "Where'd you learn how to hotwire a car?"

Speaking around the wire held in her teeth, Jenna said, "Don' worry about it."

The gunfire from Terin stopped. Kalei heard more voices shouting from the office building. She poked her head above the hood. "Terin's on his way. The other Wardens too." She ducked down and a random thought occurred to her. "Hey, do you think that big guy was Jarmel?"

Jenna no longer had the red wire in her mouth, but now sat puzzling between a blue wire and a green wire. "Nah, he went down too easy. Jarmel would've kept on coming even with a bullet in his leg."

"Good point." Kalei decided it was time to get ready to go. She crawled over to Josh's body, pulled it over to the cab, then heaved and lifted the boy into the truck. By the time she got the boy's torso in, Jenna still had not succeeded in starting the car. She knew it couldn't take this long. Half the thugs in Celan could have had the truck to Telahar by now. She knew; she had to write up what felt like a million of those missing car reports and watch the ensuing hours of surveillance tapes. She couldn't see Jenna from her position beside the back seat, so she asked, "Do you really know how to hotwire a car?"

Jenna's voice called out gruffly, "Shut up, I'm trying to concentrate."

Kalei finished laying Josh across the bench seat, then carefully climbed into the passenger side up front. Slowly, she raised her head up to peer through the window. Terin and friends were only fifteen feet away now and closing. Two Wardens created a solid vanguard, and a step behind them, two more flanked Terin on either side. All of them sported wet patches on their uniforms where Jenna and Kalei's bullets had visited. The big guy in front of Terin raised his rifle and squeezed off a series of shots. Kalei ducked just as the driver's side window shattered.

"Got it!"

Kalei looked down at Jenna. "You got it?"

"Yeah, I found the guy's sidearm! He had it right there under the seat," Jenna cheerfully responded, holding up a pistol.

"I thought you were hotwiring the car!"

"I am! Hold on." Jenna twisted a couple of wires together and the radio blared to life with the latest pop music.

Kalei turned the radio down and said, "Alright, c'mon! Let's go."

Jenna squirmed a ways out from under the steering wheel and said, "Not yet. Get over here and hold this wire while I have a nice chat with Terin and the crew. And be careful not to let it touch anything." Jenna crawled up onto the driver's seat as Kalei slid down and lay on the floor, gingerly accepting the yellow wire from Jenna.

Once she was free, Jenna popped up into the open window and took a shot at their friends. Then she paused, eyes widening slightly. "Shit! Do you see this?" She quickly ducked back under cover as three shots crashed into the cabin.

"What?"

"He just pulled the same trick Xamic did back at the mansion. The whole 'I just had my brains blown out and I don't give a fuck' bit."

"Really?" Kalei started to sit up, but Jenna waved her back down.

"Stay down there. You ain't done yet. You see the green wire hangin' there?"

"Yeah."

"When I say, I want you to touch the end of that wire to the yellow wire, then hit the gas when you hear the engine start, got it?"

Kalei retorted, "I only have two hands. How do you expect me to hold the wires together and hit the gas at the same time?"

Jenna rolled her eyes. "You don' need to hold the wires. Jus' drop 'em when the engine starts. Now stop being a pussy and get ready."

Kalei mumbled under her breath and reached for the green wire. Jenna got off three more shots, then turned and slammed the butt of her gun into the keyhole and yelled, "Now!"

Kalei brought the two wires together, but before they even touched, a bright flash of electricity jumped between them, shocking Kalei as the engine roared to life. She cursed and dropped the wires, jumping away as the yellow wire caught on her arm and shocked her again.

Jenna took another shot at the Wardens and roared, "Hit the gas!"

Kalei found the gas pedal and shoved it to the floor. The tires screamed, the truck swerved violently out into the middle of the road, and then Jenna caught the wheel and set it straight.

Jenna said, "Now get out of there. I've got it." Kalei

hastily clambered off the floor, brushing dirt off herself as she sat up in the passenger seat. "Here, take this." Jenna handed over the gun. "Keep it low."

Gunshots pinged off the truck and the back window shattered. Kalei ducked and replied, "Fuck that. I should be shooting back."

"No. Keep the gun low, keep your head low, and face forward."

Kalei wasn't sure what Jenna was up to, but the calm, determined look in Jenna's eyes convinced Kalei not to argue. She slouched low in her seat and faced forward.

The gunshots stopped, and Jenna dropped their speed down to thirty-five miles an hour. Kalei glanced back over her shoulder and saw the Wardens running to their vans. As she turned forward again, the silence that was left by the lack of gunfire was filled by the sound of sirens. Jenna didn't react, she didn't speed up; if Kalei didn't know any better, she would have thought Jenna hadn't heard them. Her only response was to turn on her blinker and merge onto Cedar Street. It was a modest, two-lane road with minimal traffic, and while Kalei noticed a kid in the backseat of the car beside them, pointing and exclaiming at the bullet holes down the side of the truck, the rest of the road utterly ignored the newcomers as just another piece in the daily commute.

A block later, the cop cars appeared two streets ahead of them, lights flashing and sirens blaring as they turned onto Cedar. The daily commuters lazily pulled to the side as the two police cruisers picked up speed on the straightaway, gunning straight down the middle of the road toward Kalei and Jenna. Kalei brought the gun forward, flicking the safety off as she prepared to fire.

Jenna held her hand out over the gun. "Don't." Jenna slowed down and pulled to the side along with the rest of traffic. Kalei wanted to scream at her sister, to demand why they were stopping, to hit her over the head, but instead, she shut her mouth and tightened her grip on the pistol.

Kalei watched Jenna for any sign of what her sister was planning, but Jenna just leaned back and lazily eyed the police as they approached.

The cops didn't slow down as they closed the distance to their target. The sisters were sitting ducks now. Kalei looked from Jenna to the speeding vehicles and realized that even if they pulled back onto the road and sped off now, it was already too late to outrun their pursuers. Was this Jenna's plan? To release Kalei, run them all over Celan in a crazy series of explosions and gunfights, just to hand her back over to the cops when she was done with her fun? Kalei had already accepted that this woman was her sister Jenna, but now she started to wonder just how much that sister had changed in the years since they were kids. Kalei realized that whether she was looking at Shenaia or Jenna, she still didn't know what this woman was capable of.

The police were four hundred feet off now, two hundred— they made no sign of slowing. One hundred feet, fifty, twenty—they passed the truck.

Kalei turned in her seat, watching as the lights retreated into the distance as Jenna casually pulled back onto the road.

Kalei didn't look at Jenna as she demanded, "What the hell was that? We were sitting right in front of them!"

Jenna turned down Seventh. "You keep goin' on about how SWORDE doesn't communicate with the cops, right? They had no fucking clue what they were looking for. They were just running down to the site like good little officers."

Later, they dumped the truck in a ditch and hitched a ride in a taxi. Kalei had donned a pair of sunglasses and a sweatshirt they pilfered from the truck, and they found a baseball cap to cover the healing bullet wound on Josh's head as they propped him up between them, claiming he was just passed out drunk when the taxi driver looked at them questioningly. The cabbie didn't seem to approve of a drunk thirteen-year-old, but it was better than telling him it was a temporarily dead thirteen-year-old.

Kalei was grateful for the sweatshirt, but the glasses had been at Jenna's insistence. "Xamic made you famous, honey. The driver gets one look at your face, and everyone goes nuts. You shoulda seen the news when you chased Xamic down that interstate. They have experts on you now." Jenna had given a short laugh as she pulled Kalei's hood over her head.

For the most part, though, the taxi driver wasn't overly concerned with Kalei's attire, or with their "passed-out-drunk" friend. He only had eyes for Jenna's half-exposed melons. Once they arrived at a grimy motel, Jenna pouted her lips, invented some sob story about losing their wallets in last night's fun, and the driver grudgingly let them go for free after a quick peek at the items of his affection.

Kalei stayed in the parking lot with Josh while Jenna worked more of her magic on the motel manager, probably sharing more than the brief flash she had given the cabbie, and soon they were climbing the stairs to their new room.

Kalei couldn't even look at her sister. She was ashamed of what Jenna had done, and even more ashamed that she had let her do it.

Once Jenna opened the door, Kalei immediately found the nearest bed and dumped Josh into it. Kalei knew this hotel. She had done guard duty for a number of crime scenes at this place. She had only seen the interior of the rooms in passing, but nonetheless, it was odd to see the cheap, garish furniture sitting neatly in their places. Usually, they were tossed about the room, or half covered in someone's blood. Almost like a recovery room, except the wreckage was ten times cheaper to replace.

As it was, a pair of twin-sized beds covered with red leopard print sat pushed against the wall, a small, wooden nightstand between them. A gaudy painting featuring a large, well-endowed woman in a cocktail dress overshadowed the drab lamp on the table, and on the opposite wall stood a pasty green dresser with a fat, cracked television on top. A door at the back led to the bathroom, but Kalei's nose told her she had no interest in investigating. The main room already smelled like sex and vomit overlaid with the sickening tang of artificial citrus. She had no desire to know what the bathroom smelled like. Instead, she plopped down on the second bed while Jenna found a short armchair near the door to fall into.

The girls sat in silence for a moment, taking a deep, mental breath after the mayhem of the afternoon. While the furnishings were distracting enough to take Kalei's mind off things, they were almost painful to look at. So instead, she found herself looking at Josh, lying perfectly limp on the bed where she had dropped him. She noticed that his head hung off one edge of the bed, and his arm was twisted in a painful angle beneath his body. Kalei leaned forward and straightened the boy out, berating herself for being so careless.

Jenna remarked, "Dumbass is slow to recover."

"Whatever. He'll wake up soon. "

Jenna kicked her feet up onto the bed and leaned back in her chair, eyeing Kalei. "So what is this? One minute, you're all, 'I'm gonna kill the Estranged!' and now you're savin' 'em? What the hell?" Jenna pulled her hands forward and started counting out on her fingers. "We've got Terin and all of frickin' SWORDE after us, Franklin's pissed, who the hell knows what Xamic is up to, and now we're playin' babysitter to some dumbass kid? Shit." Jenna flopped her arms onto the armrests. "So what now?"

Kalei looked back at Josh's body. If it wasn't for the bullet-hole in his forehead, or the fact that he wasn't breathing, he could've been just another teenager, passed out on a Saturday afternoon after a late night of video games. As it was, she knew what he was. She knew he was Estranged. But when she asked herself why she bothered to take him along, when she asked herself what they were going to do next...

Kalei replied, "I don't know."

Jenna pulled her feet off the bed and leaned forward. "I'll tell you my plan." She pointed at Josh. "I'm gonna get rid of this punk-ass kid ASAP. I can't stand the immature little son of a—"

CHAPTER SIXTEEN

Shenanigans

Jenna sat on the edge of the bed, arms animating her words as Josh watched closely from his seat on the opposite mattress. "Then I turned around..." Jenna grinned as Josh leaned in closer. "And smacked her dead in the face! And get this: the bitch falls flat on her ass and rips out the biggest damn fart I ever heard!" The pair burst into laughter.

From where she stood on the other side of the room, Kalei dropped her head back into the wall. Arms crossed, her eyes rolled back beneath closed eyelids. They had been like this for the last three days, ever since Josh woke up. Kalei was at her wit's end; she felt like a chaperone to a pair of middle-schoolers. When Josh started asking questions about whether it was a juicy fart or a loud honker, Kalei opened her eyes, pushed off the wall, and reached for the door handle.

Jenna stopped laughing. "Where do you think you're going?"

"Out."

"Hey, you know you can't go out. People will see

you."

Kalei picked a paper bag up off the dresser, dumped out its contents of newspaper and gum wrappers, then put it over her head. She poked out two holes for the eyes and demanded, "There! Better?" She didn't wait for a response. She stepped out.

Kalei strode up to the railing where it guarded their second-story walkway from the parking lot. She grabbed it with both hands and looked out at the world beyond their tiny little room. The pavement spread out in deeper, darkened hues and the cars glistened from a recent spurt of rain. A cool breeze hinted of more to come.

She didn't even know why she had bothered to drag Josh out of that office. Perhaps it was just a misplaced sense of concern. Perhaps she just didn't want to be responsible for sending anyone else to solitary. The memory of that place still stuck in the back of her throat like sour milk.

Kalei tried to take in a deep breath of fresh air, but the bag impeded her attempt. In contrast to the cool breeze that played across her exposed arms, the air inside the bag was already humid and warm. It pressed close to her face and kept any of that refreshing relief from coming in. Furious and frustrated, Kalei reached up to pull the bag off, but as her fingers closed around one corner, she noticed a man approaching and let her hand drop.

Tall, dark, and handsome, he smiled as he drew

nearer. "Why the bag?"

Kalei didn't so much as shrug as she responded, "Why not?"

The man was just a couple feet away when she replied, and at the sound of her voice, he casually stopped and squinted into her eyeholes. "Your voice sounds familiar... Have we met before?"

Kalei relinquished her hold on the railing and turned to face him. She wanted to scream in his face and tell him to just leave her the fuck alone. All she wanted was a moment's peace! Instead, she said, "How can you tell? If you haven't noticed, there's a freaking bag over my head. Tends to muffle sound, change voices a bit."

His squint deepened, and a handsome crease formed on his brow. "No, I've definitely heard your voice before."

Kalei was pissed that she couldn't even shake a damned stranger, but she knew it wouldn't do them any good if she tossed this man over the balcony and caused a scene. So she stepped past him and reached for the door handle to the room. "See ya."

As she walked by him, the man reached out for her arm.

Kalei snatched her arm away and then pointed her index finger at his face. "Back the fuck off."

She glared at him through the peepholes in her stuffy brown bag. He raised an eyebrow as he raised his arms in surrender, taking a step back as he said, "Okay, sorry."

Kalei waited for another heartbeat, daring him to try something so she would have an excuse to vent her rage, but when he didn't, she broke eye contact and stepped into the room, slamming the door behind her as she ripped off the bag. She glanced at the four garish walls; it felt as though they were closing in on her. Her companions were already too close for comfort. Even in a room of three, it felt crowded.

"I fucking hate you all." She plopped down into a nearby chair and stared at the ceiling.

Jenna looked up from her conversation with Josh. "What happened?"

"Nothing. Listen, what the fuck are we doing here? I can't stand this shithole. Let's just go already."

"And go where? I'm sure Tusic and SWORDE are already taking bets on who gets to sink their claws into us first."

Josh chimed, "Wait—Tusic? The GPS company?"

Kalei absently replied, "Don't worry about it." She continued to Jenna, "We can't just sit here on our asses. My family is still out there. Dead or alive: I need to find out which."

"You heard Franklin. They're still in the city. They're fine—"

"Are they? He didn't even say if they are still Untouched, he just said, 'They're together.' And are you really going to trust anything that comes out of that fucker's mouth?"

"Well, what do you think we should do? You

already tried calling your little friend, Lecia. She won'
answer you. Now what?"

Kalei paused for a moment. It was true; Lecia
hadn't answered any of her calls. Kalei suspected it was
because Lecia didn't recognize the number, but then,
when did an aspiring researcher turn down calls? In
either case, Kalei didn't leave any voicemails for fear
that Tusic might have an illegal phone tap on Lecia. In
fact, Kalei didn't even know why she kept calling Lecia
in the first place. Terin knew Kalei had been talking to
Lecia before her imprisonment. He probably knew she
was the only one Kalei could turn to now. It was stupid
for Kalei to call, but it was the only idea she could
come up with. Lecia was the only outside person she
had left. Except for one other person, but she was loath
to drag him into this mess. If anything, she wanted to
keep him as far away from her black nails as possible.
But then, what options did she have left?

Kalei turned and picked up the hotel phone. "I'm
calling Marley."

Jenna jumped up and pushed in the trigger on the
receiver, "Whoa, whoa. You mean your police friend?
What are you? Stupid? You call the station and the first
cop that picks up will know your voice."

"That's why I'm calling his cellphone. Now bug
off." Kalei waved Jenna away, but her sister wouldn't
move.

Jenna said, "What's gonna stop him from calling in
the reinforcements, huh?"

Kalei looked away to the undisturbed pillows on the bed beside her, studying the leopard spots closely. Jenna had never been a cop; she wouldn't understand.

Kalei said, "He's my partner."

"He's Untouched! You're an Estranged." Jenna's voice took an unforgiving edge. "He won't trust a damn thing you have to say."

That fact that Jenna was right made it that much harder for Kalei to hear. If Marley had any sense, partner or no, he would hang up the moment he heard her voice. Or turn her over to the authorities. The thought made Kalei's stomach clench. Still, she couldn't let go of the kind memories of her foster cousin, or the instinctive prodding that told her Marley wouldn't turn her in. Kalei reached for the receiver and tried to pull it away from Jenna as she said, "Whether he wants to or not, I'll make him believe me."

Kalei's attempt to free the phone failed, Jenna's grip was unyielding.

Jenna said, "You think you can *make him?* With what? Brute force? Threats? Partnerly love? C'mon, Kalei; get real. You got no skill at persuasion, and whatever bond you guys had ain't gonna fix the fact that you tha' threat now. You tha enemy to all them cops and their families."

Kalei slammed the phone down onto the receiver, narrowly missing Jenna's fingers as she pulled them out of the way. "And what other option do I have! Huh? Please, tell me! You're the big sister, right? You're supposed to have all the answers! What the fuck am I supposed to do!"

The phone rang. Everyone fell silent and stared at the device. They couldn't have been more shocked if the thing had sprouted arms and legs and begun dancing an Irish jig. It rang again.

Without taking her eyes off the beast, Jenna whispered to Kalei, "Who the fuck could that be?"

Kalei whispered back, "I dunno. Maybe it's the manager, or housekeeping or something?"

"More likely a ho lookin' for her sugar daddy."

It rang again.

Josh cupped his hands around his mouth, giggled, then whispered, "Answer it."

Jenna looked at Kalei and said, "Yeah, answer it."

Kalei furrowed her brows at Jenna and hissed, "Why me?"

"Because—"

It rang again.

Jenna yelled out, "Fuck! I'll answer it." She plucked the phone from the receiver and said, "Hello?" She paused and frowned at the painted lady portrait above the bed. "No. Who is this? ... I ain't telling you nothin' until you tell me who this is!" She put her hand over the mouthpiece and whispered to Kalei, "Check the windows." Kalei nodded, then shooed Josh out of her way as she tried to get around the bed. She hadn't made it more than two steps when she heard Jenna say, "Grasshoppers?"

The word sent a mental jolt through Kalei. She turned around and snatched the phone away from Jenna, waving off her sister's complaints as she pressed the phone to her ear and said, "Marley?"

"Kalei."

She could have cried, it was such a relief to hear his voice. She never would have expected to react that way to Marley, of all people, but it was like waking up from a nightmare and finding that the Reaper hadn't taken her loved ones after all.

She asked, "How did you get this number?"

He replied, "I'm a Detective now. It's my—"

Jenna whispered furiously, "Marley? What the fuck is he—"

Kalei turned away and pushed her free hand to her free ear to block out Jenna's protests.

Marley was still talking, "—happened since you left. But that doesn't matter; you're with SWORDE, right?"

"Not anymore."

"Thought so. Listen, you might wanna get out of there. An anonymous tip just came in saying that Kalei Distrad has been spotted at the Lazy Daze Motel. According to dispatch, SWORDE is heading your way."

"Thanks, Marley. Listen, I need to talk to you—"

"I don't think that's a good idea. Just get out of there, Kalei. ETA is seven minutes."

"Marley, wait! Chi's Diner, ten o'clock."

Marley was silent. For a moment, Kalei thought she

heard him inhale, like he was going to say something, but then the phone gave a light "click" and went dead.

Kalei hung up the phone and found an agitated Jenna standing immediately behind her. Jenna said, "What the hell was that?"

Kalei moved away from Jenna and started to collect her few belongings from the dresser. Her chapstick, her change, her hooded sweatshirt... While Kalei had been grounded to the hotel, Jenna had been busy collecting supplies, including fresh clothes. Kalei replied, "Don't worry about it. Right now, we need to get out of here."

Josh reported from the window, "I don't see anything out here." He covered his mouth with his hand as a snicker escaped from his grinning countenance. "What am I looking for? Is the boogey man coming?" He giggled like the preteen he used to be.

Kalei's eyes lingered on Josh for a moment, trying to puzzle out why his giggling sent off red flags in her mind, but she wrote it off as childish nonsense and turned to Jenna. "Someone just tipped off SWORDE. We've got about six minutes before they get here."

Kalei expected her sister to be pissed, but instead, Jenna clapped her hands and grinned wildly as she said, "Sweet, a Camaro pulled in yesterday and I've been *dying* to jack the thing."

"No." Kalei stopped her. "They'll find out the car was stolen and just send out a BOLO. We have time. Let's just go on foot."

Jenna stomped her foot and rolled her eyes as she

said, "Fine. Jus' make sure you don't take your mask off once we get out there."

"What?"

Kalei had no idea what Jenna was talking about, but the teen had already pulled away and started shuffling through the stash of grocery bags in the second drawer of the dresser. After a moment, Jenna said, "Ha! Gotchya." And turned around with a full, white opera mask in her hand. "Here. Put this on. An' make sure you pull your hood up."

Kalei snatched the mask and said, "Why the hell did you let me walk out of here with a paper bag on my head when you had this!"

"You didn' exactly wait around for me to tell you. Besides, it was funny as hell."

Kalei mumbled a series of choice curses as she pulled the mask on.

CHAPTER SEVENTEEN

Dropping By

The three finished gathering up their things and then went on their way. They had just made it across the parking lot when Josh said, "Hey! I forgot my first aid kit."

Kalei looked at Jenna, forgetting that the mask hid her raised eyebrow. She said, "He really has no fucking clue, does he?"

Jenna laughed. "Nope." Then she gave Josh a light shove on the shoulder and said, "Leave it, or I'll give you a hole your Band-Aids can't fix."

Luckily, Josh knew Jenna well enough to forget about the first aid kit.

They made it several blocks before the sound of sirens began echoing off the buildings. Kalei said, "It sounds like Marley's estimate was optimistic."

Jenna laughed. "Or pessimistic."

Kalei spotted Josh anxiously glancing over his shoulder. Casually, so as not to spook him any further, she said, "Relax. As far as we're concerned, those sirens have nothing to do with us. We don't want people wondering why you're so nervous, do we?"

Josh shook his head silently and proceeded to study his feet the rest of the way.

It was already late afternoon, although Kalei could hardly be sure from the overcast sky. A light drizzle had begun to fall as they made their way down the streets of the West End, and Kalei felt an angled drop hit her eyelid through the mask. Annoyed, she pulled her hood down further.

But Kalei, despite her annoyance, was glad for the weather. The rain brought everyone's hoods up, their umbrellas out, and made it easier for Kalei to blend in.

As the streets became more and more crowded, Jenna took her gloves off, handed them to Josh, and then put her own hands in her pockets. Kalei watched Josh put the gloves on, and she realized she still didn't know what kind of person the kid was. She didn't know if he was likely to attack some passerby, or if he'd spent enough time as an Estranged that he could control himself. And even if he could, did that mean he would? Kalei was already uneasy with Jenna, the addict that she was, roaming these civilian streets. Kalei wondered if she had unleashed a pair of time bombs onto the streets of her city, and resolved to watch both her companions closely.

They ducked into an alley when rush hour hit, waiting out the manic flood of people while Jenna scared away would-be muggers with a black-nailed bird for each. When the foot-traffic finally subsided, they stepped out and finished the trip to Chi's.

Chi's Diner was a small place, wedged between an electronics shop and a small convenience store. All three looked desolate and run-down, but Kalei knew from experience that Chi's had the best lo-mein in town. She practically had to force feed Fenn the first time she brought him here to try out the cuisine. Kalei's swirls tightened at the memory, and she quickly pushed it from her mind.

Across the street, Josh and Jenna sat down in front of an empty storefront, while Kalei continued to stand beside them. She crossed her arms and settled her weight comfortably between both legs, something she had become accustomed to as a cop, standing guard at many large events and Estranged crime scenes. Beneath her mask, Kalei's eyes carefully followed the pedestrians walking by, alert for any sign of a threat, be it a SWORDE Agent, a Tusic spy, or even just another Estranged out to cause trouble.

A man in a striped jacket walked along with his hands in his pockets and his hood pulled up over his head. He glanced at Kalei as he approached, but when his eyes found her mask, he flinched, his eyes widening in surprise, then he quickly ducked his head and hurried past. Across the street, a couple exited Chi's Diner, takeout in hand, cheerfully bantering as they walked down the sidewalk. Their umbrella caught a gust of wind, twisting inside out and fighting against the man's grip as the wind tried to pull it away. They laughed and exclaimed and fought with the umbrella for a brief moment before discarding it in the nearest trash can and running to escape the light rain.

Kalei pulled her hood lower. It was painful, watching these people go about their lives, oblivious to the danger Kalei and her companions posed. And not just Kalei; anyone on these streets could be Estranged. How many times had she walked down this very sidewalk, just as ignorant as the rest of them? She had always thought she was safe. She had always believed that an Estranged would stick out from the crowd, a crazed and hungry lunatic who chased down anyone in sight. In her police academy, they had always warned her that anyone could be an Estranged, but they had described Estranged behavior as erratic, impulsive, violent. Of course, they weren't exactly wrong, but... the fact that an Estranged could also be calm, collected, normal; that was something she had never imagined.

Kalei was ashamed of how ignorant she used to be.

A sharp, wooden clacking sound drew Kalei's attention back to her companions. The juveniles had found a pair of discarded chopsticks, and a fierce, miniature sword fight was underway. Kalei couldn't say she was surprised.

She listened to the small clack-clacks while she resisted the urge to rip the mask from her face. In some ways, it was worse than the paper bag. It clung tighter to her face, the moisture from her breath collecting on the plastic rather than absorbing into the material as it would have with the paper bag. Her face felt hot and irritated from the humidity, and the heavy hood of her sweatshirt only captured the heat, amplifying the problem. Below the mask, a cool breeze blew against her exposed neck, fueling the temptation to throw the damned piece of plastic into the gutter. But she put a lid on the impulse and felt her temptation turn to irritation.

The clacking ended with a sharp SNAP! as Josh cried out. Kalei looked down at the boy and saw him waving his hand rapidly to shake off some injury. He said to Jenna, "Sheesh, you've got some skills with the chopstick!"

Jenna leaned back against the shop doorway and crossed her arms behind her head. "I know." The teenager's smug smile sat content on her face as her eyes wandered out across the street to take in the drug store. The smile slid away as something caught the girl's attention, and Kalei followed her gaze to see a middle-aged man stepping out of the shop.

Jenna asked, "What time is it?"

Kalei heard Josh shift positions before he replied, "Seven o'clock."

Then Jenna asked Kalei, "And what time are we meeting your buddy?"

Kalei wasn't sure why the man had caught Jenna's eye, but she turned her attention back to the conversation at hand. She looked back at the two and found them watching her.

She answered, "Ten o'clock."

Jenna let out an exasperated moan. "Dammit. We're gonna be here all day!" Jenna rolled her eyes, and then her attention caught on a passing woman. She followed the woman's footsteps for a moment before slumping back against the storefront and saying, "Why don' we go do somethin' 'stead of waitin'?"

Kalei uncrossed her arms and stuck them in her sweatshirt pocket. "Like what?"

"Anythin'. It beats sittin' out here all exposed, waitin' for the good guys to roll up and take us away."

"The good guys?"

Jenna threw up her hands in defeat, then climbed to her feet. "Eh, good guys, bad guys, they all's out fo' us now. Whatevs, let's jus' get outta here."

Josh stood up as well. "Y'know, there's something I'd like to check out. It's not far. It would only take a minute."

Jenna clapped her hands together. "A'ight! We got a place to be. Let's go."

Kalei stepped in front of them, raising a hand to stop them before they could run off. "Wait a minute. Where are we going?"

Josh avoided Kalei's eyes as looked to his right, then pointed. "Uh, just up the road, about three blocks down Fifth Street."

"That's not what I meant."

Josh shrugged, looking at his shoes. "I know, but it's personal."

Kalei crossed her arms again and waited for him

to look at her. When he finally glanced up, she asked, "The kind of personal that's going to get us into trouble?"

Josh laughed, and his eyes lit up. "No, she's the last person to cause trouble."

Jenna stepped in, dropping a hand on Josh's shoulder as she demanded, "Oooo, she? Who is she? C'mon, spill!"

Josh pulled away. "What?"

"C'mon, c'mon, c'mon!" Jenna poked him in the arm each time.

"Fine! She's my mom. I just want to see her, alright? I haven't seen her since... I want to make sure she's doing okay."

Kalei uncrossed her arms and returned her hands to her pockets. "Nothing wrong with that."

Meanwhile, Jenna's upbeat attitude fell away. She gave Kalei a sideways glance, then asked Josh, "You said we're jus' gonna see her, right? We're not gonna talk to her or nothin'?"

Jenna's change in behavior surprised Kalei. It concerned her as much as it confused her.

Josh said, "Well, I would like to—"

Jenna cut him off. "You don't want to talk to her. It's better if you keep your distance, bro."

"Why wouldn't I—" Jenna held up her hand. Kalei could only see Jenna's palm from where she was standing, but she knew what Josh saw. The black steering wheels on Jenna's nails were navigating some invisible mountain road, never able to return home. Never able to be normal again.

Josh's shoulders and face drooped like a sad flower. "Oh." He looked down at his own nails, still covered with Jenna's gloves. "I guess you're right."

Kalei broke the brief silence that followed. "Well, let's go. We can still check on her."

Jenna glanced at Kalei again, her eyes somber, then quietly followed as Kalei and Josh headed in the direction he'd indicated.

It wasn't long before they came to Josh's street. It was a quiet road, with several tall apartment buildings squeezed in together, and a few modest cars parked on either side. Josh pointed to a narrow gateway on the left, wedged between a pair of brick walls. The gate was an intricate wrought iron backed by chain-link, and the walls were over ten feet high, with wrought-iron spears at the top to deter anyone from climbing. Built into the wall beside the gate was an intercom panel, a large metal square with a speaker and rows of buttons paired with names. Kalei walked up to the panel and asked Josh, "What's the—"

A quaking yell pierced the air. "Josh!"

The three turned and saw a middle-aged woman fifty feet up the sidewalk, clutching an armful of groceries. Her mouth struggled to form more words, but none came out.

"Mom?" Josh started to run toward her, but Jenna caught him around his midsection. "Let me go! That's my mom! Mom!"

Josh's mom dropped her groceries and hurried toward her distressed son. Her mouth finally asked, "Josh, is that really you? What is happening? What's going on?"

Kalei carefully pulled the darkness back from her arms and hurried forward to stop the woman. They met about ten feet from where Jenna was struggling with Josh, and Kalei held up her hands in an official "Stop" gesture. "I'm sorry, ma'am. Please don't come any closer."

The woman stared at Kalei for a moment, then her own face turned into a mask of anger. "What do you mean? That's my son! Let me see him!" The woman was only a few inches shorter than Kalei, lean and pretty despite the budding wrinkles and laugh lines that placed her somewhere in her late forties.

She tried to push past Kalei, but Kalei stepped in front of the woman, cutting off her path. The painful confusion, the relief, the love, the hot concern in the woman's eyes made Kalei wish she could let this woman go hold her son. But she knew better. It would not end well for anyone if she let that happen. She said, "I understand you want to see him, but you cannot get any closer."

Cries rang out from both Jenna and Josh as their scuffle continued. Josh yelled out again, a high-pitched shout of pain and surprise. The mom gasped, struggling to look past Kalei, to see what was happening. Tears in her eyes, she demanded, "Why are you letting that girl hurt him!"

With renewed fervor, the mother tried again to force her way past Kalei, but this time, Kalei grabbed her by the shoulders and held her in place. "You really—"

Jenna cursed and there was a loud *thunk.* Jenna screamed, "KALEI!"

Kalei spun around and saw Josh charging at them in full frenzy. Her instincts screamed, a dozen commands roaring through her mind at once— *tackle him, stop him, keep the mom back, stop him*— but her eyes met his and she froze. He was only a couple feet away and closing, but she couldn't move. What she saw in those clear green eyes, the intensity of it...

BOOM!

Josh's face exploded in an eruption of blood and gore. His body flew violently into the ground as the momentum of his dash continued to push his corpse forward. On the sidewalk, several feet behind the remains of the boy, Jenna lay on her back, gun raised, shell clinking as it landed on the pavement.

Josh's mom screamed.

CHAPTER EIGHTEEN

Separate Ways

They stole a car from a witness and escaped with Josh's body while his mom lay crying in the street. Josh's corpse bled out in the back, painting the seat red as Kalei and Jenna sat in the front, shaking.

"Shit." Jenna looked out the window. Kalei had no words. "Shit!" she repeated. "We need to get out of this car. There were *way* too many witnesses out there. We need to get the fuck out of this car!"

Kalei kept her eyes on the road as her hands twisted at the steering wheel. "And go where? Where can we go! We've got the entire fucking town after us!"

Jenna paused and bit her lip. "What about your friend? Damn, what was her name..." Kalei opened her mouth, but Jenna cut her off, jumping forward in her seat. "Lecia! I know she didn' pick up yo' calls, but if we show up at her place, then she's gotta take us in. She's all sorts a' pro-Estranged, operatin' outside the law. She'd open her doors wide open to a couple Estranged refugees!"

"And how the hell am I supposed to know where

she lives?"

"She didn' tell you?"

"Fuck no. She may be stupid, but she's not that stupid. She doesn't give out her address to Estranged." Kalei cut off Jenna before she could respond. "Even old school acquaintances. *Especially* old school acquaintances, if you know anything about our past."

Jenna sat back in her seat and replied, "Yeah, well, I know where she lives."

Kalei looked at her sister. "What? How?"

"When you was in time-out downstairs, Terin had me tied down to camera duty. And y'know, you'd think monitoring the ear cams would be hella fun. Spyin' on the whole town, get to learn everyone's dirty secrets... fuck no! That shit was boring as hell! No dialogue? Shit, and ain't no one pointing their ears at each other so you can get a proper lip-read. Shit, and some of the stuff I did see, man, there was shit that even *I* didn' wanna know!" Jenna glanced at a car passing by, then continued, "Anyway, your girl Lecia made a friend that followed her home one night. Had to send a few Wardens to take care of it. Take Main Street. We'll ditch the car at that used car lot up there."

They abandoned the car, leaving Josh in the trunk. Kalei didn't want to leave a man behind, but it was Jenna who saw reason. "Terin don' have nothin' against him. He's jus' another Estranged. SWORDE will find him and take him Downtown where he'll live happily ever after."

Kalei threw the car into park and turned to her sister. "Are you kidding? Josh has been with us since we escaped Tusic. He knows where we've been, he knows how we've been avoiding them— Terin is probably going to torture him for information!"

Jenna raised an eyebrow. "If you think Terin would use torture, then you clearly don't know him."

Kalei was insistent. "Josh almost killed his mother today. Do you think Terin will go easy on that?"

"And do you think we can carry a corpse more than a mile through town and not get spotted? 'Specially with the cops houndin' our trail? Don' worry. What's the worst that can happen? So they throw Josh in a little glass tube. So what? He'll be a hell of a lot safer than either of us."

"If that's how you feel about the tubes, then why'd you help me escape?"

Jenna looked away and unlocked her door. "That's different. You wanted out."

"And Josh won't?"

Jenna looked back at Josh where he lay on the seat. "After what he's been through, locked up is the only place he'll want to be." She stepped out and walked to the back of the car.

Kalei popped the trunk before she exited the vehicle, then proceeded to pull Josh's body out of the back seat.

She had him halfway out and was getting ready to pick him up when she noticed something. "Hey," Kalei straightened up and looked at Jenna, who still stood at the trunk, moving junk around to make room for the body. "Where's his backpack? The kid never let the thing out of his sight."

Jenna wasn't interested. "Prob'ly dropped it in the fight." She finished what she was doing and stepped back to admire her handiwork. "What does it matter?" Brushing off her hands, Jenna walked over to Kalei and the body. "Let's get this over with."

"Fine."

Together, the girls pulled out his body and carried it over to the trunk.

For the first twenty minutes, they didn't say anything. The rain had started to pour in heavy sheets, turning the world around them into a blurred dream and making it hard to see anything further than five feet away. The water soaked through Kalei's sweatshirt and poured in through the eyeholes in her mask, collecting in pools above her cheeks that slowly trickled down the rest of her face, down her neck, and into her shirt, blazing an irritating trail of tickling sensations. Kalei ripped off the mask and threw it into the gutter.

"How far is it?" she asked.

Jenna nodded in the direction they were walking. "About two miles. It's in the Wadduck district."

Kalei grumbled a curse.

They took a few more steps, and then Jenna said, "Forget about meeting Marley."

Kalei looked up at her sister. "What? I wasn't even thinking about it. That whole district is swarming with cops by now." Kalei shoved her hands into her sweatshirt pocket. "Shit, wonder if he was even going to show up."

"Hell if I know."

The conversation died, and they continued walking to the sound of the beating rain.

It was about another mile when Kalei noticed that Jenna was quivering. Her sister kept her chin tucked close to her chest, but her eyes darted out into the rain, desperate for something. It could have been that she was just cold from the rain, but that didn't seem to be it. Kalei might have been wearing a soaked-through sweatshirt, but Jenna's jacket, now that it was zipped up, was waterproof. And all the walking was already starting to make Kalei sweat beneath her layers. No, Jenna couldn't be cold. It had to be something else.

So Kalei hung back a step behind her sister and watched. A few moments later when a pedestrian walked out into the street, Jenna's head shot up and she eyed the man hungrily, but she quickly pulled her eyes away and looked at her feet.

Kalei stepped up and shoved Jenna into the nearest wall. "Are you going through withdrawals? Have you been high this whole fucking time? Who did you get a high from, Jenna? Who did you—" Kalei paused and her eyes subtly widened. She knew who. Her brows snapped together and again she shoved Jenna against the wall. "Did you get Josh high?" Jenna didn't say anything. "Fuck! What the hell is wrong with you, Jenna!"

Her sister bowed her head and grabbed her arm with her other hand. She squeezed it tightly. "I'm sorry."

"Fuck, what the hell am I supposed to do with you, huh? Give me your gun. GIVE ME your gun!" Jenna held it out and Kalei snatched it from her hand, careful to pull back her darkness as she did so, in case the bitch tried something. Kalei held up the gun. "I should just shoot you right now and leave you for SWORDE."

Jenna's eyes widened. "Don't! I can't leave—" She couldn't hold Kalei's eyes, though. She looked away and withdrew into herself. "Please don't, little sister..."

"And why not?"

"Because... because you can't do this on your own. You need me. I—"

Kalei's rage threatened to overwhelm her. This wasn't her big sister Jenna anymore. This was the teenage delinquent Shenaia, and Kalei sure as hell didn't need her help. "Really? Do I really need you? You were supposed to be my way in to Tusic, and now we know how that went, so no. I don't need you." Kalei raised the gun to Jenna's forehead.

"Hey!"

Kalei looked over her shoulder to see a man several feet behind her, completely sure of himself despite his bare, rounded torso, his flannel pajama bottoms, and a pair of slippers on his feet. She could only guess that his confidence came from the gun he was currently pointing at her. A woman shouted something from the open door to his right, and he shouted back, "Call the police, Ma." To Kalei, he said, "Let the lady—"

He didn't even finish his sentence before Jenna knocked Kalei's gun away and took off running. Kalei took another glance at the man and then ran after her.

The man shouted again, "Hey!" His gun went off, and Kalei felt a burning sensation tear through her knee. Her leg gave out and sent her sprawling to the ground.

Kalei heard the man's slippered footsteps approaching behind her. Furious, she rolled over and yelled, "Are you an idiot?"

The man stopped a couple of feet away, still pointing the gun at her. "Why were you attacking that woman?" he demanded.

"Atta—? She's Estranged! She's going to kill someone!" Kalei found her gun on the ground beside her and grabbed it.

The man shot again, hitting the pavement two feet wide of where her gun had been.

Kalei aimed her gun at the man's hairy chest and roared, "Drop your weapon!"

He shifted his stance nervously, but still managed to maintain his bravado as he bellowed, "You drop yours!"

Kalei glanced down at her knee. She couldn't see into the dark hole his bullet had ripped through her jeans, but she could feel that the wound was nearly healed already.

She said to the man, "I don't want to shoot you. Now step back inside your home and let me do my business!"

"Why do you look familiar... What? Are you a cop? Or SWORDE or somethin'? Let me see some ID!"

A man's scream tore through their argument.

"Jenna!" Kalei launched herself off the ground and took off running. She heard the man trying to keep up behind her, cursing as he discarded his slippers. She turned a corner, then another, then hit a dead end. The scream had come from the other side of the wall, but Kalei could already tell that she wouldn't be able to climb it. The cement was smooth and slick with rain. There was no way she would be able to find any footholds or traction. She bounced on the balls of her feet, pressured by urgency, but filled with frustration and indecision.

The man arrived behind her. He huffed and puffed at the entrance to the dead end, then recovered enough to shout, "This way! There's a way around."

Kalei ditched the wall and followed the man.

He took her off to the right, and after passing two more dead ends, they took another turn, which brought them to a row of townhouses. And there, at the end of the cul-de-sac, sat Jenna.

She was crouched over a man's body, crying. Bags of groceries spilled out everywhere around the man; a bright red apple had rolled away into the gutter, jars of olives were smashed and spilling out of the bags that once held them, and a box of cereal had been crushed beneath his fall, and an explosion of brown, processed morsels covered the road, growing soggy and swollen in the rain.

Jenna knelt amidst this carnage of man and food, leaning over the corpse with her face in her hands as her shoulders bounced with quiet sobs.

Kalei put away her gun and walked over. "What the hell did you do?"

Jenna raised her head from her hands, her face red and puffy. "I didn't do it, Kalei. I swear!" She sniffed, her eyes falling back to the body as she started murmuring, "I didn't do it, I didn't do it, I'm so sorry, Kalei... I didn't do it..."

Kalei followed Jenna's gaze. The man's hair fell past his ears, plastered to his face beneath the pounding rain. The muscles in his arms were lean and he sported a healthy tan... he couldn't have been any older than his mid-twenties. And he would never get a chance to see thirty.

The bare-bellied guy came up behind Kalei. "Oh shit." He raised his gun and aimed it at Jenna. "Put your hands behind your head!"

Kalei ignored him and walked over to her sister. Quietly, she declared, "This is the second time, Jenna." She reached down and grabbed Jenna by the shirt. "THE SECOND FUCKING TIME!"

Jenna was shaking from head to toe. Her face contorted as it squeezed out a stream of snot and tears.

"I didn't do it!"

"Are you shitting me right now? You have NEVER been in control, you hear me! The darkness has made you its little bitch, and now you are trying to tell me that you didn't do it?" Kalei pointed to the man on the ground. "Take a long look, Jenna! YOU did this! No one else. You! And your stupid addiction!"

Jenna stared at the body, her eyes glossed over and dazed. "I didn't do it..."

Kalei straightened up and pulled out her gun. "I'll see you later, Shenaia."

Her sister didn't protest as Kalei put the gun to the back of her head and pulled the trigger.

CHAPTER NINETEEN

Death

The vigilante was in shock at first. Then, when Kalei moved away from Shenaia, he seemed to return to his senses with renewed energy; pointing, waving his gun, shouting – the whole bit. Kalei told him to call SWORDE and ducked down a side alley to dry heave into the gutter. The image of Jenna's blood and gore on the pavement was burned into her mind's eye. When she heard the sirens coming, she wiped the spittle from her mouth, steeled herself against the image, and headed in the opposite direction. She knew that what she had done was right. Her sister had killed a man, probably not the first, but definitely the last. Kalei had made sure of that. Her action was justified. She refused to believe it any other way.

Kalei didn't know where she was heading; there was nowhere for her to go now. And she didn't care. She let her feet carry her where they wanted. When she met another person on the street, she just pulled her hood lower and changed her route. None of it mattered. Jenna didn't matter, her family didn't matter. None of it mattered. There was nothing she could do for any of them. She saw what had happened with Josh and his mom. She didn't want to lose it like he did, to endanger her husband like that. Better to just let SWORDE handle it. She was done with this game.

She didn't know how long she walked. The rain eventually slowed to a stop, and the streetlights came on, their light reaching all the way up to the heavy clouds, casting them with a faint, orange glow. But while the added light made the wet streets shine and glow, their brightness made the shadows all the darker. And Kalei's feet preferred the shadows.

Eventually, she found herself at a ladder, hanging within arm's reach and built into the side of a cement wall, extending all the way up to the roof of the relatively short building. The rungs were worn and familiar to her, and, without putting another thought to it, she began to climb.

At the top, she found that the roof was already occupied. A man sat on the far side of the small, square roof, leaning against the wall of a taller, adjacent building. It was Marley. He looked completely relaxed, legs crossed beneath him, brown jacket over his shoulders. Now that he was a Detective, he seemed to have taken the liberty of growing some scruff along his soft jaw.

Kalei stopped at the top of the ladder. "What're you doing here?"

He shrugged. "What does it look like? I'm sitting

here, waiting for you."

She stepped onto the roof, confused by his appearance. "How'd you know I'd end up here?"

Marley replied, "Don't you recognize this place? You and Fenn always hung out here. Mostly you, when you were upset, but Fenn would always find you and talk you down."

He was right. As she pushed away the haze of the day's events and finally took a clear look at her surroundings, she realized this was indeed a hangout from her childhood. It was just a few blocks from her old school, and she had spent many a summer on top of this roof. It was true what Marley had said; she had often retreated here when she was upset, but their little group had also played games here, watched the clouds from here, dared each other to stand at the edge and look down, Fenn and Kalei giggling when Marley got nauseous at the sight.

Kalei sat down beside Marley, settling her back against the bricks as he had. "Wow. You have a good memory. And good instincts too. I didn't even know I would end up here."

Marley replied humbly, "Eh, maybe that's why they gave me the job." He returned his gaze to the city stretched out beyond the roof. They couldn't see much from their short outpost; it was only about four stories up, nothing compared to the daunting heights of the adjoining buildings. But in the few gaps between the skyscrapers, she could see for miles. Kalei remembered how, on a clear day, she could see all the way to the ocean, just a speck of grayish-blue beyond the city streets.

Kalei looked down at her hands as they busily worked on a hangnail. Her swirls calmly watched the process, thick and throbbing lethargically. Finally, she asked, "Why are you here?"

He replied, "I want answers."

Kalei nodded and looked away. Then she chucked the discarded scrap of nail and leaned back again. "I don't. I'm sick of answers. And I'm sicker of questions."

"Then why'd you ask to meet me?"

Kalei rubbed a hand across her face, then she dropped it and said, "I wanted..." She looked down at her hands. "I thought I wanted to find Fenn." She took a deep breath and returned her gaze to the city view. "Now? ... I don't know..."

"You're a danger to them."

"Yup."

Marley didn't say anything for a while. Then, after several minutes, he said, "Tell me about SWORDE."

Of course. Kalei knew this wasn't a simple house call. "So you're still on duty then."

Marley smiled. "No, just sick of questions."

She knew that arguing with Marley would take more energy than she cared to spend, so Kalei explained what she knew. The sooner he got his answers, the sooner he would get off her damned roof. He asked about SWORDE, Estranged, and even Tusic, once she mentioned Landen as a player in this game. It was almost like old times. Sitting in a patrol car, shooting the breeze as they waited for a speeder to come along. They had talked about a lot of things: family, police tactics, politics. But today, it was all about the Estranged.

When she was done, Marley leaned back against the bricks and said, "I always thought SWORDE was full of super soldiers or something. People the government souped up with experimental drugs, or sent off for incredibly intense training in the mountains. When I heard on the news that you were with SWORDE, I thought, 'Hey, I guess she didn't get the bad end of that attack. Looks like she made out all right.' I guess reality isn't so nice."

"Yeah."

He turned to look at her again. "So what's the deal with Xamic?"

She fidgeted with a piece of gravel she had picked up and said, "Bad deal, that's what."

"But you said so yourself, he was at the scene of those attacks, but there's no proof he was behind them."

Now Kalei looked at him. "Hello! He snapped my neck! He caused a pile-up on the freeway and laughed about it. There's nothing good about him."

"I see your point. But why was he there? What is his motive?"

"I really don't care. I just want to see him burn in

hell." She threw her piece of gravel off the roof.

"This is why you never made Detective."

"I never wanted to be a Detective. I wanted to be a Warden."

Marley sighed. "Yeah, and now we know how that one worked out too."

Kalei scoffed. "Yeah."

"But seriously, what is Xamic's angle? We know Tusic is in it for the money and the highs, we know SWORDE just wants to keep everyone locked up behind their little gate, but where does Xamic come into this?"

"I don't know."

Out of the corner of her eye, Kalei saw Marley watching her for a few seconds, and then looked away. "Kalei, I need you to think. I need you to work with me on this. I have two dozen call girls showing up dead on the East Side and Xamic was spotted leaving the site. A bank robbery up on High Street, a small riot in the financial district— you get the picture. What I am saying is, the number of Estranged-related deaths in my city have more than tripled since Xamic showed up. I want to know why."

"Easy. He did it."

Marley sighed. "You know that doesn't work. We need motive, we need opportunity—"

"Fuck that stuff and put a bullet in his head. Problem solved."

"You know we can't do that. I'm legally bound *not*

to do stuff like that, and we don't know how to kill
him even if we could find him. See, that's the problem.
We don't know anything. We don't know where he is,
we don't know where he'll attack next, we don't even
know where he came from. I checked all of the system
records— he doesn't exist. I have Debbie going through
the archives to see if she can dig him up in the old hard
copies, but the point is, until we know more about this
guy, he's just going to keep burning through this town
like it's his playground, and I am sick and tired of him
using my friends as his playthings!"

Kalei was surprised by the anger in Marley's
voice. She met his eyes and found a burning anger and
determination she had never seen in the man before. He
was always the calm, levelheaded one; slow to anger
and always bailing out his erratic cousin and her quick-
to-cry tagalong.

She wasn't sure what to make of this new change.
She looked away and said, "Well, now you know
everything I know. Time to go out and do your detective
thing. Save the world, protect the people; it's what you
do these days, right?"

"Is that it, Kalei? Are you just going to roll over and
quit like a wounded dog?"

"Are you calling me a bitch?"

"No, I'm calling you a quitter. When you were on
the force, you were unstoppable. You didn't give a
damn about the rules, you didn't give a damn about
your safety. You just went out there and did whatever

you had to do to get the job done. You used to care about the people who live here. What is it? You become Estranged and now you don't care anymore? C'mon, Kalei. I know you. Not even becoming Estranged could rip that out of you."

Kalei watched the swirls on her nails squeeze and pulse. Her hands clenched into fists and she felt her despair coalesce into anger. He was so high and mighty. He was so sure that he knew exactly what she was going through, he was so sure he knew exactly who she was, that she was going to run into the burning building and save them all. But he was wrong. He thought she ran into those scenes to save the good guys, but the reality was, she ran in to kill the bad guys. Her hatred for Estranged, for herself, was so strong, that all she could think about was destruction. And now, she couldn't even deliver that to the people who had hurt her most. Marley could never understand that. He still had both his parents, he still had his kids, and his wife. He was Untouched. He would never know what she had been through.

"Kalei, hey, I'm serious. You've got what it takes to—"

Kalei stood up and screamed, "Shut the fuck up, Marley!"

He stood up as well, standing his ground as he said, "Kalei, I know this is hard, but—"

"What the hell do you know? You have no fucking clue what I've lost. It's not just pretty black nails and a few sweet highs, Marley. I lost *everything*. You hear me? Everything! I will never be able to kiss my husband, I will never be able to hug a friend, or hold my own child in my arms. Any chance I had at love or family is gone now, Marley. But you still have all of that. When you leave here, you're going right back to that world. Your wife is going to welcome you home, your kid is going to run into your arms, and you're going to hold him close, and that feeling will be better than any damn high my black nails could give me. Go back to your kid, give him that hug, and remember that I will never have that. *Get the fuck out of here, Marley!*"

He stared at her. Kalei could see determination still in his eyes, but the anger was replaced with pity. She hated him for that. Her fists clenched and every inch of her craved to knock those pitying eyes right out of his skull.

Quietly, he said, "I know how lucky I am. Every night when I tuck Tyrell in, I am praying that I can protect him, praying that I can keep this city from falling apart around him. But as long as Xamic is out there killing, I can't do that. Every day, the violence from Estranged in this city is escalating, and no matter how hard I try, there is nothing I can do to stop them. Do you have any idea how terrible it is? Knowing that you are completely helpless to protect your little boy? Of course you don't. There may be things I don't know, but there's a whole hell of a lot you don't know either,

Kalei. And you're not as helpless as you think. I'm helpless, Kalei, but you aren't. You haven't lost family, and you haven't lost love. Celan has always been your family, and now your brothers and sisters need you. I need you. But most importantly, Fenn still needs you. You have to put an end to Xamic so Fenn can live out the rest of his days in peace."

Kalei couldn't stand how stupid this man was. She screamed, "What the fuck kind of fairytale are you living in, Marley? Running around playing hero isn't going to change jack shit. It's all pointless. Can't you see that? Putting an end to Xamic is not going to change the fact that our city is at the mercy of Estranged, and it is just a matter of time until every one of you has nails to match mine." Marley opened his mouth to talk, but she cut him off. "Shut the fuck up and go home, Marley. Enjoy this time with your family while you've still got them, because one of these nights, hell is going to break open and we're all going to be swept in."

Marley glared back at her, all the sympathy gone from his eyes, his own fists clenching and unclenching. Finally, he said, "Fine, I'll leave you to your little Estranged world of self-pity and hellfire. But I know you still care about Celan. It's time you woke up and figured out that becoming Estranged didn't change that. As far as I'm concerned, you are still a cop, and you have been given an opportunity to do something. Remember all those rules you broke to bust into Estranged crime scenes? Well, guess what? No more rules, no more danger. You have the freedom to step in and make a difference, Kalei. You're right; if SWORDE decides to open their gates tomorrow and go nuts, I can't stop them. If Tusic decides they want to start going door to door demanding a Safety Tax, I might as well empty my bank and pray they'll feed me. I'm not Estranged. You're right Kalei, I don't know anything. I'm Untouched, and I can't do jack shit against any of them. But you can. So this is on you." He turned to leave.

"Fuck you, Marley. I'm not the only Estranged in this city. You cops have SWORDE to do your dirty work, and I'm out of that picture."

Marley turned back and yelled, "You don't get it! I don't trust SWORDE. I don't know who they are. I don't know what they do behind that gate. For all I know, they're going in and getting high with the culprits, laughing at all us weak little folk huddled outside. I don't know SWORDE, Kalei, but I know you. And right now, you're the only one I trust to help me protect my son."

Kalei glared at him, unable to find a retort, but unwilling to let go of her anger. She was still pissed as hell and convinced that his head was in the clouds.

Marley straightened his jacket, gave her one last glare, then walked over to the ladder. When he reached it, he turned and tossed something to Kalei. She caught it without taking her eyes off him.

He said, "When you get my call, you'd better damn

well be ready to answer."

Marley didn't stick around for a response; he descended the ladder.

When she heard his feet hit the pavement, she looked down at the item in her hands. It was a small, simple flip phone with just enough buttons to get the job done. She put it in her pocket and sat back down, pulling her legs up to her chest, and resting her head against her knees.

Her anger toward Marley turned into a hatred of herself. She shouldn't have attacked him like that. She shouldn't have threatened his kid and called him a moron... *Dammit, Kalei. He's your friend. He's just trying to keep his family safe, which is more than you've ever managed. Can't you understand where he's coming from?*

She had to admit, she could understand. But that understanding turned sour in her gut and sharpened the pain of her loss. Whether Marley wanted to admit it or not, she was forever alone now. She would never have a family again. The people of Celan could never fill that void.

Her grief and guilt nested in her heart and dug deeper and deeper until the hole in her chest became a festering sore. All she wanted was to take a knife and carve out that pain at its source. Or blow it out with a gun, or blow her brains out, or throw herself off the roof—anything to just put an end to it all. But even as she thought these things, Kalei's limbs turned to lead and all motivation fled her. So she just sat there with her back against the cold, brick wall.

She sat like that for a while, tilting her head to stare at her hands, to stare at the ladder, to stare at the city. As she sat there on that familiar roof, she could almost hear Fenn's voice trying to cut through her sorrow and loneliness. But thinking of him only added to the already unbearable pain.

The clouds disappeared behind the Alundai Mountains, the stars came out and spelled their sparse constellations in the sky, but still she sat there. There was nowhere for her to go. What else could she do? So she swam through her world of memories and tried to pretend the present didn't exist.

The sun had made its trip across the sky several times before the ladder rattled and gave a soft *klang*. Someone was climbing up to the roof.

Kalei's heart leapt in erratic joy, but she stuffed the emotion away. Her heart might have given in to hope, but her head knew better. Fenn wasn't coming this time.

So she waited.

A woman's face soon cleared the roof, and Kalei recognized it as Samantha, the guard from Landen's party. Kalei would have thought seeing Fenn was more likely.

Kalei gruffly demanded, "What do you want?" Her voice cracked from so many hours of disuse.

The blonde stepped onto the roof, brushed herself off, and said with a smile, "Found you!"

Kalei narrowed her eyes. "How and why?"

Samantha laughed. "You forget who I work for."

"Fine. So you're here to take me back to Landen. What the fuck could he want with me anymore?"

Samantha laughed again, a light, hearty laugh this time. "I'm not here to take you back, sweetie. Don't worry about it. This will be over quick, I promise." Samantha pulled out a gun and shot Kalei twice in the chest.

The force of the bullets at point-blank range felt like two semi-trucks hitting Kalei in quick succession, slamming her into the wall she sat against. Then the weight abruptly disappeared and Kalei pitched forward onto her hands and knees. She could feel her left lung filling with blood while pain and adrenaline blossomed through her chest.

This was exactly what she had wanted just a minute ago, and Samantha had kindly delivered it. But the sharp succession of sensations had woken up every cell in her body, and suddenly, her world came through crystal clear. She could hear the blood rattling in her throat with dizzying clarity, she could feel every sharp angle of every pebble beneath her outstretched hands, she could smell every note of car exhaust and sea salt as it was carried by the softest gust of wind. And with that lucidity, she faced the reality of leaving this world, and she knew, with resolute certainty, she wasn't ready yet. She couldn't leave Fenn alone. She couldn't see him, true, but she couldn't leave him either.

She heard the pebbles crunch beneath Samantha's feet as the woman approached.

Kalei wheezed, "You know that won't kill me."

The woman cheerfully responded, "I know." Then she took the last few steps between them, holstering her gun as she took off a glove. "But it makes you far more manageable." Samantha grabbed Kalei by the hair and pulled her head back. Samantha's cheeks were all smiles, but her eyes were cold and dead.

Kalei saw Samantha's other hand moving toward her out of the corner of her eye, but before the blonde could do anything, Kalei slammed an uppercut to into the woman's gut. Samantha took a step back and doubled over, loosening her grip on Kalei's hair. Kalei ripped her head free and followed up with a swift left hook to the cheek, sending Samantha to the ground.

Now that she was free, Kalei started to climb to her feet. But before she could get so much as a foot under herself, she was brought back down by a fierce coughing fit. She hacked and wheezed and spit out small puddles of blood as she clutched at the throbbing, bleeding holes in her chest.

Samantha managed to get up during Kalei's spasm, and came in for a second try.

Kalei spit out a final globule of blood and recovered in time to swiftly kick the blonde's feet out from under her. As the woman hit the ground a second time, Kalei climbed on top, her knees pinning the Samantha's arms to the roof, Kalei's hands around the woman's neck.

Samantha brought her own knee up and slammed it into the exit wounds on Kalei's back. The bullet holes released fresh pain and blood as Kalei cried out and Samantha used the distraction to roll her off. The woman tried to use the momentum to assert a position on top of Kalei, but Kalei caught her leg before it could crush down on her, and rolled her off again. Kalei tried to climb back on top, but Samantha was ready for her this time, and they rolled one more time before Samantha grabbed Kalei's shirt and the two women rolled off the roof.

As they fell, Kalei wrenched Samantha's hands free and gave her a hard shove. The action was instinctual; Samantha was clawing at Kalei and stabbing at her with her darkness and Kalei knew that whatever Samantha was trying to do wasn't good, but the shove ended up working in Samantha's favor. Samantha landed in a dumpster, while Kalei fell feet first into the concrete. Her legs and hips took most of the impact before the rest of her body followed, crashing flat onto her back and slamming her head into a pile of discarded newspaper. She heard snapping and cracking and crunching, but by the time the world stopped moving, she couldn't feel a thing. Kalei looked up at the blue sky, stunned.

Slowly, she became aware of someone approaching. She tried to get up; she told her legs to move, but they didn't. She looked down at her body, screaming at it to run, and discovered that everything from her stomach down no longer responded to her commands. She lay back again as Samantha approached from behind. She blinked a few times, watching Samantha pull off a glove and reach a hand down to Kalei's exposed neck. Kalei grabbed her wrist, trying to push it back, but she was unable to stop her. Samantha's hand closed around her windpipe.

Samantha's hand didn't squeeze. Instead, Kalei felt Samantha's darkness plunge into her, sharp and pointed as a blade. Kalei instinctively brought up her own darkness in defense, repelling the attack with a solid wall, but when the darkness collided with her own, Kalei heard herself cry out in pain.

Samantha pulled her darkness back, prepping for a second blow, but Kalei regained her bearings. She slammed her wall of darkness into Samantha's blade, pushing the foreign darkness out of her body. Then Kalei took a page out of Samantha's book, forming her darkness into a dagger of her own. Behind it, she put all the weight of every piece of darkness she had, every bit of anger and remorse and pain and determination – and she let loose. The dagger shot up Samantha's arm, blasted through Samantha's defenses, and pierced straight through her heart.

Something within Samantha snapped.

Then everything reversed. Samantha's body went slack and all of her darkness rushed into Kalei's as though it was a raging river flowing downstream. Kalei tried to let go of Samantha's hand, but the muscles in her arm had seized and didn't obey her orders to let go. Kalei switched to internal tactics instead, trying to fend off the oncoming torrent, but there was no stopping it. It was like she stood in front of a broken dam, trying to stop the oncoming flood with her two small hands.

The darkness swept over her, bringing with it a mixture of ecstasy and agony that was just... overwhelming would be an understatement. Kalei couldn't take it. She screamed. Visions flashed into her mind. Snippets. A gun shooting Kalei— a phone ringing– Landen's mansion exploding– someone's mother cooking breakfast in the kitchen– Flash after flash kept coming, never ceasing. The pain, the ecstasy, the images, the emotions, all of it kept coming...

And Kalei kept screaming.

CHAPTER TWENTY

Lost

It felt like an eternity. Her mind and body torn between two extremes of sensation, pain, and ecstasy waging war for her soul. The darkness churned like a storm around her, beating her down with its devastating force. She reached out to it, she tried to regain control, but it was... different. It slipped through her fingers; it moved through her in odd, undulating waves. And in those waves it brought visions – *no, memories* – memories that were not her own. Falling off a bike and scraping her knee, arguing with a woman who wasn't her mother – but she remembered her as "Mother." It was her mother. But it wasn't Kalei's mother – graduating school, going into the military... tactical training... discharge...funerals... fighting – a black-nailed hand reaching for her arm...

"Kalei. Listen to me." Kalei felt the voice before she heard it. Another darkness entered the storm, steering through her own like a boat through fog. Somehow, the new darkness maintained its shape. Her own darkness pulled and tore at it, but the foreign visitor repelled the attacks and continued its journey unscathed. Then the new entity turned the tide, reaching out into the storm like a gentle hand, corralling her unruly darkness and pulling it back to her core.

As it worked, it spoke to Kalei in a male voice, soft and weary with age. The notes of it were deep, soothing, and familiar as it said, "You need to control the darkness. Kalei."

She yelled back, "I can't!"

"Yes, you can."

"No, I can't!" She wasn't sure if she was shouting out loud, or if all sounds were captured within that dark space. "There is no way for me to grab it. There is no way for me to push it or pull it or—"

"Your darkness has changed. Samantha's darkness has diluted it and turned it into something new. It behaves differently now, that is all. You have to learn—"

"I can't!" Kalei felt herself bawling at the futility of it all.

"Stop trying to grab it."

This voice was being ridiculous. First it told her to pull it back, then it told her not to. Her emotions spun through confusion, futility, fear, and finally settled on fury. "How the hell can I pull it back without grabbing it?"

"Scoop it."

"What?"

The voice remained calm and even. "If grabbing it

isn't working, then try something else."

"I can't—"

"Scoop it."

By now, this other darkness had corralled most of her own into a pool. Kalei could breathe again. Not easily, but she could breathe. Her mind slowly began to clear as well. She thought about what he said, and she decided the voice wasn't going to relent until she tried. So, instead of reaching down to the darkness with an open hand, she closed her fingers and scooped. The darkness quivered oddly at her touch. For a second, she thought it was going to slip away from her again, but it didn't. As she pulled it closer within herself, it obeyed.

"Now, take control of your darkness."

Kalei reached out to do as he said, but when her fingers brushed against the heavy mass of her darkness, she stopped. "There's too much. I can't handle all of this."

"Yes, you can."

Her rage returned. "And who are you to tell me what I can and can't handle!"

The voice calmly responded, "I'm your grandfather. I know you can handle it."

"What?"

"I know you, Kalei, and I know the darkness. Now stop whining and take control."

Her thoughts crashed and jumbled in confusion. She tried to put together what he was saying.

"Take your darkness, Kalei!" The voice wasn't

angry, but it was stern and uncompromising.

The other entity started to withdraw. Her own darkness began falling loose of its hold; it started to spill out everywhere. "No! Don't!"

"Take it."

She scrambled to catch it all, to scoop it all in, to put it back under her control. There was so much, too much. She continued to scoop, she continued to pull it in. Any minute now, she was going to exceed her capacity and explode. She could feel her heart straining with too much darkness. Every new addition felt like it would be her last, and still she scooped and scooped, a perpetual repetition she thought would never end.

And then she had it. There was nothing left to scoop. The screaming in her body retreated, and she could breathe freely again. Kalei let out a mental sigh of relief. As she took another breath, she could feel tears of joy building in her eyes. She hadn't thought she was capable of feeling joy anymore, but there it was.

She slowly became aware of the cold cement beneath her. She could feel warm sunlight bearing down on her skin. She could hear the rustle of clothes nearby. A shoe scuffed against pavement.

But her face felt cool as something blocked the sun from her eyes. She felt a hand pull away from her arm, and the shadow retreated, allowing the sunlight to find her face as well.

Kalei slowly opened her eyes, then immediately regretted it as the bright light stabbed at her retinas.

She brought her hand up to shield her vision, squinting and blinking rapidly until she could finally see her surroundings.

She felt a hand releasing her arm as a tiny bit of foreign darkness retreated into it. She looked over, and on her right, kneeling beside her with his stoic, unreadable expression, was Terin.

CHAPTER TWENTY-ONE

Remembering

"Wait...Are you...?" Kalei sat up. She looked at her surroundings and found that she was still in the alley with the dumpster. Walker stood about ten feet off behind Terin, watching her carefully with crossed arms. Samantha's body lay beside her. Kalei's thoughts were jumbled. It was like two and two floated before her eyes, but her brain kept fumbling the four. "Did I...?"

Terin stood up. "Can I trust you?"

Kalei blinked, then squinted at him. "What?"

"You know what I did to my daughter. Your mother. You know what Josh nearly did to his mother. Can I trust you to stay away from Fenn and the children?"

His words sent her thoughts clicking back into order with sobering clarity. "Yes." The reality of what would happen if she found Fenn, the memory of what happened to her parents – for the first time in her life, Kalei was firmly resolved to never see Fenn again. Her crushed heart was a small price to pay for his life.

Still, *"You know what I did to my daughter"*... Was this some weird dream? Could he really be...?

Terin turned and walked toward the alley entrance as he said, "Let's go."

Kalei's arms felt heavy and awkward, but she complied. "So do I have to go back to solitary, or will I be free to roam Downtown?"

Terin kept walking as he said, "You're free to go wherever you want as soon as we get you back into uniform."

"What?"

"You've been reinstated to Warden."

Kalei shook her head, not sure if she heard him correctly. She glanced at Walker, and the unwavering seriousness on his face chased away all doubt.

"Who says I want to be?" Kalei took a couple steps after Terin, but then a pounding headache rushed through her skull. She reached out to the nearest wall, leaning against it as she tried to push back the onslaught.

Terin called out, "You can do that in the car."

Kalei growled through her clenched teeth, pushed off the wall, and marched past Walker on her way out of the alley.

The street was quiet, the old theater across the road sleeping in these morning hours, and the small restaurant to her left was likewise closed, both businesses seemingly recuperating before the next rush of evening traffic came for them. It was just as Kalei had always remembered it, except she had to step under a strip of "Crime Scene" tape, and at each end of the street, an officer stood watch, deterring the sparse passersby. There was also a new silver sedan parked at the curb, which Terin was already climbing into on the opposite side. Although she knew they weren't looking her way, Kalei was eager to get out of sight before the officers spotted her, so she quickly followed after Terin and climbed into the back seat.

Once inside, Kalei was relieved to be safe behind the heavily tinted windows, but the relief didn't extend to her body. Feeling heavy, Kalei leaned her head against the window, watching the buildings slide by as the car pulled away from the curb. Within her, she could feel the darkness – her new darkness – pulsing and moving. There was so much now. And every time she looked at it, she saw images that didn't make any sense.

To no one in particular, she asked, "Why do I have these... memories that aren't mine?"

She was surprised to hear the driver reply, "The darkness carries within itself not only a complete copy of your biological makeup, but it also retains memories so that when you get hurt, or shot in the head, the darkness can reconstruct you exactly as you were."

"Erit?" Kalei pulled her head away from the glass and caught a glimpse of his face in the rearview mirror. "Shit, I didn't recognize you. How are you reaching the pedals?"

Erit stiffly replied, "Don't worry about that."

Kalei chuckled as she leaned her head back against the firm, leather seat and said, "Okay, whatever. So you're saying the darkness keeps all of my memories? Why? What's the point?"

"Truly, no one can say for sure. But some scholars speculate that the darkness is something of a symbiotic parasite. Its sole purpose is to grow and perpetuate itself, which it can only do by consuming the darkness of another individual. In order to ensure optimal success in this endeavor, the darkness must maintain the health of its host."

"Okay... I'll just pretend I understood that." Kalei shook her head. "So where are these new memories coming from?"

Erit pulled the wheel right, carefully watching the pedestrians standing at the edge of the sidewalk as he made his turn. "When you killed Samantha, you absorbed every shred of her darkness and all that entails: including her memories."

Kalei looked out the window. Her eyes darted as they traced the trajectory of the passing lampposts. "So I did kill her." She turned back to Erit. "But how?"

Terin answered, "You pierced her heart."

"No I didn't. But if it's as easy as that—"

Erit interrupted, "What he means to say is, you pierced the heart of her darkness. It isn't... tangible exactly. No one has been able to establish a physical location for it within the body. It can only be found by venturing your own darkness into another person. And it can only be destroyed with the darkness."

"Oh." Kalei returned her attention to the passing

scenery. She remembered how it had felt when Samantha's heart had snapped. She remembered the rush and the dark place it had taken her... She tried not to get carsick.

Well, I think I understand why Erit and Terin wouldn't teach me this shit in basic.

"What happened to the backpack Josh had with him?"

"What?" Kalei pulled away from the window to look at Terin.

He looked at her with his usual, level stare. No new grandfather there, no touching reunion or reconciliation with the past. Just the same stoic Terin, with the same dumb questions. What the hell did she care about the kid's backpack?

She looked away and scoffed. "Josh probably dropped it during that incident with his mom. You guys found him, right? Why not ask him?"

Terin's tone gave away about as much information as his reply. "We can't."

She looked back, trying to find the answer in his weary eyes. "Why not?"

Terin met her gaze, but it was Erit who answered, "Well, technically, we could ask him. I mean, we did pick him up. It's just... it's complicated."

"What do you mean? You ask him the question, he answers. How can it be more complicated than that? Is he refusing to cooperate?"

"No, he's very compliant, but his answers... You

girls..." Erit sighed. "Allow me to put it this way. You know what I told you about the darkness being able to contain memories and reconstruct the mind? Well, in rare cases, especially when multiple head injuries are suffered within a short period of time..." Erit trailed off.

A red flag went up in Kalei's mind. Erit loved to talk about anything and everything. Stopping himself was not something he did. "What's wrong with Josh?"

Erit navigated another turn in silence. For a second, Kalei thought he wasn't going to answer. Then he said, "It seems his mind did not fully reconstruct itself ... He can talk in English and walk a straight line, all of that, but..."

Terin interrupted, "Did he tell you what was in the backpack?"

"No. Why? What's wrong with Josh?"

Josh paced the recovery room, anxiously scratching his head with his right hand while he held his left hand inches away from his mouth, the black thumbnail ready and waiting to be chewed on as needed, which seemed to be every time he paused for breath. "Trojan, bug, no... Always servers, frogs like to jump in the summer, yes, that's good..."

Kalei walked further into the room and tried to catch his eye. "Hey, Josh. Do you remember me?"

He looked at her and his eyes widened. "Frogs! Frogs are green! Frogs are green! FROGS ARE GREEN!"

Before Kalei could react to his outburst, Josh retreated to the far end of the room, muttering to the wall. Kalei was stunned. She wasn't sure if it was anger or frustration she saw in his eyes, but she felt hurt and bewildered. She didn't know if it was directed at her or... in either case, she wanted to say something, but she just... didn't know what she could say.

Terin turned and left the room, with Walker and Erit following close behind him. Kalei took one more look at Josh's quivering form, then withdrew as well.

Kalei had a hard time believing that an Estranged could be damaged like that. Josh was mentally shattered by wounds that otherwise were unable to kill him. *If I had known this could have happened, I would have put a helmet on him. I would have stopped Jenna, I—* The image of Jenna's skull falling to the cement with a fresh bullet hole on the scalp flashed into Kalei's mind.

"Wait— where is Jenna! She took a bullet to the head. She didn't... Jenna... she's not like that, is she?"

"No," Terin assured her. "She's quite all right."

"Good." The horror of what she might have done melted away with Terin's assurance. The final scraps of guilt were promptly eradicated by the recollection of *why* she had shot her sister. Kalei pushed Jenna from her mind, hoping to never see or think of her again.

She returned her attention to the people before her and found Walker already talking to Terin. "... completely useless to us. I don't know why we even bother keeping him around. He can't tell us any more

about that device than Erit can. Just let him out into
the district where he can live out whatever shred of his
miserable life he has left."

Terin replied, "I'm not going to do that. The other
inmates would be all over him. He can leave if he
wants, but we're not sending him out."

Kalei asked, "What did you need him to tell you?
You said it has something to do with that backpack he
had, right?"

Terin answered, "You already know about it. Josh
was working on Franklin's device. The same one you
were going to plug into our computers. Josh had the
latest prototype in his backpack. "

"How do you—"

Terin waved off her question. "Franklin isn't as
smart as he thinks he is."

"Okay, but what's the big deal about Franklin
getting intel on SWORDE? Sure, there will be a
political uproar and all but—"

Erit replied, "We don't think it is designed to gather
intelligence. We don't know what it is, but—"

"Yes, we do," Walker cut in. "It's some sort of
digital worm designed to take out the electric fence, the
solitary cells, and other key facilities around here."

Kalei asked, "The fence is run by computers?"

"Yes, that's how we know when the fence takes
damage, or if a section loses power."

Kalei remembered her foray through the fence with
Lecia. "You may want to get that system checked."

Erit interjected, "We don't have any evidence to support your theory that it is a worm—"

"We don't need evidence." Walker's hands adamantly emphasized his point as he continued, "We know that it needs to be hand delivered in order to work. Xamic has already proven that he can access our networks remotely. If he wanted dirt to bury SWORDE, he could get all he needed in an instant. The only systems not connected to any external network are the fence and the solitary systems."

Kalei asked, "But why would Franklin want to take out the fences? He said he just wanted to expose SWORDE. Maybe take it over himself. I don't see how releasing thousands of Estranged upon the city is going to help him."

Terin replied, "I don't think Landen is the one orchestrating this. It's true, he wants us out of the way, but I think the 'how' has fallen to Xamic. Regardless of why he made the decision, I don't think Landen realizes the danger he's put us all in."

"He might now," Kalei said.

Erit said, "Oh yes, the incident at the mansion. I'm glad you girls made it out. The stories we collected from the turned... let's just say, you managed to avoid the worst of it."

Kalei was appalled to think that the incident at the mansion could have become any worse. But if Xamic was capable of so much destruction in just one mansion... Kalei shuddered and said, "That's the least of Franklin's problems. Well, he might not have any problems anymore. He's dead."

Her companions fell silent. Even Terin looked mildly surprised, his left eyebrow raised ever so slightly higher than his right. Or perhaps it was Kalei's imagination. She couldn't be sure. Finally, Walker asked. "What are you talking about?"

"I..." Kalei studied her hands, trying to make sense of these new images, these not-memories that mingled with her own. Her swirls flexed and danced oddly across her nails. She looked back up at Terin and said, "Samantha was there when Landen confronted Xamic about the thing at the mansion..."

She remembered – Samantha remembered – Landen standing behind the desk in his Tusic office, yelling at Xamic, "What the hell do you think you are doing! You destroy my house, you kill my guests, and now I find out you are working behind my back?" Landen reached into a drawer and dropped a thumb drive onto his desk. "What the hell is this, Xamic?"

For once, Xamic wasn't laughing. He met Landen's threat with a cool, level stare. He didn't say anything.

Landen continued, "You are threatening everything we created. We made this city what it is, and now you want to tear it apart?"

Xamic replied, "*We?* You and Terin made this city, Landen, while I rotted in the ground. I made *you,* Landen. I made you Estranged, I gave you the tools to establish Tusic, I handed this city to you on a platter.

And you repaid me with eighteen years in a six-foot grave, waking up with dirt in my lungs, suffocating, never free to just die, cursed by my own creation to wake up again and again..."

"I had no idea what happened to you. It took me years to find—"

"You didn't even start looking until your little girl fell through! What if she had lived to be eighty, Landen? Would you have waited that long to dig me up? You and Terin stabbed me in the back, after everything I did for you!"

Xamic was suddenly behind Landen, an arm around his throat in a chokehold. He leaned in and said in a low growl, "I am going to enjoy tearing your empire apart, brick by brick."

Landen's eyes grew wide. Then Xamic released him, and the entrepreneur fell to the floor, dead.

Kalei realized Landen hadn't given Samantha the order to kill her. It had been Xamic.

She looked up at Terin and somehow knew that the message was meant for him. "Xamic killed Landen. He said he is going to dismantle the Tusic Empire."

Terin's eyes grew distant. Kalei thought he would say something, but Walker interrupted, "Why would he have it out for Franklin? All of our intel indicates that the two were working together. Why would Xamic choose now to take out Tusic?"

Terin looked away and studied the wall. "This obviously happened several days ago, and no word of

Landen's death has gotten out yet. If Xamic is keeping up the ruse that Landen is still alive, then it means he's using their resources." He looked back at the group. "You are not to breathe a word of this to *anyone*. If word gets out that Landen Franklin was killed by an Estranged, there will be panic in the city. Walker, rewrite the security protocols for all vital systems—"

"What! Do you have any idea—?"

Terin ignored him. "Kalei, go with Erit. He'll help you sort things out with those memories."

"I don't want to sort things out. I—"

"After that, you and Erit will track down any information you can get on Xamic, Tusic, and the device."

Kalei knew she had no grounds to argue with him. Terin was still giving her what she wanted, even if he did tack on the stupid, tedious task of messing with memories. So she relented. "Fine."

Erit started to lead her back to their old classroom, but Kalei refused. If she was going to be slotted back into the role of student, she was going to need some air. They went to the roof instead.

Once there, Erit settled himself on top of an old vent and asked, "How many of Samantha's memories can you access?"

Kalei sat down on a sturdier vent across from him and sighed. "I don't know. All of them?"

Erit raised an eyebrow. "Can you remember what

she had for breakfast yesterday?"

Kalei paused and shuffled through the back of her mind. "No."

"Then you don't have all of them. It will take some time, though. Some people never recover all of the latent memories, but don't be surprised if new memories start showing up from here on out. The trick is to keep them apart from your own."

Kalei looked out across the rooftops. "Why does that matter?"

"If you hold any value for your sanity, it matters quite a bit. Now, think back. Can you remember where Samantha was last month?"

"I don't even know where *I* was last month." Kalei looked back to Erit. "What month is it now anyway?"

Erit smiled encouragingly. "I'm sure Samantha knew."

Kalei sighed again. "Really?"

"Yes. See if Samantha recalled what month it is."

Kalei focused her gaze on a grey, crumbling building across the way. Then, she retreated from the visible world and focused her attention inward, digging and searching for the answer. It had to be in her head somewhere... but the harder she searched, the more she found nothing. "This is bullshit!"

Erit didn't waver. "Just keep trying."

The answer was August. Kalei didn't figure it out until September. Luckily, Samantha's death certificate read "August twenty-eighth."

After her sessions, Kalei usually tracked down Terin. The first time she saw him, she claimed she wanted to know more about Xamic, but she really just wanted to know how her family was doing.

He told her what she wanted to know, that Xamic was an unrepentant frat-boy genius who lived only for the high. Then, without any further prompt from Kalei, he told her that her family was safe. After that, she dropped the act and just asked him every time she saw him. He never gave any details, but he always told her they were safe. After a while, the conversations became a simple glance and a reassuring nod. Kalei could call Terin a lot of things, but she could never call him a liar.

"Grandpa" was the weirdest name to call him. She was still trying to wrap her head around that one.

At first, she was revolted to be related to the man who had killed her parents. But it made sense. The love in his eyes when he saw Mom. The hug. The tears of joy on his face. The sheer horror when he'd realized what he had done. It made sense. And now she knew why he was so adamant about keeping her away from Fenn and the girls. She got it now. And she could respect what he'd been through. She couldn't forgive him, but she could respect him.

Kalei wondered if Jenna knew, but she didn't bother to ask. She never saw her sister and she never asked to find out where she was. It was better that way. Kalei didn't want anything to do with Jenna after what she had done.

When Kalei wasn't working on her memories, or just sitting around wondering how the hell she ended up here in the first place, she found Erit and helped him track down information. There weren't many leads. Mostly just addicts who would tell them anything they wanted to hear, and dead end tips called in by concerned civilians. After a while, Erit pushed Kalei to spend more time sorting out Samantha's memories. The more their leads fell through, the more he became convinced that Samantha could provide key information.

During one of these solitary memory meditations, Mar came up and paid Kalei a visit. She asked, "No hard feelings about leaving you in that cage, right?"

Kalei shrugged. "You were just keeping yourself out of trouble. I can't hold that against you."

"Damn right." Mar sat down next to her. "You know, things have gotten a lot stupider since you left. I got assigned to a team of fucking kids. One of them spends so much time focusing on his nails that he damn near walks into a wall if you don't steer him in the right direction. I'm trying to get Terin to reassign me to whatever you're working on."

Kalei was touched that Mar wanted to work with her again, but she was also a bit surprised. "Why do you want to work with us? You don't even know what we're working on."

"I don't care. Whatever it is, I'm sure it's a hell of

a lot better than patrolling the fence with a bunch of piss-heads." Mar leaned back. "So, you visit your sister yet?"

Kalei gave Mar a sideways glance. "Since when do you know I have a sister?"

"Hell, everyone knows. I can't believe I didn't see the family resemblance sooner. But hey, your sister don't make it easy with all her crazy haircuts and makeup. Anyway, Shenaia, Jenna, whoever the hell she is, I hear she's got a pretty sweet room down on the third floor. Rumor has it she's got—"

Kalei cut Mar off and stiffly replied, "No. I haven't been to visit her. Now bug off. I've got meditating to do."

Mar grunted, bemused. "That's harsh."

Kalei didn't see the humor in it. "You want to talk about harsh? Some man is dead because of her! Who knows what kind of family he left behind, or how many people will miss—" Kalei cried out as a shooting pain sliced through her skull; it felt like an ice pick had just emerged in the core of her brain and was trying to make its way to her forehead.

"What is it?"

Kalei held up a hand to shut up Mar. One of Samantha's memories was working its way through. Kalei's own memory of the man lying on the ground shifted to one of the man standing up. But he was lying down – now he was standing up – down – up...Her mind fought the contradiction, but another burst of pain hammered into the invisible icepick. With a mental shove, Kalei forced the two memories apart. She tried to focus on the new one— to pull it through gently before it ripped itself through whatever barrier her mind had erected between herself and Samantha.

The dead man was standing; talking, even. He seemed wary as Kalei-Samantha asked him for directions. The man tried to brush her off, but Samantha pulled off a glove and showed him clear nails, assuring him that she was harmless. At that, the man relaxed a bit.

Samantha put the glove into her pocket and asked if the man lived nearby. He said he lived just up the street, and asked her to repeat where it was she was trying to go. Samantha smiled and said that he could give her directions on the way, and offered to help him carry his groceries home. She could see his well-toned muscles bulging beneath the weight of so many bags. The man politely refused, noting that he only had a couple of bags.

That was when Jenna showed up. She emerged from a side street, haggard and frantic. When she saw the two on the sidewalk, she gave a painful grunt and bit down on her fist. But then she recognized Samantha. "Hey, can you hook me up? I need—"

While the man with the groceries was distracted by Jenna's arrival, Samantha's ungloved hand shot out and closed around the man's arm. He screamed.

CHAPTER TWENTY-TWO

Sisterly Love

"Where is Jenna?" Kalei stood up and waited for Mar to answer.

"Last I heard, she was in her room on the fifth floor." Kalei started toward the stairwell. Mar called out, "I think it's room 520!"

Kalei raced down several flights of steps, down the hallway, past a half dozen doors, and stopped outside door 520. Kalei raised her hand to knock, but she hesitated, unsure of what she was going to say. She let her eyes linger on the bronze numbers tacked to the door. They still held a dull gleam, but the 2 hung upside down, making it look more like 550. Kalei took a deep breath. She decided to wing it. She knocked.

Jenna's voice called out from the other side, "Yeah?"

Kalei placed her hand on the cold doorknob and opened the door.

The room was a bit smaller than their old rooms, but the furniture was much nicer. There were far fewer scratches in the wood of the nightstands, and the upholstery on the chair in the corner was almost entirely intact, aside from a minor rip on the side. If someone bothered to give the room a good dusting, it could have passed for a real hotel room.

Jenna sat on the bed, legs crossed beneath her as she looked out the window. It wasn't a scenic view of the mountains or the ocean, but Kalei could see most of Downtown, and even the fence and parts of the grey zone. It wasn't necessarily a bad view, so long as one didn't mind the fact that most of the buildings in sight looked like something out of the apocalypse.

Jenna glanced over her shoulder to see who it was, but when her eyes alighted on Kalei, they turned grim. Jenna snapped, "Fuck off!" Then she looked away to the window again.

Kalei took a deep breath, knowing full well she had deserved that, and also knowing full well that she couldn't leave until she made amends. She shook off the not-so-warm welcome and said, "I just wan—"

Jenna turned her head, just far enough that her ear faced Kalei. "Didn' your foster mother teach you manners? I know Mom did. Get da fuck out of here!"

"Hey! I'm here to apologize!"

Jenna spun around on the bed. "Oh really? For what? Shooting me in the back of the head or leaving my body in the street?"

"I left you with—"

"Who? Who would my dear sister entrust with watching over my fucking corpse? Please, tell me. 'Cuz there sure as hell weren't no one there when I woke up."

Kalei hesitated. "He must've... I'm sorry, I—"

"No! Don't lie to me! You ain't sorry for shit. As far as you're concerned, I killed that man. As far as you're concerned—"

"You didn't kill him."

Jenna froze. "What?"

"I know you didn't kill him. I saw Samantha's memory. You—"

Surprise turned to confusion. "Samantha's memory?"

"Her memory. I—" Kalei sighed. "I just know, alright? And I'm sorry I blamed you."

Jenna stood up and took a step closer to Kalei. "No. You know what? It doesn' even matter that you blamed me. You know what pisses me off? That you write me off as some junkie. That you think it's okay to ditch me in the gutter the second I stop playing by your rules. I'm your sister, Kalei!"

"You're trying to turn this all on me? You *were* a junkie! You should have seen yourself: the way you were stumbling, pawing on Samantha to hook you up. You were nothing but a blubbering, desperate bitch trying getting her hands on another high!"

"Oh really? If that's the case, then why didn't I kill all those people in the street! Huh? Why didn't I just jump you and take what I wanted! We both know I'm stronger than you, Kalei."

Kalei scoffed. She couldn't believe what she was hearing. "You are nowhere *near* as strong as me! You can't even handle your own darkness, and you think you're stronger than me? I hate to break it to you, big sis, but I passed you by a long time ago."

"Is that what you think?" Jenna stepped back and spread her arms wide. "Look at me, Kalei. Do I look desperate? Do I look like a junkie? Or do I look like I'm in control?"

Jenna's eyes were abnormally bright, but clear. Her arms were rock steady as she held them out. Jenna dropped her arms and showed Kalei her nails, which sported five wheels, spinning out of control, but still perfectly maintained.

"You think you're all high and mighty following Terin's puritanical rules. Yeah, I know Gramps has his reasons for bein' that way, but I'll tell you what. I'm not sober! And I'm not high as a fucking kite either! I have this under control. And you know what? I'm not the one suffering. Physically, emotionally—the darkness can't touch this."

Kalei crossed her arms, glaring at her sister. "And what happens when it wears off? What happens when you need more?"

"Look around you! We're in fucking Downtown! If you haven't noticed, they've got Estranged on every fucking block of this neighborhood!"

"So what? You just stay in the area, taking and taking until nothing will satisfy you. What happens then? You take some more? You're forgetting, I was a fucking cop! I've seen this game before, Jenna. You've seen it too. You may be all fine and dandy right now, but it will catch up with you and then you will be in more pain than I ever was!"

"This isn't just some drug, Kalei. This is the darkness! It's better! We get higher, we get stronger, we don't ever fade away! We're fucking young forever! And you know what? So long as I don't touch an Untouched, I'm harmless! The darkness is harmless! It's not hurting us, Kalei; it's helping us. You just can't see it."

Kalei clenched her jaw and unfolded her arms. "Do you want to be like Samantha? Killing fucking civilians because a regular day in the park just won't satisfy you?"

"I will NEVER be like that! You just can't see it."

"Really? I think I'm seeing things quite clearly, sis. Remember that little Untouched kid from the Call? Do you remember what happened to him? He sure as hell ain't going off to college, I can tell you that much. You need to take a long look in the mirror, sister: you don't have jack shit under control."

Jenna's face turned a new shade of red, her mouth forming a furious rebuttal. But Kalei wasn't interested in hearing her response. She turned and left.

CHAPTER TWENTY-THREE

Discovery

Kalei threw herself into her work. It quickly became apparent that finding any information on Xamic's plan was a lost cause, so Kalei, Mar, Erit, and Walker switched gears to focus on finding ways to counter the threat. Counter-intelligence, increased screenings for anyone entering the building, anything that could help them stop the device before it got to them. A second and third terminal were added to the computer room so that the team could conduct their investigations while Jenna continued the day-to-day monitoring on the main terminal.

Kalei pretended that Jenna didn't exist. The treatment was mutual.

Whenever she wasn't working on the terminal, Kalei was meditating on Samantha's memories. It was weird whenever a memory involved herself. She remembered E-night, seeing herself, seeing Kalei walking up the path to Landen's mansion, and as she watched Kalei, she remembered criticizing her lack of posture and messy hair before recognizing Jenna and opening the gate. Coming out of those memories was always incredibly disorienting, so she took special care to keep them separate from her own, lest she lose hold of her identity.

Sometimes the memories came as gently as remembering where she left her keys. Other times, Kalei blacked out and woke up with her face pressed into the gravel of the roof, while memories of fights or traumatic events still ran before her eyes. Elaborate torture, sick punishments, twisted games; Landen lived in one fucked-up world, and Samantha had a front row seat to it all.

But in either case, Kalei had almost no control over which memories came back. Sure, sometimes she could nudge her thoughts into a certain direction, but more likely than not, the memory that came back would be as benign a new pair of shoes, or the latest gossip on Katy's romance with Steve. Kalei usually left the roof feeling absolutely ill from being immersed in that woman's life.

Kalei walked into the computer room and sat in a chair next to Erit. Walker was probably out running an errand for Terin, while Mar was most likely smacking some new recruits around. Jenna still didn't exist in her corner.

Erit asked, "Any progress?"

Kalei was thoroughly frustrated. Days were slipping through her fingers, and all she could come up with was, "Well, Maya finally launched her new line of perfume last fall. Oh, and Landen likes his rum on the rocks."

Erit laughed. "It seems I've had a bit more luck on my end. Jenna pointed me to a conversation between a couple of Landen's subordinates, and it sounds like Xamic is converting one of Landen's condominiums into a sort of luxury barracks. Open bar, massage parlor, the works. He's also doubled the Tusic patrols in the city."

Kalei furrowed her brows, her frustration making friends with anxiety in the pit of her stomach. "So, playing the sugar daddy even as he puts them to the grindstone, eh?"

Erit leaned back in his chair. "It gets worse. He's carting a number of Untouched into the barracks. The few that come out are turned. And, well, the recruitment process is engineered for the enjoyment of the turners, not the turnees."

Kalei's felt a touch of bile rising in the back of her throat. "What is Xamic getting at? Is he trying to build a clientele? An army? Shit, how can we stop him when we aren't even in the game?"

Erit replied, "Truly, I do not know."

Kalei closed her eyes and took a deep breath. "Well, regardless of the bigger picture, we need to stop to this Untouched trafficking before it goes any further. Maybe if we're lucky, we'll pick up more information on Xamic's plan before it blows up in our face."

"Indeed. I've already put word to the police to increase their patrols, and we have the local news stations doubling their 'Estranged Awareness' bulletins. Terin has even allowed me to send some SWORDE patrols into the city to support the police."

"Do you think that's wise? Sending Estranged, even trained Estranged, to patrol the city?"

"Wise or not, the police patrols won't do any good unless they have teeth, and our Estranged can be those teeth."

The thought of more Estranged in the city made Kalei uncomfortable. She had to agree with Erit, though; it was the only thing they could at the moment.

"Okay, you seem to have all that under control then. What can I do? Besides meditating on prissy lady's favorite brand names."

"Well, until we can pin down the 'why' of Xamic's activities, I will need aid pinpointing the 'where' of this supposed Ruffian Paradise. Landen owned a plethora of condominiums in this city, so learning its exact location is proving to be more difficult than I had originally anticipated."

"Start with the ones in T-Town. Landen favored those because they gave him easy access to City Hall and the financial district. Let me give Marley a call and tell him to keep an eye out. He might have heard something about those condos that we haven't." Kalei stood up to leave, then turned back to Erit, "Oh yeah, and any word on Lecia yet?"

"No. Unfortunately, the girl is still missing."

Kalei paused. *Where could she be?* Kalei felt her phone in her pocket and returned her attention to the work at hand. "Alright. I'll start looking for her again when I get back." She pulled out her cellphone and made her way to the elevator. While she waited for it to come back down from the fifteenth floor, she called back to Erit, "Hey, how did you pick up that conversation anyway? Ear cams don't have mics."

"The smoking buddies didn't take notice of an Estranged passed out across the street. Their faces were perfectly visible for any passing lip-reader to discern."

"And I take it lip-reading is one of your many secret talents?"

Erit smiled. "Indeed."

Once outside, Kalei dialed Marley. The two had been back on good terms since she returned to SWORDE. When she passed on Terin's frat-boy description of Xamic, Marley got all excited about building a profile and pressed her to ask Terin for more information. Terin wouldn't talk any more on the subject, but then Kalei had passed the phone over to Erit and the two had a nice long chat while Kalei left to meditate.

Otherwise, he had been a valuable asset to their investigation. Since SWORDE didn't have the manpower to track down all the leads in the city, Marley usually tracked the information down for them and sent out BOLOs whenever SWORDE needed it. Kalei always tried to return the favor. More than a couple cases had been cleared off his desk, thanks to an anonymous video file.

"Hey, Marley. It's me. I've got word Xamic is collecting his people into some sort of barracks. Any chance you can keep an ear out and let me know if you get a location?"

"Sure thing. Any word on Lecia?"

"No. I'm guessing that means no luck on your end either?"

"Nope." Marley sighed. "Damn. Y'know, this could've been a hell of a lot easier if Lecia had been a normal girl with a normal job. But nope, not our Lecia. I have reports of her spending time in every corner of the city, with no rhyme or reason. Even her contacts at the University had no idea where she could be. I'm telling you, Kalei, this case is a nightmare. I've tracked down every lead I can think of, and I still don't even know *when* she disappeared."

"Yeah, I know. But we can't give up on her."

Marley sighed. "I haven't given up yet. I just wonder if it's already too late, y'know?"

Kalei rubbed her head. "Yeah... Anyway, anything new on Xamic?"

She heard Marley's chair squeak as he shifted positions. "Not really. We haven't had any new Xamic-related attacks since last Friday. I've been giving myself a headache trying to figure out what the hell he's been up to, but now that you've mentioned this barracks thing, maybe he's had his hands full with that?"

"Let's hope so."

There was a brief silence. Kalei found herself thinking about the Untouched who had been hauled off to the new Tusic barracks. "Well, I wouldn't say you have had no 'Xamic' attacks. Apparently, he's been kidnapping Untouched and bringing them back to the barracks for his men... make sure you watch yourself, Marley."

Marley was silent for a moment. He quietly replied, "I always do." Kalei heard him take a deep breath before he continued, "So, any ideas on how to take him down when he exposes his hide again?"

"Other than tying his ankle to a rocket and launching his ass into space? Not a clue."

Marley laughed. "Okay, well, if you come up with anything better than that, be sure to give me a call."

"Of course. I'll talk to you later, Marley."

"Later."

Kalei returned to the computer room and sat down at her usual terminal in the corner. Walker now sat on the opposite side of Erit, working on his security re-writes for Terin.

While Kalei waited for the computer to cue up the latest surveillance feeds, the image of Xamic getting shot at E-night buzzed through her head, gnawing at her like an unfinished puzzle. Turning to Erit, she said, "You know what? Maybe you can tell me, Erit: how does Xamic do that thing where he takes a bullet to the head and laughs it off?"

Erit chuckled. "I've never heard it put that way before. It's nothing too incredible, really. Quite simply, he has a lot of darkness."

"That's not much of an explanation. C'mon, Mister Professor, give me the full write-up."

Erit made one more click on whatever he was working on and turned to face Kalei. "Truly? You're giving me full leave to lecture? Well, I suppose I'd better start talking before you reconsider. To begin, you know that the darkness is the energy behind healing your wounds, correct?"

"Yeah." Kalei was mildly offended he had to ask.

"Well, the greater the amount of darkness you have within you, the faster those wounds heal. Of course, if you don't have a lot of darkness, you can still take advantage of this concept by concentrating your darkness around the wound. It's quite handy, really."

Kalei was mildly surprised. "Why the hell was Estranged First Aid 101 not included in basic training?"

Erit returned to his computer and typed a few commands as he replied, "Yes, well, we still consider it to be 'advanced' training, as there are some other applications for the technique that could be quite disastrous in the wrong hands."

Kalei raised an eyebrow. "Such as?"

Erit fell silent for a moment as he finished his typing, then he turned back to Kalei again. Using his hands to animate, he said, "One particularly useful application is to use the darkness to enhance performance. By concentrating the darkness around certain muscle groups, strength and agility will see drastic improvement. Run faster, jump higher; anything you can think of. I saw the reports from your run with Xamic through the train yard, and I can assure you, Xamic's ability to vault a railcar does not come naturally."

Kalei mulled over the idea. It sounded like something out of a superhero movie, but she had to admit, she was intrigued.

Erit returned to his work as he said, "I can see you are considering trying it out for yourself. Feel free. It really is an invigorating experience, and one I am sure you will find quite useful."

Kalei was eager to take Erit up on the offer, but she knew Terin wouldn't be pleased to find out she was shirking her duties to go play. Hell, she wouldn't be pleased. People needed her right now. So, she turned back to her computer and moved the mouse to banish the screen saver. She would have time to try it out the next time she went to the roof to meditate.

But when her computer woke up, she found several of the windows blank. She gave her monitor a smack to the frame. "Some of my cams aren't coming up."

"Don't do that!" Walker scowled at her. "Some cams will be going off and on while I rewrite the systems."

Kalei dropped her hand away from the screen and replied, "But I thought the security systems weren't on the network. How can it interfere with the cameras?"

Walker growled at his computer. "It's a mess. Don't ask."

The routine continued, and the air began to cool as fall approached. The roof was especially cold, but Kalei didn't mind throwing on a jacket to go up there. It was peaceful on the roof, perhaps the most peaceful place in all of Downtown. Occasionally, she heard a shout or a siren below, but the distance muted the sounds down to a whisper, and the wind usually kicked up to carry the lower notes away. It was nice.

Until she sat down to meditate. The meditations were really just redundant, boring, and exhausting at this point. All they really did was feed her frustration, making her feel like a hamster spinning in its wheel while the world outside slowly moved along the road to destruction, a journey she was helpless to avert so long as she was stuck in her wheel. But the harder she worked, the faster the wheel spun, and the faster she went nowhere. All the while, thoughts of Xamic and his kidnapped Untouched plagued her, taunting her powerlessness. She wanted to scream.

When she became especially restless, she began experimenting with what Erit had told her about using the darkness to enhance muscle performance. It was one of the few areas where she could make progress.

She started with wall sits. Without trying anything, she could last about a minute and a half before tiring. Then, when she started shifting the darkness to her quads, she could last... well, she never really found out. She got bored after twenty minutes and went back to meditating.

After that, Kalei started testing out her speed. She found a stopwatch in the rec room and timed how long it took her to run from one end of the roof to the other. Just over eighteen seconds. It wasn't a bad time. Then she pooled the darkness throughout her legs. She ran again.

She had barely made it off the line when she had to stop because her stomach and back weren't strong enough to hold her up against the new speed, nearly sending her over backwards.

With a bit more concentration and some proper adjustments, she made the sprint in eight seconds flat. She couldn't keep the grin off her face. She sprinted across the roof for another hour before pulling herself away to get back to work. It wasn't an easy choice.

She had just sat down at her terminal when Jenna said, "Kalei."

Kalei ignored her.

"Your friend Lecia was found outside the gate. We've got a couple of Wardens bringing her into the district now."

Kalei turned around. "Why are they bringing her into the district?"

"Looks like she's Estranged."

"What?"

Jenna apathetically replied, "You heard me."

"Shit." Kalei jumped out of her seat and headed over to the elevator. "Tell them to bring her to headquarters." She hit the button.

"Roger that," Jenna replied as she went back to work.

Downstairs, Kalei pulled out her phone and dialed Marley.

He answered, "Hey, perfect timing! I just found Xamic's Grunt House."

Kalei almost dropped the phone. "Really?"

"Yeah, it's a great location too. He used the Luxury Grove Condos in the heart of Tech Town. That puts him right in the middle of everything. The Celan Bank, the State Supreme Court, the Trade Building. He can have guys at any one of those places in under five minutes if someone gives him trouble. It's ingenious, really."

"Not sure I'd call it that." Kalei was only mildly pleased to discover that her guess about the barracks being in T-Town was correct.

"Eh, call it what you will. I'll let SWORDE take over from here." Kalei heard Marley's chair rolling and squeaking as he stood up. "So, anyways, what were you calling about?"

Kalei stepped out onto the sidewalk, watching the end of the street where she knew the truck would be coming from. "It's about Lecia. We found her."

"Seriously? Alive, I hope."

"Depends on your definition."

"Then define it for me."

Kalei sighed and ran a hand through her hair. "She's a fucking Estranged."

Marley sighed. "Damn. Well, we knew this would happen one day. She couldn't play with fire forever."

"Yeah." Kalei heard an engine approaching. "Listen, she's here. I'll call you later, alright?"

"Alright."

Kalei hung up as the van pulled around the corner. She took a step back from the curb in case Jarmel was driving.

Luckily, it wasn't Jarmel, because the van stopped neatly alongside the curb. The driver, still in full Warden black, got out, and Kalei asked, "How's she doing?"

"A bit shaken, to say the least. She— well, come see for yourself." Kalei recognized Usha's voice and followed her to the back of the van.

As they arrived, a second Warden opened the door. There was Lecia, hunched over on one of the bench seats. Her usual plethora of layers were absent in lieu of a simple yellow T-shirt over a pair of jeans. She looked a bit dirty, a bit dazed, but otherwise unharmed. Lecia blinked against the light as Kalei carefully took her arm and led her out of the van. As she stepped onto the street, the woman slowly raised her head, staring at the crumbling skyscrapers, turning her head as she tried to take them all in.

Kalei asked, "Lecia? How you feeling?"

Lecia pulled away from the sky and looked at Kalei. "Kalei?" Her voice sounded dreamy. Her eyebrows came together, and then relaxed when she recognized Kalei's face. "It's you."

Seeing Lecia so disconnected bothered Kalei. She wasn't sure if Lecia was just high, or if she was seriously hurt like Josh had been. Kalei calmly persisted, "How are you feeling?"

Lecia's eyebrows puckered again, perplexed. "Feeling?"

The knot of concern in Kalei's gut tightened. She took Lecia's hand into her own gloved one and said, "Come on. Let's go find Erit and get you all sorted out." She waved off the other two Wardens and they peeled away to return to their other duties.

"Okay." Lecia followed, her gait measured and softly rolling as though she were walking on a cloud.

Inside, Kalei asked the Warden at the front desk where Erit was. She replied, "Just saw him go into the elevator not two minutes ago."

Kalei thanked her and led Lecia up to the decrepit, golden doors, pressing the "up" button a couple times. As they waited, Kalei realized that this was Lecia's first time in SWORDE HQ. The woman should be ecstatic, jumping with joy at this opportunity. She had wanted to see the inside of HQ for ages. But Lecia just stood quietly beside her, her mouth slightly open as her eyes lazily traced the trajectory of some invisible sprite. Kalei jabbed the button a few more times.

At last, the elevator dinged and the doors dragged open. A few uneasy moments later, the pair stepped out into the computer room.

"Hey, Erit, can you check Lecia out for me?"

Erit turned around. "Sure. What seems to be the problem?"

Kalei looked at Lecia, whose eyes still lazily danced around the room, heedless to its occupants. "I don't know. She just seems... out of it."

Erit stood up and walked over to them. "It's possible she is simply adjusting to her new... state. But, nonetheless, I will take a look." He looked into one eye, then the other. He gently picked up one hand and looked at her solid black nails. Lecia was oblivious to the inspection. Her eyes had finally focused on something behind Erit, and a crooked grin crept along her face, as though she had discovered a hidden paradise.

Erit asked, "Lecia? My name is Erit. Nice to make your acquaintance."

Lecia's head slowly cocked to one side, her eyes still gazing in the distance. "Funny."

Erit raised an eyebrow. "I beg your pardon?"

"Your words are funny."

Erit laughed. "Well, it seems you have noticed my accent."

Lecia ignored him.

Erit released her hand and faced Kalei. "I am sure she is fine. I recommend we take her to a recovery room, allow her a few hours to adjust, and then check in to see if we can help her become acquainted with her new life."

Kalei replied, "But this doesn't seem normal. Lecia may be stupid, but not like this. How do we know she— How do we know she isn't like Josh?"

"We cannot be certain. Everyone adjusts to the transition differently, and it is quite possible she will snap out of this. All we can do is give her time."

Lecia muttered, "I... have something to do."

Kalei looked up and found that Lecia had wandered over to Erit's terminal. She held something small in her hand, something like... a thumb drive. The same thumb drive Landen had confronted Xamic with. Kalei recognized it by the Tusic logo on the front, and a small chip missing out of the side of the plastic case.

Kalei sprang for the terminal. "Lecia! No!"

Before she could make it across the room, Lecia plugged it in.

CHAPTER TWENTY-FOUR

Reunion

"Shit!" Kalei pushed past Lecia and pulled the drive out of the computer. Still holding it in her left hand, she reached for the mouse and woke up the computer, intent on stopping whatever program might have been activated.

Walker rushed over. "What happened?"

Kalei handed the thumb drive to him. "She plugged this in. Could it be the worm?"

"Shit! Jenna, did anything happen on your end?" Walker went to the back of Erit's computer and started unplugging network cables.

"Nope. Nada."

Meanwhile, Kalei looked over the windows on the screen. Nothing new seemed to be open, and she didn't even know where to start looking for a worm. But before she could do anything, Walker came back and shooed Kalei away from the computer, sitting down in her place and opening programs she had never seen before.

"Is that the worm program?"

"No. Now stop asking stupid questions and let me do my job."

Erit joined them and asked, "What's the damage, Walker?"

Walker was quiet for a moment as he typed like mad, windows opening and closing on the screen. And then he said, "Nothing. I can't find anything."

"Maybe I pulled it out in time?" Kalei suggested.

"Maybe, but I won't know for sure until I run a full diagnostic on the system."

"Okay." Erit turned to Jenna. "Call back all the Wardens in the field. Tell them to establish a full perimeter within the fence and double the guards on solitary."

"Which? We only have enough people to do one or the other," Jenna pointed out in dull pessimism.

Erit cursed eloquently beneath his breath. "Focus on the gate and the fence. We'll provide back-up to solitary as needed."

"It still won't be a full perimeter. We'll only get about half the fence."

"Just do it. Kalei, grab Lecia. We need to go find Terin."

Lecia was still blissfully ignorant of the panic going on around her, and she readily followed along at Kalei's suggestion. They found Terin on the third floor, checking in on some new recruits as they learned to spar.

Erit interrupted and pulled Terin into the hall,

explaining the situation. When Erit mentioned Lecia's role in inserting the thumb drive, Terin walked over to her and put one hand on her left temple, closing his eyes as he did so. Kalei started to say something, but her phone went off.

Annoyed at the timing, Kalei stepped away to answer it. She didn't even bother checking the caller ID; only one person knew her number. "Marley, this had better be important, because—"

"It is. Xamic was just spotted in Tech Town. Reports say he's standing on the fountain outside the entrance to Stanley Park, yelling at pedestrians about a party. Frank says he looks like a freaking frat boy trying to get everyone pumped for homecoming. We have people heading there now, but we don't want to make a move until SWORDE gets here."

"Got it." Kalei moved to hang up, but Marley said, "Hey, how's Lecia doing?"

"It's–complicated... I'll see you in T-Town." She hung up the phone. "Terin, Xamic's been spotted outside Stanley Park."

Terin opened his eyes and slowly pulled his hand away from Lecia, showing no indication that he had heard her. He said, "Lecia should be fine now. Have someone take her to a recovery room." He turned and started walking to the stairs, Erit following after him.

Kalei shouted, "Hey! Where are you going?"

"T-Town."

Kalei caught a passing Warden and instructed him

to take Lecia to a Recovery Room. Lecia still seemed confused, but her eyes were clear and beginning to focus. Kalei chased after Erit and Terin. "What was wrong with her?"

"Xamic."

"Yes, I know we are going to see Xamic, but what was wrong with her?"

"I told you. Xamic is what was wrong with her."

"You mean he—"

"She's fine now. Get suited up before I leave without you."

Kalei took off to do as she was told. Time had finally run out; they were about to get their answers.

SWORDE responders pulled up to Stanley Park in two vans, blocking each end of the street as a crew of ten fully suited and armed Wardens stepped out. They took up positions behind the row of parked cars lining the outer edge of the park, training their weapons on Xamic, watching him carefully.

Kalei climbed out of the cabin of the first van, along with Terin and Erit, and she followed the two not-so-young men as they moved to stand behind the Wardens. Terin didn't crouch behind the car or pull out a weapon. He simply stood there in the street, not even suited up, with Erit and Kalei flanking him on either side. Even Erit had neglected to put on Warden gear, leaving Kalei to feel very out of place with her two companions.

But that was the least of her anxiety. As she looked

across a mere fifty feet to the fountain guarding the park's pedestrian entrance, she saw Xamic standing on the stonework, grinning ear to ear like a boy who knew it was his birthday. Kalei swallowed and fought off the urge to duck down behind the cars with the other Wardens.

Xamic saw the show and clapped his hands together. "You made it! Wow." Xamic fixed his eyes on Terin, his mood becoming grim. "You finally grace us with your presence. It's been, what? Nineteen years? I'm sure Erit here would say that time flies, but for me, it felt like nothing less than centuries." Like flipping a switch, Xamic's face brightened again, and he casually waved off the mood. "But that's all over with now. You picked a good day to come out of your hidey-hole, bud. You're gonna be glad you didn't miss this. Now, let's get this party STARTED!" He gave a *WHOOP!* and hopped off the fountain. "Hey, coppers! Fuzz heads! Get out here before I have to do something stupid. Yeah, I see you with the newspaper. Cut the crap. You're going to want all eyes on this baby!"

A man on the corner lowered his newspaper and turned to give his full, frowning attention to Xamic. A couple more cops stepped out of the coffee shop across the street, hands on their guns. Marley climbed out of his sedan, shotgun in hand.

Xamic noticed the shotgun and laughed. "See! He's got the right idea! You other boys better man up! Your little pistols ain't gonna do dick!"

Terin shouted, "Xamic! What's the deal?"

Xamic held out his arms and grinned. "Check it out!" He had a small remote in his hand. Kalei raised her rifle, but before she could lift in an inch, his thumb slid over and pressed the button.

Four of the Wardens dropped their heads back and released a frenzied roar. Similar sounds drifted from the park and echoed off the city streets. Then the four Wardens ripped off their gloves and tackled their comrades.

Kalei moved forward to break up the madness, but then she heard Xamic yell, "Alright! It begins!"

She looked up in time to see Xamic tear off into the park, Terin flying past her after him, shouting over his shoulder, "Erit! Find the source!"

Kalei dropped her rifle and ran after them, determined to help Terin put an end to Xamic. Breaking up the scuffles wouldn't help. They had to take out the mastermind.

They had just passed inside the gate when Terin noticed her and ordered, "Go back to Erit."

"Like hell!"

She expected him to protest, but Terin grunted and kept running. Kalei was relieved that he had his priorities in order. All that mattered now was taking out Xamic.

Xamic was already at the far end of the path, and the gap between them was only widening. Gritting her teeth, Kalei shifted her darkness to all the necessary

muscles and took off at twice the speed. She passed
Terin and started gaining ground on Xamic, unable to
contain a wolfish grin.

She was only a few feet away when Xamic looked
over his shoulder and flashed a grin to match her own.
Then his speed tripled, leaving her in the dust. Before
Kalei could react, Terin flew past her, matching Xamic's
burst of speed step for step.

Kalei growled in defiance and tried to force
more darkness into her legs, but she had nothing
left to give. The pair easily outmatched her, like a
pair of motorcycles outrunning a jogger, and as they
disappeared around a distant bend, Kalei was forced to
stop and catch her breath.

She walked over to a nearby tree and braced her
hand against it, impatiently waiting as her darkness
worked to alleviate the physical strain from her sprint.

Xamic was getting away, and there was nothing she
could do about it. Kalei screamed and punched the tree.

She took a couple more breaths, and then she heard
another scream immediately behind her. Kalei jumped
and spun around, just in time to catch a tackle from
a young woman. The two fell to the grass, the young
woman pulling and tearing at Kalei's clothing as Kalei
tried to seize her attacker's frantic hands.

Jenna's voice came over the intercom: "Attention
all Wardens, a riot has broken out in the Downtown
district. Also, the Northeast fence has been breached.
All units are authorized to use any means necessary to

take them down."

Kalei finally managed to grab the woman's left hand, and was not surprised to find that the nails were black. But the woman's right hand moved even faster now that the left was seized, and the woman shrieked hysterically as her attack failed to expose Kalei's skin. Grateful that the woman was half her weight, Kalei rolled the woman off of her, releasing the woman's hand as she reached for her Taser. The woman let off another shriek as both women climbed to their feet, and then she charged after Kalei. But before she could take more than a step, Kalei shot off her Taser and the woman dropped to the ground, her body seizing to the tune of 50,000 volts.

Kalei dropped the Taser and pulled up her comms, hailing Jenna on a private line. Her sister answered with a distracted, "Yeah?"

"Jenna, what the hell is happening?"

"Shit hit the fan, Kalei. Every Estranged in the district is goin' nuts."

The woman moaned softly from the ground. Kalei kneeled down, pulling the woman's hands behind her back and securing them with one of the zip-tie handcuffs from her belt pocket.

As she worked, she asked Jenna, "How did they break through the fence?"

"Fifty of 'em just charged straight at the damn thing. The first dozen of 'em fried, but the others broke through. Damn idiots managed to short out the entire system."

"Well, have they—"

"Shit!"

"What?"

"There's another riot being reported in T-Town. Somewhere near the new courthouse. New Port is being slammed too."

Kalei stood up, facing the path that led to Tech Town. "The T-Town riot, is it around the Luxury Grove Condos?"

Jenna paused. "Yeah, looks like that's in the damn center of it."

"Shit!" Kalei turned off the comm and took off down the path.

She had just finished shifting the darkness to her legs and was getting ready to put on speed when she heard Xamic laughing. She stopped and turned around in time to see him walk out a side entrance to the park.

He was walking.

Kalei took one more glance over her shoulder, at the wooded park path that led to the Tech Town entrance, and then turned away to go after Xamic.

He didn't seem to notice her, so Kalei followed from a distance, like a cat trying not to spook a speedy mouse. She ducked behind cars and crouched behind newspaper boxes, and as she carefully followed Xamic's steps, she realized Terin was nowhere to be found. Kalei didn't put too much thought to it, though. She assumed Xamic had lost him in the park somewhere.

Xamic led her down alleyways, across wide streets, seemingly oblivious to what was going on around him. Cars were stopped dead in the streets, locked in a sudden, mid-day traffic jam. The screams of men and women frequented the air, occasionally followed by the sound of shattering glass and crashing metal. Kalei found herself dodging through panicked crowds as police officers climbed the highest objects they could find, megaphones in hand as they ordered people to go home and lock their doors. She had no idea what had caused this mayhem, but she knew it had something to do with Xamic's red button. And she knew Estranged were probably the source of all the screams.

She only spotted one Warden running toward the attacks; more often than not, it was a group of police officers armed with shotguns responding. Kalei watched as a third group of police officers ran by, and she realized most of the Wardens were stuck in Downtown and Tech Town. The people here were on their own.

Kalei stopped. She looked at the panic around her and realized she was needed here. But what could she possibly do? Even as she scanned the area, she saw a half dozen attacks in progress, and another half dozen officers who needed help getting the mob under control. She couldn't be everywhere. She couldn't save them all. She had to choose. It was a bitter reality to swallow, but it was the truth. Kalei took a deep breath and decided the best thing she could do for all of them was track down Xamic and find out what he had done.

But as she looked across the street to where he had been standing, Kalei realized he was gone. Kalei cursed and sprinted through the crowd, pushing people out of her way and climbing over the cars. There was an alley close to where he had disappeared, so Kalei took a gamble and plunged into it.

She rushed past dumpsters and a few passed-out hobos as she rounded the corner, praying she hadn't lost him. Then she stopped short, spotting Xamic's blonde head as it disappeared through a trap door at the back of the building. A few stacks of old tomato boxes and a small dumpster for disposing of cooking oil told Kalei it must be a restaurant, and a high school job in a kitchen told her that trap door must lead straight to the basement where they stored incoming supplies. Either Xamic knew he had a tail and he was trying to lose her, or he was up to something. Probably an attack on whoever remained in the building. Either way, Kalei had to get in there. It would be close quarters in the basement, and probably her only chance to pin him down before he could take off.

Kalei loosened her pistol from its holster, praying a full cartridge of hollow points would be enough to slow him down, and then followed.

The stairwell took them past the back end of the storage refrigerators, through a sort of service tunnel, and then down a second set of stairs. Kalei waited at the top to make sure the coast was clear, still unwilling to spook him just yet. When she heard sounds of a struggle, she stopped waiting. She rushed down the stairs, gun drawn. "Hey!"

Kalei reached the bottom in time to see a uniformed Warden fall from Xamic's grasp. He turned and smiled at her. "You made it!" Before Kalei could say anything, he disappeared into a door on the far wall.

Kalei made her way across the small room, careful not to collide with the dozens of racks crowding her on either side, each one fully stacked with kitchen supplies. She slowly stepped through the doorway, her finger dangerously close to the trigger.

The room on the other side was a small living room. A couch, a TV; the full set-up. A hallway at the back led off to what was presumably bedrooms and perhaps a bathroom. Xamic sat comfortably sprawled on the couch.

Kalei opened her mouth to speak when she heard, "What's going on?" Fenn walked out of the hallway, wiping his hands with a cloth towel.

No. No. Kalei sprinted for the door.

"STOP!"

Kalei stopped at Xamic's command, one hand on the doorframe. Her whole body was shaking.

His voice was calm and mocking. "Before you leave, Kalei, I want your advice. Which one should I kill first: Teia, Kas, or Fenn?"

"You bastard!" Kalei turned around and opened fire. Xamic wasn't on the couch anymore, and tufts of cotton puffed into the air as the bullets ripped through it.

"Kalei?"

Kalei tried to ignore Fenn. She searched for Xamic and found him in the corner by the TV. Before she could redirect her gun, he closed the distance and knocked the gun from her grasp with a blow that felt like a sledgehammer. Unarmed, Kalei switched to throwing fists, but he easily dismissed them all with casual blocks. With every block, Kalei grew increasingly desperate, but Xamic appeared to be getting bored. She threw a quick right hook at his face, but he dodged low and followed up with a swift blow to her gut. Kalei doubled over, clutching her abdomen.

Before she could recover, she heard the safety clip at the back of her helmet *click* as Xamic said, "Let's get rid of this. It's time for Terin's little flower to bloom." Fresh air rushed at Kalei's face as her helmet was pulled off her head.

Kalei coughed and then straightened to retrieve her helmet from Xamic, but instead, she found herself facing Fenn. She froze. He froze.

She had a hard time believing it was him. It had been so long since she had seen his face, her memories had done little justice to—

Kalei's terror returned. He took a step toward her, but she stepped back, trying to get away from him, but unable to tear her eyes away from his. She felt herself being pulled into them, she felt her arms aching for his embrace. But she couldn't. She had to get away.

Kalei took another step back, but her foot caught on something, pulling her leg from under her and sending her crashing to the ground. She heard Teia yell, "Auntie!" Before Kalei could turn her head, she felt Teia's small arms around her neck.

CHAPTER TWENTY-FIVE

Broken

There was so much happiness. Not a high, not ecstasy, but happiness. Wholeness. She was home again. She heard Fenn shout out, but then he was with them too. And Kas. They were all finally together again. Everything was perfect. Everything was right. Kalei opened her eyes. She wanted to see their beautiful faces. Kas and Teia lay across her left leg, faces turned away. But Fenn was on her right, eyes fixed on her with an open, dead stare. Dead.

Kalei screamed. She pushed them off and scrambled back, but then she slumped over and heaved as her stomach tried to vomit. Kalei crouched there, retching, crying, her darkness ripping through her in complete chaos.

"Kalei! Run!"

Kalei looked up and saw Xamic and Terin struggling outside the apartment. Terin had both of Xamic's hands in his own, his body between Xamic and Kalei. He repeated, "RUN!"

Instead, Kalei charged at them. Terin cursed and

tried to get in her way, but Xamic let go of one of
Terin's hands and sidestepped as the teen lost his
balance. Kalei crashed into them both and they all went
down.

In the tumble, Kalei felt Xamic's arm close around
her wrist. At some point, while she was out of it, both
of her gloves had come off, and now his skin pressed
against hers. She felt his darkness coming for her.
She raised her defenses, but they were so small, so
insignificant next to the mass of violence mounted
against her.

"NO!"

Terin's hand was on her other wrist. His darkness
rushed through her and met with Xamic's head on.
Terin cried out. Kalei thought it was from the collision,
but then saw Xamic's left hand still clamped onto
Terin's right. She felt a subtle "snap" echo from Terin's
darkness.

Kalei froze. She recognized that sound. She looked
to Terin, his face contorted in a mix of pain and
surprise. Then his darkness was rushing out of her,
pouring through her left wrist and into Xamic. Terin
was fading. His hand frantically tried to pull away, but
Xamic wouldn't relinquish his grip.

Yet Terin still had time. There was so much
darkness in him. He had about as much as Xamic,
maybe even more. When pulling his hand away didn't
work, he tried to redirect the flow, attempting to push it
into Kalei, but his darkness was sucked through Kalei

and into Xamic's other hand.

Terin's reservoir began to run out. Kalei felt his presence dwindling. She felt all his sorrows, all his regrets brushing past her as they rushed up Xamic's arm. Terin's head dropped. His body sagged. A last whisper of darkness fled past Kalei's heart.

He was gone.

Kalei felt Xamic release her. She heard him step away as he screamed and hooted and shouted. It didn't feel real. None of this could be real. She felt as though she was drifting away from this world, Xamic's antics happening in some distant place, the screaming in her heart happening to someone else...

Xamic cried out, "DAMN!"

Kalei pulled her eyes away from Terin's limp form and saw Xamic jumping around the room, knocking cans and utensils off the shelves. His hair was full black now, not a hint of blonde left. Bursting with energy, he sprinted at a wall, running so fast that he ran up it, made it halfway across the ceiling, and then came crashing back down again. The fall didn't seem to faze him, though. He jumped up to his feet and stretched out his neck and arms, bouncing back and forth from foot to foot like a boxer ready to fight, or a dancer getting ready to dance. His grin seemed to be permanently fixed onto his face.

He said, "This is perfect! So fucking perfect!"

He laughed and turned that grin onto Kalei. As he approached, she stood up, looking away from the eyes that greedily appraised her skin.

Kalei held out her hand. "Here," she said dully.

Xamic's eyebrows came together. As though it were a joke, he laughed and asked, "What?"

No emotion. No rage. No sorrow. She had nothing anymore. She was nothing. She continued to hold out her hand. "This is what you want. Take it."

"Hey! Wait a minute! There's supposed to be anger here! What about revenge? I just murdered your grandfather. You just murdered your dear husband and two little nieces." He shoved her and got right into her face. "How does that make you feel?"

She had no response for him, emotional or otherwise. She repeated, "Take it."

He spun away. "NO!" He slammed a can of peas off the shelf. He turned back, grabbed her by the shirt, and picked her up, shaking her violently. "You're Kalei Distrad! You won't stand for this! You want me dead. I know you do. You want to kill me with your own hands." He looked down at those hands and grinned as he looked back at her.

She didn't respond. She was none of those things anymore. Her chest was one hollow cavern, stoic and uncaring as a cold wind blew through.

The anger returned to his face. He slammed her into the shelf, knocking a cascade of first aid supplies off the top and sending them crashing onto his head. A plastic bottle broke open on his skull, a gush of clear liquid pouring out onto his head and shoulders, releasing a strong scent of alcohol as it fell. "C'MON, Kalei!"

Kalei didn't give him a response. Her eyes traced the pattern of wetness on his shirt as the liquid expanded its reach across the fabric.

Xamic released her, grabbing a nearby shelf and throwing it across the room. He threw his arms up and screamed with rage. "No. NO! You've ruined the moment. You've ruined it!" He grabbed a second shelf and threw it into the first.

Kalei's eye alit on an old Zippo lighter sitting on a box near her hand. She picked it up. Fire seemed like a fitting thing to bring into this world. All consuming, all erasing fire. This was it. She was finally going to die. Xamic was going to kill her, and she wouldn't have to be an Estranged any longer. There was nothing left for her anyway.

Then she remembered what Marley had said to her on the roof, how he had been so mad at her for sitting there, waiting to die. *Right now, you're the only one I trust to help me protect my son.*

She let the cold nothing in her heart encase her like a suit of armor. She decided she wasn't going to let Marley's kid die, and she wasn't going to let the man who killed Fenn live.

Xamic's hair was still dripping wet, the drops falling across his torso and legs. His back was to her as he raged and kicked at the shelves. She flicked the lighter open and tossed it at him.

His body went up in flames. The fire gave a quiet

whoosh and flew towards the ceiling, devouring him entirely before slowing to a steady, ferocious burn.

Blinded by the sudden light, it took a moment for Kalei's eyes to adjust. She shielded her eyes and blinked several times, and when her vision returned, she lowered her hand to find Xamic in the center of the room, his body writhing in the flames, his clothes reduced to scraps that were already falling away in the hot blaze. He turned and glared at her with lidless eyes, his mouth fixed in a silent scream.

But he was not dying. Even as the flames consumed his flesh, it regenerated and returned, caught in an endless cycle between exposed muscle and fresh skin, muscle, skin, muscle, skin...

Kalei walked toward him. She plunged her hand into the flames and closed it around his neck. He had so much darkness now. She couldn't believe he was capable of holding so much. Now that Terin's had combined with Xamic's, it was a force to behold. But it was still finite, still limited, and at the moment, it was spread throughout his entire body, actively battling the insatiable flames. Only a paltry amount remained to protect his heart.

Xamic weakly grabbed her arm in his own, trying to pull her off even as he stared at her with wide, boiling eyes. But in this moment, Kalei was stronger.

As she reached her darkness forward, Kalei thought about Terin, she thought about Fenn, she thought about two little girls who died, and a little boy who was scared for his life.

She closed her darkness around his heart and crushed it.

CHAPTER TWENTY-SIX

Revelations

The man opened his eyes and blinked a couple of times as the grey ceiling took shape above him. He became aware of smoke crawling across its surface, consuming the stone sky until all that remained was a black cloud. He watched the smoke swirl and spin, nearly hypnotized by the undulating motion.

Am I alive? ...

He slowly rolled over and pushed himself up off the floor. The room was a disaster. Metal shelves lay askew, some resting on top of each other in a pile of twisted metal, none of them erect, their contents skewed about the floor around them: cans of vegetables, kitchen supplies, even a scattered first aid kit. A grotesque form, perhaps a body, lay burning atop a pile of boxes, the fire spreading to the other items in the room. To the right of the body – kneeling before it on her hands and knees— was Kalei.

Her face was contorted in pain, tears streamed silently from her eyes. He started to get up – he needed to say something to her – but he stopped himself.

There was something moving on her neck, just visible above her black jacket. He thought it must have been a shadow, but then he realized her sleeve had caught fire, sending up dark smoke as it ate through the material at her elbow. Instead of putting it out, Kalei reached up and violently ripped the jacket from her body, tearing her arms from the sleeve and throwing the garment at the opposite wall.

She sat there in her tank top, fists clenched on her knees as she gasped for breath. Starting at her neck and spreading down to the rest of her body, he could see black figures dancing and writhing across her skin. It was hard to tell in the dim light, but they looked like... swirls. Lines twisted in on themselves until they formed a swirl at one end. And there were dozens, swimming across her body like so many tortured fish in a pond.

He was confused. None of this made any sense. He must be dreaming...

Kalei stood up and walked away from him, disappearing into the billowing smoke.

He watched the spot where she had vanished, losing himself again in the roiling clouds. He started to cough, then realized he needed to get out before the smoke suffocated him.

Perhaps I am alive.

He groped his way across the floor, up the stairs, and along the hall, the smoke blocking out most of the light from the ceiling bulbs. Eventually, he crawled out into the alley behind the restaurant and lay there, coughing and catching his breath. Then he heard screams from the street, followed by gunshots, shouts, and the sound of a car alarm. He scrambled to his feet and ran toward the commotion.

Out in the street, it was complete chaos. Several men in business suits were running as a group of men and women in tracksuits were chasing them down. Standing on a car, a woman with an assault rifle sprayed everything she could see with bullets. A child was hunkered down behind a newsstand. Behind a car, a teen was holding a bleeding knee and screaming at someone to stop.

So many people were dying and killing everywhere.

And in the middle of the madness, he saw Kalei calmly walk up behind the woman on the car and place a hand on her exposed ankle. The woman collapsed.

He blinked. Kalei was no longer beside the car. She was across the street, the joggers falling to the ground around her. He rubbed his eyes. *There was no way – that's more than a hundred feet.* He told himself it must have been a trick of the light. Smoke was billowing just as thickly out here, and only one streetlight still lit the road while its siblings were dark and damaged.

As the last jogger finished his fall to the ground, the sound of gunshots ripped through the air again, and he saw Kalei flinch as dozens of bullets ripped through her, flesh and gore exploding out the back of her body. Her clothes became shredded, the abandoned mail truck behind her covered in blood. He started to run forward, he wanted to cry out, but then a terrible pain ripped through his chest, bringing him to his knees. His breath labored, he forced his head up to see what had happened to Kalei, expecting to see her fall. But she stood tall. In the dim light of the lone lamp, he couldn't see a mark on her.

She faced her attackers, a half dozen young men and women who looked like they had just been let out of high school, and she fixed them with a cold stare as they continued to rain bullets into her lean form. The girl in the middle, a regular Barbie, began to shout incoherently. The men and women on either side seemed to be saying something in return, but he couldn't make out the words over the gunfire. And still Kalei stood there, oblivious to the bullets tearing through her.

Then, the street went quiet.

The man on the right began to curse and hit his gun, his friends continued to pull their triggers, but the guns only made empty clicks. *Out of ammo.* Kalei didn't react to the silence; she was like a grim statue, fixed to the pavement. The young woman in the middle blanched, the others stared at Kalei, their eyes growing wider with every passing second, until the group finally broke and ran.

A heavy hush fell over the street as the footsteps faded. All he could hear was the sound of the teenage boy's whimpering. Kalei stepped into an alley opposite of where he stood and was soon lost in the shadow.

Fenn pitched forward, horrified by what he had seen. *That couldn't have been... Kalei... what happened? What* are *you!*

His black-nailed hands reached up, trying to contain the tears that fell from his eyes.

He sat there for ages, trying to wrap his head around what he had seen, trying to understand the ripping pain he felt in his heart and in his body. After a while, his open palms closed into fists and he stood up and punched the brick wall. He felt pain shoot through his arm, and he thought he heard a knuckle crack, but the fresh, physical pain gave him a moment of clarity.

He decided he didn't care what Kalei had become. Estranged, Untouched, Monster, whatever she was; that was his wife.

He was going to find her, and discover what she had become.

9

Epilogue

Kalei returned to Solitary. Behind her, the city was quiet. At her hand, the errant Estranged were all disabled until the Wardens could pick them up. The Untouched? Dead, turned, locked within their houses. Terror and shock were all that remained in the city.

Solitary confinement was empty now. All of its former occupants had vacated when Xamic's seeds had triggered. Much the same had happened in Tech Town, Downtown, in the city itself. At Xamic's command, the entire city of Celan had erupted.

Whatever Tusic, or SWORDE, or anyone had believed the device to be, in the end, it was just a decoy. He had other ways to send his signal. As Walker was causing intermittent blackouts to the ear cameras as part of his updates, Xamic was wandering the city with a different device. A signal jammer, which specifically targeted SWORDE's ear cameras. Who could have distinguished Xamic's blackouts from Walker's?

This was how he had managed to visit almost every Estranged in the city and plant his seed. Just a little pocket of darkness, tucked away into the victim's mind, ready to alter their brain chemistry and drive them to a voracious frenzy when Xamic remotely released his signal. He could do things like that. He was the genius of the darkness. He was its inventor. And he was dead.

As Xamic's killer, Kalei had now inherited not only his power, but his knowledge and his memories, as jumbled as they were with the memories of his victims.

But now things were different from anything Xamic had anticipated. Now, the darkness no longer sat within her like water in a glass. It was her. It infused her skin, her eyes, her hands, her heart. It couldn't be contained or moved; there was too much, there was nowhere to move it. From the feel of it, Kalei fully expected to look down and find that her skin had turned full black, but instead, for reasons she couldn't fathom, the darkness revealed itself sparingly, dancing across her skin in the form of living swirls.

But the swirls were a mere decoration, an icing to cover the mayhem underneath. Hundreds and thousands of dead memories pressed in against her mind, victims from both that day and days departed. Terin's victims, Xamic's victims— they would not stop. They would not tire. They wanted to be heard; they needed to be remembered.

Somewhere inside the chaos sat Kalei, more broken and desolate than she ever thought possible. Fenn was dead, at her own hands. She couldn't bear the blood on her hands. So she let go of Kalei, content to let that poor, ravaged soul be buried by the others. It was too damaged to be recovered.

As she walked through solitary, she grabbed a new remote off the counter. She sat down within one of the small circles on the floor, and she raised the glass. Her eyes fixed on the far wall and her swirls danced and flexed across her skin like so many companions. She began to lose herself in the steady ebb and flow of countless memories, each one fighting for dominance.

Then one memory slowly pushed itself to the surface. It was Terin's; he was talking to a new recruit. He told the boy, "You know you touched her. But what you don't know is whether or not you killed her. Look inside yourself. If you find her memories, you know she is dead. But if you cannot... the chances are, she is still alive, living as an Estranged."

Kalei stirred from her desolation. She heard what Terin was telling her. If Fenn's memories were among those thousands, then all really was lost. But if not...

She closed her eyes. For better or worse, she had to find him. If not here, in her memories, then out there, among the Estranged. But the search had to start here, with these tormented souls. Kalei took a deep breath and plunged into their world.

About the Author

Find out more about Alex Fedyr and the sequel by visiting the author's website, or check your favorite social media:

Website: alexfedyr.com
Twitter: @AlexFedyr
Facebook: facebook.com/alexfedyr
Goodreads: goodreads.com/AlexFedyr

CPSIA information can be obtained
at www.ICGtesting.com
Printed in the USA
LVOW04s0531061215

465580LV00004B/5/P

9 780692 509609